BRIAR ROSE

Jana Oliver's imagination has always had the upper hand despite her attempts to house-train it. When she's not on the road tromping around old cemeteries, she can be found in Atlanta, Georgia, with her husband and far too many books.

BRIAR ROSE

JANA OLIVER

MACMILLAN

First published 2013 by Macmillan Children's Books
a division of Macmillan Publishers Limited
20 New Wharf Road, London N1 9RR
Basingstoke and Oxford
Associated companies throughout the world
www.panmacmillan.com

ISBN 978-1-4472-4109-6

1 3 5 7 9 8 6 4 2

A CIP catalogue record for this book is available from
the British Library.

Printed and bound by CPI Group (UK) Ltd, Croydon CR0 4YY

To Inez, my beloved mother-in-law,
whose love knew few boundaries

'Fairy tales are more than true: not because
they tell us that dragons exist,
but because they tell us that dragons can be beaten.'
G. K. Chesterton

PROLOGUE

Inch by inch, the strange powder sifts out of the bag behind the silent figure along the journey around the darkened house. In the distance, a neighbour's dog wails, as if it senses the foul magic. Perhaps even senses the anger and the loss that brings this person here on this particular night.

Once the circle is complete, the ritual words are spoken in a thick whisper as fingers nervously clutch the paper and eyes squint to read the faint type. Then it is done: the curse is laid. It was easy, just as the conjure woman had said it would be. Still trembling, the solemn figure walks into the darkness, leaving behind the legacy of bitterness that will bear ill fruit.

Empowered, the curse stirs to life now, the powder glistening like molten silver in the moonlight. It seems to dance for a time above the withered grass, and then sinks deep into the ground, claiming one of those within the house as its own.

Over the years this curse will remain vigilant, growing in strength, changing course as needed. Then, when the time is right, it will fulfil its calling. Sate its near-human desire for revenge.

No mercy. No second chances. Only more tears to feed the bitterness.

CHAPTER ONE

A prolonged bugle blast echoed across the heat-drenched field, followed by the raucous applause of over a hundred bystanders. Briar Rose sighed in relief – the re-enactment of the Battle of Bliss was finally over.

Groaning, she rolled over on her back on the hard-packed earth, her head throbbing and throat parched. The Deep South July sun beat down unmercifully, and when coupled with the soaring humidity it was Georgia's version of a sauna.

The annual re-enactment of the battle between a ragtag bunch of rebels and a contingent of General Sherman's forces always brought tourists to Bliss. Over the years, various members of Briar's family had taken their turn at portraying their famous ancestor, Private Elmer Rose. This was her year to do Elmer's 'run', a futile sprint across the battlefield to deliver a message begging for reinforcements. A message that never reached its intended recipient and resulted in Sherman's troops sacking and burning the town on their way to Savannah.

'Good job, Briar,' one of the re-enactors called out, limping along as the final whiffs of smoke cleared over the battlefield.

A shadow passed over her, bringing brief respite from the sun. Briar blinked up at a fellow rebel soldier. The eldest of the three Quinn brothers, Joshua had curly brown hair, which was mussed around the edge of his cap. His face was sweaty and his mismatched butternut-coloured uniform spotted with red clay.

Their families *had a history*, as the locals would say. Some of it had begun before either of them had been born – their parents hadn't really liked each other for as long as she could remember – but she and Joshua had been friends until the day they'd both nearly drowned at the mill when they were six. After that awful day her folks had told her not to go near him, and his had said the same. Briar had never understood exactly why, but when her mom had grounded her for a week for trying to talk to him at a softball game a few weeks after the accident, she'd decided Joshua Quinn was more trouble than he was worth.

'Nasty people, those Quinns,' her grandmother used to say. 'That boy's momma's not right in the head, blamin' all her troubles on us. She brought it on herself.'

Because of the animosity between their families, Joshua rarely came near her, mostly because his mom had ordered him not to. When he'd broken that rule, which wasn't often, he'd paid dearly. Or least that's what Briar had heard from some of her friends. The *not being near that Rose girl* proved difficult since they were in the same class in high school and rode the same bus. Still, they'd managed to keep their distance ever since first grade.

Until now.

Above her, Joshua hesitated, and then offered his gloved hand to help her up.

4

Briar froze. That she hadn't expected from a Quinn.

'What are you doing?' she demanded.

'Helping you up,' he said simply.

'Go away! I don't want to get into trouble.'

Uneasy now, Briar stood and did a quick scan of the field around them, knowing people were watching them. Some of them would be happy to call up either set of parents and deliver the news that the 'kids' were seen together.

Briar's head continued to pound, which meant she'd not had enough water. She really wanted to unbutton her uniform coat, but no girl wanted to be seen all sweaty and gross. Instead she stripped off her cap, which really didn't help much.

When her balance faltered, Joshua's gloved hand touched her elbow to steady her. It quickly retreated at her glare. She made her way to the huge oak tree in the centre of the field, the one that had been there since before the original battle, and slumped beneath it.

Joshua crouched down near her. 'You OK?' he asked, sounding genuinely concerned.

'Just really hot. I'm kinda dizzy. I didn't eat much breakfast.'

His battered canteen came her way. When she didn't take it, he scowled, unscrewed the cap and took a big drink. 'See, no poison.' Then he wiped off the rim and offered the canteen again.

Briar felt her cheeks burn in embarrassment. 'No. Sorry,' she murmured. 'It's just . . . your mom is so . . .'

'My mom? Yours isn't any better,' he came back. 'They're both crazy.'

Crazy? 'You leave my mother out of this,' she said, defiant.

'Yeah, whatever. It's never a Rose's fault, is it? It's always us Quinns who are wrong.'

Scowling, he pushed a stray curl off his face, which only made his big brown eyes more noticeable. No doubt about it, Joshua Quinn was cute, even if his family were the enemy.

Briar looked around again, increasingly worried. 'You should go before—'

'Yeah, maybe I better,' he said, stripping off the glove and tucking it under his belt. 'This was just a waste of time.' He held her eyes for a moment, like he wanted to say more, then hiked off, no doubt to collect his horse.

Briar sighed in relief. Why had he done that? He'd stayed away from her for years, going to elaborate efforts so they never came near each other, even faking stomach flu to avoid partnering with her in gym class. Still, she'd always been aware of him watching her, but never coming close.

Until today.

Confused and still lightheaded, she slowly unbuttoned her uniform jacket and let the steamy air collide with her skin. It didn't offer that much relief, not when you were in the middle of a dusty field where there wasn't a breeze.

Usually the place for impromptu softball games, for four Saturdays each summer, this stretch of ground became the Battle of Bliss with Union soldiers on one side, locals and a small contingent of Confederate soldiers on the other. They even had cannons. Though the re-enactors were very particular about period details, the real Elmer Rose had died in the winter of 1864 during Sherman's infamous March to the Sea. It was the single most important episode in the town's otherwise dull history and that's why it had never been forgotten.

To ensure that the tourists would share that history (and their much-needed dollars) the town council had proclaimed that the re-enactment would be held during the summer, rather than in December, when it had really happened. As Briar's dad had put it, 'There's nothing quite as entertaining as watching people dying in the baking sun.'

After this summer one of the cousins would take over the role of Elmer, much to Briar's relief.

'There you are,' a voice called out.

Briar smiled at the sound of her best friend's voice. Reena Hill's corkscrew curls bounced as she walked closer. She was a senior, a year older than Briar, and the eldest of the four Hill kids.

'Hey there,' Briar said, annoyed that her head was still buzzing from the heat.

'I saw you talking to Josh,' Reena said. 'You're risking the wrath of the parentals doing that.'

'Tell me about it.' Reena and Joshua had no such restrictions, so they'd been friends for years. That had proved to be awkward on occasion.

'What did he say?' Reena asked.

'Not much.' Briar pointed at the full bottle of water in her friend's hand. 'Is that mine or are you just torturing me for the fun of it?'

'It's yours,' Reena said, tossing it to her.

Instead of gulping the water down immediately, Briar held the chilled plastic against her forehead. It felt glorious as the condensation ran down her face. She screwed off the cap and took a long drink. *That's better.*

'Did you see me bite the dust?' she asked.

'Sure did. Better than yesterday's run. Practice makes perfect.'

'I didn't look too fakey?' Briar asked.

'No. The twitching was a nice touch.'

'Good, I wasn't sure how far to push it.'

As a few tourists wandered by, Briar could tell she and Reena were attracting attention. It wasn't often you saw a tall, athletic African American girl in running shorts and bright red tennis shoes chatting with a shorter, sweaty white girl in Confederate garb. It couldn't get any more anachronistic than that.

'Is that it?' her friend asked, looking around at the milling bystanders. Some were talking to the re-enactors while others bought souvenirs or snow cones. In the distance, the heat shimmered above ground like an undulating serpent.

'Yup, let's get out of here,' Briar replied. 'Can you drive me home and turn the air conditioner down to Arctic? The heat is killing me.'

'I would if I had a car,' Reena replied as they drifted across the field to the changing tent. 'The littlest bro has a toothache so Mom had to haul him to a dentist in Savannah. I'm on foot today.'

'I swear, my parents are never going to let me get my

driver's licence,' Briar complained. 'Every time I mention taking driver's ed, my mom freaks out.'

'I don't mind hauling you around,' her friend replied.

'I know, but still. My parents act like I'm ten or something. It's getting old.'

A few minutes later Briar had stripped down to her shorts and tank top, her tennis shoes replacing the cracked and weathered brogues. Usually she wore her curly blonde hair in a ponytail during the summer, but it was so long it still cloaked on her shoulders. Today she'd pinned it up to fit under the uniform cap, which meant the sun had permission to do its worst to her neck and back.

As re-enactors and their families scattered to the picnic benches for a late lunch, Briar adjusted her tattered backpack to allow for the additional weight of the uniform and shoes.

'OK, I'm ready. Let's get out of here.'

'Here, drink,' her friend insisted, handing her another full bottle of water she'd bought from one of the vendors. 'I am not carrying your butt back to town.'

Briar knew better than to argue, having grown accustomed to Reena's take-no-prisoners attitude. Somehow they'd become friends, despite being total opposites: Reena was tall and thin, loved knitting, movie marathons and NASCAR racing. Briar wasn't that good with sports, tended to be more rounded than svelte, and was never keen about getting all sweaty. Reena was a realist and was convinced daydreaming was for little kids. Briar was a hopeless romantic. Still, somehow they'd built a solid friendship, one she hoped would never end.

As they cut across the field and on to the gravelled path that led towards Bliss, a couple of young boys on bikes flew by them, kicking up dust in their wake. In the pine woods to their right the jewelweed was blooming, bright yellow flowers against the rich green foliage. The birdsong tried to compete with the sounds from the field behind them, and failed. In the distance Briar could see one of the cotton fields, though the bolls hadn't headed out yet. Soon it'd be a sea of white.

'What did folks do before AC?' she grumbled, wiping sweat and grime off her neck. A long shower was in her future.

Her friend smirked. 'They roasted and got eaten by the bugs.'

'Ugh.' Georgia had a lot of good things to its credit, but the midges and the deer flies were pure torture.

'That's why I'm not into that dress-up thing you guys do,' Reena continued. 'You have to be ten kinds of fool running around in wool or hoop skirts when it's ninety-eight in the shade.'

'You're just lucky you're not a Rose. If you were, you'd be out there like I was.'

'You could have refused,' Reena countered.

'And get guilted forever? You know my relatives. Thirty years from now one of them will be sure to remind me that I didn't uphold "the family tradition".'

'Some tradition. Running around and playing dead.'

Briar shrugged. 'It was our big moment in history.'

'Which failed, but the town still worships Elmer like he was a saint.'

'Don't remind me.'

Briar sucked down more of the water, pleased that her head was clearer now.

'I'm getting nailed with the same family tradition guilt,' her friend admitted.

'Gran Lily after you again?'

'Yup. She says I need to learn a few more conjures before she crosses over.' Reena rolled her eyes. 'Like she's ever going to die.'

Lily Foster wasn't actually Reena's grandmother – more like her great-grandmother. Depending on who you asked, she was somewhere between eighty and a hundred and twenty years old. Briar had only been around her a few times, and each time Mrs Foster had spooked the crap out of her.

Though folks didn't talk much about it, there was a rich hoodoo tradition in the South. Carried across the oceans with the first slaves, mixed with Christianity and Native American traditions, it'd found a home in the backwoods of Georgia. Unlike voodoo, which was a religion, hoodoo was folk magic, pure and simple.

'You doing more spells now?' Briar asked, pleased that Reena was starting to open up about this. Usually her friend was reluctant to talk about that part of her life.

'Yup. We're getting deep into the rootwork.' Reena looked around like she was about to confess to some sin. 'It's kinda cool, but don't you tell anyone I said that,

OK? Not all my family is good with this.'

'You mean like your Uncle Matt?'

'Him in particular. He doesn't seem to understand you can be Christian and a rootworker at the same time. He keeps confusing it with voodoo. I think he does it on purpose, just to get a rise out of Gran.'

'So what are you doing? Are you laying tricks on people?'

'No, right now I'm working a conjure to protect folks from evil.'

'Evil, in Bliss?' Briar snorted. 'Wasting your time there, my friend. Evil requires too much effort.'

Reena gave her long look. 'Oh, you'd be surprised.'

Briar felt a shiver course up her spine. She shook it off. 'OK, name one evil thing in Bliss, and you can't count Mrs Quinn because she's just nuts.'

'All right,' Reena said, rising to the challenge. 'Remember Old Man Clayton, the guy who used to beat his wife every Sunday morning before he went to church because he thought it made him more righteous in the sight of God? Lily put a trick on him so that every time he raised his hand to hit his missus, it'd go numb. Eventually he figured it out and stopped being a douche.'

'Really? That rocks,' Briar exclaimed.

Reena reached into a pocket and tugged out a small fabric pouch. It was muted green with a subtle tapestry pattern to it. 'Gran had me make up a *gris-gris* bag. Says I'm supposed to carry it for protection.'

'Seriously? What's inside it?'

'I've got a John the Conqueror root in there to draw

12

away evil. I also have a Saint Michael's sword to defeat any bad stuff that comes my way. And something for good luck.'

'Anything for love?'

'No. Not going there.'

'Oh, come on – if I could do some spell to make a handsome prince come my way, I'd be all over it.'

Reena sighed. 'I'm too busy checking out colleges. Don't need a boyfriend. Not right now.'

'Your grades are good. You'll get a scholarship, no sweat.'

'Don't know about that. What about you?'

'Mom refuses to talk about college. Period. So my dad and I do when she's not around.' Briar shifted her backpack to keep it from rubbing against her shoulder. 'My mom went to see your gran a few times. She wouldn't ever tell me why. I only found out about it because my grandmother mentioned it.'

'Was Lily able to help her?'

'I don't think so,' Briar replied, pushing aside a damp strand of hair. 'Mom's been getting weirder over the last few months. She was always protective, but now she has to know where I am at all times or she freaks out, and all she does is bake stuff, twenty-four/seven. We have two big freezers full of cookies and brownies.'

'If there's a zombie apocalypse, I know whose house I'm hiding in.'

'It's not funny. She's been crying a lot, when she thinks I don't know. I asked my dad what was going on and he says it's no big deal.'

'Your dad always says that,' Reena replied. 'He's got an ostrich personality. If he can't see it, it's not a problem.'

'Yeah, I know. He seems so mellow about everything, especially when it comes to Mom. I'm really worried about her.'

'I think you should be.'

That wasn't comforting, not coming from her best friend. 'There's something else,' Briar said, then hesitated.

'Go on.'

'I've been having this nightmare. It's the same one over and over.'

Reena halted in the middle of the path. 'What is it about?'

'I'm walking on the old road at night then – *bang* – I get hit by a car. I wake up at two nineteen a.m. every time. Is that creepy or what?'

Her friend was frowning now. 'Did you tell your parents about this?'

'No . . . Dad would just say it was something I ate and Mom, well, she doesn't need any more hassles.'

They started walking again. 'How long has this gone on?'

'It started about a month ago. I tried waking up right before two nineteen. No go. It's like I'm destined to have the nightmare every night.' Her friend's mouth was a thin line now, the muscles in her jaw tight. 'Do you think Lily could do some sort of magic that would stop it?'

'Don't know. I'll tell her what's going on,' Reena replied quietly.

Briar could tell it was time to change the subject – her friend took this kind of stuff way too seriously. Cheers came

14

from the field behind them – apparently the baseball game was about to start.

'You going to the lake tonight?' Briar asked.

'Are you?'

'Definitely. It's the closest thing to a sixteenth birthday party I'm going to get. Anyway, *he* might be there.'

'He being Patterson Daniels?' Reena asked, smirking.

'Of course. Who else would it be?'

'Someone who isn't a jerk, maybe?' At Briar's glare, she added, 'Oh, trust me, he'll be there. Daniels wouldn't miss an opportunity to flex his planet-sized ego in front of an adoring audience.'

'Whoa, that was a slap down.'

'Damn right. God, you have the worst taste in boys,' her friend replied, kicking a small stone down the path.

Pat and his family had moved to Bliss right after Christmas last year – his dad was in shipping or something – and they'd bought the Ashland Plantation. The old house hadn't been occupied for over twenty years, so Mrs Daniels was busily having it restored, which told everyone in town the family had a bucketload of money.

Pat had immediately made a mark for himself. A football star in his Ohio hometown, he'd proved to be just as talented on the basketball court here in Georgia. No 'new kid' awkwardness for him. Pat was smart and a total hunk with gorgeous brown eyes and if this were a fairy tale, he'd be cast for the role of Prince Charming in a heartbeat.

'Daniels is too full of himself,' Reena added. 'Did you know he was hitting on your cousin the other day?'

'No way. Saralyn is just making that up. He would never pay attention to her.'

'You sure?'

'Yeah. She's just saying that to get to me. She knows I think he's cool.'

Briar had no intention of letting her cousin steal away the most eligible boy in school. Not that Pat was hers, but maybe that would change tonight.

Since most of her classmates couldn't drive yet, gathering at the lake had become the thing to do. They'd bring food, build a huge bonfire and there'd be tunes. Even some making out, not that any of their parents knew about that. As long as they kept an eye out for the occasional alligator, they were golden.

Briar had her first kiss at the lake last summer with Teddy Jenkins. It had been seriously unimpressive. So blah that she made sure never to let Teddy kiss her again. There'd been more fooling around at the lake during her short, but spectacularly doomed, relationship with Mike Roth. Which had led her to wonder why some boys were better at kissing than others. Just one of life's mysteries. She knew Pat would be a good kisser because anything he did, he did well. As she daydreamed about exactly how wonderful that might be, Reena jogged her elbow.

'Helloooo? You still there? Let me guess, you were redecorating the castle, right?'

It was Reena's way of poking fun at Briar's 'obsession', as she called it. It was her father's fault: when Briar was four, he'd read her 'Little Red Riding Hood' at bedtime.

She'd come away from that experience with a true love of fairy tales and a morbid fear of wolves. From there she'd gone through the Disney phase where all fairy tales ended happily ever after. Now she was solidly in the Brothers Grimm camp, where happy endings usually required a few corpses just to even things out.

Then Patterson Daniels had moved to Bliss, every inch a Prince Charming.

Briar wasn't about to admit to her friend she'd been daydreaming about him sweeping her off her feet, how they'd melt into each other's arms as they left Bliss in the dust.

'No, I was just . . . thinking about—' she began.

'Give it up, girlfriend,' her friend cut in. 'You keep chasing after guys with big egos and you're going to get burned. Trust me on this.'

Briar frowned, knowing this cold shower had nothing to do with her. This was fallout from Reena's last big crush, a hunky guy from Savannah she'd met at a track-and-field meet. Convinced he was the stuff of legend, she'd fallen for him hard, though he was a couple of years older than her. He'd made all the right moves at first, but it had ended badly when he'd taken her for an unscheduled ride – in a stolen car.

'Doesn't mean anything bad will happen to me,' Briar said quietly.

Reena shook her head in exasperation. 'I know – I just want you to find a nice guy. Someone whose brain isn't in their pants.'

'Like who? There's no one like that in Bliss except maybe Joshua Quinn and that's only because he's more interested in horses than girls. Anyway, it would be a cold day in hell before I let him kiss me!'

Reena rolled her eyes. 'Forget it. Josh is hot and he's not an asshat like Pat. You're just too blinded by your weird family grudge to notice.'

Unbidden, the darker memories came now, how when she and Joshua were small they'd played together at pre-school, then in kindergarten. They'd spent every minute together, until one of them had died and come back to life. It had never been the same from that day forward.

And it never will be again.

CHAPTER TWO

To take advantage of the re-enactment spectators, a flea market had sprung up underneath the century-old magnolia trees in Bliss's city park where folks browsed and bought stuff they didn't need. Nearby, the bandstand hosted a group of local guys playing bluegrass music, each sporting new beards in honour of Elmer Rose Month. Like many location traditions, it didn't make much sense: Elmer had never lived long enough to grow a beard.

As Briar and Reena headed towards the shade, a visiting family rolled across the street, the littlest child in a stroller. She had bright red hair and was clutching a rag doll. As the elder kids raced forward towards the swings, the doll tumbled on to the ground, left behind in the street. Briar stared at it, riveted by its button nose and the line of dark stitches for its mouth.

The little girl turned and began to wail, pointing at her lost treasure. Reena didn't hesitate, but dashed out to grab it, trained by her younger siblings that it was the only way to end the racket. As she reached the middle of the street, a car turned the corner and accelerated, heading in her direction.

Briar froze. Her voice wouldn't come; her mouth wouldn't work. She heard the screech of brakes, the crunch of body against metal as the car struck her friend, tossing her into the air along with the doll.

'Hey, you OK?' Reena asked, joggling her elbow. She stood beside her now, the doll already retrieved and returned to the beaming toddler. The car had parked along the sidewalk.

There'd been no accident, only Briar's mind playing tricks on her.

'What's wrong?' her friend asked.

'Nothing.'

But everything *was* wrong. She'd not told Reena the truth: the nightmare was starting to creep into the daylight now, showing up at random times, slowly taking over her life. *Like now.*

The town already thought her mom was strange. Now she was acting the same way.

I'm not nuts. It's just because I'm not sleeping well.

'Come on, you need food,' Reena said. Like a hummingbird to a blooming flower, she zeroed in on a bake sale, her drug of choice. From what Briar could see, the heat wasn't doing anything good to the frosting on the cakes, or the Methodist Church ladies running the booth.

Relieved that the weird sounds had finally retreated from her mind, she scratched at a bug bite. 'Same old stuff,' she muttered. 'Nothing ever changes here.'

Briar tagged along with her friend, kicking at the dirt like a sullen child. She found herself wishing, for the millionth time, that something magical would happen to their home town. Unicorns running rampant in the streets, a smoking dragon curled round the city hall bell tower, anything that would nullify the 'norm'.

When Briar was little, it hadn't felt that way, but after you'd seen fifteen Fourth of July parades with the same people *every* year there was no excitement, just the grim realization that she was trapped in what had to be the dullest part of the universe.

Tomorrow she would be sixteen, and absolutely nothing would change.

As soon as I graduate, I'm out of here.

She sighed to herself. Her escape was as much a fairy tale as any the Brothers Grimm had collected. Once you were here, you never escaped. Bliss was a life sentence.

Reena looked over at her, pointing at a plate of apple fruit bars. 'Want some?' she called out.

Briar shook her head. 'Nope. Thanks.' Not with the acres of baked goodies at home.

The area just in front of the three-storey city hall was home to Elmer Rose's statue, erected on the hundredth anniversary of his death. To the left of the statue was another monument of sorts, but this one wasn't for one of Bliss's heroes. The dry patch of red dirt and a gnarled tree stump indicated where Jebediah Rawlins, a notorious traitor, had met his end, executed for conspiring with the Yankees.

The Rawlins were distant cousins to the Quinns in some way, though the latter refused to claim them. That was probably best: the traitor's name had been used to scare Bliss's children into good behaviour for decades. Even now, townspeople wouldn't walk over that section of dirt, as if it were an entrance to hell.

After Reena had bought a dozen macadamia-nut

cookies and scarfed down two in short order, they parted company at the bandstand. With a wave, her friend headed east towards her house, her face pensive. She'd been that way since they'd talked about her gran. In fact, she'd been a lot more solemn the last couple of weeks or so, for whatever reason.

During the heat of summer, life slowed in Bliss. As Briar hiked home, she kept to the side of the street that offered shade. Something made her turn and look back towards the centre of town. The grin came unbidden. She'd been wrong – there was something new. The water tower had received a fresh coat of paint earlier this week, white, like usual, except now bright red spray paint announced that this side of the tower was HOT. She was willing to bet the other side said COLD. Someone was going to be pissed off about that.

'That rocks,' she said. Most likely it'd been Ronnie and Ben, a couple of the troublemakers from her class. She'd be sure to ask them tonight at the party.

She cut down the road that led to her house – aptly named Rose Street after dear dead Elmer, again staying in the shade. Along each side of the road were individual rose gardens, but this afternoon the blooms wilted in the heat, even though some of the gardens had been recently watered.

Bliss might be dull, but it did have pretty tree-lined streets. Magnolias, mostly, and Briar loved how their fist-sized blooms smelt like heady perfume in early summer.

What would have happened to her if she'd lived in a

bigger city like Savannah or Atlanta? Would she still be the same person? Did your hometown indelibly mark you for life?

Lost in her depressing thoughts, it took her time to realize that someone had called her name. Looking around she found Mrs Parker rolling a wheelbarrow full of junk up the sidewalk behind her. At present she was clad in a worn T-shirt, ratty cut-offs and her greying hair pulled back with a scrunchy.

As odd went, Mrs P was off the scale by Bliss standards. She loved to collect junk. Folks might have thought that was strange, but it was an easy way to get rid of a mismatched set of dishes or a broken lawn chair. Mrs P took it all home, welded the metal together into bizarre statues and stored them in her backyard.

'Happy birthday, Briar!' the woman called out, sounding nothing like a homicidal maniac. But then how would a homicidal maniac sound?

'Thank you, Mrs Parker.' The woman was a few hours early on the greeting, but it never hurt to be polite, especially with adults. They gave you less trouble that way.

'You know, you shouldn't believe any of the rumours,' Mrs P added.

You mean like how you hacked up all your husbands and are using them as fertilizer in your backyard?

Just to be safe, she called out, 'What rumours?'

No answer was forthcoming as Mrs Parker was already headed across the street, her wheelbarrow squeaking with each turn of the wheel. She began to hum something that sounded suspiciously like a song from the musical *Sweeney Todd*.

You're so freaky. Maybe Reena was right about there being evil in Bliss. It did have its share of macabre residents, like Mr Nelson, who left his Halloween decorations up all year and mowed his lawn every other day, even in the heat of the summer, claiming if he didn't the zombies would rise and kill them all.

At least that would be cool.

CHAPTER THREE

Before she entered the house, Briar paused on the broad porch to hang up the uniform coat and trousers on a pair of hangers her mom had supplied just for that purpose. They needed to air out before next week's re-enactment or she'd really reek. That would be a little too authentic.

After fanning open the shoes, she laid her damp socks over the arm of a rocker. As long as the neighbour's basset hound didn't bury them like he had last year, she'd be in good shape.

The house wasn't as big as the mayor's stately house near the town square – it was only a two-storey affair with a wrap-around porch. Though the wooden floors creaked and the plumbing needed updating, again, it always felt like home.

There was something odd about the place, especially the unexplained draughts in the bathroom late at night when Briar showered. Doors opened and closed when no one was upstairs, stuff like that. Her father said it came with living in an old house, but she wasn't so sure.

Briar pushed open the back screen door – no one locked their houses in Bliss – and found her mother fussing around the kitchen, icing cupcakes. She paused in wonder: it looked as if a rainbow had exploded over every available surface. Her mom always baked for special occasions:

engagement parties, weddings, baby showers. Even funerals.

That thought made her shiver, despite the heat.

'Hey, Mom, I'm home.'

Though usually full of energy, when Mrs Rose turned towards her, she appeared to have aged since early this morning. Her skin was sallow against her pale blonde hair and the dark circles under her eyes were more prominent now.

Not good. 'Are you feeling OK?'

'It's nothing. Just tired.'

Briar dropped into one of the wooden chairs at the kitchen table. Now that her mom no longer worked as a school nurse in Statesboro, it seemed all she did was cook and clean. 'Why were you baking brownies at three in the morning?'

'How did you know that?'

'I woke up drooling from the smell.' Which wasn't exactly true – she just hadn't fallen back to sleep after the recurring nightmare.

'I was up because I needed to get a few things done,' her mom replied in a flat tone.

Which is so not an answer.

'What are all these for – my birthday?' Briar asked.

'No, the library. They're having a fundraiser.'

From experience, Briar knew asking more questions would get her nowhere, so instead she homed in on the closest cupcake. It was pink, her fave colour.

'Hands off,' her mom said, shaking her head.

'Ah, come on. Just one?' Briar wheedled. 'I died really good today.'

Her mother's face went ashen and she turned away, her fingers gripping the edge of the counter top.

'Mom? What's going on?'

Mrs Rose shook her head and said softly, 'Have as many as you want. It doesn't matter now.'

It doesn't matter? Feeling feisty and keen to test that theory, Briar collected a dinner plate and placed five cupcakes on it, each a different colour. As she poured herself a glass of iced tea, she waited for the 'That's far too many of those, young lady' reprimand. It never came. Her mom kept her back to her the entire time, even as Briar headed upstairs for a shower, plate and glass in hand. With each creaking step her worry increased.

Once inside her room, she pushed the door closed with a foot and sank on her bed, still holding the plate and the drink. That wasn't her mom in the kitchen. She might look like her mother, but that was a robot, someone just going through the motions, phoning it in, one cupcake at a time.

Though overly protective, her mom was pretty even-tempered, unless one of the hags on the library board got to her, though recently she'd been snappish and prone to crying fits. She'd been going to church twice a week and she had one of those *gris-gris* bags like Reena carried. None of that seemed to help.

Briar had spent a lot more time in her room to avoid getting into fights over stupid stuff like how much laundry detergent to put in the washer. One of her classmates had suggested that her mom was going through *the change*, but didn't they have medication for that sort of thing?

She set the food aside and then flopped down on her bed, staring up at the stars her father had put on the ceiling when she was little to watch over her at night. To her left, the bookshelf was crammed with fairy tales. A Disney princess poster was positioned on one wall and on the other was one from *The Hunger Games*. It was like she wasn't sure who she wanted to be.

Some day I'll know. Then it'll all be good.

But when?

Between the shower, the yummy cupcake and the tea, Briar felt human again. She carefully styled her hair, letting it fall in loose golden curls down to the middle of her back. It was her greatest asset or her biggest headache. If it behaved itself, it was gorgeous, like a movie star's. If not, it was as if Medusa had bleached her hair blonde and all the snakes were PMSing at once.

Briar grinned at herself in the mirror – despite the brain-numbing humidity, today was a good-hair day. Hopefully Pat would love it. She carefully applied some make-up and dug through her closet in search of the perfect thing to wear to the lake. Something cool, but kind of sexy would be good, but so far nothing was right. She tossed clothes on the bed, trying to decide. Dragonfly, her cat, took residence right in the middle of her black silk top, littering it with white hair.

'No, don't!' she said, rescuing the garment before the claws did any damage. After it was safe, she cuddled the feline for a few minutes and a loud purr was her reward.

'So what do you think is wrong with Mom, Dragonfly?'

The cat yawned in disinterest, displaying a rough pink tongue. In Dragonfly's brain, if it had nothing do with the food bowl, it was unimportant.

After another rummage through her closet, Briar settled on a pair of skinny jeans and a red top that always made her hair look especially good. Too many people had seen her all grimy at the re-enactment and it was time to banish that image from folks' minds, at least those of any cute guys. Not that there were that many in Bliss. Pat, for sure. Even Joshua Quinn, and a couple more. The rest were just barely OK and so not on her radar.

When Briar trudged downstairs, she found her mom washing dishes, by hand, though they had a dishwasher. The cupcakes were gone, probably collected by one of the library people. In their place was a selection of freshly baked cookies painstakingly layered in a series of tight circles with precise spaces between each of them, evidence that her mom's OCD was once again in full force.

Briar took a deep breath. There wasn't much she could do if her mother wouldn't talk to her, so it was time to go for gold.

'Ah, Mom, tonight's the party at the lake. Can I stay out until, um, midnight? I mean, I'm almost sixteen so—'

Her mother stiffened as she looked over at her. 'No, you're not going out tonight. You need to be at home.'

'But the party's sorta for my birthday. I have to be there.' That wasn't quite true, but it sounded good.

'Not tonight.'

Reena had been right – her parents were going to ruin everything. Pat would meet some other girl and fall in love and she'd never get another chance at happiness again.

'Mom!' she wheedled. 'I've been doing all the extra chores you gave me—'

'And complaining the entire time,' her mother cut in.

'That's in the teen operational manual. It's totally required,' Briar replied. 'I've been home on time all summer. I just want one night out.'

'Not tonight.'

'Oh, come on! If you're going to ground me, you have to tell me why. You owe me that.'

'Briar, please, not tonight—' her mom began, her voice rising.

The door swung open and Briar's dad entered the kitchen. Franklin Rose was frowning, his brown hair far too short to be fashionable, and his suit rumpled from the heat. A computer bag hung from a shoulder, his job as a pharmacy salesman keeping him on the road part of the time.

'What's going on here? I could hear you two from the driveway.'

'I want to go to the lake tonight, to the party. Mom says I can't go, but she won't tell me why.'

'She *has* to be home tonight, Franklin,' her mom said, sudsy hands on her hips. 'You know why.'

'Not this again, Maralee,' he said, shaking his head as he placed the computer bag on the floor near the pantry. 'I thought we'd settled this.'

'No, you're just ignoring the truth,' her mom said, her voice tightening more now. 'She *has* to be home tonight.'

'I will be. I'll be home before midnight,' Briar said. 'What's the big deal? It's just a party, and it's my birthday tomorrow. This could be like an early present.'

But it was as if they had forgotten she was in the room.

Her mom moved a few steps closer to her dad, eyes moist. 'Please, Franklin, this is important.'

'This has to end, Maralee. You know what the doctors said,' he murmured, gently touching her shoulder. He looked over at Briar. 'You can go to the lake tonight. Just . . .' Her father sighed in resignation. 'Be home by . . . eleven thirty. *No* later. You understand?'

Briar broke out in a grin. He'd come through for her.

'Thanks, Dad!' she said, and gave him a quick hug. The victory didn't feel as awesome when her mother slowly turned and then walked up the stairs without a word.

'Mom?' No response. The door to her parents' bedroom closed behind her.

'What's up with her?' Briar asked, her voice lower now. 'Is she sick?'

Her dad shrugged, though she could see the worry in his eyes.

'It depends on who you talk to. She has this . . . fixation about you turning sixteen. That it's a bad thing.'

'She's always been strange about my birthdays. Why is this one a big deal? Does she think I'm going to run off and get married or something?' Her father wasn't meeting her eyes now. 'Come on, Dad, I'm not stupid. What's really going on?'

He waved her out on the porch, closing the screen door behind them. They settled on the old porch swing, rocking it back and forth. They hadn't done that in a long time, and she realized how much she missed those moments together. Her dad could be a pain sometimes, but she loved him a lot.

He squeezed her hand. 'Your mom has always been a bit different. That's what I loved about her. Some of the women in this town . . .' He shook his head. 'She started behaving strangely after that day at the river, the day you nearly drowned. From that point on, your mother believed you'd been . . . cursed. That at midnight when you turn sixteen you're going to . . . die.'

'What, so tonight?' Briar blurted. Of all the things she could have imagined, that one wasn't on the list. 'You're messing with me, right?' Her father did have a quirky sense of humour sometimes.

'No. She honestly believes that someone put a curse on you and nothing I've said will shake her of that.'

'Nope. Not buying that, Dad. That's too weird.'

'I'm serious, Briar,' he replied, his brow furrowing deeply. 'Haven't you ever wondered why she won't let you take driver's ed?'

Briar *had* wondered about that. 'I just figured . . . I don't know, I just thought she was sad about me getting older. Moms can be that way.'

Her father's expression was now a mix of disbelief and something harder to discern. 'It's not because of that. She doesn't think you're going to be here tomorrow.'

A tremble coursed through her. 'For real?'

He nodded.

'But it can't be true, can it?'

'She thinks it is. Me? No. It's too crazy to think about.'

That was good, right? Her dad had always been pretty sensible so maybe this was just in her mom's mind. 'You'll get her some help, right? I mean . . . have her see a doctor or something? Have her take some pills?'

He put his head in his hands. 'She's seen psychiatrists and it hasn't worked. We even went to Atlanta last spring to talk to a specialist. Remember when you stayed over at your cousin's house and you thought we went to see a basketball tournament? I was trying to get her some help even then.'

Briar would never forget those three days. It was when she'd discovered that Saralyn really was an airhead and that they had zip in common other than the Rose name and the blonde hair.

My mom is nuts. So all those rumours hadn't been wrong.

'Who does she think put the curse on me?'

Her father shook his head. 'Since it's not real, there's no need to act like it is. That's why I insisted we never tell you about it in the first place.'

'All right.' Briar pulled her hand out of his and leaned forward, her elbows on her knees. As she thought it through, Mrs Parker went by, waving. Briar and her dad returned the gesture automatically.

'Is everyone in this town crazy?' she asked.

'No. Just us Roses and a few . . . others,' her father

replied, his eyes tracking the lady and the wheelbarrow.

'Well, there's an easy way to fix this,' Briar said. 'When I don't croak tonight, then it's all good,' she said, trying to make this sound as normal as possible. 'Mom will know I'm not cursed and she'll get better. Right?' Briar added hopefully.

'That's what I'm counting on. Or maybe she'll come up with some other whacked-out notion that we can't shake out of her.'

She heard a tinge of anger in those words. How bad was it getting between them?

'You . . . still love her, right?' Briar asked, almost in a whisper. 'You're not thinking of . . . divorce or anything, are you?'

'I still love her,' he replied, 'and, no, I'm not thinking of divorce. I will always love your mother, even if she's a bit delusional.'

Briar sighed in relief. 'You remember what Granny Rose was like. She was totally odd. She said she had tea parties with Jeb Stuart's ghost.'

'I'd forgotten that,' he said, shaking his head. 'It's a fact: our kind of Rose crazy isn't just for show — it's bone deep.'

Briar laughed. That was true. Since her mom was a Rose as well — a third cousin who'd married in the family — Briar had all the genes working against her.

Her father stood, distracted. 'You'd best be going to your party. I'll go up and talk to your mom. Maybe I can settle her down.'

She took his hand and squeezed it. 'Thanks, Dad. You're awesome.'

'You know the rules: stay away from the booze and the boys.'

'Yes, sir.' She'd follow one of those rules, but the other . . .

He dropped a kiss on top of her head. 'I'm really proud of you. You're a great daughter, even if you forget to clean the cat box. Now go have some fun, but be home before midnight. We don't want your mother completely freaking out, do we?'

Warmed by her father's love and his support, she smiled up at him. 'Don't worry, I'll be home on time.'

Just in case her mom wasn't nuts after all.

As she hiked on her own along the old road to the lake, Briar found it hard to get into the party spirit after the buzz kill her dad had dropped on her. Though the exercise made her sweatier than she preferred, she decided against calling Reena for a ride. She needed time to think.

Mom really thinks I'm going to die. No wonder she'd been acting so strange the last few months. In her mother's case, that irrational fear would take on more power than for most. The reason was just up ahead, a roadside shrine that had been there since before Briar was born. It consisted of a white wooden cross inscribed with the words 'Rest in Peace'. There were always roses in front of it, and today there was a tiny teddy bear wearing a Statesboro High School Blue Devils T-shirt.

Briar stopped in front of the cross and adjusted the bear

so it sat upright. This was a family memorial marking where her Aunt Sarah had died in a traffic accident years ago. Sarah had been Briar's age, just sixteen, when it had happened. Her mom never wanted to talk about it, so she hadn't asked for details. She just remembered to stop every now and then, and pay her respects to a relative she'd never met.

A truck rolled up and came to a halt, causing her to turn in surprise. It was Ronnie and Ben, the two pranksters from her class. Cigarette smoke wafted out of the driver's side window in a thin blue haze.

'You want a ride?' Ronnie called out.

'No, I'm good. Thanks!' No way would she get in the truck with them or she'd smell like an ashtray by the time she reached the lake. She could fix her make-up, but not her clothes.

'OK, see you there,' he said.

'Hey, did you guys tag the water tower?' she asked.

Both of them lit up in grins. *I knew it.* She shielded her face from the dust as they drove on.

Maybe I should have asked Reena for a ride.

As she walked on, birdsong accompanied her. Ahead, a squirrel bounded across the road and then vanished into the woods. Her phone buzzed and she checked the screen. It was Reena. She let it roll over to voicemail, not wanting to talk right now.

Was this curse thing going down or not? Her dad didn't think so, but Reena and her gran believed in such things – that was part of their hoodoo beliefs – so to them this would be for real.

What if this is my last day alive? That would totally suck.

Briar had too many things to do to end up in a grave this early. She'd never been to Europe or to New Zealand to see if hobbits really lived there. She hadn't been to Disneyland and she didn't even have her learner's permit yet. And she definitely didn't want to die a virgin.

I'm obsessing again. She did that a lot nowadays. But not tonight: there was a party to enjoy and a hot guy to snag as her very own. All this craziness could wait until later, and then, when midnight came and went, her mom would know everything was all right.

Because it just has to be.

CHAPTER FOUR

Bliss's lake, located south of town just downstream from Potter's Mill, had gone through a number of ups and downs in its watery life. By the mid-sixties it was a dumping ground and its beaches a mess. A concerned group of locals had laboriously cleaned the shoreline and constructed a series of floating docks. Even folks who'd griped about the nature nuts messing with 'their lake' began to enjoy it once again.

According to Briar's grandfather, the local kids had always congregated at the north-eastern edge of the lake, mostly because it was sheltered from sight. Besides a nice beach, there was a handy set of woods right behind the parking area in case you wanted some privacy. He'd admitted to taking her grandmother there on more than one occasion, which was just too much information in Briar's opinion.

Without breaking her stride, Briar headed for the restrooms located near the parking lot, hoping that nobody had seen her. She ducked inside and was happy to find no else was there, unless you counted a lone wasp buzzing along the ceiling. She pulled the cosmetics case out of her bag and fixed her face, trying to deal with all the sweat and oil. After more lip gloss and a spritz of body spray, she was ready to go.

Once she was presentable, Briar headed towards the parking lot. It was already crowded with cars and trucks, with a few bikes in residence, as not everyone had a driver's licence. The music rolled up towards her from the shoreline and the bonfire was already lit. The scent of roasting meat and citronella candles hung heavy in the air. Kids were scattered around, some in groups, some on their own. She guessed there were about thirty of them, ranging from freshmen to seniors, the majority of them from her high school.

As she wove her way through the parking lot, Briar looked for Pat's car, but it wasn't here. What if he changed his mind and stayed home? That would screw up all her plans.

She stopped to talk to friends, to find out what was new. Some mentioned the re-enactment; others had fresh gossip to share. Most of the kids were clustered around the bonfire, which was set inside a pit ringed with concrete blocks and positioned far enough away from the woods to avoid a conflagration. A bucket of water sat nearby, probably some adult's idea of a fire extinguisher, though by the end of the night it was a good bet it would be dumped over someone's head.

The *clip clop* of hoofs made her turn towards the road. Joshua angled his four-footed ride on to an open stretch of grass, climbed down and then tied the horse to a tree with a long lead. As he petted the sleek black mare with genuine fondness, a Border collie trotted up and parked herself at his feet, tongue lolling.

'There you are. I wondered if I'd lost you to that rabbit,' he said.

'Hey, it's horse boy!' someone called out.

A muscle in Joshua's face twitched, but he didn't reply. A couple of girls went over to *ooh* and *ahh* over the mare. He was polite with them, answering their questions, but Briar could tell he was uncomfortable with the attention.

Joshua wasn't a regular at the lake parties. *Why is he here tonight?*

'Hey. Happy almost birthday,' Reena called out as she crossed from the parking lot. 'How's it going?'

'Pretty good. I nearly didn't get to come. My mom is totally freaking out.'

'And that's different, how?' her friend replied.

Joshua headed their way, the dog on his heels. 'Hi. Sorry I'm late,' he said, addressing Reena. 'Lots of tourists at the stables this time of year so my boss wouldn't let me leave early.'

It sounded as if he and her best friend had planned to meet at the party.

'No sweat. I just got here,' Reena replied.

Joshua was staring at Briar now, a faint redness to his cheeks. He was dressed in a pale blue T-shirt and jeans that were worn at the knees, and, as usual, his hair was doing its own thing. On him it looked good. Briar had to admit she'd caught herself checking him out at school more often than was wise. At least when she thought no one was looking.

She started in surprise when the collie's cold nose nudged her palm.

'Come here, Kerry,' Joshua said, slapping his thigh. 'Leave her alone.' The dog complied, though the awkwardness of the situation didn't change.

After Reena cleared her throat, he fumbled in his jeans pocket for something.

'Umm, Briar, I have a—' A spike of panic filled his eyes as if he'd just found himself head to head with a nine-foot grizzly bear. 'Ah . . .'

Reena raised an eyebrow, but didn't weigh in.

'I should get Kerry some water,' he said, and hurried off towards the lake, the dog in tow.

Her friend huffed. 'Wimp,' she muttered.

'What was that all about?'

'Give me a sec, will you? I need to talk to him,' Reena said, already on the move before Briar could reply.

Everybody's weird tonight.

Briar's cousin waved her over to the picnic bench. Though everyone said they looked similar, Saralyn had shorter hair and bigger boobs, which she liked to show off by wearing tops that were too small. That little trick bought her a lot of male attention, which she thrived on.

'What's up with Joshua?' she asked. 'Why's he hanging around you?'

'No idea.'

'He's just cruising for trouble.' Saralyn watched a guy walk past, checking him out from head to toe. 'Cute. Do you know who he is?'

'He's a sophomore this year. Name's Greg something or other,' Briar replied.

Saralyn adjusted a bra strap, tucking it underneath her sleeveless tee. 'How's Aunt Maralee doing? Is she going off the deep end yet about the curse?'

Curse? 'You know about that?' Briar hissed under her breath, stunned that Saralyn would blurt out that kind of thing in front of everyone.

'Yeah. Most of the family does,' her cousin replied. 'From what my parents said, your mom's been nutty since your Aunt Sarah died, only she's much worse now.'

'It's not like that,' Briar replied. Though it really was.

'I never believed the curse was for real anyway. I think it's just her wanting attention. She's such a drama queen.'

Before Briar could respond, a familiar sound cut through the party noise. The laugh belonged to her ex-boyfriend and it took her only a few seconds to find him near the bonfire, his arm round a tall redheaded girl clad in a micro bikini.

The ex.

Mike was an athlete, with a cocky smile and an impressive set of pecs. His light-brown hair had gone summer blond and his eyes were a dark brown. In short, he'd been the perfect boyfriend and everything had seemed great between them, at least until he'd dumped her a few weeks back.

The memory of that dumping rose along with a thick coat of acid in the back of her throat. Now here he was with another girl hanging all over him. No break-up grief there. Briar checked the girl out and found that she wasn't that special: her legs were short, her neck too long and her hair needed serious help.

'Bet you miss going out with him,' her cousin observed.

'What? No way.' But that was a lie.

She'd liked Mike. He'd been pretty cool, though his constant pushing for them to go all the way had doomed their relationship. They'd sorta come close one night in the back of his car, but she'd decided it didn't feel right. When she'd said no, he'd been mad, even though they hadn't even got their clothes off yet.

Mike had accused her of being a stupid kid, which in guy speak meant he was angry that she wouldn't put out. From what she'd heard, his new girlfriend didn't have that problem.

When Briar rose from the bench, eager to go somewhere where she couldn't see the pair of them, Mike smirked at her. He said something to his date and she laughed. When they turned away, he made sure to put his hand on her butt.

Now he was just being cruel. *Jerk.*

Another check of the parking lot told her Pat hadn't arrived yet. The evening was starting to suck.

Maybe I should have just stayed home.

If she left now, Mike would know he'd won, and she'd lose her chance at Pat, the chance to catch herself a really good guy. That would be the ultimate revenge, letting Mike know just how much she wasn't missing him.

Needing a friend, Briar looked around for Reena, but she was still talking to Joshua, so she forced herself to wander around, making the rounds half-heartedly. There were lots of happy-birthday wishes and hugs, which she appreciated, though it was hard to muster sufficient good cheer.

There were also whispers behind her back, and it made

her nervous. Did everyone know about her mother's illness? Were they laughing about it?

Probably. Bliss loved a good rumour even when it came at the cost of one of their own.

'Too much drama,' she muttered.

When someone offered her an unopened can of beer, she broke one of her father's rules and accepted it. *Why not? I'm almost sixteen.*

After popping open the top, Briar took a sip and quickly discovered that the stuff didn't taste that great. Since a couple of her classmates were watching her, she nodded and smiled like it'd actually been good. Maybe that was why beer was so popular – everyone acted as if it was good just to impress their friends.

'You better hope the cops don't bust this party,' Saralyn said as she walked by.

'Now you sound like my dad,' Briar replied.

Her cousin muttered under her breath, but she couldn't catch a word. Briar suspected it hadn't been very nice. The second sip of the beer made her head buzz and by the third she was feeling pretty happy. Her worries about her mom were fading, at least for the moment.

She smiled as Reena wandered up. 'Hey! What are you and Joshua up to? You guys going to hook up or something?'

'What? No.' Her friend frowned at the beer. 'Josh is just having . . . issues.'

'A Quinn with issues? Who knew?' Then Briar giggled, rather enjoying the bubbling feeling coursing through her. 'Sort of like us Roses. We're all screwed up.'

'Just how many beers have you had?'

'Just one,' Briar replied. She lowered her voice conspiratorially. 'For the record, this stuff is yucky.'

'So I've heard.' The frown was still in place.

'Guess what? You're *so* not going to believe this one. My mom thinks I'm cursed and that I'm going to croak at midnight. Can you believe that?'

Reena didn't respond, her eyes wider now.

'This is the part where you say, "Yeah, your mom's nuts. Sorry about that, girlfriend."'

'She actually said that?'

'Dad did. It's why she's been so crazy recently.'

'A curse isn't something to joke about.'

Briar's attention swung to the parking lot and she smiled. 'Score! He's here!'

Her dream guy unfolded himself from his car, and when Pat's eyes lit on her he smiled in return.

'Wow, did you see that?' Briar said. 'He's totally hot.'

Her friend gave Pat a cursory glance. 'Look, he's just a dude. He's not a handsome prince and he doesn't have a fancy castle. Live in the here and now, girl, OK?'

Briar shot her a glare, furious that her friend had peed on her daydreams . . . again.

Reena pulled her phone out of her pocket. 'I'm going to call Gran to see what's going on.' She stepped away, turning her back to muffle the party noise.

Briar kept watch on Pat as he made his way towards her, stopping along the way to talk to other kids. His dark hair was softly tousled, just short of collar length, and he had a rich tan from his job as a lifeguard at the local pool. He wore faded jeans, a black T-shirt that moulded to his chest, and a runway model smile.

When Reena turned back towards her, her eyes were wide and her shoulders stiff as she ended the call.

'Hey, you OK? Something wrong with your gran?' Briar asked.

'No . . . she's . . .' Reena's eyes met hers. 'She didn't pick up. Gran Lily always picks up.'

'She's probably just having a nap or something'.

Reena shook her head. 'Something's wrong here. I'm scared that the curse is for real, Briar.'

'Oh, come on. That's total crap. I know all the stuff your gran is teaching you is kind of spooky, but seriously – a curse? That's kids' book stuff.'

Her friend didn't respond, but the way she stared at her made Briar take a step back. 'OK, if you think this curse thing is righteous, what if tonight's all I've got left? What should I do to make it perfect?' she said. 'Here's a clue: no one wants to go to their grave a virgin.'

Reena's deep frown told her she'd struck a nerve. 'Don't be stupid. Don't trust that loser. Pat's not like you think.'

'Whatever,' Briar murmured. 'Go be a bummer somewhere else, OK? I've got a guy to charm and you're not helping.'

'When you're ready to go home, find me. I'm going to try calling Gran again,' Reena said, then cut off towards the water.

Now Briar felt like a jerk. She didn't like arguing with

her best friend. Besides, if tonight was her last night, she wanted it to be special. Memorable.

Feeling her cheeks warm at what that might entail, Briar returned her attention to Bliss's star athlete and full-time chick magnet. He'd already dated a few girls, but word was that he was on his own at the moment and she knew that wouldn't last long. To Briar's amazement, he'd been paying more attention to her ever since she'd broken up with Mike.

He tracked right for her like she was the only girl at the party.

'Hey, birthday girl,' he said. Then, to her surprise, Pat leaned close and dropped a kiss on her cheek. The scent of musky aftershave tickled her nose.

'Thanks!' Suddenly self-conscious, she felt lots of eyes on them. In particular, she noted the stern frown on Joshua's face.

Like he had any reason to be upset.

'Briar?' Pat nudged.

'Huh? Oh, sorry. What did you say?'

'I said I was hungry. Let's go stoke up on some food.'

They wandered through the party, chatting with other kids. She couldn't help but notice the jealous expressions of some of the other girls, including her cousin.

Finally they reached the twin picnic tables, which were laden with munchies. It was the usual summer fare – lots of meat for the guys and vegetables and carbs for the girls. Pat threaded three hot dogs on a skewer and took them over to the fire. Briar wasn't hungry, not with her stomach churning around, so she grabbed a paper plate and loaded it up with buns and chips for Pat.

When she was finished, Briar placed the plate on an empty picnic table. Pat was joking with one of the other guys, taking his time doing the grilling thing. It was then that she had the unusual feeling of being watched far too closely.

She turned to find Joshua standing behind her, the Border collie at his feet. He looked nervous, twisting something in his one hand.

'What is it with you?' she said, trying to keep her voice low. 'You want to get us grounded?'

'No. But . . .'

Pat called out to her that the hot dogs were about done.

'OK,' she called back. 'What's up, Joshua? Why are you even talking to me? You know we'll get into trouble.'

'I . . . ahhh . . . have something for you. I was going to give it to you at the battle today, but . . . it's . . . a birthday present.'

'What?' she said, completely caught off guard. 'Do your folks know about this?'

He shook his head. 'Best you don't tell yours, either. There will only be hell to pay.'

And then some. Her suspicions rose. 'Why would you give me a present?'

'Because we used to be . . . friends,' he said, continuing to twist something in his hands. Somehow the answer felt incomplete.

Why would that matter to you?

48

Joshua stretched out his hand. A curl of silver sat in the middle of his calloused palm.

Briar gasped.

He lifted up the charm bracelet and held it in the air with two fingers. 'Please, take it. Act like I'm not a Quinn, just for one second, OK?'

He was so sincere that she'd feel awful if she turned him down. But if she accepted the gift and her mom found out . . .

I don't care. When Briar flattened out her palm, he dropped the bracelet into it. The metal tingled against her skin, like it had a faint electrical charge. She leaned closer to study it, moving it about with her fingers. Once she realized what she was seeing, her eyes met his in wonder.

'All these charms are from a fairy tale. How did you know?'

'I remember you read them all the time at the library,' he hedged. 'I hope you like it.'

'Ohmigod, it's awesome, Joshua. Thanks!' She hesitated. 'I don't understand. Sure, it's my birthday, but—'

'This is just between us,' he said solemnly. 'I don't care that my mom hates your mom or the other way around. That's their thing, not ours.'

'This afternoon you said—'

'Doesn't matter what I said. I was . . . upset.'

He had been, but he wasn't now. If anything, he was hopeful. 'I don't want you to get in trouble for this.'

'Same for you,' he said.

'Briar? Where's those plates?' Pat called out.

The dude's timing sucked. This was way awkward.

Though she wanted to hurry over to Pat, she put on the bracelet and watched the little charms twirl round on their jump rings. *So cool.*

'Briar?' Pat called out again.

'Ah, sorry, I gotta go,' she said. 'But thank you. I *really* love it, even though I have to disavow any knowledge of where it came from.'

'You're welcome. Happy birthday, Briar.'

As he walked away, Joshua looked back over his shoulder, a faint smile in place. For a brief moment Briar wondered what it would have been like to kiss him.

CHAPTER FIVE

If Pat had seen what had gone on between her and Joshua, he didn't act like it. Instead, he led her further down the lake to an empty picnic table. Fortunately the moon was fairly bright and it cast a lovely glow over the woods and the water beyond.

Just like in a fairy tale. But in this one the princess dies.

Where had that come from? Briar shoved the ridiculous thought as far back in her mind as possible, not wanting to ruin the moment. They settled in at the table and she watched Pat eat. Briar tried not to be nervous, but it was futile. This was the guy she'd been dreaming about since the first time she'd seen him in the school hallway, leaning against the lockers. Even then he'd looked as if he owned the place.

'So what did the horse dude want?' Pat asked before loading more chips into his mouth.

That hit an unexpected nerve, especially after the awesome gift. 'His name is Joshua.'

'I know, but he's always on that old nag so that makes him a horse dude.'

Joshua's mare certainly wasn't a nag. If anything, Arabella had been a race horse in a previous life.

Though aggravated at his attitude, Briar bit her tongue, not wanting to mess up their time together. She knew the other girls were just waiting for her to make a mistake, and then one of them would swoop in to claim him.

'Joshua gave me this for my birthday,' she said, extending her arm so he could admire the bracelet.

Pat peered at it and then smirked. 'Is that an axe murderer on that thing?'

'What? No, silly. That's the huntsman from "Snow White".' She pointed at another charm. 'This is a prince, probably from "Cinderella" or "Sleeping Beauty". And that's a flying horse and a—'

Pat leaned over and stole a kiss, breaking her recitation. Her body began to glow at the attention, especially when he pulled her closer on the bench seat.

'How's about we go for a walk down by the mill?' he suggested.

The warm glow from the kiss fizzled and died. The mill was the last place Briar wanted to go. It was dark and kind of creepy, and Pat had no idea that she'd nearly drowned there. But how could he? He wasn't a local boy.

Her old fears went to war with her hopes. In the end, the hopes won.

'Ah . . . OK.' It wasn't like they were going into the river or anything.

After discarding their trash, they headed down the tree-lined path to Potter's Mill. Briar found herself shivering at the thought of their intended destination. When Pat's arm curved round her waist, she tried to relax. This was exactly what she'd been wishing for ever since the last day of school. She'd be safe with him. Why ruin it?

Briar knew everyone was checking them out as there were whispers behind them. She shot a glance over her shoulder and found some of the kids pointing and snickering. What was that all about? Then she saw Joshua and he was frowning, his hands clenched at his side.

Briar stumbled and that made her pay closer attention to the uneven path before them. In the distance, she could hear the river coursing over the sluice gate, the rattle and clank of the aged wheel as it turned. The mill had been built before the Civil War by slaves from the Ashland Plantation, and while damaged by the Union troops during the battle of Bliss, it had only ceased grinding grain in the early 1930s. Though a local group of preservationists had restored it as best they could with limited funds, it was still weather-worn in many places.

As the sound of moving water grew louder, it was nearly impossible not to remember that summer day ten years before. She and Saralyn, who had been five at the time, had wandered away from a family picnic and found themselves by the mill. It was something they were never supposed to do as alligators sometimes sunned themselves on the banks.

Oblivious to the danger, they'd clambered up and down the stairs, proclaiming the mill was their castle. Joshua had joined them and it'd been great fun until Saralyn had lost her footing. Briar had grabbed for her, but in the process had hit the railing that overlooked the river. It had broken in two, pitching her into the churning water below, leaving Saralyn safe far above.

Over the years Briar had heard different versions of the

tale, often by people who hadn't been there that day. How Joshua had pushed her into the water, how both of them had died. How it was all her fault that they were at the mill in the first place, which was another lie.

While her cousin ran for help, Joshua had gone into the water after her. It had been him who had drowned, not her. She still remembered that part as clearly today as when it had happened, Joshua's hand clutching on to hers, his brown hair floating around him in the churning water as they were pushed along by the current. That strange jolt of sensation that had passed between them right after he'd stopped fighting and given in.

Briar was still breathing when she was pulled from the river, crying, begging them to help her friend. It'd been her uncle who had done CPR and brought Joshua to life. Finally he'd coughed and sputtered and choked out a bellyful of water. Then Joshua had begun to cry.

No matter the tale or who told it, from that day on, the river had been Briar's mortal enemy. From that point forward Mrs Quinn had begun a personal vendetta against the Rose family, blaming her for what could have been a personal tragedy.

With the memories dragging her down, Briar halted abruptly. 'Ah, I don't like being near the water.'

Pat turned and studied her. 'You can't swim?'

'No.' He didn't need to know her past. She didn't want him to pity her.

'Then relax, will you?' he said. 'I was thinking of us doing something else.'

The boy of her dreams stepped closer, cupping her face with his strong hands and then kissed the end of her nose. Briar smiled up at him, caught up in his spell. This really was like a fairy tale. The moon, the prince, the princess. All they needed was a white horse and a castle.

The next kiss was full on her lips. It was genuine, not the half-hearted kind Mike had always given her.

Briar found her heart pounding when it ended. 'Wow,' she said, her eyes widening.

'Yeah,' Pat replied, smiling. The next kiss lasted a lot longer, his hands sliding round her waist and pulling her tightly against him. His body reacted to their closeness and Briar found herself blushing. This was so perfect.

When it ended, Pat kept his arms around her as if he couldn't bear to let her go. He angled his head towards the mill. 'We could go in there,' he suggested. 'No one would know where we were. We could be all alone.'

The mill part didn't sound that good, but the *all alone* part did. Unless . . .

'Umm . . .'

He gently touched her cheek. 'I promise I won't tell anyone. Not like Mike.'

Her ex's name broke Pat's intoxicating spell. 'What's Mike got to do with this?'

'Nothing. Come on,' he said, taking her hand. 'We have some time before anyone misses us.'

When he tugged her forward towards the mill, he didn't realize he'd triggered more of her memories. Saralyn had pulled her along in much the same way only a short time before Briar had fallen into the river.

'No,' she said, sliding her hand out of his. 'Let's go back to the party, OK?'

'Why?' he said, stepping close to her again. His hand caressed her cheek. 'It'll be fun.'

Briar stepped backwards, suddenly aware that there was no one else around. Still, her reaction made no sense. Pat wasn't a threat. He was too cool.

'No, I gotta go,' she said, turning away. Pat quickly caught up with her.

'What's going on?' he asked, catching her by the wrist. Then he suddenly broke his grip and stared at his hand. His finger was bleeding. 'That damned bracelet of yours bit me.'

'Sorry. The axe is kinda sharp, I guess.'

He sucked on the wound, and then wiped his finger on his jeans. 'Look, I thought we were good together. Why can't we just hook up tonight?'

Briar blinked. 'Hook up?' He nodded. 'You mean like . . .' Pat gave another nod, a slightly irritated expression on his face.

This wasn't just a kissing expedition – he was talking about going all the way.

'It'd be good. I promise,' he said, deploying that devastating smile of his. As if that would be reason enough to take that final step.

For a few precious seconds Briar actually considered it. This was Pat, and she liked him a lot. If the curse was for real, what would it matter? She deserved some happiness.

No. Not this way. It felt too needy. Desperate even.

'I can't. I'm not like that, Pat. I don't know why you thought I was.'

He frowned now. 'You've already done it with Mike, so it wouldn't be like it was a big deal.'

There were so many things wrong with that statement she didn't know where to start. 'Who told you Mike and I hooked up?'

'It's all over his Facebook page. He didn't use your name, but everyone knows it's you.'

It can't be. She'd unfriended Mike when they'd broke up, but he wouldn't say things like that about her.

'You're lying!' she said, growing angry.

Grumbling under his breath, Pat dug out his smart phone, hunted around for something, then handed it over.

'Look!' he said. 'He put it up yesterday.'

There it was right on his page: Mike's post, a response to the question 'Have you ever done it in a car?' was about the night he'd spent with a girl whose initials were BR. He went into *graphic* detail of their time in the back seat of his car, none of which was true because she'd called a halt long before they got *that* far.

Briar's cheeks burned as if someone had doused them with gasoline and set them on fire. *Ohmigod.* Her ex had told the world they'd slept together. That's why the others were laughing. They thought she and Pat were out here getting naked.

How many people had read this and believed it was the truth? Mrs Parker had said she didn't believe the rumours.

Is that what she meant? Did the whole town know?

Of course they do. That lying piece of . . .

Briar threw the phone back at Pat and took off at a run, her stomach close to heaving, frantic to find Reena and get out of here.

If this really was her last night on earth, it had just become a total disaster.

By the time Briar made the journey from the mill to the lake, she was crying and furious at the same time. She heard Pat behind her, calling her name, but she kept moving, desperate to find her friend.

Faces turned towards her as she ran up the path. Some showed concern, others were sneering.

'Couldn't handle him, huh?' one of the girls said.

'Briar?' her friend called out, and hurried over. When Reena saw her tears, her eyes narrowed. 'What happened? What did he do to you?'

'He thinks . . . Did you know what Mike is saying about me? That he and I – went all the way?'

'What? her friend blurted.

'Yeah, on Facebook. Now everyone thinks I'm a slut who'll put out for any guy who asks,' Briar retorted, fury warring with mortal embarrassment. 'That's all Pat wanted. You were right about him.'

Sniggers came from some of the other kids, who'd gathered around to witness her mortification.

'Hey, if the shoe fits,' one of the guys called out, then laughed.

Briar glared the offender, a classmate who should have known better. 'It doesn't fit. It never will.'

'Briar, look I'm—' Pat began as he caught up with her.

She whirled round, waving a finger at him like a weapon, bringing him to a halt. 'You stay away from me, you jerk!'

'Hey, I'm sorry. No harm, no foul,' he said, raising his hands in surrender, but he didn't appear that upset. More disappointed than anything.

'Just so we're clear – Mike lied. We *never* went that far.'

'All you girls say that,' one of the guys called out, then yelped when his girlfriend smacked him on the arm.

Briar zeroed in on Mike's braying laughter as it was the loudest. For once she wished she was a guy – she'd flatten him in front of all the others and kick him when he was down.

'I want to hurt him so bad,' Briar said, her hands clenching into tight fists.

'Makes two of us, but now's not the time,' Reena said, taking her arm. 'Let's get you home.'

Jeers accompanied them across the parking lot. Just as they just reached Reena's car, Joshua caught up with them.

'What happened with Pat?' he insisted. 'What'd he do to make you cry?'

'Why do you care?' Briar snapped.

'Come on, tell me what happened. Did he hurt you?'

Why would a Quinn give a damn?

'He needs to know,' Reena said, unusually solemn. 'I'll be in the car. Don't take too long.'

Briar leaned against the vehicle, not caring if her jeans

got dirty now that her whole evening, her life, was ruined. She folded her arms over her chest, heart thudding and felt another tear roll down her cheek.

'What did Daniels do to you? Just tell me,' Joshua asked, closer now, but not so close that it made her uncomfortable.

'He didn't do anything bad. We just . . . kissed.' Which had been great until he'd ruined it.

'Then why are you crying?'

'It was Mike,' she said, and then spilt the details of her ex's sick joke.

Joshua's mouth dropped open as unexpected fire ignited in his eyes.

'That bastard,' he said. 'And Daniels is just as bad. He shouldn't believe rumours.'

There was irony for you – her family's enemy sticking up for her.

With deep-seated regret Briar realized that Joshua had been really cool all along and she had never been allowed to see it.

She wiped away the tears. 'You've been really sweet, even if you are a . . . well, you know. Thanks for the present. I love it.'

Right on cue, Joshua looked embarrassed. Thankfully, Kerry provided the perfect distraction, proudly bringing a stick, which she dropped at Briar's feet.

'It's never been fair what our parents did. I don't . . . hate you. Never did.'

He smiled. 'I never hated you, either.'

The passenger-side window rolled down. 'We need to get you home. It's eleven fifteen.'

'You better go,' Joshua said. 'Don't want you to get into trouble.'

Like it would matter. What would my parents do? Ground me? Can't do that if the curse is real.

As she saw it, not being around tomorrow might actually be a good thing.

Briar dejectedly climbed into the car and buckled her seatbelt. As they backed up, she found herself watching Joshua. He was kneeling now, his arms round his dog. On impulse, she gave a wave and he returned it. He seemed so sad, lost even.

'You never knew Josh really liked you?' Reena asked softly as she pulled out of the parking lot.

'No. Not much we could have done about it anyway.' Briar took a deep breath. 'You know what my mom's like and his mother's even worse.'

'Yeah. He got grounded last spring because of you.'

'Me?' she asked, shocked. 'Why?'

'You were standing near him at a basketball game. You didn't know he was there, too caught up in the game I guess, but his mom heard about it. She went ballistic. Josh said his dad stood up for him, but it was still really ugly.'

'Wow, I didn't know that. What is it with adults? Why are they so mean?'

'Sometimes they're that way because they're scared,' Reena replied.

Before Briar could ask what Mrs Quinn feared, her

cellphone pinged. It was her dad asking if she was headed home. She texted back that they were on the way.

A fat tear rolled down Reena's face, her hands gripping the steering wheel so tight her nails blanched.

Oh, man. 'Hey, it's OK,' Briar lied. 'This curse thing . . . it's not going to happen.'

Reena didn't reply as another tear coursed down her cheek, following the one before it.

Trembling, Briar laid her head against the side window and watched as the car's headlights spotlighted the trees along the road, like candid snapshots of her life. If this really was the end, had she made a mistake turning Pat down? What would it have been like? Would it have been good or . . . What else would she regret not doing?

As they passed the roadside memorial, Briar wondered if her family would build her one, leave a cupcake in remembrance on the anniversary of her death. Remember her for what she was, not the lies others had told.

It's not real. It can't be.

But Reena's silent tears told a different story.

CHAPTER SIX

As Reena pulled into the driveway, Briar's parents were waiting for her. They sat on the front steps as ambitious bugs flitted around the porch lights. Though her mom's eyes were dry now, her father's were red and puffy. Both of them seemed to have aged in the last couple of hours.

What really ended Briar's doubts was her friend's great-grandmother, parked on the porch swing, her feet dangling in the air as she rocked back and forth. Tiny and birdlike, with silver hair and mahogany skin, Lily Foster held a Bible in her hands.

If she was here, then the curse was for real.

It can't be . . .

Briar fumbled with the door latch and then was outside the car. Lily looked up at her and she swore the woman could see right into her heart.

Is it true?

The old woman nodded in return.

'Oh my God,' Briar said, her knees hitting the lawn as her will to stand vanished. 'It's real. It's really . . . true.'

Her parents were at her side now.

'Mom? Dad?'

They all collided in a big hug.

'I'm so sorry, Briar,' her father said, touching her hair. 'I never believed . . .' He raised his head to look over his shoulder at the woman on the porch. 'Not until tonight.'

Hearing her dad so emotional shredded Briar's heart. As she tried not to cry, the screech of grinding metal catapulted through her mind, followed by piercing screams. The nightmare again. She began to shake, her stomach nauseous, her head pounding.

'Get me inside,' Briar whispered, clutching her stomach. She refused to die on her family's front lawn and give the neighbours something to talk about. She could hear it now: *Did you see that Rose girl? Just belly flopped on to the grass like a dead carp. Got cursed, I heard. Can you believe it?*

Her mom helped her into the house, through the front room and past the kitchen where a mound of tissues sat on the table next to three empty cups. As they made their way up the stairs, there was muted conversation behind her, Reena and Lily talking about something. Her friend's voice was trembling, bordering on panic.

Once Briar reached her room the nausea had passed and with her mom's help she stripped off her make-up.

'I don't understand,' she said, staring at her mother's reflection in the mirror. 'Why me? What have I done to anyone?'

'It isn't your fault. It never was.'

Briar's anger burned brighter. 'Why didn't you tell me? Why wait until today? I could have done . . . . things.'

'I just couldn't tell you,' was the soft reply.

Oh, God. She could rage at her mother until midnight, shout and curse about the unfairness of it all. Then what?

She'd just be leaving all the pain on her mom's shoulders. *Mom has enough.*

Briar sighed and donned her favourite *I'm a Princess* nightshirt. It seemed the right choice.

What will they bury me in? Probably that sunny yellow dress she'd worn to church last Easter. She could still remember that day because she'd seen Joshua there, minus his parents. He'd made sure to sit a number of pews away, maintaining that required distance. What would he think when he found out she was dead?

Her mother was strangely calm now, loaning strength to her daughter. In her own way she was helping Briar get through this final night with dignity.

'I love you, Mom,' she said.

'I love you, too. I am so sorry this has happened.'

Standing behind her, her mother combed Briar's hair and braided it just like she had ever since Briar was little, making soothing noises as she did so. When their eyes met in the mirror, her mother's were brimming with tears.

'Who did this to me?' Briar asked.

'Someone who was very angry. Someone who couldn't forgive,' her mom replied. 'It is not important who it was, Briar. She will be punished for the rest of her life.'

She?

Her mother finished the French braid. Out of habit, Briar smoothed it with her hands, admiring the intricate weave.

'What's this?' her mom asked, pointing at the charm bracelet.

'Ah, a birthday present.' *Please don't ask who gave it to me.*

'It's very nice. Did you have a good time . . . at the party?'

Just tell her. 'I found out that . . . Mike's been spreading lies about me. He's telling people we went . . . all the way.' Briar held her breath, waiting for the reaction.

Her mom touched her cheek. 'I know, honey. I heard about it.'

'What?' *Oh, crap.* 'Does Dad know?'

Her mom shook her head. At least that was some good news.

'I didn't believe it. You're smarter than that. You always have been. I haven't given you credit enough for that.'

They hugged and for once Briar wished she was still a little kid. They had had an evening ritual: her mom would braid her hair, her dad would read her a story, then she'd fall asleep knowing everything would be all right. Those days were gone.

She climbed into her bed. When she found the pillows weren't right, Briar added an extra one so she could sit up, not stare at the ceiling like a corpse.

God, am I morbid. It was hard not to be.

From downstairs came the mournful chimes of the antique mantel clock tolling the three-quarter hour. A coarse shiver rippled through her body.

Fifteen minutes to go.

After a tap on the door, Briar's father and Reena entered the room. Her best friend's eyes were swollen and she kept sniffling. Right behind them was Gran Lily, who looked like a wizened little doll with those all-seeing eyes.

Lily took possession of Briar's study chair, shuffling it round so that it sat next to the bed. 'Good evenin', child,' she said as she settled into it.

Briar sucked in a sharp breath. 'Please – Lily, I don't want to die! Isn't there any way you can stop this?'

'No, we can't.'

She detected something in Lily's tone that sounded off, like the old woman was shading the truth. She had a million questions but she couldn't quite form the words. 'Am I going to throw up or my head spin round or something?'

'No. Ya'll just fall asleep. Reena and me are here to help ya cross over,' she said in her thick South Georgia accent.

Oh, man. What would it be like over . . . *there*? Would there be angels or devils? Briar really hadn't given much thought to that.

Lily nodded at her great-granddaughter, who began to pull items out of a grocery bag. Reena's hands shook badly, her movements jerky as roots and herbs appeared one by one. The old woman began to place them round Briar.

'What is all this?'

'A little somethin' to help ease ya over, girl,' Lily replied.

Reena gave her a satin pouch, a *gris-gris* bag.

'What's in this thing?'

'Lemon balm and some . . . other things you don't want to know about,' her friend said. They stared at each for a time as things went on around them.

'God, I can't . . .' Reena began.

To see her friend so emotional was more than Briar could stand. She sat up on her elbows. 'Why are you guys bothering? I mean, if I'm going to die, all this stuff . . .' she said, gesturing at the bed, 'isn't going to make a bit of difference. Why don't you just go home and let it . . . happen.' That way Reena wouldn't have to watch her die.

'Just lay back down, girl. Let us do what we do best.'

Lily applied a line of some sort of oil down the centre of Briar's forehead. It smelt of fresh mint and patchouli.

Briar grew increasingly frightened and sought re-assurance from her parents. Her dad was frowning – clearly he wasn't on board with all this magic stuff – but her mom gave a reassuring nod, despite the tears.

'Lily is trying to help you,' she said softly. 'Please don't fight this. It'll make it harder. We just might be able to—'

'I think it's time for the candles, Reena B,' Lily said, cutting her off.

Confused at what wasn't being said, Briar slumped down in bed, frowning. She couldn't believe what was happening to her. Her eyes followed Reena as she placed white candles all around the room, then lit them, one by one, so solemnly you'd think it was a church. The larger one by the bed seemed to have something scratched in the side of it. Briar strained to read it, but couldn't make out the letters.

'It's your name,' Reena said. 'It helps absorb the evil. Helps you . . .' Her friend choked up, a hand clamped to her mouth now.

Briar's composure fled. 'Oh God, I'm scared,' she whispered. She knew she should be doing something, fighting this – but she just felt paralysed. It was as though the curse had been waiting for her all this time and she had no choice but to let it happen.

Her mom sat on the edge of the bed, careful not to disturb any of the magical items. She took Briar's hand in hers and kissed it.

'I'm here,' she said. 'So is your dad. We won't leave you.'

Her father was on the other side of her now, near the headboard, taking her right hand in his.

'I love you. I'm so sorry. I don't . . . listen sometimes,' he said.

'Only sometimes?' Briar said, trying to joke. It fell flat.

'It's my fault,' her mom said. 'It always has been. I see now we should have told you a long time ago.'

What kind of life would she have led if she had known? Why follow the rules? Why not drink or use drugs or sleep around? What would it have mattered?

Then I wouldn't have been me.

It was too late to apologize for the million little mistakes she'd made over the years. The regrets for the things she'd done, and left undone. It all came down to this last moment and she knew whatever she said would weigh on her parents for the rest of their days.

'I love you, both of you,' Briar said. 'I will always love you, no matter what.'

Both her parents were weeping now, Reena as well. In all her years, Briar had never seen her friend cry like that, not even when she'd totally wiped out on her bike.

Lily rose and moved to the end of the bed so Briar's dad could take her place on the chair.

'The curse will take effect – we can't stop that,' the old woman said. 'But yer a strong girl and ya got too much to live for. Ya need to fight it. Fight hard. Don't let it win. Ya understand?'

'I can fight it? Will that really work?' Briar asked. *Please say yes.*

'Don't know,' Lily admitted, her steel-grey brows furrowed. 'But givin' into evil is never right.'

'I'll try,' Briar replied, though she had no idea how to do that.

Her dad's hand encompassed her wrist, causing the charm bracelet to dig into her skin. She remembered Joshua giving it to her. Now she wished she had kissed him.

Downstairs, the clock began to chime the hour. It was nearly midnight. Reena clicked off the overhead light, leaving the room bathed in the candles' gentle glow.

This is it.

As her parents and her best friend gave way to their grief, only Lily seemed calm. Her creaking voice prayed, 'By the power of the Almighty and the grace of Saint Peter and Saint Expedite, the healin' strength of Archangel Raphael . . .'

Briar grew uncomfortably sleepy, her eyelids heavy as her vision tunnelled, her vision greyer with each breath. It was as if her body were disconnecting her from this world, one sense at a time.

Is this what it's like to die?

As the clock struck its final note, she felt a ripple of cold roar through her body. She startled at the sensation.

A life for a life, a dark voice whispered deep in her mind.

70

'A life for a life,' Briar repeated as faint gasps came from around her. 'Goodbye.'

Then she forgot how to breathe.

Briar found herself on a road that seemed familiar, like the one near Bliss that led to the lake. A thin moon hung high in the air and the night was muggy. She became aware of someone walking next to her, a boy, but she couldn't tell who it was. He was talking about a movie they should see.

No. Not again.

She knew this dream. It'd haunted her for the last two weeks. Was this her personal hell, to die over and over for eternity?

From behind her came the sound of a car engine and she turned, only to be blinded by the oncoming headlights. There was the screech of brakes, the skid of tyres on gravel. The boy issued a warning cry, then rending pain cut through her the instant the car struck her straight on.

Briar felt her body fracture as metal met mortal flesh. With a thud, she hit a tree, cracking her spine like a brittle chicken bone. As she lay on the warm ground, she could hear the boy sobbing, the sound of someone wailing. She felt the blood as it poured out of her body, taking her life with it.

Then it began again: Briar found herself on her feet, unharmed. The boy was talking to her like before and then from behind her came the sound of the engine.

'No!' she screamed as the car ploughed towards her. She tried to move out of the way, but it made no difference.

Down she went, and then she was up again, standing helpless, like a virgin sacrifice to an insatiable god.

Over and over she died, each time becoming weaker, more eager to give into the pain and let go. She heard the car again, turned to see the lights. How many times had this happened now? Five, ten, a hundred?

Deep down Briar knew this would be the last time. She couldn't take it any more. She should just give up and end the agony.

Ya have to fight it, girl.

'Lily?' she called out. 'Help me!'

But the old woman wasn't here.

Fury filled her that someone was trying to kill her just because she was Briar Rose.

'I'm not giving in!' she shouted. 'I will never give in!'

As the car moved closer, with crossed fingers and a whispered prayer, she closed her eyes and walked directly towards her fate.

'She's not breathing,' Mr Rose said. 'Oh God, she's gone.'

'Hush now,' Lily commanded. 'She's still out there, but she has to do this herself.'

Reena touched her friend's hair. 'Come on, Briar,' she urged. 'You can do it.'

'Baby, don't give in,' her mother whispered, caressing her daughter's cheek.

Lily placed an aged hand over Briar's chest. 'Ya have to fight it, girl. Yer a Rose – show some backbone. If ya give in, the darkness wins. Now get to it!' she ordered.

With that, Briar took a deep, shuddering breath that shook the bed. Her eyes flew open for a second, and closed again. The next breath was softer, as was the one after that as she fell into an easy rhythm, a deep sleep, her face no longer contorted in agony.

'Hallelujah,' Lily said, smiling. 'Lord a' mercy, it worked.'

'All right! Go, Briar!' Reena said, pumping a fist towards the ceiling.

'She's OK?' Mrs Rose began, her voice quivering. 'She'll wake up soon?'

Lily's smile dimmed. 'That all depends on her. She's somewhere between this world and what lies beyond.'

'I'm not understanding this. I thought she was supposed to die,' Mr Rose said, his voice hoarse as he wiped away tears with a shaky hand. 'And now she's . . .'

'She shoulda died, but I'd hoped Briar might be strong enough to change the curse a bit. She's done that. She's sleepin' for now.'

'Just like Sleeping Beauty. But for how long?' Reena asked, her joy fading.

'I have no notion,' Lily replied. 'Ten years, a hundred? Maybe she'll wake up, maybe she won't. That's the way of it.'

Reena hadn't expected a miracle, but the thought of her friend shrivelling up, day by day, all sad and withered, wasn't one she could face. 'So that's it? She sleeps . . . forever?'

Her great-gran's eyes bored into hers. 'I told ya it wasn't no simple curse. It's grown over the years, twisted itself. Be thankful she has a chance.'

73

'But—'

'I'm not God, girl. I can't fix everythin'.' Lily hesitated. 'None of us can. Ya'll learn that soon enough when yer doin' yer own rootwork.'

'But if we can't help Briar, what's the point of doing any of this?'

'Because you've given her a chance. That's more than she had before,' Briar's mother murmured as she smoothed a strand of hair off her daughter's face.

Lily gazed down at the sleeping girl. 'The curse still has power over her and it can kill her if she isn't strong enough. Y'all have to prepare yerselves for that.'

Mrs Rose's eyes met Reena's, filled with both raw fear and desperate hope.

'No, she's strong inside,' her mom said. 'Briar will come back to us. I can feel it.'

'From yer lips to the angels' ears,' Lily murmured.

CHAPTER SEVEN

As she fought her way back to consciousness, Briar became aware that she was no longer in the nightmare. The car, the road and the blinding pain were gone and in their place was hard ground that made her back ache.

'Mom? Dad?' she called out as she pulled herself up. Her head spun and then righted itself as more of the cobwebs seemed to fall away.

She wasn't in her bedroom, but in an alley and it appeared to be just after sunset, with barely enough light left to discern her surroundings. The smell of woodsmoke and manure filled her nose with each breath, along with some other scents she couldn't place. None of them were nice.

Her sleep shirt had been replaced by a long dress over what appeared to be some sort of chemise. The dress was homespun in a watery blue and a darker blue corset was laced over the top, but not so tight that she couldn't breathe. Her hair was still plaited, but now was secured with a dark cord and lay over her shoulder. A pair of patched leather boots covered her feet.

Further inspection revealed that the red fingernail polish Briar had so carefully applied before the party was gone. In fact, all her nails were broken and encrusted with dirt, her fingers calloused as if she'd done manual labour.

What is this?

To her relief, the charm bracelet was still on her wrist, and for a fraction of second she swore it glinted in the dim light. A quick pat of her clothes proved that nothing else had made the journey, not even the *gris-gris* bag Reena had given her. It felt strange not having a cellphone.

Unable to make any sense of her situation, Briar examined her surroundings with increasing apprehension. The building to her right was constructed of rough-hewn wood, the one on the other side made of stone. She rose and took a few steps forward, unsteady. Finally her eyes focused on a small figure sitting at the end of the alley, a mangy cat that had managed to score itself a mouse. The fur seemed odd, not like hair at all. It looked up at her, its victim's tail hanging out of its mouth.

'Ewww . . . gross,' she said, waving her arms. 'Go away!'

It took off like a shot, making a strange noise as it moved.

Was she really dead? Was this heaven? *No. It wouldn't smell this bad.*

As she reached the street, the world seemed alien to her modern eyes. There was no tarmac, no streetlights, no cars or people. The buildings were a confusing blend of stone, wood and . . . metal.

Briar stepped in something squishy and recoiled, shaking her shoe to remove the dung. *If this is heaven, I so want a refund.*

A house on the right looked familiar, as if it belonged in Bliss, but the next one had a thatched roof with ivy scrambling up a ramshackle stone chimney. There were lights inside the dwelling, along with furtive moments. Someone peered out of a window, then slammed the shutters closed as if she were a thief on the prowl.

As Briar moved along in a daze, she passed a bakery and a cobbler's shop, then more strange houses. Despite the increasing darkness, she swore she could see the outline of a great stone edifice in the distance, its turrets lifting high in the air.

A castle? No way. How cool is that?

There was a sound behind her and she whirled, desperate to find someone who could explain all this to her. A man dressed in peasant clothes hurried by, hunched down as if he hoped that made him invisible.

'Hey, excuse me . . .' she said, trying to catch up with him. 'Wait! I need some help.' He fled down the darkening street, his terror evident. 'Boy, thanks!' she said, irritated.

What is it with this place? Why was he so freaked?

A deep metallic sound began to reverberate through the town, much like a gong, with each strike evenly spaced after the other. It must have been a signal of some kind as door bolts slid home and shutters closed all around her. The town was closing down for the night, which meant Briar was going to have to sleep on the streets if she didn't find help soon.

'And I thought Bliss was bad,' she muttered. She picked a house at random, but pounding on the door got her no reply. She tried the next place, then the next, her panic rising.

What are they afraid of?

As if in answer to her question, a tormented howl filled

the air. Briar had heard coyotes before, but this sounded different. *Dogs?* A pack of them could do a lot of damage. Maybe they were the reason why the guy was in such a hurry to get off the streets.

The first howls were soon joined by another, then even more. The hair on the back of Briar's neck rose.

'Wolves? No, it can't be.'

Some primitive reflex urged her forward and Briar jogged back down the way she'd come. Perhaps if she kept moving she'd find someone who would take her in for the night. Or she'd wake up from this nightmare and be in her own bed, safe and sound.

'Yeah, that's it. I'm going to wake up now and it'll all be fine,' she said.

The scene didn't change, and instead the howls grew closer. When Briar took a quick look over her shoulder she saw them. They were wolves and somehow their eyes glowed unnaturally in the twilight.

'Oh, crap!'

Panicking, Briar took off at full speed, trying to avoid the muddy holes and the piles of manure. For a couple of streets she stayed ahead of them, but they slowly gained on her. Knowing she couldn't outrun them, she raced up to the nearest house and pounded on the door. 'Help! Let me in!'

'Go away!' someone shouted from within.

'But there are wolves!' she cried.

'You broke curfew – it's your fate,' was the stone-cold response.

Briar whirled to find the beasts trotting round the corner. One was sniffing the ground, tracking her. She took off at a run again, barrelling down a side street, only to find it a dead end. Judging the height of the stone wall that blocked her way, she tried to find hand and footholds to climb it, but slid back to the ground and landed on her butt.

A throaty growl shot icicles into her blood.

The wolves lined up in front of her now, one in front – the leader – and four behind. She could better see their unnatural sparkling eyes, as if they were lit from within by some nefarious magic. Their fur was patchy, and where it was missing metal had replaced it, cutting deep into their flesh. Perhaps that was why their howls sounded so tormented.

What are these things?

The leader's growl grew in intensity as it took a step forward. Heeding the warning, Briar flung herself at the wall again, digging with her fingers, trying to find some handhold. Her boots slid against the stones. She nearly cheered when her hand managed to reach the top, but she couldn't gain any purchase with her feet. Reena would already be over this thing, racing away, but Briar had never been great in gym class. Now that was going to cost her everything.

With a snarl, the lead wolf leaped forward, its teeth catching hold of the bottom of her dress, trying to drag her down. Briar yelped in fear just as the fabric ripped, setting her free, and she frantically clawed her way higher on the wall, scraping her palms in desperation.

A hand clamped on to hers and tugged. Gasping in surprise, she pushed harder with her feet against the stones, trying to help. When she didn't budge, another hand grabbed hers and she was pulled on to the top of the wall. See-sawing on her belly against the rough stones, she tried to focus on her rescuer, but it was too dark to make out the face clearly.

'Quickly, over the top!' His voice was male and he was short of breath, like he'd been running.

With tremendous effort, she went over the stones, landing directly in her rescuer's arms. Claws ripped against stone on the other side of the wall as the wolves tried to climb the barrier.

'We must run,' the man said, dragging her up on to her feet. 'They will scale it soon. Hurry!'

Briar staggered after him, still winded. When she didn't move fast enough, he caught her hand and pulled her along. Grimly, she knew she really had no choice but to trust the guy – it was either go with him or become supper.

She barely noted their surroundings as he wove them through tiny alleys, over wooden fences and through abandoned houses. From behind came the constant howls as the wolf pack continued its hunt.

When the noises grew distant, Briar was finally allowed to rest. She slumped up against an old building.

'Those are really . . . strange . . . wolves,' she said, finding it very hard to breathe. 'They climb walls. They're . . . metal. That's not . . . right.'

'They will hunt anyone on the streets, at least until

daylight.' The man pointed above her at a window set in the wall. 'Up you go.'

'In there?'

'It is best we are both inside until the sun rises.' His face was still in the shadows, so she had no way to judge his intentions.

Her caution took hold. 'Look, you were great, but . . . I don't know you. I don't know if—'

'I am trustworthy? That is a puzzle, isn't it?' he said, his voice harder now. 'What shall it be – the wolves you know, or the one you don't? That is a difficult choice, is it not?'

In the distance, the howls rose again and Briar shivered in response. A single, high-pitched screech of agony carried through the night, following by silence.

'What . . . ?' she began.

'Apparently you weren't the only one breaking curfew tonight,' the man observed. 'So what will it be? Remain here and hope they don't find you or go inside the stable and sleep in peace?'

'Why aren't we going in the stable's doors?'

'It's quicker this way.'

She knew what the wolves would do to her. This guy? Not so much. Unfortunately, there wasn't any other choice. 'You win. I'm inside for tonight, but I'll need a lot of questions answered.'

'I shall do my best to satisfy your curiosity,' he said, making a cradle of his hands.

Briar stepped up into them, then caught on to the bottom of the window sill. Pulling herself up, muscles straining, she straddled the opening and then lost her grip entirely. With a short cry she plummeted down into a pile of something reasonably soft. It was hay, fragrant and fresh. She rolled out of the way so her rescuer could join her.

The young man landed with considerable grace, which told her he'd done this manoeuvre a number of times. Next to him, she had all the climbing skills of a whale.

'Stay there. I'll light a candle so you do not have stumble your way through in the dark.'

Briar lay back in the hay and tried to let her racing heart return to a normal pace. Was this part of the curse, like some giant role-playing game? If you survive the car-wreck dream, then you move to another level, one with killer wolves?

The yawn caught her off guard, and before she had a chance to stifle it she found her eyes drooping. She fought them, desperate to stay awake, if nothing more than to have a chance to run if this guy got creepy. Unfortunately, the desire for rest proved stronger and Briar fell asleep for the second time that night.

Something snuffled her hair.

'Go away,' she murmured, waving an arm. There was another snuffle, wetter now.

As her sleepiness ebbed, she began to recall images from the night before. None of them was good. She remembered the old clock striking the hour, her parents weeping, Lily whispering something to her. The solid impact of the car striking her over and over. And then waking in a world where there were bizarre wolves and houses made of brass.

There was more snuffling near her right ear. Despite her pounding headache, Briar forced her eyes open and discovered something white and woolly staring back.

She shouted, scrambling backwards in the pile of hay as the ewe bolted away, just as shocked as she was. Briar wiped something off her face – sheep snot she guessed – then tried to get a grip on her surroundings.

Looking around, she remembered climbing in through the window above her, helped by some young guy who'd saved her from becoming wolf chow. A quick glance proved her clothes were still rustic and her boots covered in dried crap.

There were no Pearly Gates, no Saint Peter peering down at her and asking why she'd kicked Becca Fingle in the shins when she was three.

Maybe I'm not dead. But she certainly wasn't in Bliss.

Besides the sheep, a mud-spattered cow was tethered a short distance away, methodically chewing its cud. A really big horse took up a position near the front of the structure, the sturdy kind of beast farmers used before tractors were invented. Four riding horses were tethered on the other side.

This did not qualify as heaven unless you were a member of the Future Farmers of America.

She started at the sound of voices coming from just outside the barn. One was quiet, with a hint of a rustiness to it, the other higher-pitched, aristocratic, enunciating each word with precise care, as if they were bladed weapons. As Briar peered round a stall, two men entered the building.

The first had dark hair that ended at his broad shoulders, and an aquiline nose. He was tall, wearing homespun clothes along the same lines as hers, and held the reins to a horse that would never be used for ploughing if the fancy saddle was any indication. Briar smiled in recognition – this was the guy who'd saved her butt the night before.

The man next him was blond and better dressed, clearly from a higher rung on life's ladder and eager to flaunt it. Once the horse was secured and the saddle removed, its owner began to issue orders.

'I'll need my mare to remain here for today only,' he said, giving the stablehand a condescending glance. 'I'll send for her after I have completed my business at the castle.' He tossed a coin in the air, one the groom caught with some dexterity. 'Don't scrimp on the hay, or you shall feel the bite of my sword.'

'Is it your intention to visit the princess?' the young man asked, brushing aside the threat.

The nobleman blinked at the bold question. 'Yes. Why do you ask?'

'I wouldn't advise it.'

'I do not need the advice of those beneath me,' he replied crisply. 'I hired you to tend my horse, nothing more.'

The stablehand gave a half-hearted bow. 'I apologize, my lord. No doubt, you know what is best.'

The man seemed mollified. 'Perhaps there will be a position for you at the royal stables when I become king. Providing my mount is well cared for, of course.' Then the imperious fellow spun on a heel and strode out of the barn.

Once the noble was gone, Briar's rescuer patted the horse's flank. 'Your master's a glittering fool. If he tries to see the princess, he'll be dead before sundown. I'll be sure to find you a smarter owner the next time around.'

Princess? Briar slumped back into the hay, stunned. *Ohmigod. I'm inside a real fairy tale. You have got to be kidding me.*

The young man walked to where she was located, and leaned against a timber support, arms casually crossed over his chest. His raised eyebrow hinted at amusement.

'So you're awake,' he said, his voice richer now than when he'd been talking with his customer. 'It is not often I find young women curled up in my hay.'

Briar's headache made her cranky. 'Where are they normally curled up?'

The roguish smile on the young man's face gave her the answer.

'You're not from here.' He hadn't posed it as a question.

'Why do you think that?'

'Because you were out after curfew. Those who live in the village know that's a death sentence.'

'You were out after curfew,' she said.

'I heard you pounding on one of the doors, trying to gain access. I knew you wouldn't.' He leaned closer and pointed at her face. 'You should not allow yourself to be seen in such a manner.'

'What's wrong with me?'

'Your hair, it's the colour of gold.'

Apparently he didn't like blondes. Even worse, he was watching her more closely than Briar preferred.

'What is your name?'

'Briar . . . Rose.'

He was older than her, maybe eighteen or so, and his eyes were a deeper brown. He was quite handsome in a rugged kind of way, and reminded her of an older version of Joshua, but that was probably because he worked with horses.

'You have yet to tell me why you were alone on the streets,' he said.

How was she going to explain this? If she told him the truth, they'd probably roast her at a stake for being totally crazy. 'What is your name?' she asked, hoping to buy time.

'Ruric,' he said, executing a full bow with a great deal of expertise.

'Good to meet you, Ruric.'

'Why are you on your own in such a place?' he asked, moving a step closer. Clearly he wasn't going to let it drop.

'This is going to sound strange, but where am I?'

'In the town.'

'And the town's name is . . .'

'Kursian, though hardly anyone refers to it as such.'

'Oh.' That didn't help. 'I was sent here . . .' She trailed off. 'And I don't know how to get back to my home.'

He blinked. 'What village do you call your home?' he asked.

'Bliss.'

The corners of his mouth curved upward. 'That is a curious name for a hamlet. Is it truly so blissful for those who dwell there?'

'No. It's OK, I guess.' *At least it doesn't have wolves in the streets.*

'Oh . . . kay?' he asked, puzzled.

Briar realized she needed to translate. 'OK means . . . it's good. Nothing really fancy, but good.'

'I see,' he said, frowning. 'Our village is not blissful. It is dangerous here, what with the wolves and the fata.'

'The what?'

'They are—'

Someone called out for Ruric and he quickly waved her into a corner. 'Stay out of sight until I have finished with this one. Then I will help you if I can.'

Briar did as he asked, though she wondered why he was so nervous about her being seen by anyone.

Once another man and his horse had departed, Ruric returned. During that time, he'd apparently given her situation some thought. 'Perhaps I can find someone who knows where your village lies,' he said. 'Then I can arrange an escort to return you safely to your family.'

'I don't think it'll be that easy,' she said, that admission crushing a bit more of her hope. 'I think I'm here for some reason.' Not that she had a clue why she felt that way. It was more instinct, like knowing she should walk towards the oncoming car in her nightmare, rather than trying to dodge it.

When she looked back up, Ruric's frown had reappeared. 'You are most peculiar, Briar Rose.'

'I know,' she said, flopping down in the hay. 'Tell me more about your village. Why do you have a pack of wolves roaming the streets? I mean, that's pretty . . . drastic.' She'd almost said 'medieval'.

'They are only part of what keeps this village in thrall.'

Which wasn't an answer. 'What about this princess?'

'She is part of the problem. Aurora has been asleep for a long time, you see.'

Aurora? Oh wow, I'm in 'Sleeping Beauty'. That was her fave tale ever, but why did it feel wrong?

'Why hasn't some prince kissed her and broken the spell?'

'You know of her plight, then?' Briar nodded. 'In truth, many have tried, prince and commoner. They all failed because of the regent.'

'What regent?' she asked, puzzled.

'The one who rules the kingdom until Aurora is restored.'

That's not right. While in some of the versions of 'Sleeping Beauty' the curse had put the entire kingdom asleep, in others it was just the princess, her family and the servants, trapped inside a wall of thorns. None of the tales had ever spoken of someone *running* the kingdom while they waited for the sleepy royal to rise and shine.

'Who is this regent person?' she asked.

Ruric's face clouded. 'That is a very dangerous question.'

He beckoned her further back inside the stable. She noted he kept himself positioned so he could see the doors at all times.

'Aurora was cursed to die when she reached her sixteenth birthday,' he replied in a lowered voice.

There's a lot of that going around.

'When the princess pricked her finger on a needle, she fell asleep.'

'And her family too, right?'

'Yes, but . . . they did not survive. One by one, they died from some mysterious illness, or at least that is what the regent claimed. Now the only one left is Aurora and none can awaken her.'

That was so wrong. Before she could follow up on that, somewhere in the village a gong began to sound.

'Another curfew?'

'No.' Ruric's face fell. 'I knew that fool didn't have a chance.'

'You mean the guy that left his horse here?'

'Yes. That sound means we are being summoned to a Reckoning.' He stared at her. 'We must cover your hair.' Ruric hurriedly dug around in his possessions until he found a coarse piece of fabric, which he handed to her. It smelt musty and even though she tried to talk him out of it, he wouldn't budge.

'Just cover all of it. Tuck it up tightly.'

'Why?'

'Because it's dangerous for you to be seen the way you are. I'll explain later. Hurry now, we are running out of time.'

Once she'd done as he asked, he hastily smeared dirt on her face, taking special care to darken her eyebrows. His fingers were calloused, but gentle, and it was disconcerting to be this close to him, to see so deep in his eyes.

As if made uneasy as well, Ruric stepped back, wiping

his hands on his breeches. 'That will have to do.' He pulled on a grey cloak, tying it at his neck.

'What is this Reckoning thing?' she asked as he secured the stable doors behind them.

'It is . . . a summons by the regent. All in the village are required to attend, unless you are at death's door.'

'And if you're not . . . dying?'

'Then you soon will be.'

CHAPTER EIGHT

Ruric took off at a pace that made Briar scurry to catch up with him. It didn't help that he was blessed with long legs.

When she protested, he refused to slow down. 'We must hurry. It is never wise to be late,' he said.

'Why?'

'It is best not to draw attention to ourselves.'

Briar growled under her breath. Still, Ruric was so serious she clamped her mouth shut. Eventually she'd get her answers.

As they hurried along, she stole quick glances at the other villagers. Some had pockmarked faces, or missing teeth. A few limped along using makeshift crutches. A young woman with a baby in her arms hustled past, her face flushed. She looked familiar.

'Mrs Bailey?' Briar called out. The woman didn't act as if she'd heard her and kept moving.

Briar thought maybe she'd been wrong, but then she saw two other people from her town, as well. One man looked straight at her, but there was no sign of recognition.

OK, this is freaky. Part Bliss, part . . . whatever.

Next to her, a portly man puffed along, flour dusting his clothes. A baker perhaps? A small boy sped past them with a scraggly dog barking at his heels.

In the daylight the village looked just as confusing as it

had at dusk. Ramshackle houses with uneven roofs crouched over the street like arthritic vultures. The street itself was dirt and mud, or worse, depending on where you put your feet.

This is too real to be a fairy tale. The storybook villages were littered with clever boys, hideous giants, brave princes and evil stepmothers. Princesses were everywhere, most of them in dire need of being rescued. The only thing in abundance in this hamlet was people who really needed a bath.

Hasn't anyone invented soap yet?

Despite the smell, Briar really wanted to slow down and check it all out. Even if this was a dream, how often did you find yourself inside a story? Unfortunately, Ruric didn't alter his pace until they reached some sort of crossroads when the increasing foot traffic slowed him down. Five lanes – they could hardly be considered streets – converged at a hub, like spokes on a wheel. In the very centre was a well.

Just like Bliss used to have. Briar had seen pictures of it at her grandparents' house.

After much jostling, more villagers spilt in around them from all sides, then they all channelled down one street in particular. Luckily, it was the widest of the bunch.

Ruric touched her arm. 'Stay close to me,' he said, his tone worried.

A woman walked by, a shiny area on her cheek catching Briar's notice. For a second she thought it was some sort of jewellery, but blood oozed around it, dark and weeping. Then she spied another villager, this one with pieces of metal replacing two of his fingers. He seemed in pain, his hand swollen and infected.

'What is wrong with those people?' Briar asked, angling her head in their direction.

Ruric shot a quick glance at them. 'They have accepted the regent's metal as a talisman against our enemies.'

'Why would anyone do that if it hurts them?'

'They will do anything not to fear, even if the threat is nothing compared to the cure.'

Out of the corner of her eye Briar caught sight of a man hunched over in an awkward position, his arms and head secured in some sort of wooden framework. He was smeared with rotten produce and covered in swarming flies.

She tugged on Ruric's sleeve. 'What did he do?'

'He was one of the night watchmen and was caught asleep at his post. He's fortunate all he got was the pillory.'

Eventually they entered an open area just outside the village. To Briar's relief, it was broad and green. The air was cleaner here and she took a deep breath, savouring it.

'Oh, that's better,' she said. 'Where are we going?'

'To the common,' her escort replied. 'It is where the villagers graze their livestock.'

The flood of people continued on, and in time they approached an open field. There weren't many cows or sheep, but a substantial crowd had gathered, clustered in tight knots. Briar guessed there were over two hundred souls with more still streaming from the village. Some were fully human; others had that metallic talisman of which Ruric spoke. The way the brass twisted into their flesh seemed more torture than protection. It reminded her of the wolves.

Ruric paused for a moment, eyeing the crowd. 'Come, let us head for the oak,' he said, pointing to a massive tree in the very centre of the field. In many ways the field reminded her of the one outside Bliss. It had that same pastoral vibe. Before they had a chance to move on, a man with bulging biceps and a leather apron joined them. He had big bristling eyebrows and a crooked nose, like it'd been broken, but not set properly.

'Smithy,' Ruric said, inclining his head politely.

'Ruric. How are you today?'

'Well, and you?'

'The same. Who is this, then?' the man asked, nodding his head at Briar.

'My . . . cousin, Briar. She has come to visit me, no doubt to report home as to how I am faring.'

Briar made sure to nod and go along with the ruse.

'Welcome, maid,' the smithy said, then frowned. 'Poor day to be here, though,' he added, shooting Ruric a knowing glance.

'True, but none of us were given a choice,' he replied. 'I need a new horseshoe. I'll bring the damaged one by this afternoon so you can judge the size of it.'

'I'll be watching for you,' the smithy replied, and headed off. Briar tracked him for a time until he joined a dark-haired lady with broad hips.

'Cousin?' she said, giving Ruric a raised eyebrow.

'It has to be that way,' he said in a low voice. 'You don't resemble me so I cannot claim you're my sister.'

He had a point. 'So why did you have me cover my hair?' she asked, making sure to keep her voice so quiet only he could hear her. 'A lot of girls here don't.' Almost all of them, in fact, at least those of her age.

'Do you notice anything in common about them?'

Her eyes hopped around, checking out each young female she could spy. They ranged from tall and scrawny to heavy and round. One even resembled her cousin Saralyn, except with dark hair, which was really creepy. Then she saw the one thing they weren't.

'None of them have the same hair colour as mine.'

'That is it.' He leaned closer now. 'It is said that the regent dislikes any that have hair the colour of gold because it is an insult to the sleeping princess.'

'So what does he do? Give you a haircut?'

'She,' he corrected her. 'Yes, there is a haircut, in a way. She has you beheaded.'

'You're not . . . joking, are you?' Briar replied, aghast.

'No. I saw a young woman die in this very spot only a few weeks ago. She had come to the village with her husband, but no one warned them of the fate that might befall her.'

'What did her husband do?'

'He died at her side, ripped to pieces by a—' Ruric shook his head. 'Those are not things you should know about.'

In lieu of a reply, Briar's stomach somersaulted. *They kill people because of their hair. What kind of hell is this?*

As he led her across the field, people greeted them pleasantly and there were more questions as to who *the fair maid* was. Briar also received a few glares along the way, mostly from younger girls.

The tree they sheltered under was gnarly and huge and had to be centuries old. As Briar rested her back against the trunk, enjoying the leafy shade, she couldn't help but notice a few women frowning at her.

Ruric noted it as well. 'Ah, they'll be wagging their tongues when this is through. You are seen as a threat to all those mothers who have marriageable daughters.'

'But cousins can't marry,' she said. When he gave her a bemused expression, Briar gasped. 'They can?'

'Most certainly. In my village as well.'

'Not where I come from.' *And for good reasons.* 'You're not from here?'

'No. I arrived in the spring. Quinton, the elderly man who owns the stable, needed help. He's been pleased with my work, so I've stayed on.'

'People seem to like you,' she said. Especially the girls, who tracked him wherever he went. Some primped their hair or swayed their hips enticingly whenever they thought he was looking in their direction.

'Only because I am young, healthy and unwed. I'm prime game,' Ruric admitted.

'I can see that,' Briar said before she had time to think. 'I mean . . .' Her cheeks grew warm with embarrassment.

Ruric smiled wolfishly. 'Thank you.'

'Why haven't you married one of them?'

'In truth, mostly I spend my time with tavern wenches. There are fewer expectations that way.'

'Oh.' Now she regretted asking the question.

He hesitated, and then added, 'Do you have a suitor in your village?'

Suitor? Briar shifted gears to medieval-speak. 'No, they have proved false. One spread rumours that I was . . . well . . .' Just how did she explain that?

'Free with your affections?' he questioned.

That was a nice way to put it. 'Yes, and the other just wasn't what I thought he was.' Which really sucked.

'I am sorry,' Ruric replied. 'Truly. You appear to be a fine young woman, not coarse like some.'

Is he hitting on me? That would totally rock if she wasn't in the middle of some death curse.

'What about you? Is there someone waiting for you back in your village?'

Ruric nodded. 'She would be the reason I am *here*, and not at home.'

It appeared that the stable dude had as much trouble with love as she did. Who would have figured? He was very handsome, in a Romeo sort of way. No wonder some of the village girls were hoping she'd die of the plague or something.

A vendor walked by, selling talismans off a tray woven of rushes. Many of his wares were metal. 'Keep your family safe from evil!' he cried, holding up something that looked like a small coin.

'How do they work?' Briar asked. 'The talismans I mean?'

Ruric gave her a curious look. 'The fata fear metal, so the villagers have long worn small adornments believing that will keep them safe. Then the regent came to power and offered her own metal as protection, but hers is different: it pierces the skin and it is said it corrupts your soul.'

Briar thought of Joshua's gift. 'But things like coins . . . or bracelets . . . everyday stuff doesn't grow on you, right?' she asked, nervous now.

'No. Only metal the regent has enchanted.'

Briar whooshed out a sigh of relief. 'So what's a fata anyway?'

Before he could answer, a series of trumpet blasts split the air and, as if someone had flipped a switch, all conversation ended.

Ruric bent close to her ear. 'Do not call attention to yourself in any manner. Do you understand?'

She agreed, if nothing more than to keep him from worrying.

Her ears picked up the sound of many horses' hoofs on packed ground. It took a moment to see the riders headed towards them, each clad in bluish silver armour that glinted in the sunlight. With their visors down, and even their hands and fingers covered, they resembled robots rather than men.

'Those are the regent's elite warriors,' Ruric explained.

Behind them was a coach pulled by a skittish pair of greys. It was made of iron and oddly ornate, like something a goth Cinderella would love. From the way the beasts strained in their traces, the conveyance had to be heavy. A servant sat at the back of the coach on a small seat, his eyes forward, half his face covered in a brass mask. Briar gaped at him: he was dressed in a Yankee uniform.

What's a bluecoat doing in a fairy tale?

Apparently sensing her confusion, Ruric took her hand in his. The simple gesture reassured her, and Briar smiled up at him in gratitude.

As the coach pulled to a stop in front of the crowd, the armoured horsemen formed a solid line of menace just to the right of it. From behind the coach came more riders who formed a similar line to the other side. The message was clear: you mess with whoever was inside, and your life would be brutally shortened.

The servant hopped down and strode to the door of the coach. He hesitated, as if awaiting some command, then swung it open.

'Is it the princess?' someone whispered. 'Has she been awakened?'

'Would that it be so,' another man whispered in reply.

A dark figure emerged from the coach, a woman clad in a ground-skimming steel-coloured dress that flowed over a bell hoop. The dress was classic Civil War garb, the kind Briar had seen at Bliss's re-enactment balls.

When the regent turned towards the crowd, Briar could only stare in incomprehension. The woman wore a mask, not the fancy kind you'd encounter at a masquerade ball, but a copper one that covered her entire face, with only the eyes and a small slit at the mouth left open to scrutiny. Her hair was hidden by a stylish hat, and a fingertip-length black veil trailed down over her shoulders.

Ohhkay . . . 'That's the regent?'

Ruric nodded. 'Perhaps we will be fortunate and there will be no Reckoning. Sometimes she just summons us for no reason at all.'

'Why?'

'To remind us who truly is in charge,' he said in a tight voice.

Oh, goodie. A sleeping princess plus *a dictator.*

The regent walked forward a few paces and then ascended a low wooden platform that must have been custom built for the purpose as it put her above the crowd, like a ruling monarch. The footman hurried forward and placed a small wooden table in front of her, upon which she set a dark leather bag. It also looked of Civil War vintage.

Then their leader just stood there, as if waiting for something. There were murmurs from the crowd, but apparently no one dared leave the field. Finally, in the distance came the creaking of wheels, and this time it was a small cart. Inside it was a man, his shirt ripped and his back bloodied, as if he'd been whipped. Heavy shackles hung from his wrists.

'It's him!' Briar hissed. 'The man who boarded his horse.'

'Yes, it is,' Ruric replied flatly. 'I warned him, but they never listen. At least I got a good mare out of the deal.'

She stared up at him, surprised at his callousness. 'That's really cold.'

'I am certain it is, but I shall make no apology.'

Townspeople began to yell insults at the poor wretch as he was marched in front of the crowd. After another trumpet blast, the footman came forward and unfurled a piece of paper.

'This man,' he cried out, 'from the village of Henkel, did attempt to harm the Sleeping Princess, the one known as Aurora. In her mercy, the regent has granted him death for his heinous crimes.'

'That's mercy? What's worse than death?' Briar exclaimed, drawing looks from some of those around her.

'A number of things,' Ruric said. 'I'll explain it all *later*.'

The prisoner was forced to the centre of the field and given a sword. From Briar's vantage point, it looked old and rusty, as if it was just a prop, not a true weapon. The man shouted his anger, but he dared not attack, not with the mounted horsemen watching his every move.

'There is no princess!' the noble cried out to the crowd. 'It's all a lie! I have seen the truth for myself.'

Boos came from the villagers, along with a few rotten vegetables, which he ducked as best he could. As the missiles continued, the regent opened the top of the voluminous bag and extracted something round and spiked, like a curled-up metallic hedgehog. Placing it on a black-gloved hand, she blew on it, her breath turning into a fine copper mist the instant it left her mouth.

'What is she doing?' Briar whispered.

'Magic,' Ruric replied grimly. 'Watch carefully.'

To Briar's delight a tiny bird formed on the woman's palm. After another breath, its creator tossed it in the air. Briar watched in fascination as it grew larger, and then larger still. So large that its wingspan was at least twelve feet.

The villagers murmured in awe. A few little kids began to cry, fearful of the creature. From what Briar could tell, it appeared to be a buzzard, one with a cruel hooked beak and long talons. As it glided into the air, the sun glinted off it, nearly blinding her.

'It's metal,' she exclaimed, astounded at the sight. 'It shouldn't be able to fly.' *Unless it has an engine somewhere.*

'Alas, flying is not all it does,' Ruric replied.

As it sailed overhead for one long pass, testing its wings, the bird momentarily cast a shadow over the man below. Without warning, it dived at him out of the sun, as if it knew the condemned man wouldn't be able to see it. A few of the villagers cried out in alarm and that was the only reason it didn't hook its claws into him as it swooped low above the ground. He vainly tried to stab at a wing to wound it, but missed. Knocked off his feet, he scrambled to avoid one of the talons as it raked near him. The buzzard rose high in the air, gained speed and then made another run, again with the sun behind it.

Birds were smart, but this thing had a vicious cunning to it.

Briar began to shiver when the metal monster managed to grab on to the prisoner and haul him off the ground. The man tried to hack at one of the legs, but the sword had no effect. When the buzzard reached the zenith of its flight, it set its captive free and his piteous screams lasted until he impacted the ground with a solid thump.

'Oh my God!' Briar cried.

Ruric pulled her close, burying her face in his shirt.

'Is it over now?' she whimpered.

'No,' Ruric said. 'The beast has landed.'

Against her better sense, Briar turned in time to see the buzzard perch on the man's body, then plunge its beak into his chest. It pulled out his heart and devoured it in one greedy gulp.

She clamped her hand over her mouth, sickened, fearing she would vomit.

'The man died swiftly, not like some of them,' Ruric said quietly.

Ohmigod. Why am I here? What did I do to deserve this?

Briar swallowed hard and then turned away from the carnage. 'These executions. Do they happen a lot?'

'Yes, usually whenever some fool tries to wake the princess. They believe if the spell is broken the regent will step aside.'

'Is that likely?'

He shook his head. 'Some are allowed inside the castle – like this fellow, probably because he was of noble birth. Others steal their way in. The result is the same.'

Why don't they overthrow this tyrant? The villagers outnumbered her warriors. All they had to do was gang up her on her.

Ruric must have divined her thoughts. 'No further questions,' he said uneasily. 'Too many ears are listening.'

The next sharp blast of a trumpet made Briar jump in panic.

'Justice has been done!' the footman cried out, then handed his ruler into the coach. After he leaped up on to the seat at the back, it rolled away, sandwiched between the two lines of heavily armed horsemen.

The bird executed a few hops and took wing. All eyes followed it, wondering who would be its next victim. To Briar's astonishment, it shrank in size until it was tiny again. It flew along the side of the coach and then popped into the window, no doubt to become a tiny metal ball once again.

Monster recycling. That's not good news.

It was only as the villagers began the trek back home that Briar wondered what would become of the dead man's body. When she posed the question, Ruric looked towards the remains.

'He'll be buried in an unmarked grave.'

'But his family? How will they ever know what happened to him?'

He looked at her curiously. 'Why do you worry about him, a man you did not know?'

'Because if it was me . . . I'd want my family to know how I died.'

Ruric's face softened. 'As would I, Briar, as would I.'

CHAPTER NINE

Dawn found Joshua awake. He hadn't been able to sleep, not after all that had happened at the party. Some of it had been because of Briar, at how upset she'd been at Mike's lies. He'd wanted nothing more than to tear the bastard apart after he'd seen how much that loser had hurt her.

I still might.

Which was at war with everything he'd been told over the years. The Roses are bad people, they'll hurt you; and yet now he found himself caring for one far more than was sensible.

As the night wore on and sleep continued to elude him, he'd thought about the moment he'd given Briar the charm bracelet. How he'd wished it had gone differently . . . better somehow. *If Daniels hadn't been there . . .*

If he hadn't been born a Quinn.

After Briar had left the party, her cousin had started talking about some curse and, at first, he hadn't paid much attention.

'We'll know in the morning if it's real or not,' Saralyn had said to one of her friends. 'I think it's total crap. Who would put a curse on Briar, anyway? She's nothing special.'

Even now he couldn't believe it. A curse was just crazy talk. Yet he had this gnawing anxiety that something was very wrong, and it had begun at the stroke of midnight. The pressure in his chest still hadn't let up, even though it was past seven.

With considerable effort, he forced himself out of bed and chose a clean pair of jeans and a T-shirt from a drawer, though he wasn't expected at the stables until noon. Out of habit, he gave a tap to the dream catcher suspended from the ceiling, causing it to turn in lazy circles.

He was stalling, knowing there'd be another inquisition from his mom. It happened nearly every morning when he'd been out the night before. Who had he talked to? What had he done? Had he been anywhere near that Rose girl? That was one question that always came his way.

Last night he had been *very* close to that Rose girl, and it was a good bet someone had already blabbed about it. He never understood how his mom heard about such things; it was almost like she had a network of spies watching his every move.

Joshua sighed as he trudged down the stairs and entered the kitchen. They'd remodelled it the year before and so it was all gleaming stainless steel and granite countertops now. His mother was at the gas stove cooking breakfast, her posture tense, his father hunched over the newspaper at the table. It was clear that things weren't right between them and had been that way for a long time. It was quieter than normal this morning: his two younger brothers were in North Carolina, at summer camp. They, at least, got some time away.

Joshua headed for the coffee out of habit. From out on the porch he could hear Kerry eagerly tucking into her own breakfast, her metal dog tags banging against the ceramic bowl with each bite.

His father looked up and gave him a smile. He appeared older than his thirty-seven years. His hair was the same colour as Joshua's and he had a quick smile for everyone. Much like Briar's dad, his job took him on the road more than any of them liked.

His mother, in contrast, was fair-haired, somewhere between brown and blonde. She used to smile more when he was little, but that had all changed. Most of the time she was pensive, caught up in her own thoughts. None of them were happy.

'You're up early,' his father said. 'How was the party last night?'

'Good,' Joshua said, dumping a mound of cereal into a bowl. The milk followed. He took his place at the table, setting his phone by the coffee cup.

'Was the Rose girl there?' his mom asked, not turning round.

He didn't reply. It worked better that way.

'Was she?'

His dad's eyes met his and the message was passed: just get it over with.

'Yes,' he replied.

'You talked to her?'

For some perverse reason, Joshua decided not to hide the truth. 'Yes, for a little bit.' His hand shook as he took another sip of coffee, waiting for the repercussions.

His mom turned, her eyes widening, and he swore he

saw fear in them. 'Did you . . . touch her?'

'No!' Josh said, annoyed. 'I didn't touch her.' *I just gave her a birthday present and I would do it all again just to see her smile.*

His mother joined them at the table. It was then he noticed that her hands were shaking. 'It's her birthday,' she said evenly.

'I know,' Joshua replied. 'She's sixteen, like I'll be in a couple of weeks.'

His dad's eyes moved back and forth between them, as if trying to read between the lines. 'Then if she's sixteen now, it's over. About damned time,' he said. 'Maybe now our families can get on with our lives.'

He dropped the paper in disgust and rose from the table. 'I'll be back Tuesday night. I've got a meeting in Atlanta, and it'll run long, so I'll stay over Monday. I'll call you guys this evening.'

He ruffled Joshua's hair. 'Hang in there,' he whispered.

'I'll try,' Joshua muttered.

With a concerned glance at his son, his father was out of the door and headed towards his car. It was as if he couldn't leave fast enough.

Joshua began to count down from ten, waiting for his mother to take the next step, to do the full inquisition. Instead, her face grew pale and her hands shook harder.

'What's wrong? Are you sick? Do you want me to get Dad to come back?'

'No. It's . . . just so hard.'

'What's hard?' he asked.

It wasn't as if she was listening. 'I'm relieved, but that's wrong and I know it. I'm so confused. I can't imagine what Franklin and *she* are going through right now.'

Briar's parents?

His mother wasn't making much sense, but she hadn't for a long time. As he'd grown older, he'd come to realize there was a Before Mom and an After Mom. Before that day he'd nearly drowned in the river, she'd been fun, full of laughter and love. After? She was afraid, scared about everything that had to do with the Rose family. No matter how many times he'd asked, she'd never tell him why.

As he'd recuperated that summer after his time in the river, she wouldn't let him out of the house for weeks on end, even refused to let Briar visit him. When he'd finally returned to school, she'd gone to his teachers and told them something that had made them treat him differently from all the other kids. It had all centred on the Roses' only child.

'Mom, what's going on? Why are you like this? Briar isn't some demon. She's just . . . a girl.' A pretty one with bright eyes and a great smile. Not that he saw it that often.

His mother's eyes were full of tears now. 'There was this curse. It was one of those hoodoo things. It was put on you when you were born.'

Joshua's heart skipped a beat. *It can't be . . .* 'A real curse?'

His mother nodded. 'You were supposed to die on your sixteenth birthday.'

'So I'm like . . . dead in a couple of weeks?' he asked, blindsided.

'No, not now,' she said, shaking her head. 'Lily, Mrs Foster, that old hoodoo lady, said the curse left you when . . .

you were in the river. When you almost . . .'

'Died. Yeah, I got that part. No one ever lets me forget it,' he snapped. 'But what does that have to do with Briar?'

His mother wiped the tears from her puffy eyes. 'When you stopped breathing, Lily said the curse moved to Briar, because she was holding your hand.'

This was so fantastical he couldn't even wrap his mind around it. 'Come on, that's totally bogus.'

'No. Lily called me this morning to let me know that the curse took hold last night. Briar is . . .'

Dead? No way. She can't be.

'You are so lying!'

'No,' she whispered, 'I'm not.'

Not trusting his mom's sanity, he texted Reena.

Is it true? Is there really a curse?

His eyes met his mother's brimming gaze. If she was right . . .

The text pinged on to his phone. **It's for real.**

'Oh my God.' The chair fell over as he shoved away from the table, his hand clenched round his phone. 'Oh God, no.'

'I'm so sorry, son,' his mother said, touching his arm now. 'That's why I kept you away from her, why I was so . . . insistent about it. I was afraid that somehow that curse would come back on you somehow. Then you'd be . . .'

Dead.

'Who . . . did this?' he whispered. *Who hurt her? Who took her away just when . . .*

'It's not important,' his mother said, reaching out to

soothe him. He flinched away. 'God, I'm sorry, but you're alive, son. That's all that matters to me right now.'

He stared at her, seeing this woman in a different light for the first time. Not crazy, but a mother, one that would shed tears for someone else's child, but still rejoice that hers was alive.

His phone dinged again.

We need to talk. Meet me @ bandstand in an hr.

'Why didn't you try to stop this, have Lily break the curse?' he demanded.

'She tried years ago. It didn't work. But don't you see? At least now you're safe.' Her eyes were brighter now. 'Now you'll grow up and have kids of your own and—'

With a sharp cry of despair, Joshua barrelled out of the side door.

It was hard to saddle Arabella and talk on his cellphone at the same time. His balance was off, as if something inside him was missing.

'Reena? It's Joshua,' he blurted out. 'Tell me she's not . . . Tell me this is all some damn sick joke.'

'It's not a joke.'

Joshua lost the grip on the saddle blanket and it tumbled out of his hands. Backing up, he bumped into one of the barn supports and slid down the pole until he hit the ground beneath. There wasn't enough air to breathe, like when he'd nearly drowned. Arabella turned her head in his direction, as if to wonder if he was ill or something.

'Josh?'

'Tell me what happened,' he said, feeling the sting of tears. 'Tell me how she died.'

'What? No, she's not dead, she's . . . asleep. But we don't know if she's ever going to wake up.'

Briar is still alive? He uttered a silent prayer of thanks.

'But I thought—'

'She fought the curse somehow. It was a close thing. Real close.'

Joshua closed his eyes to bottle up the tears. Kerry nudged him and he laid his head on her shoulder.

'You there?' Reena asked.

'Yeah.'

'I'm so sorry, Josh. I know how much you care for her.'

'I'll see you at the bandstand.'

The phone went silent.

'She's alive,' he said, and the collie thumped her tail as if she approved.

Joshua rose and hurriedly saddled the horse, the tears at bay now. Reena would tell him the truth. Only then would he know what to do, how to bring Briar back to them.

CHAPTER TEN

Joshua tied his horse to a post near the town's bandstand, his fingers stiff and hard to work. The mare took full advantage of the location, leaning her head down to graze on a patch of grass while Kerry, a stick magnet if there ever was one, had already found a likely candidate. She trotted it up to him and he mechanically gave it a toss to keep her occupied.

It was close to nine in the morning now and Bliss's residents were going about their business. In some ways, that irritated him – Briar had nearly died last night, but you wouldn't know it here. Across the street Mr Dale, the pharmacist, entered his shop, his hands full of boxes. Next door, the restaurant was open and the smell of bacon hung in the air.

Who cursed me? Somebody here in town?

Joshua refused to believe that. There were a number of squirrelly characters in this place, but for the most part people liked his family, at least when his mom wasn't raising hell about the Roses. Still, the curse had to come from someone who knew them. Strangers didn't bother with stuff like that.

After a few more stick retrievals, Kerry curled up at his feet, panting, reminding him he'd have to find her water pretty soon. Leaning back against the tree trunk, he stared up into the branches, too many dark thoughts tumbling through his mind for such a sunny day.

He heard the slam of a car door, then Reena walked across the grass towards him, causing Kerry to thump her tail in greeting. From the way his friend moved, she hadn't slept any better than he had. She slumped in the grass next to him.

'When did you find out about the curse?' she asked.

'This morning. My mom dropped that bit of news on me over breakfast.'

'Ouch. I found out last night, at the party.'

He looked at her, his temper flaring. 'And you didn't tell me? I thought you were my friend.'

'I wanted to, but Lily wouldn't let me. She said it'd only mess things up worse.'

'That's debatable.'

She broke off a blade of grass and began to tear it into thin strips. 'You know what happened, I mean, at the river, with you and Briar?'

'Mom said I was cursed, then I died, and Briar got it next.'

Reena nodded. 'Lily knew something had happened between the two of you, but it took a while for her to figure it out. Then she told your mom and tried to break the curse. It didn't budge.'

'Which is why my mom was so fanatical that I should stay away from Briar. Not to touch her.'

'Yeah, Lily wasn't sure if the curse could go back – you had to die for it to move across the first time, but she didn't want to take any chances.'

He didn't like that very much. 'Does Briar know it came from me?'

'No.'

That, at least, was good news. 'Who did this?'

'I . . .' Reena sighed. 'I can't tell you that.'

'All this damned secrecy doesn't work for me. I need to know!' he stormed.

She glared at him. 'You have no idea what you're messing with here. Hell, I don't and that scares me. This trick is off the rails, and blaming folks just gives this thing more power, do you understand?'

'How can a death curse get any worse?'

'It can, so that's all you're going to get from me. Down the line, if Briar makes it, I'll tell you, but not until then. That's Lily's orders and I won't cross her.'

'You know, that old lady is starting to piss me off,' Joshua said, glowering at her. 'Who is she to tell us what to do?'

A deep frown settled on Reena's face. 'I'm going to ignore what you just said. You're upset. So am I. Let's not make this a personal battle, OK?'

'I'm just . . .' Joshua shook his head. 'I don't know what I feel right now.'

'Same here,' she said, gently touching his arm. 'Last night was . . . hell.'

'Oh, God.' That was what he'd felt, that deep emptiness, as if some of his own life had faded away with Briar. Maybe it had.

'I was sure she was gone,' Reena whispered, 'then she fought the curse, hard, and that's why she's not dead. I'm hoping that means she might come back to us some day.'

'That's possible?' he asked. 'Please say yes.' *Even if it's a lie.*

'Lily thinks if Briar can break the curse she'll wake up again.'

'Is there anything I can do to help?' Reena shrugged at that, which made him feel useless. Kerry nuzzled his hand and he petted her silky head. 'Now that I look back, I'm guessing my dad knew about this, but I don't think he believed it was true.'

'Like Mr Rose, then,' she said. 'He didn't accept it until Gran showed up at his door last night.'

'I swear, if I'd known I had a curse in me, I never would have gone anywhere near Briar,' he said.

'If you hadn't tried to save her, she would have died that day too,' Reena replied. 'You forget, I was there when they pulled you guys out. She didn't let go of your hand until they started CPR. She *willed* you to live, Joshua.'

'That worked out well for her, didn't it?' he said bitterly.

'You gave her a few more years.'

'So I could kill her now? That's no comfort,' he said, his anger ramping up again. But who was to blame? His mom? She only wanted to protect him. No, the person who deserved his fury was whoever had cursed him in the first place. Some day he'd learn who that was, and he'd make sure he or she paid for it.

Joshua exhaled heavily, placing his arms on his knees and leaning forward. 'So we just wait and hope she gets better?' He shook his head even before Reena could answer. 'What if I talk to your great-gran? Do you think I can convince her to help us?'

'It didn't work for me, but I guess you can try.' Reena rose to her feet and dusted off her jeans. 'If she doesn't change her mind, I have an idea.'

'Whatever it is, I want to be part of it. I want to make this right.'

She studied him for a moment. 'Don't blame yourself. This is *not* your fault, Josh.'

'I know,' he replied, though he was lying.

It is *my fault.* He felt it deep in his bones. *I have to make it right.*

When Joshua brought the mare to a stop in front of the old cabin, a couple of guinea hens trotted off into the woods, raising a holy ruckus as they disappeared into the underbrush. Joshua had always thought the things were God's idea of an inside joke, nothing more than round feather-covered balls with stubby legs.

A caramel-coloured hound raised its head from the porch and gave a single deep woof. Then it lay back down, its job done.

After Reena's car pulled into the drive, he dismounted and joined her.

'Why does your gran live out here all alone?' he asked.

'That's the way she wants it. We keep trying to get her to move in with us, but she won't do it and she won't go into one of those "dying places" either. That's what she calls a nursing home. We check on her every day and hope for the best.'

'But is it safe for her? I mean . . . someone could rob the place or something. It's out in the middle of nowhere.'

'Most folks aren't that dumb,' Reena said. 'If they are, they'll find themselves in a world of hurt. Of all the people in this county, you do not want my gran mad at you. Root magic is for real, and it can do a lot of harm if needed.'

'Really. I hadn't noticed,' he said sullenly.

Reena sighed. 'I know you're upset, but park that attitude out here. Lily doesn't take any crap from anyone, not even me.'

After considering that solemn warning, Joshua reluctantly followed his friend towards the porch, avoiding the chicken droppings that lurked in the grass. Just in front of the door was a line of red grainy powder.

'What's that for?' he asked, pointing.

'It's brick dust. It's used as a ward to keep the folks inside the house safe. If you've got bad intentions, you can't cross it.'

OK. 'Just how old is this place anyway?'

'It was built right after the Civil War,' Reena replied. 'Not much has changed since then, except for indoor plumbing.'

Reena paused on the porch to pet the dog. Then she took a deep breath and moved to the door, but she didn't open it and barge in even though she was family. Instead she knocked and waited. It was that respect thing she'd talked about, and Joshua took note of it.

'That you, Reena B?' an aged voice called out.

'It is. I brought Joshua Quinn with me.'

'I know. Carl told me.'

Apparently she means the dog.

He followed Reena inside the cabin, and the moment he crossed the threshold he felt something slide over his skin, as if it were scanning him. His eyes must have widened and Reena nodded in understanding.

'Told you,' his companion said.

The small space was neat, everything in its place, not that there was much in the way of possessions. The floor was hand-hewn wood and it creaked as he took each step. The exposed rafters were put to good use – herbs hung from them in bundles, as well as some old baskets. A small kitchen held a table and a few chairs and down a short hall was a bedroom. A worktable sat along one wall, covered in roots and herbs. On it a mortar and pestle rested near an open book, and above the table was a portrait of Jesus at Gethsemane, flanked by pictures of John F. Kennedy and Martin Luther King, Jr.

Mrs Lily Foster occupied a rocking chair near the big window that overlooked the backyard. On top of the chairback was a tabby cat that nimbly rebalanced itself each time the rocker moved. It had big green eyes and a crooked tail, as if it'd been hit by a car sometime during its nine lives.

'Come hug me, girl. It's been too long,' the old woman said, opening her arms.

'We just saw each other last night,' Reena replied.

'At my age, that's a long time.'

As they embraced, Joshua could feel the love between them. It'd been like that with his grandmother until she'd passed away

119

a couple years earlier. She'd always been a counterbalance to the underlying discord in the Quinn household. Once she was gone, it'd only got worse between his parents.

'Come forward, boy,' Lily said, waving. 'Don't be frightened. I know yer family's story, and their sins. They ain't yers.'

He moved nearer to her, but not as close as Reena. 'I . . .' he began, but didn't know the right words. 'Good day, ma'am.'

She grinned, revealing worn teeth. 'Polite, that's good. Need more of that in this world.'

This wasn't getting them anywhere. Surely this woman knew why they were here.

'Patience,' Reena whispered, as if she'd read his mind. She pulled a kitchen chair closer to her eldest relative while Joshua chose the floor. It was a bit cooler there as it seemed Lily wasn't into air conditioning, and the ceiling fan only stirred the heat around like a big spoon in a pot of boiling stew.

'Briar needs your help, Gran.'

The old woman closed her eyes and kept rocking back and forth like she'd not heard her great-granddaughter. When the cat grew tired of the movement, it jumped off and wound its way to Reena, brushing against her jeans. Then it moved to Joshua. Peering up at him, it placed its front paws on his leg in a frank bid for attention. As sweat ran down his back, he scratched the soft head and the cat began to purr.

'Hobbes likes ya,' Lily said, her eyes open now. 'That makes sense, though. Yer much like a cat, always watchin', real quiet and thoughtful.'

'Don't have much to say,' he replied.

'But what ya do say is worthwhile. It means ya have good sense.'

He'd never thought of himself like that. He'd just thought he was shy.

'Reena tell ya what happened last night?' Lily asked.

'Yes, ma'am.'

'I did some scryin' this mornin',' she said.

Joshua gave Reena a confused look, unsure of what the old lady meant.

'My gran uses a mirror so she can divine things.'

'Sort of like looking in a crystal ball?' he asked.

'Yeah, just like that.'

Lily kept rocking. 'That curse took her deep inside herself, in some sort of dream. It's up to her to find a way back.'

'Is there some way we can . . . go help her out?' Joshua asked.

Lily's piercing eyes zeroed in on him. 'What happens if that dream is more like a nightmare, and it tried to kill ya?'

Did he care? 'Doesn't matter. This is my fault.'

'No, it's not. Ya did what was right all those years back at the river. This curse isn't on yer head, boy.'

'You're wrong – it is. At least I feel it is,' Joshua said, his voice rising.

One of the woman's silver eyebrows crept upward, but she didn't chastise him for his mouthiness. 'There are only a few ways for ya to get into a curse dream and none of them are easy. Ya'd have to borrow power to do it, and that's always dangerous.'

'Borrow power?' Joshua asked. Next to him, Reena stiffened.

Lily didn't reply, but rocked a bit faster now, her eyes on her great-granddaughter now. 'If ya did get inside, who's to say that if Briar died in there that curse wouldn't go right back where it came from?'

Josh grew cold, despite the stifling heat. 'Back to me, you mean? Can it do that?'

'Maybe. Or the dream could kill ya outright.' She shook her head sadly. 'This conjure's out of control. It's taken strength from both sides of this wrong, and it's doin' what it wishes now. I've never seen nothin' like it before.'

Which was really bad news as this lady was ancient.

Reena took a very deep breath and then slowly let it out. 'We should be going,' she said, rising from the chair. 'I'll come by and see you tomorrow and bring you some of Mom's homemade rolls.' She dropped a kiss on the old woman's cheek.

'I'll be lookin' forward to it,' Lily said, rocking away. 'In a couple weeks we'll do that trick ya've been workin' on. Ya know, the one at the crossroads. Ya should be ready by then.'

Reena hesitated, as if sorting through some hidden subtext. Then she nodded, her eyes moving towards the table. 'Can I borrow your spell book tonight? I need to read up on it.'

'Surely. Just bring it back tomorrow.'

After Reena had taken the thick book, Lily called out to them. 'Don't y'all do anythin' ya'd regret, ya hear?'

'Yes, Gran,' Reena replied, but her voice held more resolve now, as if she'd come to some momentous decision.

Once they were in the yard, Joshua felt like punching something. Mike maybe. Yeah, that would make him feel a lot better, for about three seconds. Even after talking to Mrs Foster they were no closer to helping Briar escape the curse.

'*That* was a total waste of time,' he said.

Reena slowly drew the spell book out of a paper bag. Now that he saw it up close, it seemed rather ordinary. She leafed through to a page near the middle, and smiled down at the spidery handwriting skittering across the paper.

'Gran isn't plain sometimes – it's just her way. I figured out what she was hinting at when she talked about borrowing power. That's the next conjure I'm studying. It's a crossroads spell.'

'Whatever,' Joshua said, not really listening.

Keeping her back to the house, Reena used her free hand to pull a purple ribbon from under her shirt. Attached to it were two old-fashioned skeleton keys. Before he could ask why she was wearing them, a tiny spark of magic danced from the book to the keys and back.

'Did that just . . . ?' he began, eyes blinking.

Reena nodded. She looked over her shoulder at the cabin and then back again. 'These are crossroads keys and I can tap into the power with these. That power might get me inside Briar's dream.'

Joshua gaped. 'Hey, that's the huntsman charm from Briar's bracelet,' he said, pointing. 'What are you doing with it?'

'I took it this morning when her folks were downstairs.

123

I needed a connection to Briar, one that also links to you since you're where the curse started. This is it.'

'You said you didn't know about the curse until last night,' he said, suddenly suspicious, 'but you were the one who found the bracelet on the internet and said I should buy it for Briar's birthday. You set this up all along.'

'No,' she said, glaring over at him. 'I didn't. I thought the bracelet was a good way for you guys to get closer, maybe . . . end this bullshit between your families. I had no idea I'd be using it to try to save Briar's life.'

'Oh . . .'

'I've never tried the trick, but I know which spirit to call up now. Gran had the book on the worktable opened to the exact page I need.'

'So why is she messing with us? Why doesn't she do it herself?'

'I don't know. Maybe she can't for some reason.' Reena replaced the skeleton keys down her shirt. 'It might not work, but I have to try.'

He gnawed on that for a time. 'What happens if it goes wrong, the spell I mean?'

'Nothing good,' she said, her expression sobering. 'I might end up asleep like Briar . . . or dead. Same for anyone around me when it goes down. Keep that in mind, if you're going to join me in this.'

Joshua took a deep breath, but there was never any doubt as to his answer.

'Just tell me when and where.'

CHAPTER ELEVEN

Briar and Ruric walked back to the stable in silence, though around them many of the villagers spoke in hushed voices. One man said the prisoner had it coming because he'd tried to harm the princess.

'Don't be a fool,' a grizzled woman barked. 'He was here to break the curse. I saw it in my dreams.'

'Nightmares, more likely,' the man retorted. 'The princess will never be free unless—'

'Hush! You know what happens to traitors,' an older woman warned. 'Be careful of that tongue of yours.'

Silence fell after that. Given what Briar had seen in the field, they were right to be afraid.

How did the regent gain so much power? What was that magic of hers?

There were no answers, not yet at least, so Briar forced herself to examine the little details she'd missed on the hurried journey to the field. Maybe that would give her some idea of how to return home. At the very least, it would help block out the graphic images of the dying man.

The Village of the Damned, as she'd begun to think of it, had houses and shops jammed together so tightly it was impossible to see daylight between them.

As if he knew what she was thinking, Ruric pulled her out of the flow of the foot traffic. 'Note the houses here,' he said as they stopped in front of one structure. This house was half wood, half brass, as if the builders couldn't quite make up their mind which they preferred.

'Watch closely,' Ruric murmured.

Briar wasn't sure what she was supposed to be watching, but she did as he asked, feeling like an idiot. Who stood around and stared at houses for fun?

As she waited, her eye caught on a small piece of the metal. It rippled, then cloned itself, layering over the neighbouring wood as if it were a scale on a dragon's wing.

Whoa. 'Why does it do that?' she said, astounded.

'It is the regent's magic,' he said quietly. 'She seeks to make everything metal. She loves it more than she does flesh or wood or stone.'

Now that's creepy.

'It is like her warriors, the ones you saw in the field. At one time they were men, now they are covered in metal.'

Ohmigod. She'd just thought they were some sort of robots.

As they moved on, Briar peered inside one structure and spied the man she'd seen earlier, selling a loaf of bread to a thick-waisted woman. Two grubby children sat at her feet. Briar winced when she saw one of them had a band of brass round its throat. It was crying, tugging on it as if it hurt. Maybe it did.

Why would anyone put that on their child?

Ruric cleared his throat nervously. 'How are you faring, cousin?'

She realized he wasn't just being polite: there was deep concern behind his words.

'I'm . . . scared,' she admitted. 'I've never seen someone die before.'

He took her hand and squeezed it gently. It was a kind gesture.

'Surely there have been deaths among your family or friends,' he said. 'It is the way of things.'

'In my village you die when you're really old, unless you get really sick, which doesn't happen very often.'

He didn't reply, a slight frown creasing his forehead now.

Deep down, the longer she was here, the more Briar kept thinking about the car dream. How things kept happening *to* her until she took control. Was that the lesson she was supposed to carry into this dream? If she did take control, could she beat the curse and go home to her parents, her cat and the real world?

No clue.

Her stomach took that very moment to rumble, loudly.

'When did you last eat?' her companion asked.

'A long time ago,' she said. *At a party by the lake where the guy of my dreams broke my heart.*

'Then I shall share my food and, in gratitude, you will help me clean the stable. It's honest work, or so my father always claimed. He sent me to work in the stables when I was eight. He said it would keep me from frivolous behaviour.'

'Did it work?'

A lopsided smile lit his face. 'No, it did not.'

I bet you're a player. The way the girls fawned all over him, that was a given.

Since he was talking about his family . . . 'What does your father do?'

'He is . . . sort of a reeve, the man in charge of it all. And your father?'

Her dad sold pharmaceuticals so she worked on a term Ruric would understand. 'He's an apothecary.'

'An honourable profession.'

By the time they reached the stable there were two men waiting for them, one who wanted to collect his horse, and the other who wanted to buy one. Ruric took care of the first customer and then told the second he had nothing to sell.

'You must. The prisoner had a mount and he has no use for it now,' the man replied gruffly. He was stocky with a burgeoning stomach. His clothes were fairly nice, which suggested to Briar that he had a steady income. Some official maybe.

'The mare is not for sale,' Ruric replied evenly.

'Does Quinton know you're not handling business like you should?'

Uh-oh.

The look in Ruric's eyes promised trouble if this man kept pushing. 'Quinton is quite pleased with my services. I repeat, there is *no* horse for sale. Should there be one, I shall send word to you. Now good day, sir.'

The man's attention shifted to her. 'This is your cousin I hear tell?'

His tone was caustic – apparently he wasn't used to having someone tell him no. She resisted the urge to check that her hair wasn't showing.

'Yes, this is my cousin Briar,' Ruric replied.

'It would be a shame if something happened to you. What would become of her?'

'Then I shall have to be very cautious.'

The man huffed, then strode away, muttering under his breath.

When Ruric entered the stable, he headed directly for the mare. He patted her flank fondly as if to reassure himself she was OK.

'I thought you planned to sell her,' Briar said.

He half shrugged. 'I'm becoming increasingly fond of her. In fact, I shall keep her. Hopefully her new master will have better sense than the old one, though I doubt it, given what I've just done.' At her puzzled expression, he explained. 'That was the village reeve. He answers directly to the regent.'

'Oh . . . and he's not happy with you.'

'No. He's not an evil sort, but he never questions his orders. That makes him as much a threat as his mistress, for he has no conscience.' Ruric patted the horse again, then moved away. 'Come, let us eat.'

'I have to wash my hands. Seriously.'

He gave her a confused expression and then pointed to a wooden bucket. She peered into it and was pleased to find it wasn't yucky or anything. She wet first one hand, then the other. It took some work rubbing them together, but finally they looked cleaner, though her nails were a complete disaster. It was the best she could hope for.

'Are you fit to dine now, my lady?' Ruric said, his eyes dancing with mirth.

Briar bit back a snarky reply. 'Yes, I am, my lord,' she said, executing a rather clumsy curtsy.

Ruric led her round to the back of the stable where there was a small grassy patch under a tree. There he laid out their meal on the thick grass: yellow cheese, two hunks of dark bread and a liquid he poured into a heavy metal cup. He handed the cup over to her.

'What is that?' she asked, giving the contents a sniff.

'Mead. It is particularly fine.'

She wrinkled her nose, worried about the taste.

'If you wish, perhaps I can ask a dairy maid to draw you some fresh milk from one of the cows.'

Briar almost agreed, then remembered that their milk wasn't pasteurized. Just how many germs could be in the stuff? *Squillions.* All of them designed to make her very, very sick. There was no guarantee she had any immunity to the illnesses this village harboured, and there had to be a lot of them.

'No, I'll just have a little of this.'

Briar took a test snip and was surprised to find it was sweet and quite tasty. Thirsty, she took a good half of it down before returning the cup to Ruric. Then she attacked her portion of the bread and cheese. By the time those were gone – along with more mead – she was feeling much better.

'My head is buzzing,' she said, grinning. 'This stuff is way better than beer.' *Maybe I can get Dad to make some for me.*

Ruric eyed her pensively. 'You are unlike anyone I have

ever met. You've never tasted mead, you've never witnessed someone dying and you speak very oddly.' He leaned forward. 'Tell me the truth, Briar. What is your story? You may trust me to keep your secret.'

'You're right, I do have a story.' *Boy do I.* 'I didn't lie, I *am* from a village named Bliss, but it is not . . . around here. In fact, it's not even in this world. I think.'

Ruric's eyes widened, though he did not respond to such an outrageous claim.

'I was cursed, like your princess. I was supposed to die when I turned sixteen, but I fell asleep instead. When I woke I was here, in an alley, and then the wolves came after me.'

As her companion continued to stare, she could only imagine what was going through his mind.

'I know it sounds crazy, but where I come from there aren't magical metal birds or things like that. Well, unless you count aeroplanes, I guess.'

'Aero . . . planes?' he asked, finally speaking.

'Never mind.' The cup was empty again and she held it out for a refill.

'I think that wouldn't be wise. You have *no* head for drink.'

That comment annoyed her, even though he was probably right. 'You said you wanted to know the truth. That's it.'

'I find it truly fantastical.'

'I figured. We have a story about a princess much like yours. She was cursed and fell asleep with all her family. Many years later a prince kissed her and the curse was broken and then they lived happily ever after.'

Ruric took a cautious look around to ensure that no one was near enough to hear them. Given the everyday village noises, it was doubtful that anyone could eavesdrop.

'So if you are telling the truth, and I must admit I find this quite a tall tale, all we must do is have someone kiss the princess, and she is freed?'

'Yes, but you already know all that.'

He nodded slowly. 'Indeed, but here it is not as simple as in your tale. The regent insists that only *she* shall judge which man may kiss the princess, and that all others only mean to harm her. In the end, none are judged worthy and they are put to death.'

'That's clever. She keeps all of them away in case one of them is the right guy. If the princess wakes, she's out of a job.'

'Yes, that's it. In your tale, how is the regent defeated?' he asked. 'Perhaps that will offer us hope in our present situation.'

'That's the problem, Ruric,' Briar said, feeling bad that she was about to rain on his parade. 'There *is* no regent in our tale. She isn't supposed to be in charge of the kingdom. No one is, at least until Aurora is awakened.'

'There has to be someone responsible. You cannot allow a kingdom to rule itself.'

His tone of voice had changed. It sounded almost regal, which triggered her suspicions. *Maybe your dad isn't just a reeve.*

'Is this story of a sleeping princess well known in your village?' he pressed.

'Yes. It was one of my favourite tales.'

'Why?'

'Because . . . there's a happy ending. The princess falls in love with the prince. It's all good.'

He was staring at her so intensely she automatically checked that her hair wasn't showing. 'You believe me, then?' she asked.

'For the moment. Or it's possible you're quite mad, though in a harmless fashion.'

'I'm not mad. I know where I came from.'

'But do you know how to return there?' he asked.

Briar felt deflated. 'No, I don't.'

'Well, then we shall tackle one obstacle at a time. We shall have to battle the tyrant to free the princess,' he said. 'Then perhaps we can find a way to get you home.'

'Battle? Wait a minute. I'm pretty decent with a bow and arrow, and I've used a rapier . . . you know, fenced? But those warrior guys have big swords and all that armour.'

It took him some time to work out what she'd said. 'Then you shall have to use your cunning.'

Briar rolled her eyes. 'Riiight. I'm just full of that.'

'Your cunning and the fact that your hair is the same colour as our princess. If we can make others believe she has been awakened, perhaps then we have a chance. But the timing must be perfect or—'

'Ruric?' a girl's voice called out. 'Are you here?'

He sighed audibly. 'I am,' he called out as he rose.

A young girl with jet-black hair and big breasts strode towards them.

Saralyn?

Except for the wrong colour hair, this girl could be her cousin, but, like the other villagers who resembled folks from Bliss, there was no recognition in her eyes.

Ruric turned towards the newcomer. 'Good day to you,' he called out, though his voice held little warmth. 'Briar, may I present the miller's daughter, Dimia.'

Dimia? 'Hi,' Briar replied.

A stiff nod came her way. Apparently the instant dislike was mutual.

Dimia's attention returned to Ruric. 'My father sends his good wishes and asks if you would join us for a meal in two days' time.'

'I would be honoured,' he replied. 'However, I do not wish to leave my cousin on her own until she knows the ways of the village.'

He'd purposely put Dimia in a corner.

'Oh . . . I . . . you can bring her along,' the girl said, though clearly she'd hoped it wouldn't come to that. 'One more will not matter.'

Wow. Thanks. I'm touched. Don't go out of your way or anything.

'That is very generous,' Ruric replied. The corners of his mouth were trying hard not to form a smile.

'I am eagerly awaiting our time together.'

Ruric didn't return the sentiment. Instead, he turned back to Briar. 'Come, cousin, the stable needs our attention.'

'Oh . . .' Flustered, Dimia fluttered for a second, and then took his arm. 'Can it not wait? I wish to talk to you . . .

alone. I promise, we shall not go far. I have much to tell you.'

I bet you do.

Ruric sent a look Briar's way. 'I'll be fine,' she said. 'Go on, catch up on the village gossip. I'm sure it's really important.'

That earned her a scowl from the miller's daughter, who clearly saw Ruric as the ideal husband and Briar as a liability.

'After our walk, I shall visit the smithy. One of the horses needs a new shoe,' he said, graciously giving in to his fate. He put his arm through Dimia's and they set off at a leisurely pace round the side of the building.

Briar stood, brushing the crumbs from her skirt. Was she jealous? Maybe a bit. Ruric was a hottie, and he'd been very good to her. But cat-fight jealous? *No.* The clock was ticking in this Village of the Damned: either she figured how to get home or her hair was going to be the death of her.

CHAPTER TWELVE

It had taken Ruric some time to free himself of the miller's clinging daughter – Dimia was not easily shaken off, much like a burr in a horse's mane. Now, as he entered the smithy's hut, he felt more anxious than usual. With the man's death today, he knew his time here was coming to an end.

It had been a fine game of cat-and-mouse he'd been playing over the months, gathering information on the regent and her servants. Now there was more at stake – his 'cousin' could die because of his fanciful plans.

'Ah, there you are,' the smithy said, looking up from his work.

'Here is the shoe,' Ruric said, handing it over. 'The nail holes have worn too much to hold it in place.'

'A common problem,' the smithy replied. He began applying the bellows to the fire, his eyes not on Ruric, but at the entrance to the hut. 'Your cousin presents a problem. Is she truly of your blood?'

'No, she's not,' Ruric said. 'But she needs our help. She has . . . something that will cause her to *lose her head* if it was discovered.'

The smithy thought for a moment, then nodded in understanding. 'That is to our benefit, then. You never saw our princess, but I did, and your cousin looks strikingly similar.'

That knowledge only complicated matters. 'I wondered if that was the case. I also wonder why she's here at this moment in time.'

Ruric positioned himself so he could see the door, though to any who might walk by it would appear he was having a leisurely chin wag with the smithy.

'Have you had luck in finding more . . . supplies?' he asked.

'I have,' the smithy allowed. 'They are tucked away safe. All we await is for you to make your move.'

'I know. I have not felt it was the right time yet.' He knew what would come next. They'd had this argument before. 'I am aware that we cannot wait forever.'

'If the princess is dead, perhaps we can use your cousin in her place, since she looks so much like her.'

Ruric wasn't sure what he thought of that notion, so he did not reply.

'We are running out of time,' the smithy warned.

'I know,' he replied. 'I'll talk to our . . . friend at the inn tonight. See what she has learned.'

The smithy smashed the hammer on to the molten metal, flattening it. Then his eyes sought Ruric's. 'We must master the metal, before it masters us. We have no other choice.'

Ruric inclined his head and left the man to his work, his heart heavy and his mind full of doubts.

But what if the metal proves stronger?

Once inside the stable, Briar applied herself to the pitchfork. She'd done this kind of duty two summers ago when she'd taken riding lessons, the ones her mother had reluctantly allowed after much badgering from Briar's dad.

Briar had found immense freedom on the back of a horse, but it'd only lasted one summer. The next year Joshua had taken a job there and the stables had become off limits, like so much in her life. She wondered if Mrs Quinn had done that on purpose, or had she even known that Briar was taking lessons when her son applied for the job?

At the thought of Joshua, she held up the arm with the charm bracelet, watching the little figures turn in the air. Instead of making her feel better, it only made her feel lost.

I want to go home.

On top of everything the huntsman charm was missing, something she regretted. And she had developed a lovely set of blisters.

Argh. So much for being a real princess.

When her back began to cramp and her arms twitch, Briar jammed the pitchfork into the manure pile and then leaned on it, trying to catch her breath.

'You're doing well for an apprentice,' Ruric said from the doorway.

She welcomed the break. 'Enjoy your ramble with the buxom maid of the mill?'

'Not really. Dimia's mother is keen to have her middle daughter wed by autumn. Both of them feel I would make a suitable choice.'

'I don't have to go eat with them,' Briar said. 'I can stay here, out of sight, if you want.'

'You would throw me to the wolves, dear cousin?' he asked, amused.

'Oh . . .' He really wanted her to run interference. 'Or I can be there and make sure that you don't agree to anything you'll regret.'

He nodded. 'That would be wise. The reeve's son accepted an invitation to dine with the miller and his family two months back. From what I've heard, the ale flowed heavily and it is said he was very deep in his cups when he made the proposal to Dimia's older sister.'

'Does he regret that now?'

'Of that you can be sure. I hear that his lady wife is a shrew.'

Briar's mind obediently coughed up the image of a small, needle-nosed rodent. She pushed it away. 'I'm definitely going along with you.'

'As I'd hoped. Your hair is coming loose again,' he warned. 'Hold still.'

Ruric stepped closer and then gently tucked the errant piece under cover. This time his hand didn't retreat, but remained in place for longer than was necessary.

'Ah . . .' she began.

He smiled, then stepped back. 'There, perfect.'

Perfect. No guy had ever called her that before.

'Thanks,' she said, feeling her cheeks flame. Eager to change the subject, Briar asked, 'Have you ever thought about trying to wake the princess?'

Ruric stilled, as if she'd just slipped a knife between his ribs. 'Why would you think I would do that?'

'Everyone else seems to want to.'

His brow furrowed in thought, then he beckoned her further into the stable, away from the door. His voice fell low. 'I do wish to wake the princess as much as any man, but since I've been here twelve men have been caught and executed in the field. That doesn't count the ones who perished inside the castle and were never seen again.' He gave her troubled look. 'I have the courage, but I do not want to be torn apart by some magical beast or turned into a . . . monster.'

'Why do you want to do this? Why risk your life?'

'To free the village from the regent's tyranny, of course,' he said loftily.

No, it's more than that. She could hear the longing in his voice, and she suspected it wasn't for the princess or some vague notion of right or wrong.

As if discomfited by the conversation, Ruric shook his head. 'Enough of this,' he said. 'Come, let's go find you a proper scarf before someone discovers your secret.'

He fell silent as they walked to the small market at the edge of the village. This wasn't the main market, Ruric explained, but a lesser one. As some of the other townsfolk walked by them, she felt eyes scrutinizing her. Briar tried to ignore them, but couldn't help wondering if one of them was a spy for the regent.

'Why are they out here? Wouldn't they want to be in the middle of the village where they could make more money?' she asked, surprised that this market wasn't that busy.

'Not all care to be that close to the castle,' he said.

Ruric paused at a stall to inspect a selection of herbs. As he talked with the owner, Briar grew bored and wandered on her own, but never so far as to lose him from view.

She felt the sense of menace grow with each passing hour. It wasn't just the regent, but the village itself, as if somehow it deemed her a threat and wanted to dispose of her.

Get a grip.

It was then she saw an old woman sitting on a tree stump, a piece of colourful red fabric laid on the ground in front of her. Resting on it was a set of crudely drawn cards, probably some version of a tarot deck. Curious, Briar moved closer.

'I shall tell your fortune, maid, if you dare to seek it,' the woman said, eyeing her with some intensity. Her hair was frizzled grey and her hands gnarled, one eye milky and unseeing.

'Umm . . . sorry, I have no money.'

The woman cocked her head, studying her closer. 'For you, I will not require coins. Sit, child, and learn of your future.'

It was tempting. Maybe this lady knew something that would help her get out of here. When she checked on Ruric, he had moved to another stand and was chatting up a girl. She could tell from the way he was holding himself he was in full charming mode. As if realizing he was being watched, he held up a scarf for her inspection and gave her questioning look. She shook her head. Brown never was her colour. He held up a second one, which told her he wasn't going to stop until he found one she liked. This one was robin's egg blue and rather pretty, so she gave a nod.

He pulled out the proper coins, which earned him a bigger smile from the stall's owner.

The old woman tugged on Briar's skirt. 'You must sit, child, and listen to my cards,' she said. 'If you do not, it will go ill for you.'

That didn't sound good. Besides, she had nothing to lose as it would make her look like any other villager. Blending in meant a better chance of survival.

Briar sat on the grass opposite the fortune teller and watched as the woman gathered the strange cards in her knotted hands and painstakingly shuffled the deck. Then she had Briar pull four of them and place them in a row on the fabric.

Turning over the first card revealed the image of a golden-haired maiden frolicking in a field of blooming roses. Behind the flowers was a thicket of briars.

Roses and briars? OK, that's spooky.

'This is you, all innocent and trusting,' the woman said. 'For you are not from here.'

Of course I'm not. She was Ruric's 'cousin' from wherever the heck.

The second card revealed a dark forest dotted with glowing yellow eyes and glittering fangs. Briar couldn't suppress the shiver that rode through her.

'This is you now. You are lost and afraid. You think you are alone, with no one to protect you.'

The fortune teller's eyes rose and sought out Ruric as he traded jokes with one of his neighbours. 'You must find the strength to defeat the evil that controls you, but you are not alone. You must find your prince, one who is worthy. One who will stand at your side. Only then will you find your way home.'

Ruric laughed now, slapping his thigh at some jest.

The third card flipped over. It was the girl again, surrounded by three torches, each lighting the way out of the darkness. 'There are those who wish to help you in your quest. They will come from a great distance.'

What could that mean? There was no way for Reena to get here. Even if there was some magical way to do it, Gran Lily wouldn't send her own kin into this kind of hell.

Briar swallowed the sudden lump in her throat. 'What happens if I don't find that help? Or . . . my prince?'

'Then the darkness wins,' the woman said, turning over the fourth and final card. It was the gold-haired girl lying on a stone slab, a line of swords piercing her from throat to stomach. Deep crimson flowed down her sides on to the floor, forming patterns that eerily resembled decaying roses.

I'm going to die here.

'Briar?'

She jerked at the sound of her name and found Ruric standing over her. 'Ah . . . sorry, I wanted to get my fortune told.'

'The teller of fortunes is not here today,' he said.

'What?' Briar turned back and found that the woman and her cards were gone. Even the piece of cloth had vanished.

OK, that was really weird. Did I just dream all that?

'We can return tomorrow if you wish,' he offered. 'Perhaps she will be here.'

'No, it's OK.' The cards had showed her two possibilities: either she found more help or she died. It couldn't be simpler than that.

Briar fell quiet, unnerved by what the old woman had revealed. As they strolled through the market, Ruric handed over the scarf and she tied it round her neck for the time being.

'It will look fine on you,' he replied.

'Thank you,' she said. *Are you my prince?*

An apple came her way and Briar eagerly dug into it, hungry once again. Unlike the supermarket kind at home, this fruit was actually good. When juice ran down her chin, she wiped it off. Briar was about to take another bite when she hesitated. A thin worm crept out, waving its head above the fruity flesh.

The worm was all metal.

'Ruric . . .' she said, panicking. Had she eaten of some of that?

With a growl, he took the apple and tossed it away. 'Now she is poisoning our food. When will this madness end?' he said under his breath.

A commotion made them turn in unison and it centred on a pair of uniformed men stomping through the market. One carried a large leather bag and the other glowered menacingly, his sword drawn. They stopped at each stall or cart where the merchant would grudgingly place an item or two inside the bag.

'What are they doing?' Briar asked.

'Collecting the duties. They come through every day and it is expected that each merchant give them some of their goods.' He touched her elbow and angled his head. 'This way.'

He led her away, moving casually as if he were in no hurry, so as not to attract attention. Briar matched his pace. Once they were a short distance from the market, he led her down a narrow alley, which proved to be a dead end. Instead of being upset at the obstruction, he deftly moved aside a portion of woven fencing and crawled through. Trusting that he knew where he was headed, Briar followed along. Behind them, he replaced the barrier.

'You know this village really well, don't you?' He nodded. But it was more than just curiosity. 'You're mapping an escape route, in case something goes wrong.'

Ruric seemed impressed at her assessment. 'I do not believe it is as simple as kissing the princess to wake h Too many men have gone to their deaths for that to b case, some more worthy than me.'

'So you're going to wait then? Make sure y right before you try.'

'No,' he said, shaking his head, as if res 'I am done waiting; too many have died Meanwhile the regent's power increa day. That creature in the apple w such things will be in all of us, ea

'But if you don't wake the like the others.'

'I know. Does that trouble you?'

She nodded. 'Yes. A lot.'

He smiled and then paused, pointing down an alley. 'There is an abandoned wine cellar just there. It's through that old blue door. Do you see it?' When she nodded, he continued, 'It is fairly safe if you ever need to take shelter. I have supplies laid back there.'

They set off again. 'You were talking to yourself in the market. Do you do that often?' he asked.

'No.' When Briar told him about the old woman and what her cards had shown – leaving out the part about finding her prince – his face grew grave.

'You have been given a sign. You should heed it, for you are a clever girl.'

No matter what Ruric thought of her, she wasn't an extremely clever girl, or a lucky one for that matter. To survive in this make-believe world, she'd need to be both.

CHAPTER THIRTEEN

When it grew close to the time when he was supposed to meet Reena at the crossroads, Joshua took off on foot into the woods. It was about a twenty-minute hike and he knew the path well, even in the middle of the night. He'd crept out of the house, careful not to wake his mom. For the first time in months, there hadn't been a light under her door and he hadn't heard her crying.

Kerry trotted along beside him now. To the dog this was an adventure, but to Joshua this was trouble in the making. He didn't like sneaking around, feeling he was breaking his parents' trust. If his mom knew what he was up to, he'd be grounded for the rest of the year.

As he tromped through the woods, his mind continued to churn. He knew nothing about magic other than it had hurt someone he cared about. What would happen if Reena could break the curse? What if Briar found out he'd been the one to give it to her?

One thing at a time. They had to get Briar awake and then he'd worry about the rest.

Reena had insisted he meet her at Potter's Mill. Joshua reached the site early, so he sat on stairs that led to the mill. It was a clear and muggy night, and a froggy choir s⸻ him from the riverbank. The mosquitoes were ⸻ and he slapped at the ones that thought him edi⸻

From above came the drone of a private jet heading towards the Savannah airport. He peered upward and finally found the flashing lights among the brilliant stars. He liked nights such this. They seemed to heal some of the damaged places in his soul.

He wasn't exactly sure when Briar had gone from classmate to something more, someone worth caring about. Part of it had been when his mom had immediately made all things Rose off limits. That had just piqued his curiosity.

Still it wasn't all her fault. Maybe it was Briar's pretty eyes or her hair. He'd always liked her hair and had been upset when she'd cut it short one summer. Fortunately it had grown back, long and thick, and now, that he was older, he found himself wondering what it would be like to touch it.

Are you crazy? She's never going to talk to you again, not after she finds out who cursed her. Even if they could shake their parents loose, that would be kiss of death for any future they might have.

Still, he'd found the courage to give her the charm bracelet. He'd bought it weeks in advance of her birthday, had it sent to Reena's house so his mom didn't know what he was up to. His biggest fear had been that Briar would laugh at him when he gave it to her.

Instead, her eyes had lit up. He shouldn't have worried – Briar was kind like that, but he knew it had nothing to do with her caring about him. That had been made clear when she'd taken off into the woods with Pat Daniels and ruined the entire evening.

'Josh?'

He jolted in surprise. 'I'm here.'

A flashlight swung in his direction and then promptly arched to the ground so as not to blind him. As his dog splashed at the river's edge, trying to catch a bullfrog, Briar's best friend joined him on the bank. She tucked her knees up to her chin and hugged them.

'Kerry, get up here,' Joshua called, and the Border collie reluctantly obeyed. You never knew when an alligator might be trolling for a meal.

'This place has bad memories for all of us,' Reena said.

'Yeah.' It was the reason why Briar feared any body of water. For Joshua, the fear hadn't taken root. It'd been hard the first few times he'd tried to go swimming after the accident, and then the panic had left him behind. As he saw it, if the water hadn't killed him then, it never would.

'Pat picked a bad place to try to get lucky,' Reena observed.

Joshua snorted. 'At least she knows he's a jerk now.' Then he sobered. 'She'll hate me too, once she knows the truth.'

'Is that your way of saying you don't want to do this?'

'No. But what *are* we doing? You haven't told me jack.'

'I will when the time's right. Come on, we need to get going.'

Joshua offered to take her backpack, but she refused, so he followed behind. They walked along the old road, the one that wound from up north down to the lake. Night sounds kept them company, and every now and then something would rustle in the bushes near the road.

Ahead of him, Reena's posture was taut, anxious. Whatever she was going to do was spooking her big time.

Maybe this isn't a good idea.

'You know anything about hoodoo?' Reena asked, breaking the silence.

'Some,' her companion replied. 'They sacrifice chickens, don't they?'

'That's voodoo you're thinking of. Hoodoo is folk magic. They . . . I do root magic.'

'OK, so where are we headed?'

'We're going to a crossroads. They've always been places of power, even before Christianity.'

'They used to bury suicides at a crossroads so the ghosts wouldn't haunt them, didn't they?'

'That's right. There's a spirit there and I'm going to summon him. The Dark Rider has a lot of power, and if I do it right he'll share some of that with me. I'm hoping I can get inside Briar's curse and help her find a way out.'

'Ohhkay . . .' Joshua said, not quite believing her. 'What's this spirit dude like?'

'The Dark Rider is more of a trickster than anything.'

'Like Loki, you mean?' When Reena gave him a sidelong look, Joshua shrugged. 'I'm kinda into Norse mythology.'

'Yeah, I guess he's like that.'

'If I remember anything about gods or spirits,' Joshua replied, 'they never give you anything without a price.'

'Not in this case. I should be able to borrow the dude's power without costing me anything.'

Riiight.

They walked to the intersection in thoughtful silence. The road had been abandoned once the new highway was built further to the east. Occasionally the locals would come down this way, but only if they didn't care about the exhaust-ripping potholes or if there hadn't been a heavy rain.

Reena shifted off her backpack. 'If you're having second thoughts, now's the time to leave.'

Joshua hesitated for a fraction of a second, and felt bad about it. 'I'm good,' he replied. 'Anything I can do to help?'

'Keep an eye out for traffic,' Reena said, her voice tighter now, evidence of the strain. 'There shouldn't be any, but with my luck some moron will come driving down here when I'm in the middle of the conjure. I don't want to be a big brown bug on someone's windshield.'

'Consider it done.'

He sent Kerry off to sit on the side of the road and then moved closer to watch Reena's preparations. He'd never seen magic up close before and until recently he'd not believed in it.

His friend retrieved a dark canvas bag from inside the backpack. From that bag came smaller pouches, along with candles and a box of matches.

'Why would a rootworker put a curse on a kid?' he asked.

Reena gave him a sharp look. 'Lily thinks that the conjurer was inexperienced, did something wrong, and that somehow the trick got out of hand. She doesn't believe it was targeted at you. It happens. Magic is . . . touchy.'

'Does this happen a lot?'

She shook her head. 'A trick to find a lover or gain

money, sure. Killing someone? Not so much.'

When Reena finally had everything she needed, she moved to the centre of the crossroads and knelt in the dirt where she carved out a hole with a short-bladed knife. Once the hole was about seven inches deep, she removed the ribbon from beneath her T-shirt and pulled it over her head.

'I've been wearing the keys for about a month now so they're part of me. I'm going to bury one here and keep the second one. Once I do that, I'll have a conduit to the power at this crossroads, power that might take me to Briar.'

Reena began to refill the hole, covering the first key. Once she'd tamped down the earth, she cut the ribbon. After retying it, she dropped the remaining key and the little charm under her T-shirt.

'That's it?' Joshua asked, growing more nervous as time passed.

'No,' Reena replied. 'That was just the beginning.'

As he kept a wary eye out for any cars, she sprinkled something on to the ground from the small pouches. When she'd finished, the piles of herbs formed four corners, with a dot in the very middle of them.

'A quintux,' he murmured.

'Yup. Since the veil between the worlds is supposed to be thinner here, I've created an altar. Well, sort of.'

The scent of the herbs opened his mind to new possibilities. Seeing Reena here in the dark, lit only by a pale moon, made him wonder how many of her ancestors had conjured in just this way, both here and in Africa. How many centuries had they woven magic and tried to fix the evils of the world?

Joshua watched in growing fascination as she laid out a series of small bones. Next came the candles – four of them. Before he could ask, she explained their significance.

'The white candle is for healing. The orange one is to open the way, the purple one for power and control.'

'And the black one?'

She looked over at him. 'Freedom from evil.'

'That works,' he murmured.

Reena fussed with one of them, adjusting its position, her hand quivering. After a deep breath, she nodded to herself.

'I'm going to light the candles now, then I'll summon the Dark Rider. I need you to turn round and don't look back. You're not supposed to see him. And don't say a word, no matter what happens. You understand?'

'So if I'm not going to help, why am I here?' he asked, annoyed.

'You're here in case it all goes wrong. That way you can tell Lily what happened to me.'

His blood chilled. 'Briar wouldn't want you to get hurt because of her.'

'I know. Like you, I have to do this.' Reena looked down at the crossroads. 'Say your prayers that this works. If not, I don't know how we'll ever get her back.'

As Joshua turned away, he whispered that prayer, and added one of his own.

Reena had spent most of the evening trying to determine what song she should use to call the Dark Rider to her. The tune itself wasn't important, but her delivery had to be pure and true. She needed to convince the spirit that she was worthy of notice, worthy of him sharing his power.

After much debating, she'd finally chosen 'Bye and Bye', an old negro spiritual her great-gran used to sing in church. Now she had to make the song hers.

Reena cleared her throat, whispered a prayer under her breath, and began.

> O, bye and bye, bye and bye
> I'm goin' to lay down my heavy load.
> I know my robe's gon' to fit me well;
> I'm goin' to lay down my heavy load.
> I tried it on at the gates of hell;
> I'm goin' to lay down my heavy load.

Like the other women in her family, she'd always had a good voice, but now it sounded weak and thready, as if the trees along the highway had sucked the life out of it. By the time she'd finished the first verse, nothing had happened. Not one twitch of power.

Was her great-gran's faith misplaced? Had all this work been for nothing?

I have to do this. It was that or go back to the Roses' house and watch her friend's life ebb away. 'I'm going to try again.'

'You can do it,' Joshua replied without hesitation.

At least he believes in me.

This time Reena closed her eyes and thought of her very best friend, what it would mean if she remained inside the curse. If it didn't kill her, Briar would sleep through the rest of high school, through prom, graduation. She'd lose her chance to attend college, to get married or even to have children. The world would move on and Briar Rose would know nothing of it.

Reena would lose her best friend and Joshua would lose . . . well, something he'd only just realized he wanted.

No way.

Reena began to sing again, visualizing the inside of the old church where Lily had taken her as a child. It'd been built in the late 1800s and the floor creaked a warm welcome with every step. The pews were wood and hard on her butt. The women always wore their Sunday best, clad in their fancy hats and dresses. The men were in dark suits, their shoes polished, their ties straight. That old building was filled with love and faith, emotions stronger and richer than anything else in this world.

She'd just reached the second verse when the earth began to crack open. Her voice faltered and went silent.

I did it! Reena Bulloch Hill, Lily Foster's great-granddaughter, had pulled the Dark Rider from his slumber.

Kerry went frantic, barking at the intruder. Joshua ordered her to be quiet and the collie fell back, low growls filling her throat.

'Why have you summoned me, child?' a chill voice demanded.

Reena's heart lodged in her throat. The Dark Rider never spoke to anyone. Had she screwed up the conjure?

'I . . . I need . . .' She corrected herself. Everything she'd

155

read said that she had to keep control of the situation, not beg for what she wanted. 'I need to break a curse. I need power to do it.'

'You are of the old one's blood,' was the reply. 'Her I respect. You are but a pup.'

'A pup who summoned you,' she shot back. Attitude counted, or at least that's what Lily had always told her. 'Here's the deal,' Reena began, resisting the urge to turn and face the spirit head on. 'My best friend, Briar Rose, is cursed and she needs our help.'

A bone-dry chuckle came from the spirit behind her as footsteps drew closer. Reena's knees were knocking now and she clutched her personal *gris-gris* bag tighter. Joshua was shivering as well, though he kept his back turned as she'd asked.

'I see this curse,' the spirit said. 'It is a dark one. She lives not inside a dream, but a nightmare, one built of her own imagination. One that will kill her in time. So you wish me to break it?'

'You can do that?' Reena blurted.

'No. I cannot.' Another chuckle. 'What is it you wish of me?'

'I seek the power to go inside the curse with her,' Reena said. 'Then I'll help her break it.'

'Is that so?' She felt his breath on her neck, bitter cold, and gave out a sudden yelp of fear.

When Joshua whipped round, his eyes connected with those of the Dark Rider.

'Oh my God,' he whispered.

If was as if black had taken on a new dimension, with its own weight and intensity, far beyond the simple lack of light. The Dark Rider was made of this nothingness, from his hair to his skin to his eyes and his clothes.

'You idiot! I told you not to turn round!' Reena cried.

'You smell of horseflesh,' the spirit said. 'Do you ride?'

Joshua gave a dry swallow and nodded.

'Hey, no, this thing is with me, not him,' Reena insisted.

'No longer,' the spirit replied. '*This* one has seen me. For that revelation *I* shall name the price of the power you seek, pup.'

Joshua's heart was pounding so fast he could barely breathe. What would this thing want? His heart? His soul?

'No,' it said, reading his mind. 'Something far more entertaining. You will rid me of the burden I bear, for it is much like a curse to me.'

'What burden?' Joshua asked, confused.

The spirit pointed at the crossroads. 'There is a dark soul that lies here with me. He gives me no peace and I would have him gone.' He looked over at Reena, who kept her eyes off him. 'For the power I will grant her, there will be a horse race. If you win, then you will live. If you lose, all those you hold dear will fall by his sword. Either way, he is gone.' The Dark Rider tilted his head. 'Do you agree?'

Joshua's eyes moved to Reena, but she was already shaking her head. 'Not a good idea,' she said.

But what choice did he have? If he said no, Briar was lost.

He pulled his attention back to the spirit. His body shook

harder now and it shamed him. 'You will send *both* of us into this curse where Briar Rose is being held. You will bring us back once we've helped her break it.'

The dark man shook his head and pointed at Reena's back. 'This one will send you into the curse and retrieve you. I will only grant her the power to do so. I will not guarantee your safe passage, nor your survival.'

It was a bargain even the devil would have turned down.

'Joshua, don't do it!' Reena said. 'Not this way. You have no idea—'

'It's a deal,' Joshua cut in. 'But I'll race at the time and place *I* choose.'

'You dare set terms on me?' the spirit retorted.

'Yeah, I do,' Joshua replied, feeling his courage stir. 'You want this as much as we do.'

A nod of respect. 'Indeed. The race must take place before the next full moon, one week hence. If not, you will have no choice but to come to me and pay *any* price I demand.'

'Done,' Joshua said, sweat rolling down his face.

'The key and the charm are the way into the curse. Your blood must be shed for the power to spark.' The unholy grin that spread across the spirit's face made Joshua's knees weaken. 'This was too easy. I expected a harder bargain.'

Ripples of chilly laughter echoed around them as the Dark Rider vanished into the night.

Joshua sagged in relief. They had a way to get to Briar. He'd worry about the rest of it later.

Reena grabbed him by the shoulders and shook him,

hard. 'Do you know what you just did?'

'I think so. I'm going to race some . . . thing. I'll just have to win.'

She shoved him and he staggered backwards a few steps. 'Why in the hell did you turn round?'

'I thought he'd hurt you.'

Reena groaned. 'He was playing with you, and you fell for it. I told you he was a trickster.'

'Then consider me tricked. We got what we came for − that's all that matters.'

'I didn't intend for you to go into the curse. It's too dangerous. That is my job.'

'Not any more,' he said.

Reena swore under her breath, then waved him forward into a hug, the kind that friends share when they're scared.

'You're an idiot, but you're an awesome one,' she said, embracing him.

'Right back at you,' he murmured, relieved she wasn't going to stay mad at him forever.

After they broke apart, Reena retrieved her pendant and pulled it off. Next came a penknife, and she winced as she stuck it in her palm. Wrapping her hand round the small charm, she let her blood mingle with the silver.

Once she was satisfied the charm was properly anointed, she had Joshua do the same. As he trapped the woodsman in his bloody palm, he closed his eyes and thought of Briar. A prickling coursed through him, as if the bracelet had somehow bonded with him.

'Joshua?'

He blinked open his eyes. It was still dark and they were still in the middle of the road.

'It didn't work,' he said, his panic kicking in.

'I haven't done the conjure yet,' she explained. 'It's about four thirty now. I'll begin the spell in an hour. That should give us time to get home and . . . get ready.'

Now it made sense – she wanted to leave a note for her parents. He should do the same.

Joshua returned the pendant and waited as she began to methodically obliterate the markings in the centre of the road. When Reena had finished, she took hold of his arm.

'I'll see you in about an hour,' she said. 'Wherever that might be.'

He nodded and then, without thinking, hugged her again.

'We'll bring her home,' he whispered. 'I promise.'

CHAPTER FOURTEEN

Once the chores were done, Briar had curled up for a nap in the fragrant hay while Ruric shod a horse. When she woke sometime later, the shadows were beginning to lengthen. Ruric sat on a low stool, carving a figure out of wood with sharp flicks of his knife. Briar yawned as she joined him and he smiled up at her, slipping the blade into a scabbard at his waist.

'You were weary,' he said. 'Are you revived now?' Briar nodded. 'And hungry?' She nodded again. 'I swear, I shall have to inherit a kingdom to feed you, my lady.'

She reached up to tuck a strand of his hair out of the way, and in a flash he caught her arm.

'You remind me of someone I once cared for. She was . . . very special.'

'Was?'

'She died three years ago. Thrown from a horse. I still remember that day,' he said, his eyes growing distant. 'I had no way to save her.'

'How awful. I'm so sorry,' Briar said. 'It still hurts, doesn't it?'

'Yes, I shall always miss her.'

For a second she thought he was going to kiss her, but instead he frowned at her wrist. 'What is that?' he asked.

'A . . . charm bracelet.'

'Do you mean it's magic?'

'No, it's just what we call them.' When he let loose of her hand, Briar held it up so he could see it better. 'It has different figures on it. They come from some of our favourite stories. We call them fairy tales.'

'It is most fetching. Did your family give it to you?'

'No, it was from this boy I know.'

One of Ruric's eyebrows rose. 'I thought you said you had no suitor,' he teased. 'A young man who offers such a fine gift is clearly worthy of your affections.'

'Not really. Joshua is . . .' How could she explain the whole mess? 'His family hates me. Well, his mother anyway.'

'Yet he must have defied his parents to give this gift.'

'Yeah, he did,' she said, not trying to hide the smile.

'Did his family put the curse upon you?'

Ruric had asked the question she'd tried so hard to avoid. Because if his mother or father had done this to her, that meant Joshua knew about it. 'I don't think so.'

'Now I've made you sad. I am sorry.'

'I just don't understand it all. Why I'm here, how I get home.' *Why I met you.*

'While you're working all that out, we should find somewhere more comfortable for you than the stable. There is an inn near the main gate. It is decent and the food is good there.'

This isn't right. 'I don't have any money, Ruric. You can't keep paying for everything.'

'I'm sure there is some way you can pay me back.'

He didn't mean . . . When she tensed, he caught it.

162

Ruric shook his head. 'Do *not* think I seek favours of that nature. I can be quite disreputable, but not in this case.'

'Disreputable? You?' Briar said, surprised. 'I don't see it.'

'You would be astonished at my churlish behaviour. My father always was.'

'I still have no money.'

'We shall find a way for you to earn a living, something honourable. I promise.'

Rogue or not, she'd just have to trust him to keep his word.

As the afternoon moved towards nightfall, it was as if there were two villages: the one that bustled with life during the day and the terrified one that hunkered down in the evening. Briar was used to small towns and how they 'rolled up the streets' at sundown – Bliss could be that way sometimes. This wasn't quite like that. There was an edge of uncertainty, almost dread, in the villagers' hurried movements. As the sun went down, people began to take shelter indoors. Doors were bolted, shutters locked, at least those on the ground floor. It didn't matter if it was a business or a house, it was as if the citizens felt they were under siege.

Ruric had done something similar, ensuring that the animals were fed and comfortable, then he'd bolted and locked the stable doors, hanging the large key round his neck, secured to a thick leather cord.

'You do this every night?' she asked.

'No. I usually eat my meal before the curfew, perhaps

have a pint of ale and then sleep here if one of the beasts is unwell or unusually skittish. I'm thinking they'll be fine tonight.'

Always her mother's child, Briar began to catalogue the negatives. 'What if there is a fire?'

'The smithy is nearby and he holds a key to the stable. He will free the animals.'

'What keeps someone from breaking in and stealing a horse?'

'No one is out after curfew,' he said curtly. 'You well know what that's like.'

She did indeed. Nevertheless, if something happened to Ruric, she wouldn't last a day. Briar forced herself to shake off that thought and hustled to catch up with him. Long-legged guys were not always a good thing.

'I'm taking you to the Inn of the Seven Fools,' he explained. 'It's the best of the lot. Since there are only two inns in the village, that doesn't say much.'

The Seven Fools was brightly lit, and from the noise issuing from the open door, it was doing a brisk business.

'I thought you said people weren't out after curfew.'

'They won't be. They're having one last ale before they head to their hearths.' Ruric leaned closer. 'Be cautious. There are spies everywhere and they will willingly sell your secret to the regent. Give them no opportunity to do so.'

Briar nodded her understanding, even more nervous now. As they stepped over the inn's threshold, the scent of roasted meat and yeasty ale assaulted her nose. Instantly her mouth watered and her stomach growled. More troubling, voices stilled and eyes turned in their direction.

'Good evening, chandler,' Ruric said, clapping a pockmarked man on the back. 'How was trade today?'

The man looked up from his meal. 'It was fair. And yours?'

'Not bad. Worth getting out of bed.'

A snort from a nearby table where the reeve studied them with sharp eyes.

'You have a new mare in your stable that has no owner,' he said. 'I'd count your day went very well.'

Ruric's smile faded. 'If I were so callous, perhaps. We must remember what it cost that mare's owner for it to become mine.'

The reeve huffed. 'I see you still have your cousin tagging after you.'

'As it should be.' Ruric gestured for her to join them. 'Briar, this is John of Leeland, our reeve. John is a man of many talents, most of which involve the consumption of ale.'

A hearty laugh returned. 'Do not let this young man lead you astray, girl. He has his *own* vices, though I doubt he will be parading those in front of his cousin.'

Ruric's good humour faded. 'Too true. How is the stew tonight?'

'Good. Worth the coin,' the man replied.

'I shall take that as a recommendation.'

Briar was led to a corner table, one with uneven legs, and she found it greasy like everything else in the inn. She gingerly sat on the bench, tucking her feet underneath her skirt.

'I'll get us some food,' Ruric said. 'Mead or ale?'

Ale didn't sound that good. 'Mead's OK. I'll deal.' At his puzzled expression, she added, 'I'll make do.'

While Ruric waded back through the crowd towards what seemed to be the bar, Briar checked out the other patrons. There were only three other women in the room, one of whom appeared to be the innkeeper's wife. Another was sitting with a young man, laughing at something he'd said. At her feet a spotted mongrel gnawed on a bone.

Most of the others were deep in their cups, beyond the point at which they should be drinking. Voices rose as a vigorous argument began between two men as to how bad the winter would be and if there would be adequate hay for the livestock.

It all felt wrong somehow. The patrons' laughter was forced, often interrupted with glances over shoulders, as if they were unsure of whom to trust – except the reeve, who kept a critical eye on everyone, no doubt to report to his boss. His eyes were on her right now, judging her.

What did he see? Ruric's cousin or someone who didn't belong here?

For a brief moment, the bustle of the establishment faded away, as if she were standing outside the curse, looking in. There were the tables and the people and . . . the darkness, the part of the curse that wanted to kill her. It hovered in the corners like mutant shadows, growing stronger, moving closer the longer she was inside the nightmare. There was no place to hide. She would always be the foreign body here, the disease the curse would seek to eradicate. It hadn't been able to do it when she'd first arrived, so now it was recalculating, looking for weakness. Like a predator stalking its prey.

It was the first time she'd thought of the curse as a sentient thing and it frightened Briar to the core.

As Ruric waited for his food, the third woman sauntered up to him. He smiled as she pulled him into her arms and collected his kiss on a cheek. She whispered something to him, then she gave a pointed look over her shoulder towards Briar, daring her to intervene.

You skank.

The moment she thought it, the fortune teller's warning came back to her. Briar had to find her prince or she wasn't getting out of this alive. Was it possible for Ruric to fall in love with her? And did he realize just how much she wanted to kick that girl in the shins?

His admirer was still joking with him, but Briar could tell he wasn't interested. It was the way he held himself, the way he kept his eyes on her, not the wench.

Why did the curse allow Ruric to save her from the wolves? Wouldn't it have been smarter to leave her unprotected? Or was there a counter-curse at work here, one that had sent her the fortune teller so she could find a way to survive?

Briar was deep in her thoughts when someone breathed in her face. It wasn't a good experience. She looked up into two red-rimmed eyes and an overly large crimson nose. The man was so drunk he was lurching around, unable to keep on his feet.

'You're a right fair maid,' he said, grinning. She smiled back, not sensing any menace.

Ruric returned at just the right moment, jested with the fellow and then made sure he left her alone. Once he'd placed the bowls of stew on the table, he sat down opposite her.

'What's wrong with him?' she asked, following the drunken man's uneven progress towards the door.

'Benton lost his son last year. The lad was sure he could break the enchantment so he found a way into the castle and he's not been seen since. Then Benton's wife died only a few months later. He has no solace but the drink now.'

That made Briar's heart ache. This might seem like a fairy tale, but there was no joy here, no happy ever after. It would be the same for her: in time, the curse would crush her. That was its job and it wouldn't stop until it had fulfilled its prime directive.

Pushing that depressing realization aside, she dug into the stew with a crude wooden spoon. A tentative taste told her it was really good and she began eating at a pace that would have earned her a reprimand from her mother. Ruric didn't seem to mind, a hint of a smile in place as he addressed his own meal. The dark crusty bread he provided offered the perfect means to soak up the remaining juices at the bottom of the bowl. By the time she'd finished off her meal, her stomach felt as if it would burst.

Briar slowly sipped on the mead. It was less strong than the drink Ruric had given her earlier in the day. Apparently the innkeeper watered his drinks.

'Better?' he asked.

'Yes. Thank you.'

'My pleasure. It would do the family no good to believe I starved you.' He leaned closer and delicately wiped something off her chin.

Embarrassed, she felt her cheeks warm again. 'It's a good thing you're my cousin,' she said.

Ruric laughed. 'Am I that enticing?'

'You're . . . nice.' *And handsome and, though you live in a fairy-tale curse that wants to kill me, you might be my prince.* Or maybe not.

'I'm only *nice*?' he said, sounding genuinely offended. 'How degrading. I am known as a scoundrel in my village, the black sheep of my family, who gambles and drinks and frequents the bordellos. But to you I am only . . . *nice*.'

Briar frowned. 'It was a compliment,' she insisted. 'You're nice and kind and you don't scare me, not like some of these people,' she said, her eyes trailing across the room. Three men in particular made her very uncomfortable. They'd been staring at her since she and Ruric had entered the inn.

Her companion's eyes followed hers. 'Ah, yes,' he said, his voice quieter now. 'Your instincts are good.' He pushed back from the table. 'I think it is time we retired, cousin. I have secured us a room for the night.'

He didn't wait for her reply, but was already on his way to collect a candle from the innkeeper. When he motioned for her to head upstairs, Briar threaded her way through the crowded room, embarrassed at the ribald comments that came her way. Even the tavern wench gave her a knowing wink.

Knowing it was best to keep up the ruse, Briar headed up the rough-hewn steps, muttering under her breath. Ruric held back, taking his time to light the taper and she realized he was listening to the men in the corner, the three that had spooked her. When he finally joined her at the top of the stairs, his face was stern.

'Are they following us?' she asked, worried.

'Not yet. It could be said that you're too pretty for your own good.'

Briar doubted that. She had dirt on her face, her clothes had horse crap on them and she needed a bath and deodorant, both of which seemed to be lacking in this village.

He led her down the hallways to a dinky room, all of about eight by eight feet, if that. There was no bed, and it was only after Ruric had placed the candle in a holder that Briar saw the two rolled pallets in a corner. Surely he didn't think they were going to share this tiny bit of real estate? Sleep so close together?

Ruric must have seen the concern on her face. 'I'll sleep by the door,' he said. He pushed open the shutters that covered what served as a window, and leaned out to study the view. A moth took immediate advantage, fluttering in to check out the candle.

As she watched, Ruric laid out one of the straw-filled mattresses for her and then added a blanket. The other pallet went in front of the door. As soon as he had arranged it the way he liked, he stretched out. Propping his head on a palm, he watched her inspect the situation.

This is cosy. Her parents hadn't let her double date until she was fifteen and now here she was all alone with a guy only a couple of years older than her. One who admitted to wenching and being a black sheep. If they had known, her folks would be flipping out right now.

Briar turned back to the 'bed' and prodded the mattress with a toe, sure it was probably full of fleas and lice and other bitey things. She looked back over at Ruric and found he was suppressing a smile.

'Not like in your village?' he asked innocently.

'No. We sleep up off the ground and the mattresses are . . . thicker.' *Way thicker.*

Briar eased herself to the floor and sat on the pallet. It wasn't so bad, sort of like a lumpy sleeping bag. It was then she realized that he'd given her the thicker one.

Their eyes met.

'Thank you,' she said. 'For everything.'

'I must admit that I wish I wasn't so honourable. However, that is not the case.'

He does care for me. That made her feel good. 'Why are you doing this? You didn't have to help me.'

'I would like to think that if my sister were on her own, someone would take care of her without trying to take advantage.'

That was cool. 'What's your sister like?'

The smile finally bloomed. 'Devilish. Sofia climbs trees and dislikes the gowns my mother purchases for her. She

171

wed this last spring and has settled down now, though her husband did remark that she is still rather wilful. I suspect her daughters will grow up much like her.' His smile told Briar that he didn't mind that at all.

He'd made a big slip – poor people couldn't afford to buy gowns for their daughters. They made everything by hand or bartered for it. It was clear that Ruric was of noble blood, maybe even a prince.

The fortune teller was right. I did find him. But now what?

Briar decided not to call him on his verbal slip, holding the secret close to her heart.

'I climbed trees when I was younger, until I fell out of one,' she said.' My mother was always too protective of me. I didn't get to do much.'

'It could be said you're making up for that now.' He lay down, staring up at the ceiling as the candle cast subtle lines of light and shadow on the side of his face. 'Tomorrow I will buy black dye so we may make your hair less golden.'

Briar opened her mouth to protest, but then closed it. He was right – she had to hide her hair to remain alive, at least in the short term.

In the semi-darkness, she touched the charms on the bracelet one by one, thinking of her friends and her home and how much she missed them. Of Joshua and the courage it had taken for him to defy his family.

'You're very quiet,' Ruric observed.

'I was thinking of my friends back in Bliss.'

'And the young lad as well?'

'Yes.'

'I did not see love written upon your face when you speak of him. Why is that?'

'He's . . . not my type.'

'What sort of man do you seek?' Ruric asked.

'A prince,' she said, before she could stop herself.

He looked at her long and hard, his expression unreadable.

'I hope you will find what you seek.'

CHAPTER FIFTEEN

Joshua stared at the bedroom ceiling, feeling the minutes slip away. What if he died inside the curse and his parents found him all stiff and cold in his bed? His mother would lose her mind after being so convinced he was safe now. And when she learned that he'd willingly put himself in danger to help Briar . . .

Joshua's cellphone vibrated and he jumped in surprise.

It was Reena. 'You freaking yet?' she asked.

'Totally.'

'I'm going to start now.'

'OK. Use that dude's power for all it's worth.'

'I will, Josh. Thanks . . . for everything. See you soon.' She hung up.

Joshua put the phone on the nightstand on top of the lengthy note he'd written to his parents. If something happened to him, he wanted them to understand why he'd had to do this. Why Briar's curse was his burden.

With a tortured sigh, Joshua lay back and resumed his study of the ceiling. For a time nothing much happened except that an owl hooted outside his window, which he didn't think was a great omen. Then his mind began to fill with an eerie darkness and that same sting of magic he'd felt at the crossroads. It slithered across his body, encasing him like an invisible shroud.

He swore he could smell the pungent scent of herbs and hear Reena's rich voice along with the pounding of drums.

'Come on, you can do it,' he said. 'Take us to Briar.'

Then he'd make it right.

Even if she hates me for the rest of my life.

The sound of the door creaking open roused Briar from a troubled sleep. She rolled over, her back tender from the hard floor. Ruric stood in the hallway, and in the dim light of the candle she saw him carefully shift his feet so as not to create any noise on the loose boards.

She sat up. 'What's wrong?' she whispered.

He returned, closing the door behind him. 'We have to go. The men are planning to pay us a visit.'

'But you can take them, right?'

'I'm a trained fighter, but three large ruffians in a very small room might prove more than I can handle, if I'm also trying to protect you.'

'Won't the innkeeper help us?' she asked, rising to her feet.

'No. He will remain blind as long as a few coins are offered and none of his property is damaged.'

He stuffed his mattress in the corner, as it had been when they arrived. He indicated she should do the same and Briar hurried to comply.

There was the sound of voices and boots on the stairs.

There was nowhere to hide. 'Oh, God. What do we do?' she asked.

'We become invisible,' was the reply. Ruric pointed

towards the window. 'I'll go first, then you follow me.'

He vanished through the opening and then his hand appeared. 'Come on. There is little time.'

Briar peered out and down, queasy at the sheer drop off the end of the wooden planked roof.

He has to be kidding.

Ruric waved his hand again, more urgently this time. 'I vow I will not let you fall, but you must hurry.'

The drunken men were in the hallway now. They were coming for her.

Briar hefted up her skirts and climbed out of the window. The moment she was out, Ruric's arm carefully guided her along the slippery roof.

'Don't look down,' he said.

'Wasn't planning to,' she murmured back.

Once he was certain she was settled into a niche by the stone chimney, he skittered back like a monkey and closed the shutters. Briar continued to quake in fear – she was sure she'd lose her balance and hit the ground, cracking her skull open. When Ruric's muscled arm went round her again, she huddled against him, shivering in fright. His cloak settled around them, fending off the night wind.

'Stay very quiet,' he whispered.

The noises came quickly now – the door being forced open, coarse laughter, then the swearing began. Boots stomped around as the shutters were thrown open.

'Curse that rat. Where has he taken the wench?' one said.

There were more colourful oaths, some of which were

quite crude. In time – after loudly debating the merits of accosting someone else, especially one who might be better armed – the trio retreated downstairs, their dark intentions thwarted.

Briar sighed in relief. That had been too close, even with Ruric there to help her.

In the moonlight she could see her companion's pleased smile.

'You outwitted them. You're really smart, you know that?'

'That remains to be seen. I have learned much about those kinds of men over the years. I used to hunt them and bring them to the gallows for their crimes.'

Which is why there is that hard place in your heart. Apparently there was more to Ruric than just being a noble. When she started to speak again, he held up his hand for silence.

There were shouts on the street now, followed by deep-throated snarls. A piteous scream pierced the air and then there was silence.

'The wolves?' she whispered.

'Yes. Those men were not from the village, so they went out after curfew to try to find us.'

'They're . . . dead, then?'

'That or they have been captured and taken to the castle.'

Briar's shivering returned, despite the warmth of Ruric's cloak and he hugged her closer.

'You are safe now. Do not worry.'

'I know, it's just so different to my home.'

'Then it was fortunate that I found you running from the

wolves last night, was it not?' he said simply.

Or fate.

With great caution, Ruric helped her across the roof and back into the room. The pallets were tossed around and so he moved them back into their original positions.

'I will leave the candle unlit. I have no wish to let the innkeeper know we're still here. As it's after curfew, he will not rent the room to anyone else.'

Briar would never know what made her tug her own pallet closer to his, but she did. Not touching, but within a foot of him. It was her way of saying she had placed her complete faith in man she barely knew.

Ruric solemnly observed her actions. 'I am honoured by your trust,' he said. He rolled on his side, his face towards the door, ever on guard.

At one time, she would have thought his behaviour so very noble, just what a prince should do for a princess: slay the dragon, rescue her from the tower. But this was Ruric, someone she truly cared about, not some abstract guy in a fairy tale. He'd already shown that he would do anything to protect her, even risk execution or being changed into one of those metal monsters.

Maybe you are my prince, but I can't be your princess. I have no kingdom for you.

All she had to offer him was a gruesome death.

The dark tunnel gradually gave way to sunlight. As Joshua clawed his way back to consciousness, his skin prickled as if impaled by scores of needles. He shook himself awake, trying to throw off the magic, which caused his stomach to roil.

When he finally opened his eyes, he found he was lying underneath a tree, an old oak whose massive branches shielded him from the sun. He peered up at it, puzzled. It seemed familiar in some way, like the one under which he and Briar had sheltered after the re-enactment.

The thought of her made him struggle harder to clear the cobwebs.

Taking stock of his surroundings, he was amused to discover cows and sheep grazing nearby. A young woman sat on a low stool, milking a nanny goat, dressed as if she'd just stepped out of the Middle Ages.

Did it work? He'd have to assume it had. But why this pastoral scene?

When Joshua pulled himself to his feet, the surprises kept piling on. His own clothes had changed, now being a pair of dirty leather boots, dun-coloured breeches, a beige linen shirt and a dark-brown leather jerkin, belted at the waist. A scabbard was attached to the belt, and he pulled the knife free to examine it. Satisfied it was for real, he re-sheathed it.

'Josh?'

He turned to find Reena hurrying across the field towards him. Her curly hair was down on her shoulders, and she was in a peasant dress, a homespun cloak floating behind her. Slung over a shoulder was her canvas bag.

As she grew near, he beamed. 'It worked!' He picked her up and spun her round as if she weighed nothing.

'OK. Good,' she said, taken aback at his enthusiasm.

'Colour me surprised.' She eyed his garments. 'Hey, look at you. It's good you're my bud, or I'd be all over you in a flash. You're smoking, dude.'

He laughed. That was one of the reasons Reena had become a good friend – she had a great sense of humour even when things were scary.

They turned as one towards the town in the distance. 'Oh look. It's got a castle. Go figure,' he said.

'Makes sense. I mean, where else would Briar end up but in a fairy tale?'

'Yeah, but which one?' he asked.

'Hopefully one that isn't lethal,' Reena replied.

'There are very few of those. The Dark Rider said that this is a nightmare, more than a dream.'

'Yeah, I remember.'

When they approached the milkmaid, she stared up at them. Or, more accurately, stared at Reena.

'Ah, good day to you. We're looking for a friend of ours. A girl named Briar,' Joshua said.

'Ah, her,' the woman said. 'She's at the stable.'

'Thank you, good . . . lady.' They hustled on before she could ask more questions.

As the pair drew closer to the town, Reena slowed her pace, thoughtful.

'The stable doesn't sound like Briar's kind of place. Knowing our girl, she's inside the castle trying on fancy princess dresses and glass slippers. Probably hitting on a prince.'

'She better not be,' Joshua replied tersely. Especially not

the *hitting on a prince* part. 'Let's just find out where the stable is and get Briar out of here. I don't like the feel of this place.'

'I don't think it's going to be that easy,' Reena cautioned. 'The curse brought her here for a reason. We need to know what's going on before we start stirring things up, or we might make it worse.'

Joshua thought that through. 'What if she doesn't want to leave? She might not realize it's a dream.'

'Don't go there. No need to feed the curse with anything it can twist.'

He stared at his companion. 'You make it sound as if it's listening to us,' he said.

'Magic isn't static, Josh. It feeds on what you give it.' Reena studied the village around them. 'We're in the middle of a giant-assed spell and we don't want it to get mad at us.'

'You serious?' he said, hoping he'd misunderstood.

'Totally. The curse didn't plan on us showing up, so there's no telling how it's going to react. We need to be very careful.'

Joshua's good mood flagged. He'd figured it'd be a quick in-and-out rescue mission, snag up Briar and go home. Not a covert action with a hidden enemy that had its own vicious agenda.

So what else can go wrong?

CHAPTER SIXTEEN

The next morning the innkeeper gaped at them as Briar and Ruric descended the stairs into the tavern. He gave them a curt nod and went back to counting his coins, though she could tell he was flustered. That unease proved prophetic when Ruric strode to the counter. He leaned over, then deftly sorted out four copper coins and dropped them in his pouch.

'What are you doing? That is my money!' the innkeeper protested.

A thick-bladed knife rammed down into the wood only a few inches from the man's hand. He jerked back in surprise.

'As I see it,' Ruric began, his voice full with menace, 'you should be pleased I am only reclaiming the payment for the room. You told those roughs precisely where to find us and that placed my cousin in mortal danger. I should cut your throat for such perfidy.'

'I had no choice,' the man said. 'The reeve . . .' His ruddy complexion paled.

'Go on.'

The innkeeper drew a heavy breath. 'The reeve urged them to pay you a visit. If I had refused, those men would have torn my inn apart.'

'Would you have wished the same if it had been your daughter?'

The man mumbled in the negative.

'You always have a choice, innkeeper,' Ruric replied. 'Mind that you make the proper ones in future.'

The man huffed in disgust. 'You are barred from my inn from this day forward.'

Ruric stepped back, sheathing his knife as he did so. 'As you wish, though I shall miss your most excellent stew. Good day, innkeeper. Do mark my warning.'

As they stepped outside into the morning air, Briar couldn't help but notice a pile of torn and blood-stained clothes at the edge of the road.

'It would appear our ruffians met a bad end,' Ruric said. 'I, for one, shall not mourn their fate.'

'Neither will I,' Briar replied, then realized how heartless that had sounded. That wasn't like her.

'You are learning, cousin,' her companion replied. 'There are good people in this world, and there are bad. The trick is to keep the former as your friends and the latter as far away as possible.'

'So says Ruric.' He nodded and smiled. 'Why did the reeve do that?' she asked.

'If I was killed or injured, he could easily claim the mare as his own. It appears I have made an enemy.'

'You could just give him the horse,' Briar suggested.

'If I appease him on this matter, what if his next request is for you?'

Her heart skittered. 'He wouldn't do that, would he?'

'Maybe not, but he has power enough. I do not need to grant him any more,' was the curt reply.

Instead of going directly to the stable, they headed towards the main market, after more food and dye for her hair, he explained. She began to wonder what the dye would be like in this place. Would it stink? *Probably.*

As they turned a corner on to a broader street, Briar caught her first close-up view of the castle and was immediately disappointed. Where were the pointy spires, the elegant stained-glass windows, the perky princess striking a pose on the balcony?

Instead, this was a fortress with thick stone turrets, broad defensive walls and a deep, smelly moat. Guards stood high on the curtain walls, patrolling back and forth, all human. Over the bridge, others stood in front of a portcullis, questioning anyone who came too near.

Walt Disney would not have approved.

'There is no way you can get in there,' she whispered, mindful that someone might overhear them.

'Of course there is,' he said. 'I know at least two different ways. There are more, no doubt.'

'No,' she said, touching his arm to make him pay attention. 'You'll end up dead, Ruric. It's not worth it.'

He sighed at that point. 'Most likely, but I have always been a lucky soul. Nevertheless, it is a grand castle, is it not?'

Not by her way of thinking.

Briar found this market was larger and had a better selection. She also felt more eyes on her, not only from the merchants and the other shoppers, but from the castle behind them. She forced herself to act normally, buying the items Ruric had said they needed, often from people who looked remarkably similar to people back home. It proved difficult figuring out which coin was of what value. She grew smarter at it when one of the merchants tried to shortchange her.

As Ruric chatted with a pair of townspeople, Briar caught the elusive scent of baked goods. In particular – cake. Her mouth watered and she did a slow turn to try to figure out where it'd come from.

Wandering through the stalls, she kept tracking the scent like a bloodhound, because it reminded her of her mother and home. It grew stronger as Briar approached a narrow alley, one with all the doors and windows boarded up. Various hex signs were scrawled on the walls like graffiti, some in what appeared to be dried blood. Curiously, none of that frightened her. Instead, she felt at peace, as if the brooding darkness that shadowed her couldn't reach her here.

More steps brought her close to an abandoned well, all boarded up with symbols scrawled on every surface. What did they mean? One of the boards had fallen aside and she peered down into a deep black hole. From somewhere below came the steady *drip drip* of water. Knowing Ruric would be worried about her, she looked back down the street towards the market, but couldn't see him.

Though she knew she should go find him, that he might be worried about her, Briar didn't want to leave this place. She sank down on to the stone kerb of the well, fanning herself with her hand. Her new scarf was hot, but she didn't dare take it off. It'd be better after she dyed her hair, then she could braid it and wouldn't be so warm.

Briar closed her eyes, feeling at home for the first time since she'd arrived. A faint noise came from behind her and she swore someone tapped her on the back. She looked round, but there was no one there. Had to be her imagination.

Ruric appeared at the end of alley and she waved her hand so he'd see her. There was another tap, followed by a loud giggle. Briar spun round and found . . . nothing. No, there was a teal feather lying on one of the boards and she knew it hadn't been there before. She retrieved it, entranced by how it glistened in the sunlight, almost iridescent.

Where did it come from?

'Briar! Come away from there!' Ruric called out as he ran towards her. 'It is not safe.'

Just as she stood, he raced up and took hold of her arm, pulling her down the street like she'd been a naughty child. She was just about to show him the cool feather, but something stopped her. Instead, Briar stuffed her treasure inside her shirt.

'I wasn't like I was going to fall in,' she grumbled.

'The well is very dangerous. *They* live down there. They kidnap mortals and suck the life from their bodies. I doubt the metal on your wrist would have saved you.'

'They who?' she asked, bewildered.

'The fata. They are the ones who laid the curse on the princess. It is why the regent sends her beasts out at night, to keep them at bay, if not we would all die.'

Was a fata something like a fairy? That was who had laid

the curse in the Grimms' version of 'Sleeping Beauty'.

'What do they look like?' she asked.

Now that they were approaching the end of the alley, Ruric slowed his pace and let go of her arm. 'Their skin is very bright and colourful, sometimes covered in feathers. They have eyes that shine like a cat's. It is said that once they pull you underground they change into hideous monsters. They are fond of mortal males in particular.'

Which I'm not. Briar didn't want to call BS on him, but none of this sounded right. Still, her companion's fear was so palpable there had to be something behind this. For now, she decided to keep the feather hidden, at least until she had the time to figure out what it meant and why someone, or *something*, had given it to her.

The time passed without incident as people came and went, collecting or dropping off horses. Briar had found some time to dye her hair, which had proved to be a smelly process. Ruric had helped her with her eyebrows and when she was done, he pronounced her fit to be seen without a head scarf.

'Your hair is like a raven's wing now,' he proclaimed, touching her drying braid. 'It is magnificent to behold. You're as beautiful as any princess.' Then he delicately placed the lightest of kisses on her forehead.

Is he flirting with me? It sure felt like it.

Despite the warmth in her cheeks, she didn't mind.

CHAPTER SEVENTEEN

Once they were further into the village, Joshua asked a local where they could find the stable and was provided with directions. To his relief, people weren't taking a lot of notice of them.

The heavy tolling of a gong stopped them in their tracks.

'What does that mean?' Reena asked.

'Probably time to drown a witch,' Joshua joked.

Reena glared at him. 'Oh, like someone who works with herbs and roots and does magic?'

He winced at his mistake. 'Sorry. I say stupid stuff when I'm . . . worried.' Scared was more like it, but he wasn't going to admit that, even to his friend.

As the gong struck a final note, the villagers stopped toiling, talking or whatever it was they were engaged in, and began to file towards the castle. Even if Joshua and Reena had wanted to go in another direction, it wasn't an option with the tide of bodies surging forward.

'Maybe we'll see Briar somewhere along the way,' Reena said. 'Save us a trip to the stable.'

That he doubted. When Joshua caught a glimpse of a man who looked exactly like Bliss's mailman, he nudged Reena and pointed at him.

'The curse is pulling things out of Briar's mind,' his friend explained. 'Remember, the Dark Rider told us that.

That's not good news – she has a really vivid imagination.'

Yet another reason to get her out of here as quickly as possible.

The mass of humanity finally halted outside the castle's massive front gate as the portcullis was painstakingly winched upward, foot by foot.

'You'd think it'd be like one of those fairy castles,' Reena said, craning her neck up to get a better look. 'This is—'

'Not good news,' Joshua replied, keeping his voice low. 'That is one seriously fortified castle. Someone isn't feeling secure on their throne.'

Reena gave him a nudge. 'Check out the building on your right,' she said under her breath. 'It's like . . . metal.'

Joshua followed her gaze and gaped. One side of the structure was wood, the other brass. Before he could comment, a phalanx of armoured warriors exited the main gate. They were heavily armed, carrying either pikes or swords. A lone rider followed them.

'Look!' Joshua exclaimed. 'The horse is metal.'

Reena checked it out. 'OK, that's seriously weird.'

Joshua admired the beast from its shiny copper ears to its long tail. It had the grace of a real horse, but with each footfall requiring a series of complex motions as if it were a clockwork toy.

Its rider was dressed in a hat and a long black gown that flowed down the flanks of the steed, her face obscured by a mask made of copper. A black iron falcon perched on her shoulder, its green eyes scanning the crowd as if it were searching for its next meal.

'This isn't like any fairy tale I've ever read,' Reena whispered.

'Not unless Stephen King wrote it,' he replied.

A servant in a Civil War uniform and a half-mask stepped forward, and, after a trumpet blast, unrolled a piece of paper.

'As there have been those who question the existence of the Sleeping Princess known as Aurora, the regent has ordered that she be brought forth so that all may see Her Highness and know she is unharmed.'

Excited murmurs broke out around them.

'She's here? Is it true?' someone called out.

'That means she is still alive,' another replied.

Joshua nudged his companion. 'Sleeping princess?'

Reena shrugged. '"Sleeping Beauty" is Briar's fave tale, but I don't remember a regent in the story.'

As they watched, a quartet of liveried servants exited the castle bearing a small filigreed bed. Resting on it was a young woman, one with flowing blonde hair that cascaded over the side of the mattress. Her hands were folded over her chest and nestled between them was a single metallic rose.

'It's Briar,' Reena said, her voice telegraphing her surprise. As she tried to move closer, Joshua caught her arm.

'No . . .' he said. 'Wait and see what happens.'

As the sleeping form paused in front of the crowd, there were gasps of delight. Many of the villagers fell to their knees as if the princess was some sort of religious icon.

'This is way off the creepy scale,' Joshua said.

'You sure it's not Briar? We can just grab her and take off.'

'No,' he said. 'It's not her.' That earned him a frown. 'Trust me on this.'

'If you're wrong . . .' Reena warned.

He knew it wasn't. The girl on the bed was remarkably similar, but he'd spent too many hours studying the lines of Briar's face to be fooled.

'You're right,' Reena conceded. 'It's not her. Her boobs aren't that big.'

Joshua snorted and that earned him a frown. 'You said it, not me.'

A young man suddenly dashed forward, intent on reaching the princess, but he fell short of his goal, knocked down by two guards. With a nod from the regent, his throat was cut, the gushing blood spilling forth. The instant it left his body it quickly turned to metal, flowing into the soil beneath him like molten silver as his eyes turned sightless.

'Oh, God,' Reena blurted out. 'Did you see that?'

From behind them, someone shushed her. 'Be silent. If she hears you, you'll be next.'

Joshua tentatively took hold of his friend's hand and it shook in his.

What is this nightmare?

As the young man's body slumped to the ground, a feminine wail came from the crowd. A young girl ran forward and cradled him in her hands. As she wept, the princess was ferried back into the castle, her part in this drama complete.

'No!' someone cried. 'Free her!'

That person was promptly hushed by his neighbours.

The servant unrolled another parchment. 'An enemy of the Sleeping Princess has been discovered within the village. To threaten Aurora is to warrant death.'

Joshua shifted weight on his feet, uneasy at the increasing tension in the crowd. They were angry, he could feel it rolling over him in waves, yet still none of the townspeople wanted to share the fate of the man whose flowing blood was anointing the dirt.

The jeers and shouts began the moment guards hauled a small form through the castle gates. Thinking it was a child, Joshua gasped. It wasn't until the prisoner was dragged closer that he realized it was something entirely different.

'Cursed swine! Burn it!' someone called out.

The being was multi-coloured, its skin dappled with oranges and rusts with vivid blue encircling its eyes. Its hair was a light shade of green and small pale flowers were woven with the locks. It was clothed in feathers that fluttered as it moved.

'What is that thing?' Reena asked.

'A fata,' one of the villagers replied. 'That's what it looks like in the sunlight. I've heard that at night it changes and it will kill you if it can.'

Joshua touched the sleeve of a man standing next to him. 'Why do you hate it so much?'

'Their kind cursed our princess. It is why Aurora sleeps and none can wake her. Why the regent is our —' the man hesitated — 'ruler.'

Though he'd meant to say more than that, Joshua got the picture. 'What's with all the metal?'

The older man gave him a strange look. 'It's to keep them fata at bay. Everyone knows that. Where are you from?'

'We're new to your . . . village.'

'Why in God's sweet name would anyone come here?' the man replied, then pointedly moved away from them as if they were contagious.

The crowd grew louder as the small figure cowered, crying blue tears that splashed on its toes, its whole body shaking.

The servant cleared his throat. 'The sentence is slow death. There will be no mercy shown,' he announced, then dutifully rolled up his parchment.

With faint cries, the fata was forced inside a gibbet, one lined with iron. It shrieked when its skin touched the sides, but there was no way it could avoid the metal. It was a cruel way to die.

At the regent's gesture the gibbet was hauled up on a pole for all to see. Only now did the crowd vent its displeasure, both with oaths and rotten fruit. The anger was real, though Joshua suspected it was also meant for their ruler.

'Should have torn the accursed thing apart. It is an abomination,' a woman said.

Joshua turned to see who had spoken and then his attention locked on a girl, one that looked remarkably like Briar. Her build was similar, the way she held her head, but it couldn't be as this girl had jet black hair and the man next to her had his arm round her in a comforting gesture, as if they were a couple.

'Come on, let's get out of here,' Joshua urged.

As they broke clear of the throng, Reena looked back at the creature hanging in the gibbet. 'Even if those things cursed the princess, that's just sick, letting it die that way.'

'Not our problem,' Joshua replied. At his friend's startled expression, he added, 'I know that sounds really cold, but our only job is to get Briar out of here, before someone decides to cut her throat.' *Or ours.*

'Now you see why I have been so cautious,' Ruric said as they walked back to the stable together. He was still holding her hand and she appeared to like that, but Briar wasn't smiling now, not after what had happened. A sensitive soul lost in a dark world, he knew she grieved for both the dead man and the fata.

'Aurora looks like me. You knew that, didn't you?' she said.

'Yes, I was told you resembled her.'

Why am I so keen to throw away my life for the princess? Is being a king that important?

It was the same question Ruric been asking himself for the last few months, just one of the issues that had held him back from his quest. Now Briar's presence made that question more pressing. His 'cousin' was a fine young lady, and if he didn't need to secure a throne of his own she would make a good choice for a wife, if she would agree to such a thing.

Perhaps if he woke the princess and helped overthrow the regent, he could choose another path for his life. A path that didn't require a throne, but might include a pretty girl with no home.

As he looked over at her, pondering that future, someone called out.

'Briar?'

She came to a halt, and then slowly turned. Her eyes widened in astonishment. 'Reena?' she cried.

Then there was a flurry of embracing as she and the other girl greeted each other. The newcomer's arms were dark, her face the same underneath her hood.

'Josh is here too,' the girl said. She waved at someone and a young man moved closer to them.

Ruric took the measure of the young man and found little fault. He was younger by a few years, but handsome in his own way. This must be the lad Briar had claimed wasn't a suitor, yet the way he looked at her said she was mistaken.

So he has come for her.

Ruric couldn't miss the deep frown that came his way. He knew that expression well enough: this one was jealous. How had Briar missed the signs?

'How did you get here?' she asked, clearly baffled.

'Reena got us in,' the young man said.

The look he shared with his companion said there was more to it than that.

'What's with the hair?' the one named Reena asked.

Briar shook her head. 'Not here,' she said, looking around nervously. 'I'll tell you later.'

Ruric gently cleared his throat. 'Would you care to introduce me, cousin?'

'Oh, sorry!' Briar began, her voice registering her excitement. 'This is my friend, Reena, and this is Joshua.

Ruric runs the stable. He has been taking care of me since I came here.'

'I am pleased to meet you both,' Ruric said. He resisted the temptation to take hold of Briar's hand to see what the one named Joshua might do. Given the fire in the fellow's eyes, it might result in a brawl.

'You do know how to pick them,' Reena replied, waggling an eyebrow. 'So, Ruric, you wouldn't happen to have a brother, would you?'

'Yes, two of them.' He smiled, studying her features. 'Both wed.'

'Guys, we need to be going,' Joshua cut in.

'But . . .' Briar's enthusiasm waned. 'Right now?'

'Ah, yes,' Reena replied. 'Sooner or later the curse is going to take you down. We don't want to be here when it does.'

So there really is a curse. That saddened him, for he realized that she might truly leave him behind. *Perhaps I am only a dream to her.*

'Oh . . .' Now Briar appeared to be on the verge of tears. 'Can you give us a moment, please?'

Reena nodded immediately, but the young man didn't look pleased. It took her shoving him down the street to gain them some privacy.

'You are wrong,' Ruric began, feeling an unexpected ache settle into his chest. 'That young man does care for you.'

'He . . .' Briar shook her head. 'It doesn't matter, not once I get home. His mom will see to that.'

'Then . . .' Ruric summoned his courage. 'Perhaps

you might . . . stay here with me.'

Briar's mouth dropped open. 'Oh . . . but . . . I . . .'

In her eyes he could see her emotions play out: the promise, the doubt.

'Ruric?' They turned in unison to find the reeve headed towards them, four of the regent's guards behind him.

'The horse is still not for sale,' Ruric snapped, aggravated at the interruption. He leaned closer to Briar. 'Allow me to get rid of this fool. I have more I must say before you make your decision.'

'I'll . . . wait.'

That gave him hope. Ruric turned towards the overbearing official. 'What do you want, reeve?'

'You.'

Ruric was immediately set upon by two of the guards, who spun him round and rammed him up against the side of the stable, mashing his cheek into the wood. A sword poked him in the back, ensuring he gave up the fight. The remaining muscle kept watch in case some of the villagers decided to intervene.

'What is this? What's going on?' Ruric demanded.

'You are under arrest,' the reeve said. 'You are to be taken to the regent for trial.'

'What have I done to warrant such unpleasant attention?'

'You have profited from the enemies of the princess.'

'Oh, I see. I didn't sell you the mare and now you're seeking your petty revenge.'

'Teach him some manners,' the reeve ordered. A guard

buried his first into Ruric's side and he grimaced in pain.

'Stop this!' Briar said. She tried to get closer, but one of the guards held her back and she was no match for his strength. 'Leave Ruric alone. Just take the stupid horse.'

The reeve eyed her closely. 'Best be silent, girl, or you'll be joining him.'

'Stay out of this, cousin,' Ruric urged. 'It is a simple matter once I speak to the regent. I shall be back here soon enough.'

Briar had seen too much death in this kingdom to believe that.

Once his arms were secured in front of him, Ruric requested the opportunity to say farewell to her. To their surprise, the reeve granted it.

He knows I'll never see Ruric again.

Ruric looped his arms round her, and pulled her against him. He leaned close to her ear. 'Go home. You do not belong here. Give that young man a chance to tell you how much he cares for you,' he whispered. When he broke the embrace, he gently touched her cheek. 'Remember me kindly, Briar Rose.'

Tears escaping, she nodded, then tipped up on her toes and kissed his cheek.

'I had wondered what it would take to get you to do that,' he said. His kiss went on her cheek as well, though she swore he would have preferred to kiss her mouth.

'Please don't let the regent hurt you.'

'I'll endeavour to make it so. And, look, I have found yet another way inside the castle,' he said, winking.

As the guards led him away, Briar didn't try to hold back her tears. A few of the townsfolk paused to watch the procession, whispering among themselves, but none intervened.

Divide and conquer. Take away one troublemaker at a time and the others won't stop you.

She rounded on the reeve, all fury. 'He's innocent and you know it. You just did this to get the horse.'

The man's hand shot out and grabbed on to her braid, dragging her close to him. He smelt of scented oil and greed.

'You would be wise to hold your tongue, girl,' he snarled. 'I know what you have done with your hair. You'd best keep on my good side, or the regent will learn your secret. Then you will be silenced forever.'

When he shoved her away, she nearly fell. 'Saddle the mare. She is mine. From this day forward, I will expect you to pay me one-fifth of your profits. Do you understand?'

Even though she did not own the stable, Briar had no choice but to agree. Her hands trembling and the tears falling, she readied the horse.

'Kick him,' she whispered in an ear. 'Kick him hard.'

She led the beast out of the stable and handed over the reins.

'What will the regent do to him?'

The man heaved himself up on the horse. 'Cut his throat. Make him one of her own. Feed him to one of her monsters. It is of no importance to me. I have what I want.'

Swinging the mare round, he cantered up the street, his head high, his victory complete.

CHAPTER EIGHTEEN

'How long is this goodbye going to take?' Joshua growled, scratching under his shirt. He swore fleas were leaping on him from all directions, though he'd found no evidence of their presence.

'Listen to you,' Reena replied, grinning from under the hood. 'You keep that up and you're going to glow green.'

'I don't care. You saw how he was looking at her. She was even holding his hand. What was that all about?' he asked, stomping along.

'He's a hunk. That's what I'd do. Just chill, will you? Once we get back home she'll forget all about him.'

Home. Back in Bliss. How is that going to make things better?

As they entered a broader street, Joshua kept muttering his breath. 'Come on, let's go get her. I want to get out of here.'

'All right! If it keeps you from bitching, I'm all for it.'

As they turned round, Joshua shot a glance towards an open area where a few small boys had gathered. There were two pillories there, one of which was occupied. As the boys issued taunts and threw rotten produce and mud at the prisoner the guy's arms and legs shook from the unnatural position he was forced to hold.

'Talk about having a bad day,' Reena said. When the prisoner raised his face, she gasped. 'Pat?'

It sure looked like him. 'Can't be,' Joshua replied. 'How could he get here unless you brought him?'

She moved closer. 'It's him. I swear it.'

The prisoner's eyes moved to her. 'Reena?' he called out. 'Oh God, get me the hell out of here!'

'I'm thinking that works for me. Just wish I had my cellphone to capture the moment.'

Instead, Joshua tapped one of the small boys on the shoulder and asked for what he was holding. The lad gave it up with a knowing nod.

'Thank you.' He weighed the squishy, overripe apple in his palm.

'You wouldn't dare—' Pat began even as the fruit flew towards him.

Joshua's aim was true and it smashed directly into Pat's forehead, oozing its rotten flesh downward. Pat spat and swore.

'That's for Briar, you jerk,' Joshua said, then laughed. He looked around and spied a pile of fresh horse manure.

Reena caught his intention. 'Josh Quinn, don't even think it,' she ordered. She charged up to the prisoner and began to tug on the bar holding Pat in place. One of the townspeople interceded, an older gent with a balding head.

'No, girl, leave him be. We put him there because he's been uncivil.'

'But it's inhuman,' Reena said. When her hood slipped off, she made no attempt to pull it back up.

The man stared at her now. 'He's lucky it was just us and

not the regent who put him there. It's no more than what he deserves.'

'What did he do?'

'He insulted my good wife, called her a hag when she'd not tell him what he wanted to know. And he's been blaspheming.'

Reena eyed Pat. 'Did you do all that?'

'Yeah, maybe,' he mumbled. 'I was trying to get someone to tell me what was going on. I mean, what is it with this place? Is this like one of those Renaissance fairs or something?'

'I'll explain later. Just hold it together, OK?' She smiled up at the villager. 'How long does he have to stay like this?' she asked, turning on the charm.

'If he apologizes, I'll set him free.'

'I won't—' Pat began.

Reena slapped her palm over his mouth. 'How long will he stay if he doesn't apologize?'

'Half a day should do it.'

She looked back at the prisoner. 'Well, Daniels, what's it going to be? Half a day of getting hit by crap, or just sucking it up and being polite?'

'Polite,' he mumbled against her palm.

'Good plan.' She removed her hand and the prisoner stammered out an apology for being a total jerk.

Joshua cracked a smile. *This has to be a first.* Once they got Briar home, he'd savour this memory for years.

In a short time, Pat was free of the contraption, groaning in agony as his muscles protested. He shook himself to dislodge some of the fruit. 'God, I stink.'

He headed for the closest water trough, and after dunking his head he scrubbed until his face was clean. Joshua decided not to point out just how filthy the water might be.

Pat's efforts resulted in his hair plastered against his head, water dripping down. Joshua began to snigger.

'It's not funny,' he said through gritted teeth as he shifted his full attention to Reena. 'If this is a hazing thing, just tell me.'

'It's not. I'll explain later.'

'Yeah, later,' Joshua urged. 'Let's grab Briar and get out of here.'

'Briar? She's here too?' Pat's expression changed. 'Oh, I got it. This is some sort of payback for coming on to her, right?'

'I wish it were that simple,' Reena said, tugging on his arm to get him moving. 'I'm not sure why you're here. What happened?'

'I went to sleep and I woke up dressed like this,' Pat replied, gesturing at his damp clothes. 'Everybody I talked to was stupid. I couldn't get a straight answer.'

Probably because you were an asshat.

'What time did you fall asleep?' Reena asked.

'Ah, a little after four. My folks are in Savannah for the weekend so I stayed up and watched some TV.'

'It was the same for us,' she said, looking over at Joshua. 'There has to be a connection.'

Smoothing his hair out of the way, Pat ran a hand across his face, leaving a trail of red in its wake.

Reena stepped closer to him. 'You're bleeding.'

He looked down at his palm. 'Yeah, I did it at the party. It was that dumb bracelet of Briar's.' He frowned at Joshua. 'Why would you ever give a girl something sharp like that? You know they're klutzes.'

A low growl formed in Reena's throat. 'I'll act like you didn't say that.'

Suddenly it all made sense. 'The charm that cut you, was it the woodsman with the little axe?' Joshua asked.

'Yeah, why?'

He and Reena traded looks.

'It's possible,' she said, lowering her voice. 'If he got his blood on the charm before I did the spell, he would have been included in the magic.'

'Magic?' Pat blurted.

'Shush!' Reena replied, looking around uneasily. 'These people are not going to be good with that kind of thing. OK?'

'I don't care. I'm going to start yelling that word at the top of my lungs if you don't tell me what the hell is going on,' Pat retorted.

'The dude's losing it. Better calm him down,' Joshua said, which earned him a glower.

Keeping her voice low, Reena began to explain, though to any normal person it sounded quite insane. From the expression on Pat's face, he was thinking the same. As they retraced their steps to the stable, he went through a number of stages: first he laughed, then told her to stop lying to him, and finally grew really angry.

None of which had played well with Reena.

'I told you the truth,' she retorted, her fists clenched, looking like she wanted to punch some sense into him. 'I'm sorry you have your head so far up your butt you can't deal with it.'

Pat glared over at him. 'Is this crazy chick for real?'

'She is. Hoodoo brought you here and it will get you home, unless you keep being a total dick and she decides to leave you behind. Frankly, I'm all for that.'

Pat shook his head. 'This is just bull. It was that pizza I had right before I went to sleep. I'll wake up in the morning and it'll be fine.'

Reena nailed him on the arm and he winced. 'You feel pain in your dreams?'

He blinked a couple of times, then checked out their surroundings with increasing concern. 'This is for real?'

She nodded. 'Welcome to Briar's nightmare, dude.'

Briar was still crying when her friends found her. She ran into Reena's arms, weeping so hard she could hardly catch her breath.

'Honey, what happened?' Reena asked. 'Are you OK?'

'They arrested Ruric,' she gasped. 'They've taken him to the castle.'

'I'm so sorry. He seems like a nice guy.'

'We need to leave before something like that happens to us,' Joshua insisted.

Briar stared at him through the tears, stung by his

insensitivity. Then she saw Pat and her mouth dropped open. 'What is he—?'

'Long story,' Joshua replied. 'We need to go now.'

Go? Was that even an option? Could she leave Ruric behind, never knowing what had happened to him?

Even as she thought that, she felt the darkness growing again, gathering strength. Her friends being here had changed everything. Before, it had been a matter of keeping her head down, trying to figure out how to help Ruric wake the princess. Now, if she tried to save him, she'd be putting the others in danger.

Who did she owe more?

'I'm with the horse dude,' Pat said, angling a thumb at Joshua. 'This isn't my idea of fun. Can we go now?'

'No,' Briar replied, pulling away from Reena. 'I'm not going anywhere until Ruric is safe.'

'What?' Joshua shot back. 'Are you crazy? You know what it's like here.'

Townspeople began to watch them more closely than was prudent. Having this sort of argument in the middle of the street wasn't a smart move.

'Come on, we need to talk this out somewhere else,' Briar said, beckoning them forward. 'Somewhere less . . . public.'

Somewhere the regent didn't have any spies.

CHAPTER NINETEEN

After a brief stop to talk to the smithy, who had promised to deliver the bad news to the stable's owner, Briar herded her friends through the village. To ensure they weren't followed, she'd led them on a circuitous route.

Finally she swung open the blue door to the building that supposedly held the wine cellar. The moment she stepped inside she wondered why Ruric had thought this was such a great hiding place. The roof was history, birds flitting around in the open rafters, which meant the floor was covered in little white mounds of bird poop, and the hearth was home to a hissing creature of some kind.

'This pretty much blows,' Pat began as he checked out the dusty interior. 'You really live here?'

'No!' she said, irritated, pushing the door closed behind them. 'It's a hiding place if things go wrong.' *Like now.*

It took a bit, but Briar finally found the door that led to the cellar and creaked it open, nearly tearing it off the weakened hinges. A wooden box sat on the top stair. Inside she found six beeswax candles and a candle holder, along with a flint, a crude piece of steel and other items. Ruric had planned ahead.

'Either of you a boy scout?' Briar asked.

Pat shrugged. 'I was when I was a kid.'

'You? Really?' Reena said. 'My middle bro is into all

that. He's working on some first-aid badge and he keeps bandaging up the dog because the rest of us won't let him near us.'

'Been there, done that,' he replied sullenly.

Briar pointed at the candles and the flint. 'Can you get one of those going? We're going to need it to use the cellar.'

'I can try,' he said, scooping up the items and retreating back into the sunlight. There were a couple of muffled curse words along with the repeated sound of flint striking steel. Then a 'Score!'

Pat returned with the burning candle. 'Don't let it go out. It was a pain in the ass to light.'

Briar took the taper and the holder, mating them. She slowly descended the stairs, taking care not to trip. 'Can one of you bring down the box?'

'I live to serve,' Pat replied.

Compared to the upper level, the wine cellar itself was pretty decent. Dusty, but not as bad as she'd expected, probably why Ruric had selected it. She set the candle on a broken barrel and tried to clean off a place to sit. Then gave up.

Pat slumped on the floor. 'You got any food in there?' he said, gesturing at Reena's bag.

'No. This isn't a picnic.'

'I just asked,' he replied, crossing his arms over his chest and closing his eyes.

Joshua had gone silent, besides his occasional sneezes, and parked himself some distance from Pat. Reena sat in between the two guys, as if she was a referee. Which was about right with this pair.

'Look, I'm sure that staying here sounds like a good idea to you right now,' her best friend began, 'but I'm not sure how long the magic is going to hold for us to get back.'

'Did Lily help you?'

'Sort of. Not straight out, though.'

Still not a complete answer. 'You're not even sure if I can leave, are you?' Her friend gave a reluctant nod. *Thought so.* 'This isn't negotiable,' Briar continued. 'I need to get Ruric free. I don't know why, but it feels really important. I think it's a way to fight the curse on my own terms.'

Joshua pounded a fist into the dusty floor. 'This Ruric guy is not real,' he exclaimed. 'He's just some fantasy in your head.'

'He's real to me, as real as you are,' she said. 'Maybe more so.'

Something changed in Joshua's eyes, as if a massive steel door had just slammed shut inside of him.

Briar looked away, feeling bad. Why had she said that? 'I'm sorry.'

Reena's expression grew pensive as she fiddled with a ribbon she wore round her neck. 'We saw that guy get his throat cut and the fata thing put in the cage. This regent of yours is red-lining the evil scale, so we're outgunned here. I know you care for Ruric, but—'

'Fine,' she said, disappointed. All those years she'd been there for Reena and now her friend was not willing to take a risk for someone Briar truly cared about. 'You guys can wait for me here, or go home. Whatever works for you. I'm going after Ruric.'

'You can't just knock on the castle's doors and ask if he can come out and play,' Reena argued. 'You have to have a plan.'

Briar was only half listening. For some reason the captive fata kept coming to mind. *Why does the regent fear them?*

Was it because they were incredibly dangerous and she was trying to protect her subjects?

No . . . Nothing about the tyrant said she gave a damn about her people. Which meant if the fata weren't their enemies, they might be potential allies.

Was that why I was given the feather?

'I need to free that little creature in the cage,' she announced.

'Why? What would it gain us?' Reena asked.

Us? Briar knew that tone: her friend wanted to be convinced.

'I want to see if the fata can help us. Maybe it knows a way into the castle. We need those guys on our side.'

'You only need allies in a war,' Joshua argued, 'not in some punked-up fairy tale. We're not here to overthrow a tyrant. We're just here to get you home.'

He was pushing back on everything she said and that pissed her off.

'I know why Reena's here, but what about you? Your family hates me. In fact, I bet it was one of them who put the curse on me.'

Even in the dimly lit room Joshua's face paled. His eyes

lowered as he shook his head, more in resignation than anything. 'You're just like the rest of the Roses,' he said, not looking at her now. 'I don't know why I thought you might be different.'

'OK, this is serious drama overload,' Pat said, opening his eyes. 'Time to blow out of here. Make with the magic, will you, Reena? I want to be home before my folks know I've been gone.'

Reena blew out a breath through pursed lips. 'No go. I'm staying with Briar.'

He frowned. 'Fine. Just zap me out of here.' There was a silent pause as the light dawned. 'You're not going to do it, are you?' She shook her head. 'I didn't ask to be in whatever the hell it is.'

'I know, but you're here now so just deal.'

'Reena,' Joshua warned.

'Same for you.' Reena turned her back on him. 'So what's the plan?'

It was the first time Briar could remember taking the lead in anything. Definitely the first time in her friendship with Reena. It felt good, and really scary at the same time.

'If the fata escapes, the guards will go crazy trying to find it because they fear the regent. While they're running around, that'll give us a chance to get inside the castle.' Not that she had a clue how to do that. *If only Ruric had told me what he had planned . . .*

'Well, that's a long shot,' Reena said, rising to her feet.

'I know.' As plans went, it was way thin.

'We'll need a diversion while you and I get that thing

211

out of the cage. Say . . .' Reena looked over at the guys now. 'Two dudes beating the crap out of each other?' she suggested.

Pat grew an ominous smile. 'That could be fun, right, horse boy?'

'Yeah,' Joshua replied, a strange light erupting in his eyes. 'If I'm stuck here, I might as well have some fun.'

Briar picked up the hostile vibe. 'No, you guys will go too far.'

'It has to look for real,' Pat replied. His *I'm so going to enjoy this* smile had grown in size now.

Joshua rose, dusting off his hands. 'Some bleeding would be good. Can't get more realistic than that.'

Briar shot her best friend a *Don't let them do this* look, hoping Reena might introduce some sanity into the situation.

'Let them go for it,' was the quiet reply. 'What can it hurt? They've been working towards this for a long time.'

Which was exactly what Briar feared.

It was later in the afternoon when they returned to where the fata was imprisoned. When Briar saw the little creature, she regretted waiting so long. The poor thing was keening in a crackly voice, punctuated occasionally by a faint sob. Its pretty colours were nearly gone, faded to a sickly grey. At that moment, she knew this was the right thing to do.

After scoping out their surroundings, the guys decided they'd stage their brawl just inside the market to attract maximum attention.

'Pat is going to flatten that boy,' Briar whispered.

'You want to bet on that?'

'What? There's no way Joshua is going to win.'

'You don't know him very well, do you?'

'And why would that be? Oh, yeah, he's a Quinn and it's not like I've been invited to his family reunions. Besides, I don't have anything to bet, not here at least.'

'You do at home. I'm jonesing for that royal-blue sweater of yours,' Reena replied. 'If Joshua wins, it's mine when we get back to Bliss.'

If *we get back to Bliss*. To make her friend happy, Briar played along. 'What if I win?'

'You know my cool owl necklace? It's yours.'

'Throw in the earrings and you got a deal,' Briar replied. They shook hands.

Briar looked back towards the market. 'I don't get what's going on between the guys,' she said.

Her friend cocked her head. 'You really are clueless. That's kinda cute, you know.'

'Then make me less clueless.'

'For Pat, it's his ego. His need to feel more important than anyone else. Joshua isn't going to let him grind him down, now that he has a reason to man up. Any guess why that is?'

Briar shook his head.

'You, doofus. He's got a serious crush on you. He's worried that Pat is going to carry you off on that white horse you're always talking about.'

'Pat? He's pretty much out of luck. He shouldn't have assumed I was a slut.'

'What about Josh?'

'He's still a no-go even when I get home.' She frowned. 'I'm not even sure I can trust him, you know?'

'Whoa, that's harsh. OK, what about Ruric?'

Briar sighed at the thought of him. 'It's . . . complicated. He's probably a prince, you know? A real live one.'

'So you finally got to meet one,' Reena said, grinning. 'And a babe at that.'

The sound of raised voices carried across the market. Both of the guys were standing near the stall that sold potatoes, Pat within inches of Joshua's face now. He was yelling at him, something about messing with *his* girl.

'Oh, not smart,' Reena said, shaking her head. 'He just pushed Josh's *Don't go there* button. Probably on purpose.'

The two guys began shoving each other, trading insults as their testosterone-fuelled emotions heated up.

'You're a swine,' Joshua called out. 'You treated her like a tavern wench.'

'At least I don't spend all day shovelling horse shit like you.'

Reena whistled. 'That was below the belt.'

The shoving moved quickly to punches being thrown.

Briar joggled her friend's elbow. 'That's our cue.'

While a knot of curious onlookers formed around the two combatants, Briar and Reena edged closer to where the gibbet was tied off. Holding her breath, Briar began to work on the knot, her fingers cramping from the effort. They weren't that close to the castle, but that wouldn't keep one of the guards from figuring out what they were doing.

'Hurry up!' Reena urged.

'I'm trying.'

'Uh-oh,' her friend said, looking back towards the fight. 'The crowd is getting bored. Can you do this on your own?'

'What? Yeah, maybe.'

'Good. It's time to get their attention again.'

Reena walked away about thirty paces, and then dropped her hood. Her whole stance changed as she sashayed through the crowd. Whispers began, followed by frank pointing.

'Is that a Moor?' someone said.

'Why is she in our village?'

'What is this nonsense?' Reena demanded as she came to a halt in front of the guys, hands on her hips and eyes blazing.

Wow, look at you.

Pat wiped a line of blood off his chin, assessing the change in plan. He pointed at Joshua. 'This cur insulted you.'

'Me? It was you, you son of a goat,' Joshua shot back.

Briar stifled a giggle as she worked on the rope, relieved that the trio had everyone's attention again, even the guards. When the knot gave way, she slowly inched the cage down to the ground, wincing when it made a creaking sound. She did a quick look around, but no one was paying attention, not even the sentries high on the castle walls. In the background she heard Reena unleash a crude joke at Pat. That got the crowd laughing and, more importantly, not paying attention to the fact that Briar was fata-napping.

Then it all went wrong – the moment the cage reached

the ground she saw it had a special metal lock, one that she hadn't seen from the ground. The fata looked up into her eyes and began to cry. It knew it was doomed.

'You'll need this,' a voice said.

Briar whirled round to find a guard behind her. He was one of the human ones and in his hand was a small brass key.

Was this a trap of some kind?

'Hurry,' he said. 'You do not have long before someone sees what you're about.'

With a shaking hand she unlocked the cage door and gently pulled the fata out of its prison. It shook with fear.

'Why did you help me?' Briar asked, looking up at the guard.

'The terror must end,' he said. After he'd stuffed some old rags inside the cage and then closed the door, he pulled on the rope. The cage rose into the air. It was done.

Briar wrapped her cloak round the fata to shield it. Her heart thudding, she skirted the crowd, making sure not to move too fast so that no one would notice. When she glanced over her shoulder, the guard who had helped her was gone. Had he been real?

As she passed by her friends, she caught Reena's eyes. The two guys stepped back, each a mess. Pat's shirt was ripped and bloody. Joshua was no better, both cheeks bruised. It looked like a draw which meant no one had won the bet.

'The fata! It has escaped!' someone cried.

Briar nearly panicked and bolted, but she forced herself

to walk slowly as if nothing was wrong. As if she wasn't harbouring one of the regent's enemies.

'Find it!' another shouted. 'It will kill us all.'

That wasn't likely. The creature was half dead, shivering against Briar's body like a sick child.

Orders were being barked now. 'Search the village. Find the creature. Kill anyone who aids it.'

Which would be me.

Briar had barely reached the edge of the market when a gruff voice called out to her. 'You! Stop, girl!'

She kept walking. Beneath her cloak the fata stirred and a faint buzzing came in her ear, then cleared as if someone had tuned a radio.

'Go to the well . . . Be with my kind,' it whispered.

'I'm trying,' Briar whispered back.

'Stop!' the voice shouted again, closer now.

This time Briar took off at a run, barrelling through people who got in her way. Rounding a corner, she nearly tripped over a rooster pecking in the dirt. As she slowed to avoid it, Reena caught up with her, her friend's track expertise paying off.

'The guys are behind us,' she called out, looking over her shoulder. 'Man, are those guards mad. Steal one little fata and——'

'This way!' Briar dodged down the alley towards the abandoned well, slipping in the mud. Reena caught her before she fell and they ran on. Soon Joshua and Pat were right behind them, pounding along down the deserted alley, past the hex signs.

Briar skidded to a halt in front of the well, and then carefully unwrapped the fata. Bending over, she rapped on one of the boards. 'Hey! Down there! Hello!' she called out. There was no response.

The creature whimpered and tried to crawl out of her arms so she laid it gently on the well kerb. A board shifted and bright green hands came up and cradled it. It whimpered again and then disappeared below.

'Wait! We need help! We need to get inside the castle to save a friend.'

Nothing.

'You have to help us. Maybe we can stop the regent, you know, together.'

There was a chittering sound, almost like an argument.

Briar looked over at Reena and got a shrug in reply. Shouts came as the guards closed in.

'We have to go!' Pat called out.

Then another head popped up out of the well, one that was bright orange with pink circles round its eyes. The fata blinked up at Briar as if it hadn't seen the sun in some time. Something dark green was placed on the well kerb.

'Ah, what is this?' Briar asked, taking what appeared to be a pouch made from sewn leaves.

To save you from the metal, the creature said, then disappeared. Before Briar could ask any further questions, the board slid back in place.

'OK, then . . . thanks.' It wasn't exactly what she'd hoped for, but Briar stuffed the pouch under her corset, intending to examine it later.

'Ah, guys, we got a situation here,' Pat said.

The guards drew closer, a solid line of menace marching in lock step towards them. All were armed.

'Plan B?' Reena called out as the men fanned out in front of them.

'Run?' Briar said. Before any of them could respond, one of the doors further down the alley shuddered and after another blow it sheered outward and collapsed into the dirt. A guard stepped through the opening, followed shortly by three others.

They were trapped.

'Well, this sucks,' Reena said. 'Plan C?'

'Go home?' Pat suggested.

'I need time to do the spell, and we don't have it,' she replied.

'That leaves fighting our way out,' Joshua said with sigh.

'Yeah, now that's a great idea,' Pat muttered.

Without any discussion, he and Reena lined up on one side of the well, Joshua and Briar on the other. Joshua offered up his knife, but she shook her head. Instead, she found a piece of board and tested its weight in her hand.

'Stay behind me,' he said. 'If you can run for it, take off.'

Not happening.

A guard lunged at her and when Briar whacked him on the knee with her board, he went down. To her left, Joshua was doing his best to stay out range of the swords. When he slipped and fell, she cried out, but he rolled back up on to his feet in one swift move. It was a nice manoeuvre.

Another guard advanced on her.

'Come on, girl, give it up. You're not going anywhere.'

Briar swung at him and missed, which allowed him to grab her wrist and pull her towards him. The guard yelped and set her free, his arm bleeding courtesy of Joshua's knife.

As the fight continued, they were pushed closer and closer to the well. When Pat cried out, Briar risked a quick glance over her shoulder. A solid blow to his chest had sent him reeling over the edge of the well kerb. He lost his footing and landed, hard, on the weakened boards.

Reena rushed after him, offering her hand. As he reached out to take it, a guard shoved her forward. She banged her knees on the kerb, then fell shoulder first on to the boards. For a second, she and Pat just stared at each other until the ominous cracking of weathered wood came from beneath them. He grabbed on to Reena's arm and then extended his towards Briar.

'Pull!' Pat shouted.

Briar grabbed his hand and wedged her feet against the kerb, her arms and back feeling the strain. Behind her she could hear Joshua trying to hold off their attackers, but he was seriously outnumbered.

Pat's eyes met hers. 'Oh, damn,' he said quietly.

His final words were nearly drowned out by a sharp series of cracks when the boards gave way beneath them. As the pair plunged downward into the well, he purposely let go of Briar's hand.

'No!' she cried, trying to grab at him.

It was too late: her friends were gone.

As she tried to see down into the darkness, hoping maybe

they'd not fallen too far, she was grabbed roughly round the waist and hauled backwards. Briar kicked and cursed, but to no avail. Using her long braid to control her, the injured guard slammed her to her knees. Tears of pain and loss swam in her eyes.

Joshua fell next to her, a knife at his neck.

'Please get them out of there!' she begged.

'They're accursed fata lovers,' one of the guards said, and then spat. 'They'll learn what it's like to care for the regent's enemies.' Then he laughed. 'Trust me, soon you'll wish you were down there with them.'

CHAPTER TWENTY

I should have made Briar go home.

Joshua had never felt so powerless. It'd all gone wrong. Pat and Reena were probably badly injured, perhaps even dead, while he and Briar were being marched to the regent and whatever gruesome death that lunatic felt they deserved.

It was a true nightmare on steroids, something right out of the Brothers Grimm. Those two had always gone for the darker tales, like the one where a queen's feet were clamped into red hot iron shoes, and she was forced to dance herself to death. Or the one where a father had to chop off his daughter's hands so the devil wouldn't carry her off.

They'd love this tale.

Reena had been right – the curse was changing and adapting. It was a chess game with no rules and all the pieces were on the other side. How could they defeat something like that?

Joshua thought of his family, his hometown. What if four of Bliss's teens died in their sleep? How would the reporters spin that one? The town would become infamous.

Enough. He was shovelling fuel to his fears and that only made them stronger. Joshua gritted his teeth and tried to clear his head as best he could. Coldly evaluating their chances of escape told him the odds sucked. There were too many guards, all armed, and all motivated to keep the regent happy.

He gave Briar a quick glance. Her eyes were wide and her breath was coming in little gasps, proving she was as freaked as he was. Even if Pat and Reena had been with them, they couldn't fight back. The only option was to meet with the regent, try to reason with her.

That was a plan doomed to fail. This was a tyrant who had a guy's throat slit just because she could. Appealing to the regent's sense of fairness was like trying to explain to a ravenous tiger that you'd not make a tasty snack.

As they were led through the streets, Joshua expected the same boos and rotten fruit the fata had received. There were none. Instead, there were whispers and, occasionally, Ruric's name was mentioned. No one came to their aid. What would it take for these people to fight for their freedom?

The instant they crossed under the castle's portcullis Joshua sensed the sting of cold magic pass through his body like an electrical charge.

'Whoa,' he said. 'Did you feel that?'

Briar nodded. Her mind kept replaying the desperate look in Pat's eyes, how he'd let go of her hand rather than pulling her down into the well with him. He might be an arrogant jerk, but he had a good soul.

If he and Reena were dead, those last few seconds would haunt her for however many days she had left in this life. Considering who they were about to meet, it couldn't be that many.

When viewed from the outside, the fortress seemed immensely large, threatening even, but from the inside it wasn't as impressive. The majority of the regent's servants were twisted half-human creations, part flesh, part metal. The metal didn't mesh well with the skin, but burrowed into it like some sort of ravenous parasite. A young girl hurried by, one side of her face swollen and oozing a thick silver fluid. Her one eye was completely metal and it swivelled in its socket.

'Is that what's going to happen to us?' Briar whispered.

'No. Nothing like that,' Joshua replied as he winced at the sight. 'Don't worry. We'll be fine.'

He is so lying.

'Now that's hospitality for you,' he said, angling his head towards a line of eight wooden poles placed along one side of the courtyard. Severed heads decorated each one of them, and crows perched on a few, tearing pieces of flesh away with their sharp beaks.

'Oh, gross,' Briar said. She looked away, her stomach roiling.

'There's some good news – your friend isn't one of them.'

She sighed in relief. 'Thanks.' He'd saved her the stomach-emptying task of checking each head herself. It meant Ruric might still be alive and that gave her hope.

They were led inside the castle proper, up a short flight of stone stairs, then into a vast chamber. The sight of it took Briar's breath away. The walls were stone, no doubt part of the original castle's design. A vaulted ceiling rose high above them, each roof support clad in shiny brass. The floor was constructed of the same metal, with an intricate pattern of wheels nestled within wheels. Situated in the centre of the biggest wheel sat a throne, of sorts. It wasn't one in the traditional sense, but an elevated platform with pikes of brass and iron arrayed in a semi-circle round the seat.

It spoke of power and of something else. Sanctuary, perhaps? As Briar stood, transfixed, she swore she could hear the room breathing, assessing them to determine if they were friend or foe.

'Go on,' one of the guards said, and gave them a shove towards the front of the chamber.

Once they were closer to the throne, they were ordered down on their knees.

'Is this the part where you try on the glass slipper?' Joshua said under his breath.

Briar couldn't stop the grin. If this had been anyone else but Joshua, she would have hugged him in thanks.

She felt the regent's presence before she saw her, like a river of ice water coursing through the marrow of her bones. The ruler crossed the chamber with silent steps in a dark black dress. Her mask was in place, but this time Briar could see her dull brown hair, plaited in short braids that reached her collar. The woman was taller than her by several inches and she moved oddly.

Briar let loose a cry of recognition at the figure behind her.

'Ruric!'

He observed her solemnly, but did not reply.

'What's wrong with you?'

Still no reply.

What has she done to you?

When the regent took her place on the throne, she revealed her feet, which were clad in leather boots with peculiar buckles. Despite her height, her feet didn't reach the floor.

'Why have you come to my kingdom, child?' the regent demanded. The voice was deeper than Briar expected, like that of a heavy smoker.

'I was sent here by a curse,' she replied.

'Who laid this curse?'

Joshua shifted uneasily next to her.

'I don't know. I just want to go back home.'

'If you wish to leave, why do you side with my enemies?'

'We . . . felt sorry for the creature,' Joshua jumped in. 'We did not mean to anger you.'

What is he doing? Playing to her sympathy was a waste of time.

'Why are *you* in my kingdom, boy?'

He gave Briar a look. 'I came to get her.'

Which still didn't make any sense to Briar.

'What of the others in your lawless band?' the ruler asked.

'The same.'

The copper face turned in her direction. 'Who are you to warrant such attention?'

Briar really didn't have answer for that, so she shrugged. 'I'm just lucky, I guess.'

'Or you are very important. But you are not this man's

cousin, as you claim,' she said, indicating the silent Ruric. 'He admitted as much.'

'No, I am not.'

The regent leaned closer now. 'I smell magic on you. Perhaps your father is a sorcerer?'

Magic? Me? Maybe it was the curse she was sensing.

'What is your ransom worth?' the ruler asked. 'How much gold or silver will your family pay for your freedom?'

'She can buy her freedom with a bracelet of finest silver,' Joshua said.

It took a moment for Briar to catch on, and she nodded energetically. 'Yes, I can.'

As the regent shifted on her throne, an earthy odour struck Briar's nose, one that spoke of caves and soil and no sunshine.

She held up her wrist, displaying the bracelet. 'In exchange for this rare bracelet made of silver, you will let us go.' She realized she hadn't been specific enough. 'That means me, my friends and Ruric.'

He maintained his silence, staring at her as if he had no idea who she was.

What has she done to you?

'Silver, you say?' the regent said, her voice huskier now as she rose from the throne. A few steps forward and her gloved hand secured Briar's arm. The masked face moved even closer, inspecting the bracelet, a strange sniffing noise coming from behind the metal. 'Yes, it is silver. Such workmanship. What metalworker crafted it?'

'An old family in our kingdom, Your Grace,' Joshua

replied, his voice silken. 'They are highly . . . regarded.'

Nice apple polish.

'I can take it off, put it on your arm,' Briar offered. Anything to get this thing to step away from her.

Before she could move, the regent's free hand reached out to touch the bracelet. When the gloved fingers closed round it, there was a fat, crackling spark as rivulets of magic flew along the bracelet's length and into each of the charms.

The regent shrieked and lurched backwards, grasping her hand in pain.

'Foul sorcery!' she cried.

The blow struck Briar's face before she could duck, and sent her reeling away across the smooth floor.

'You bitch!' Joshua cried, trying to wiggle free of the hands that pinned him in place. 'Let me go!'

Even before Briar's head stopped spinning, she sat up, if only to show Joshua she wasn't badly injured. When she gingerly touched the side of her face, it was numb and her fingers came away slick with blood from the cut on her mouth. She'd never been hit in her life and it gave her a new fear on which to gnaw.

The regent was back on her throne now, her hands clenched like claws.

'You would have cast a spell upon me. That was a mistake.' She gestured and Ruric instantly moved forward. 'Show her what you have become.'

On command, he pulled back the sleeve of his shirt. Metal had flowed over the flesh on his arm as if he'd been dipped in silver. Once the process was complete, he would be one of the regent's elite warriors, human no more.

'I am hers now,' he said, his voice barely a whisper. 'I pray for death, but it does not come.'

'Ohmigod,' Briar exclaimed. 'Why are you doing this to your people?'

'My enemies would destroy me,' the ruler replied. 'I cannot let them do so.'

'The fata, you mean? How could they hurt you?'

'They and I cannot exist in the same world. They would destroy my metal and that would make me weak. I shall never be that way again.'

The regent gestured. 'Bring the boy forward. Let him pay for her arrogance.'

'No!' Briar tried to grab at Joshua, but he was dragged to the throne. Then he was on his knees again.

She couldn't let him get hurt. 'Look, we're sorry for what we've done,' she began, 'but maybe we can work something out.'

'Watch in sorrow as one of your own becomes mine.'

'No, don't you dare—' Briar called out, but the regent had already seized hold of Joshua's throat. As he struggled, a torrent of unintelligible words flowed from the small mouth-opening on the mask, and the overwhelming smell of dirt and metal shavings filled the chamber.

Though Briar thrashed against her captor, she couldn't get to Joshua. When the spell ended, he was on his knees, glistening tears running down his reddened cheeks.

'Joshua?' *Please be OK. Don't let him be like Ruric.*

'Show her, boy. Show her who owns you now.'

With a grumbled oath, Joshua pushed away his shirt. Briar had expected to see herself reflected in the silver, but instead the skin was only faintly red. There was no metal.

She gaped in wonder. *How did you do that?*

The regent lurched backwards in surprise. 'What shield keeps my magic at bay? Is it the same as hers?'

'Yes,' Joshua said, shooting Briar a sidelong glance. 'You just need to let us go. Your metal can't harm us.'

Their enemy pondered on that for a time, then waved them away. 'Take the prisoners to the pit. We will see if your magic is stronger than mine when darkness falls and the metal reigns supreme.'

As she was roughly yanked to her feet, Briar tried one more time to reach her friend. 'Ruric? You have to fight her. Don't give in.'

'It is too late,' he said, his voice but a whisper. 'I am sorry.'

As she and Joshua were marched out of the chamber, Briar took one last look over her shoulder. Ruric was on his knees in front of his ruler now, his head bowed in reverence.

Like she's a god or something.

CHAPTER TWENTY-ONE

Though the drop into the well had been horrifying enough, the sudden dunking into the chilly water was a brutal wake-up call. Reena clawed herself to the surface, gasping and coughing as bubbles rose around her. Next to her came a huge splash as Pat did the same.

After another round of coughing, she called out. 'Josh? Briar?'

Only Pat's laboured breathing returned. Just them, then. 'You OK?' she asked.

'Hell, no,' he spluttered.

Though it was hard to see in the limited light that wormed its way around the broken boards high above them, Reena groped along until she found the side of the well. The stone was cold to the touch and slick with moss. She worked round in a circle, hoping to find a place where there might be a ladder or a foothold that would allow them to climb out. If they remained in the water too much longer, hypothermia would claim them.

When she'd just about given up hope, she found a flat section of stone built into the wall. She didn't know why it was there, but it would give them a place to rest. She made her way back to where Pat was weakly treading water. Reena grabbed on to his damaged shirt and tugged.

'This way, dude,' she said.

With effort, they beached themselves on the damp stone. There they lay, trying to regain their breath as the chilly air sent shivers down their spines.

'Now what?' Pat said as he rolled on his back. 'How do we get out of here?'

'I don't know.'

As she waited for her vision to adjust to the dim surroundings, Reena remembered the skeleton key and frantically dug for it under her sodden clothes.

No key. No way home.

When her fingers closed round it, she sighed in profound relief. Unfortunately she had left the canvas bag full of herbs and roots on the surface, but maybe she'd find more somehow.

From what she could see, the well wasn't like the ones at home, but had an elaborate set of stairs cut into the sides that wound all the way to the top. They were composed of smooth, weathered stone, as if countless feet had trodden them over the years. The flat area they were lying on was probably where the locals knelt to fetch their water.

'Hey, look. We got steps,' she said, pointing. 'We can get out of here once you're ready.'

'Good. Give me a minute,' Pat said, but his voice sounded off.

'What's wrong?'

'My arm hurts,' he replied, which for a guy meant it was somewhere between a bump and a compound fracture.

Before she could follow up on that, a colourful face came close to hers, causing Reena to start in surprise. It was one of the fata, who had no notion of personal space. It twittered at her in a high-pitched voice that was almost out of her hearing range.

'I don't understand what you're saying,' she said.

Then, suddenly, she did.

Come, now, it said, beckoning with yellow hands.

'No. We have to go help our friends.'

Gone, it said, looking upward sadly.

'The guards got them?'

A nod.

'What's it want? Can it get us out of here?' Pat asked.

'I don't know.'

They both rose with some effort, all the aches registering now. With a groan, Pat stared up at the top of the well and shook his head in disbelief.

'We fell that far? It must be two miles at least.'

A bit of an exaggeration, but she was good with it.

Instead of leading them up to the surface, one of the fata extended its arms towards the water and issued a single melodic tone. It reminded Reena of birdsong, but even richer, if that were possible. Gradually the water level began to change, lowering some ten feet or so. As it receded, it exposed more stairs.

The creature beckoned to them and, though Reena wasn't sure if this was a good idea, she followed along.

Pat didn't budge. 'No way. I'm not going any deeper into this thing.'

The fatas began to chitter in agitation and she caught their concern in the tangle of voices.

'They say it is too dangerous to go up right now.'

Pat cradled his right arm to his chest, his face pale. 'How do we know they're not lying to us? How do we know we can trust them?'

Before Reena could argue, one of the fata marched over to him, waving a thin green finger at him. Once it had his attention, it pointed downward.

'Nope. Not going. You can't make me,' he said defiantly.

A teal foot lashed out and caught Pat squarely on the knee. He yelped and as he reached down to check for damage the hand grabbed his uninjured arm and tugged him along. He tried to break free, but got nowhere, skidding over the stones. 'Hey, this thing is really strong.'

Reena grinned. 'Then don't be a jerk. We need to find out what's going on and they might have some answers.'

One of the beings shyly took hold of her hand. Its skin was soft, like delicate silk, and a curious shade of pumpkin orange.

He does not trust us, the fata said in her mind.

'I don't think he trusts anyone,' Reena murmured back. 'Will our friends be all right?'

Unknown.

With the fata as escorts, they wound their way further down into the well and eventually halted in front of a solid wall. Reena's fata waved a hand in front of the stone and it melted away, revealing a wooden door. Once they were through the portal, the wall sealed behind them. She heard the rush of water as the well refilled, putting the entrance beneath its chilly surface.

Clever. There was no way the guards could get to them now.

The hallway in front of them was tunnelled out of rock and warmer than she'd expected. Since the fata didn't strike her as miners, Reena wondered if someone else had built them. Maybe they weren't the only ones who lived underground.

Along either side of the hallway were exquisitely carved flowers attached to the walls, each petal providing a muted source of light. Though there was no breeze, they moved of their accord. When Reena reached out to touch the closest flower, her fata swiftly pulled her back.

Only for us.

'What happens if I touch one?'

You are no more.

Reena lowered her hand to her side. 'Thank you.' Unsure if Pat had heard that bit of news, she relayed it to him, and received a grunt of acknowledgement.

He must really be hurting.

Eventually they entered a large chamber, an open space filled with black earth and high humidity, like a botanical garden. The same flowers grew on the walls here, but higher up, beyond her reach. Some of them were dark and shrivelled as if they were dead.

When they are gone, we are no more, the fata said in her mind, its violet eyes peering up at her.

'You eat them?'

A shake of the head. *We gain life from them. We are not meant to be under the earth. We are not of that kind.*

235

'Then why are you down here?'

The drazak hunts us. We are safer here. For now.

'What is a drazak? Is the regent one of those?'

Yes. She is an earth dweller.

'Why does she hate you guys?'

We are not of her kind.

Which wasn't very helpful, but Reena let it pass for now. At least now she knew that the regent was something other than human.

They were led to a bower, one comprised of soft ferns and delicate flowers. Reena found herself wondering where those had come from. Did they grow down here?

As she gingerly took a seat, Pat held back.

'What's going on here?' he asked, his jaw clenched. He had beads of sweat on his forehead and he was still clutching his arm.

'You're hurting, aren't you?' she said. He gave a nod. Reena patted the ferns next to her. 'Park it, dude.'

He did as she asked, his frown deeper now.

'Let me see it. I took first aid, so maybe I can help,' she said.

With great effort Pat gradually moved the arm away from his chest, still steadying it. She carefully stripped off his torn shirt and wasn't surprised to find his chest was sculpted with classic six-pack abs. She hadn't expected any different from someone like Pat: image was everything to him.

'You work out, don't you?' she asked, trying to find some common ground.

'Yeah, why?'

The trick was to keep him talking so he wouldn't notice the pain as much.

'How much can you bench press?'

'Two twenty.'

'Not bad.' She did a cursory examination. 'Well, cheer up: no bones are sticking out. That's a good sign.'

'You're not funny.'

'Wasn't trying be,' she retorted. Feeling along length of the arm she knew she'd found something when he flinched.

'Stop that – it hurts!'

'Wow, you're a weenie,' she said. When he gaped at her, she shook her head. 'Just kidding. I know it hurts like a bitch.'

'How would you know that?' he challenged.

'I was in a car accident and broke my arm in two places. Luckily they gave me the really good drugs or I would have screamed myself hoarse.'

Pat let out a lengthy breath. 'Wish I had some of those now.'

Which told her this was hurting like a bitch.

Reena examined the area more closely and found the skin was darkening – evidence of bleeding underneath the skin. It was a pretty good bet he'd snapped a bone during the tumble into the well.

'Looks like it's toast,' she said. 'Sorry. We can make a splint and—'

The light touch of a fata made her turn.

We will help.

'I'm not sure about this,' Pat began. Apparently he'd

finally begun to hear the creatures' thoughts as well.

'Let's see what they can do for you. Briar trusts them – we should do the same.'

A huff was his only response.

The fata moved closer, looked up in Pat's face and then nodded to itself.

You do not believe in us. You do not trust your eyes.

'You're right,' Pat said, then frowned. 'This is a bunch of crap, like one of Briar's fairy tales.'

Tales have a purpose. They teach. They give joy. They warn.

'Just do whatever you're going to do and get it over with.'

The fata, a female as far as Reena could tell, carefully laid her dainty azure hand on Pat's arm and began to sing. A shimmering melody filled with half- and quarter-notes came forth, like the marriage of a harp and a flute. The other fata picked up the song and soon Pat's eyes began to blink. He yawned, loudly, and Reena gently laid him back on the bower as he fell asleep. The song trailed off and ended on one long note.

'Thank you,' she said. 'At least he won't feel the pain now.'

Sleep. It is best for all. We will tell you when it is safe to leave.

That did sound good. There wasn't much they could do for Briar or Joshua. When they woke, if Pat was feeling better, they'd try to find their friends and go home.

Reena curled up in the bower, inhaling the relaxing scent of the leaves. Her aches began to disappear one by one, and she wondered if the same was happening to the guy next to her. Her worries wouldn't disappear as easily.

What would happen to them if Briar died inside the curse? Would the three of them wake up in their beds? Or would her death destroy them all?

A nervous twitch rolled through her muscles, as if she was being watched. Opening her eyes, she thought she saw something grey in the shadows of the cavern above. Then it was gone.

Reena drifted off to sleep, lulled by the conversation of the fata around them. On the edge of her mind was the suspicion that her trust was misplaced.

CHAPTER TWENTY-TWO

As they were marched out of the rear of the castle, Joshua kept shooting glances at Briar. The blood had dried on her cheek, but her eyes told him she was still frightened. He wanted to take her hand, even though they were both bound, but he dared not. The curse might pass back to him, and all those years of distrust and hostility between their families would finally come to fruition.

But what if the curse did revert to him? If Briar were free, maybe she'd wake up in Bliss, all safe and sound. Then Reena could get the rest of them home.

And on his sixteenth birthday . . .

I'll be dead. That was the one flaw in his plan.

'Better uses for a wench than the pit,' one of the guards muttered.

'You saw her magic. You touch her and you know how it'll end,' another said.

'It'd be fun for a while,' the man jested.

The leader kept them moving along until they reached an open stretch of ground near the rear wall of the fortress. Unlocking a metal gate they entered an area that supported no plant life, not even a weed. Its only feature was a gaping hole.

The pit.

As they walked closer, Joshua did a quick survey: he

calculated about thirty feet from the edge of the pit to the wall behind them, where a lone man stood guard. Was he there all the time, or did he walk along the wall at regular intervals?

When Joshua was inches away from the hole, his boot sent a small cloud of soil over the edge. He peered downward, figuring there'd be a tiger or a bear prowling around at the bottom. Instead there was a pile of dirty rags, but nothing else.

A crude rope ladder was dropped over the edge, shaking loose some of the shale. After Joshua's bonds were cut, the poke of a sword in his back encouraged him to make the journey deep into the earth.

He didn't dare leave Briar alone with these guys. 'Ladies first,' he said.

'Go on, lad,' the leering guard replied. 'She'll be down soon enough.'

Briar's eyes widened as if she'd suddenly realized there was more danger here than just the pit. When she stepped towards the ladder, the man grabbed her arm. 'No reason to hurry. I'll keep you company.'

'She goes first,' Joshua repeated. 'Or someone is going to get hurt.'

That only earned him laughter, but to his relief the senior guard interceded. He sliced Briar's bonds and pointed. 'In with you, girl. Make it quick.'

She descended with considerable haste, which set the guards laughing.

'Look at her. She won't be coming back up that fast.'

'So what happens here?' Joshua asked. 'Do we starve to death or what?'

The leader shook his head. 'Nothing that painless, boy,' he said solemnly. 'Go see to your girl. It'll be dark soon.'

'And then?'

The man's eyes betrayed unexpected pity. 'Then the metal will reign.'

His teeth clenched, Joshua climbed down the twisty ladder. The moment he touched the earth floor the ladder was pulled back up. Their captors didn't hang around, but headed off into the castle, joking back and forth.

Now that he was below ground, he examined the sides of the pit more closely to discover it had been dug out of shale, which was sharp and brittle. Not ideal for climbing – especially since he had no gear – but not impossible if he was very careful. Joshua had some experience free soloing, so if the rock would hold his weight he might be able to do it. All they had to do was be patient until it was dark, then escape when the sentries would be less likely to see them. Once up on the surface, he'd toss down the ladder and Briar could be free as well.

This feels too easy. What am I missing?

Briar sank to the ground. 'This is bad, isn't it?' she said, her voice quavering.

'Sort of. At least nothing's trying to eat us,' he said. *Yet.*

'I thought she was going to make you like Ruric.'

He looked over at her, hearing her concern and not understanding why she would care. 'You have any idea why that didn't happen?'

Briar shook her head. 'This . . . nightmare is familiar,' she admitted. 'I think some of it's from my own imagination, but where did the regent come from? I must have dreamed her up. Same with the fata.'

'Or it's a blend of your mind and whoever created the curse in the first place,' Joshua suggested. When Briar didn't respond, he sat on the opposite side of the pit from her, always careful to maintain his distance.

She noticed and the frown was instant. 'Can we give it a rest? Our parents aren't here,' she said. 'Enough with the hate, OK?'

'No hate, it's just best not to get too friendly. It'll make it harder when we get home.'

'*If* we get home,' she replied. 'And, if we do, my mom is going to owe me big time. I'll *make* her tell me who did this to me.'

Should he just admit it and get it over with? *Not yet.*

'We'll be OK,' he said.

Briar shook her head. 'Nice try, but I'm not buying it. Ruric is going full metal, and Pat and Reena are hurt or . . . dead.'

'Pat die? Are you kidding? That ego of his wouldn't allow it. Besides, Reena will watch out for him.'

Briar's gloom lifted a bit. 'If she doesn't kill him first.'

'There is that.'

'He really did nail you,' she said, pointing at his bruised cheek.

'Yeah,' he said, touching it gingerly. 'But I got a few hits in myself.'

'You know, our new home sucks,' she said, gesturing around now. 'No food or water, no cable. Worse, no toilet. This really blows.'

He couldn't help but laugh. Was it his imagination or was that defiance in her voice now? A different girl emerging out of the shell of the old one, someone who had no choice but to stand on her own because Mrs Rose wasn't running interference this time.

Neither is my mom. For once they could be themselves.

He pointed at a series of marks on the stones. 'I wonder what those are for?'

'Prisoners keeping track of how many days they're down here before they—'

'Escape,' he cut in. 'Possible.' Still, that didn't seem right, not with the slashes reaching almost all the way to the top of the pit.

Briar peered upward. 'Why isn't there a guard up there? What keeps us from getting out?'

'Nothing. I've done some rock climbing. Once it's dark I'll go first and toss down the ladder to you. Then we'll have to figure out how to sneak out of the castle.'

Briar shook her head. 'No, then we find Ruric.'

'He'll just turn us in. He's one of her soldiers now.'

'I want to know that for sure before we take off.'

'Briar, he—'

'I owe him, Joshua. I can't leave him here to die.'

He sighed at her hard-headedness. 'Well, at least Pat isn't around to give us any grief. It's just the two of us.'

Briar weighed that last statement and apparently wasn't

happy with it. 'This isn't a date, you know.'

'I'm not saying it is, but if I had to be stuck in a deep pit with anyone, you'd be my pick.'

'That's such a lie. Until the other day, you couldn't stand to be near me. It's like I've got the plague or something.'

'That's not true.'

'Yeah, right. So why *did* you give me the charm bracelet?' she asked, her voice rising. 'That completely violated the Thou Shalt Not Go Near That Rose Girl rule.' Not that her family was any different when it came to him.

'I know, but I've always thought you were cool,' he said. 'I wanted to give you something and Reena said you'd like the bracelet. She said I should try and be friends with you.'

Really? 'That doesn't explain why your mother told you to stay away from me.'

Joshua clenched his teeth and held his silence, probably hoping she'd back off or change the subject.

'Come on, just tell me,' she persisted. 'Why was it so important that we don't share the same airspace? What is your mother worried about?'

He began to dig in the dirt with a piece of shale, but didn't answer.

Briar sank back on to the ground, trying to get a read on the guy. This felt really important, so she came at it from a different angle. 'We used to hang together all the time. We were friends, Joshua. We played together, even held hands. Until after you almost died.'

He looked up at her now and she could see the worry. She was getting closer to the truth.

'Why did you try to save me that day?' she asked. 'You couldn't swim that good, not then at least.'

'I was too young to know I could die,' he replied. 'Six-year-olds are immortal, you know.'

'Yeah, until they're not.' Briar shuddered. He was staring at her now, no doubt reliving the scene in his own mind just as she was.

'I remember you squeezing my hand so hard it hurt,' she said. 'And then . . . I felt when you . . .'

'Don't say it!' he snapped.

'Why not? You died, Joshua. We both know it. But how did I feel that? How could I know the *second* you stopped breathing?'

He shook his head. 'We were kids. It was scary. That's all.' He was rushing his words now, as if trying to hurry past a bad memory. Or deflect her from the heart of matter.

'No, it was more than that,' she said, softer now. 'I was still holding your hand when they pulled us out. I wouldn't let go until my dad made me. I cried so hard, but they wouldn't let me near you, even after they'd put you in the ambulance.'

Joshua's face was paler now, two crimson spots resting on his cheeks.

'I should have let you go when I died,' he said. 'This is my fault.'

'This?' Briar leaned forward. 'What do you mean?'

He shook his head, refusing to answer. Rising, she walked to within a few feet of him and then sank on her knees. Their eyes met and she could see dread in them.

246

'Why won't you touch me, Joshua?'

No reply, but his eyes still held hers. She was so close.

'Am I so . . . gross . . . you can't stand the thought?'

He gasped, as if something had cracked deep inside him.

'No, it's not you. It's the curse,' he said.

Curse? 'I don't understand.'

'My mom . . . believes that if I touch you . . . it'll come to me.'

'What? How did she know I had it?'

'Because it used to be mine,' he said, his voice so quiet it was difficult to hear him. 'That day I died in the river – the curse moved from me . . . to you.'

As if touched by a live wire, Briar shot her feet. '*You* cursed me?'

'Yeah,' he said, looking away now. 'I didn't do it on purpose. I guess it thought it didn't need to be inside me any more, didn't have to wait until I was . . . sixteen to kill me.'

'Sixteen? That's why I was supposed to die on my birthday, because you were?' He gave a weak nod. 'What did I ever do to you?'

'Nothing,' he replied. 'Oh God, nothing. I swear I never meant to hurt you.'

Joshua pulled his knees to his chest, wrapping his arms round them. 'I didn't even know I'd been cursed until after you fell asleep. Mom never told me.'

His mother never told him. Did she really believe that? Now that she looked back, she could. Her mother hadn't told her the truth, either.

'So you're the reason I'm in this hellish nightmare. In

this pit?' she said, waving her arms around. 'You!?!'

'Me,' he said quietly. 'It's all my fault.'

Briar paced for a time, though it was difficult given the size of the hole. She wanted to make him hurt as much as she did. He'd killed her future, taken away her family and landed her inside this twisted fairy tale.

The longer she paced, the more she noticed that he hadn't moved, staring blankly at nothing. As if the admission of his sin had hollowed him out inside.

Briar returned to her part of the pit and slumped down. She unconsciously mirrored Joshua's pose, knees tucked close her chest. A sort of crinkling noise caught her attention and with some digging she retrieved the leafy pouch. She'd forgotten about it.

'What is that?' he asked, his eyes suspiciously moist.

'One of the fatas gave it to me.' Briar carefully opened the pouch to find glimmering dust inside. It was lavender and when she dipped her fingers into it, it made them tingle. She held them up. 'Great. We got sparkles. Just what we need.'

Their eyes met again.

'I'm sorry,' he said. 'I really am.'

Briar tucked the pouch back under her corset. Oddly her anger had burned out like a damp firecracker. 'You really didn't know about the curse?'

'No. I have no idea who put it on me or why. Nobody will tell me.'

That sounded familiar.

She raised her head. 'With me carrying the curse, you

were golden. What are you doing here? It's way dumb for you to be anywhere near me.'

'I'm here to make it right.'

'How? You'd be stupid to take the curse back. Even if you could, it might not make any difference. I might just be . . . doomed.'

'Or not,' he insisted.

'Does Reena know all this?'

'Yeah. Lily told her after you went to sleep.'

'Of course, the entire world knows and somehow they never got around to telling me,' Briar sniped. *Like they never told me about Mike and his lies.*

'They didn't get around to telling *us*,' Joshua said, his eyes narrowing. 'Remember, you're not the only victim here.'

'You know, you could have fooled me.'

The silence between them, heavy with words unspoken, made Briar curl up for a nap to block it out. That meant lying on a dirt floor, one that smelt faintly of copper and of oil. She dreamed of water, the relentless kind that had nearly killed her. Once again she experienced the panic, felt the unyielding pressure, sustained that tingling jolt between her and Joshua as they tumbled in the rolling darkness.

When she struggled up out of the dream, dusk was settling in. It took her a moment to recognize the walls of the pit and then their current situation returned full force. She stifled a sob.

Across from her Joshua stared at nothing, still digging at the ground with a piece of shale.

Her drowning dreams were always harbingers of bad things to come, like the fierce windstorm that had damaged the high school when she was a freshman, causing her and the other students to take shelter in the hallway. Or when Reena had been in that traffic accident on the way to South Carolina. She'd dreamed of roaring water the night before it had occurred.

'Something bad is going to happen,' she announced.

'Worse than being trapped in a pit with no toilet?' Joshua mumbled.

'Yeah. Way worse. I . . . just know it. I . . . get these premonitions.'

Briar tensed, waiting for the laughter or the derision. It didn't come.

'OK, I'll go with that warning,' Joshua said. 'Something bad is going down, but what is it?'

'I don't know. Just . . . bad.'

He stretched, a couple of bones popping, then moved to the pile of rags and gave it a kick. Suddenly his posture changed. 'Ah, hell,' he said.

Joshua rarely swore. 'What's wrong?'

He picked up one of the pieces and brought it closer for her inspection. There were rust-brown spots in the fabric and it appeared as if someone had taken a pair of scissors to it, leaving dozens of slashes behind.

'That's dried blood.' Joshua dropped the garment, frowning. 'Why don't they have a guard right on top of this pit?' he asked, pacing now. 'Because they know once it's dark we're never coming out of here.'

'I don't understand.'

'Remember what the regent said? "When darkness falls and the metal reigns supreme."'

'So?'

'Those scratches in the rock?' he said, more agitated now. 'They're not from someone trying to get out. They're from something that lives *down here*.'

Briar was on her feet in a heartbeat. 'What kind of something?'

'Don't know and don't want to find out. We are out of here.'

Joshua moved to the closest wall, one with a number of stone outcroppings.

'If I can get enough handholds, I can do it. Don't stand underneath me in case I fall,' he urged. He gave her one last look. 'I promise, I won't leave you down here.'

'I didn't think you would,' she said, wanting that to be the truth.

Joshua nodded as if he appreciated her trust, then began to climb.

'The shale is bitchy stuff,' he said. 'It breaks easily and it cuts you up. Probably why they dug the pit here.'

It proved a painstakingly slow process. He'd find a handhold and a corresponding place for a foot and pull himself up. Then repeat the process. One time he slipped and he barely caught himself. Another time the rock broke and he had to quickly readjust. He wiped his hands on his trousers a couple of times and she could tell they were bleeding.

Briar found herself holding her breath, becoming dizzy. Forcing herself to breathe, she called out, keeping her voice low. 'You're doing great!' And he was. She'd never known he was capable of this.

Joshua had just reached halfway up when suddenly he cried out.

'What's wrong?'

'Something bit me!' he said, waving his hand. He examined it, and moved another notch up.

'Go on, you're OK,' she urged. 'You're almost there.'

He'd climbed another few feet when he cried out again, and this time he slid down the wall of the pit, desperately trying to grasp on to something. It proved futile and he hit the ground hard.

'Oh my God. Are you OK?' she asked, kneeling beside him.

When he looked up and found her so close, he shied back. It'd been reflexive on his part, but the message was passed. He still feared her, feared that the curse could claim him even if she wasn't dying.

Briar stepped away, trying to contain the hurt. 'So that's how it is, huh? Even now?'

'I'm sorry. It's . . . hardwired.' He lifted his hand. It was bleeding and starting to swell. 'Something was in one of those holes. I thought I saw it just for a second.'

'It was probably just a bug. Take a rest. You'll get it. You were doing great.'

'No, we need to get out of here. *Now.*'

A dry, metallic rustle began just as Joshua regained

his feet. To Briar's ears it sounded as if someone were pouring a truckload of nails on a concrete highway, in slow motion. The rustle continued and then grew in volume.

Joshua whirled round in an effort to pinpoint the source. 'Where is it coming from?'

'Everywhere?'

The first rust-coloured creature poked its head from a hole near the top. It slithered out, wriggling like a girl trying to pull on a pair of tights that were one size too small.

'What is it?' Briar asked, squinting in the gathering darkness.

Before Joshua could answer, a dozen more of the things began to descend the pit wall.

'Centipedes,' he said, his voice registering surprise. Curiosity claimed him and he moved closer to check one out. It returned the scrutiny by arching up, displaying its sharp mandibles and snapping at him.

'These things are metal!' he exclaimed.

'Then get away from it, you idiot!'

There were more of them now, undulating down the wall like copper snakes as the rustling noise grew. When one of the creatures headed directly towards Briar, she squealed and stomped on it. It twisted to right itself, unhurt. Then it came after her again.

'Oh God, why did I wait?' Joshua batted at one that had climbed up his trousers, then tramped it hard with a boot heel. It stopped moving.

'Joshua!' He whirled round to find Briar encircled. She

was jumping on the creatures as hard as she could, but it wasn't slowing them down.

He yelped when one sliced into his flesh. Even after he'd destroyed that one, hundreds more closed in, eager for blood. They crushed the creatures as fast as possible, but it was no use. The tide of centipedes scrambling over each other to get a taste of human was overwhelming.

It was ironic. All her mother's protectiveness had been a waste of time: her daughter was about to become supper for a ravenous family of magical arthropods.

'I am NOT dying in some damned pit!' she shouted. 'That is not going to happen!'

Something clipped the side of her head and Briar almost went down. The something was the rope ladder.

'Go!' Joshua called out. He was about to push her towards it, then checked himself.

She didn't take time to think it out, but grabbed the ladder and began hauling herself upward at a frantic pace. She felt the rope go tight below her and knew that Joshua was following right behind.

Though she was off the ground, the danger was still present as a wave of their attackers followed them up the walls. Briar kept climbing, sometimes having to slap one of the things off the rope so it wouldn't bite her. Beneath her she heard Joshua cry out again, but he kept moving.

A hand pulled her out and she landed hard on the ground. As she rose to thank her rescuer, she gasped. It was the guard who'd taken too much of an interest in her. His knife was now busily sawing on the rope, a move that would send Joshua to an agonizing death.

'Wouldn't want him to get free, would we?' he wheezed, grinning at her.

Blind, murderous fury catapulted Briar forward: she kicked the man hard in the side causing a rib to snap. He swore and dropped the knife. Off balance, his arms windmilled, his hands seeking hers.

'Help me!' he cried. Then he was gone, tumbling over the side of the pit with a hoarse scream.

Briar dropped on her knees at the hole's edge, fearing the guard had hit Joshua on the way down. To her relief, he was still climbing towards her. A centipede scurried up the ladder ahead of him and as it reached the top, she smashed it with her fist. It rolled over on its belly, legs quivering in the air.

To her horror, the weakened rope began to unravel where it'd been cut.

Briar offered her hand without thinking. 'Hurry,' she called out as one side of the ladder broke free. Joshua's eyes went wild with panic as he swung in the air.

'Take my hand!' she cried out.

'Move,' a voice commanded, and when she rolled away she saw Ruric reach over and yank Joshua out with almost superhuman strength. Joshua fell on his side, panting, his hands bleeding.

From below them came an unholy shriek, high pitched and frantic, the plea of a man who knows he has no escape. The screams suddenly cut off, leaving only a thick gurgling noise as the metallic rustling intensified.

Ruric pulled her away from the edge. 'Don't look,' he said.

Joshua sat upright, staring at her with wide eyes. She'd let a man die for him, and they both knew it.

'Thank you,' he said simply.

With a quick slice, Ruric cut the other side of the ladder and let it fall in the pit.

'We must go,' he said.

When he turned towards them, Briar clamped a hand over her mouth.

Half of his face was solid metal.

CHAPTER TWENTY-THREE

Something brought Reena out of her slumber: a low murmuring noise. She sat up to find a cluster of fata talking quietly among themselves. Their posture and gestures told her they were agitated.

'Hey, wake up,' she said, shaking Pat. He mumbled for a bit and after another good shake he finally awakened, groggy and confused. His hair fell over his face and he had sleep wrinkles in his skin.

'I'm *still* in this dream?' he said. 'God, won't it ever end?'

Reena pointed at the fata. 'Something's up. They're spooked.'

'You woke me up for that?' Pat rolled over on his side, and then he was sitting up again, running his fingers down his injured arm.

'What's going on here?' He cautiously moved the limb and then blinked in surprise. 'I thought you said it was broken.'

'Let me look.' Reena gently checked the area where the bone had fractured. Then she smiled. 'I'd say you're in good shape, dude. Magic. Better than a cast any day.'

He yanked his arm away from her. 'You're messing with my head, right? This is all some sort of trick.'

'Why would I bother doing that?' she asked.

'You're pissed off at me because of Briar. I know you're a witch. They talk about it at school.'

Reena rolled her eyes. 'I'm a rootworker, not a witch. There's a difference.'

'Not to me. I don't know how you got me here, but I don't belong in this nightmare. You need to fix this, now.'

The arrogant jerk was back now that he wasn't hurting.

It was so tempting to do exactly as he wanted, to get this thorn out of her side. Except she didn't dare. If she sent Pat back on his own, then she and Joshua might be trapped here forever. Or until the curse killed them. Given that it'd been making life rough for them, that was a definite possibility.

'I know your ego isn't going to believe it, but this *isn't* about you, Daniels. Not even close. So think of other people for a change, OK?'

'You can be a real bitch, you know that?' he said, his words coated with acid.

She leaned closer, narrowing her eyes. 'When it comes to protecting my friends, yeah, I am. Trust me when I say this, you're *not* one of them.'

'Like I care,' he said, but she noted his eyes were at chest level. Checking out her breasts, no doubt, even while he was dissing her. It was only then she realized the skeleton key lay outside her clothes. She tucked it away, Pat watching her every move.

The tension was broken when a fata approached and placed her canvas bag on the floor in front of them.

'It's my bag.' Reena opened it to find her herbs and roots. But there was more inside now and she pulled bread and cheese. 'How did you get this food?'

The fata pointed upward and then retreated.

'They sent someone for takeaways?' Pat asked. 'That's crazy. They know what happens if they get caught.'

'I'm guessing hospitality is a big thing with them, like it is with my great-gran. You don't disrespect your guests,' Reena said. She broke off a hunk of the bread and handed it to Pat, their fingers touching for a brief moment.

'Do you think we should eat this?' he asked, quieter now. 'I mean, what if it's poisoned?'

'If they wanted to kill us, they could have done it while we were sleeping.'

'Unless they're really sadistic and want to watch us die in agony,' he retorted. At her frown, he shrugged. 'I watch a lot of horror movies.'

'Really? I think we're good here.' She took a munch of the bread and found it to be filling, at the very least.

'Just how do we get home?' Pat asked.

His conversational tone spiked her scepticism. 'I do some magic and we're gone. At least the three of us. Briar will have to fix the curse somehow or I don't think she'll ever go home.'

'Saralyn told me she's a vegetable. Is it true she can't wake up?'

'That's a jerkwad thing to say to her best friend,' Reena snarled.

'Whoa, tone it down. Are you like PMSing or something?'

'You don't want me as an enemy, Daniels. Not ever.'

'What are you going to do? Turn me into a frog?' he jested.

'No, but I can leave your ugly ass here.'

'You can't do that,' Pat retorted, the piece of cheese in his hand forgotten. Then he must have realized he might be wrong. 'Tell me you wouldn't leave me here.'

Reena barely heard him, caught by the dark emotions seething just under her skin. Lily had warned her about this, how there would always be a temptation to use the magic for harm, especially on a loser like Pat. She closed her eyes, trying to clear the anger, and then she blew most of it out in one long stream of air. When she opened her eyes, Pat was staring at her as if she'd sprouted horns and breathed fire.

'I'll get you home when the time is right,' she said, working to keep her tone even. 'Not before. You understand?'

There was a nod of the head, almost respectful. Except that his eyes tracked to her chest again, but this time she knew it had nothing to do with scoping out her breasts. He'd figured out the skeleton key was important in some way. She'd have to guard it more closely from now on.

Was this the curse at work? Was it trying to drive them apart, leave them isolated, so it could pick them off one by one?

That was not a comforting thought.

The next fata to come near them was shivering, glancing upward at every few steps.

'What's wrong?' Reena said, rising to her feet.

You must go.

'Something's here, isn't it? Something . . . bad.'

A nod. *Come. Now. Hurry.*

Reena clutched on to the bag as they retraced their steps down the long corridor towards the well. The hair on her neck began to rise.

'What is that I'm feeling?'

Darkness, the fata said. *What we are, after . . .*

'After what?'

After the metal changes us. We burn. We kill.

Reena shot a glance over her shoulder to ensure that Pat was following. He wasn't. Instead, he'd halted along the way, an expression of total bewilderment covering his face.

'Daniels? Come on!' she called out.

His expression remained unchanged, as if somehow he'd lost the will to move.

'Pat? What's going on?'

The fata tugged her arm, pulling her along. *Go now!*

Before Reena could break her grip, a wave of the small beings fled past them. Each was toting one of the flowers and talking in agitated tones, their movements frantic.

Using the confusion to her advantage, Reena broke free and worked her way back towards Pat. He still hadn't budged.

'Hey, guy. Time to go.'

His eyes tracked to hers and his mouth opened slowly, as if it were a monumental effort. 'Help me!'

Reena sprinted down the corridor, which was devoid of fata now. What were they running from? Could the regent's guards have got into the caverns somehow?

Just as she'd reached Pat, a low wail echoed through a tunnel, like the keening of a hungry soul.

'Come on!' she said, grabbing his arm and tugging, but he didn't move, as if he were rooted to the spot.

'I hear them. They're coming for me. Don't leave me!' he pleaded, terrified.

'No way they're getting you,' Reena said. *Whatever they are.*

There seemed to be no physical reason why he was stuck in the middle of the corridor, which meant it had to be something in his mind.

What could break it? *What is so important that he will want to follow me?*

Reena knew the answer in an instant. She pulled the ribbon out from under her clothes, holding the key up at Pat's eye level.

'See this? This is the way home. You have to follow me or you don't get there, do you understand?'

He nodded, still terrified.

'Take my hand. That's it, now take a step.' He strained and his foot moved only a few inches. 'That's it, take another.' He moved a bit further now.

'You won't leave me?' he asked breathlessly.

'No. You may be a total jerkwad, but I'm not leaving you.'

Pat took a huge breath, gritted his teeth and lurched forward, nearly falling into her arms. She shoved him down the hall and he picked up his pace, though it was stilted.

Voices called out to her in her mind. They sang her name in a twisted melody, similar to that of the fatas, though this song was of darkness and death. Of the loss of life and the hunger to find it once again.

With one last look back at the shadowy grey figures creeping along the walls like ghostly vampires, Reena and Pat sprinted for their lives.

CHAPTER TWENTY-FOUR

'Does it hurt?' Briar asked as she reached out to touch Ruric's metal cheek.

When her hand grew closer, he pulled away, as if the contact might harm him.

Joshua couldn't help but notice her fierceness fading away as she peered up at their rescuer. It was replaced by something softer, more vulnerable. It was the way he wished she'd look at him, if only things were different.

'What about my friends? Are they OK?' Briar asked.

'They are not in the regent's custody. That is all I know,' Ruric replied. He held out two pieces of rope. 'I shall have to bind you both. I will make the knots loose so you can get free if needed.'

'How do we know we can trust you?' Joshua asked.

'I did just save you from certain death,' came the terse reply.

That wasn't what he'd wanted to hear. Joshua turned to find Briar standing near the edge of the pit, nudging a dead centipede with her foot. She studied her hand and then gave it another nudge. As if unable to resist, she peered downward into the pit and then began to tremble, her arms encircling her chest.

'I told you not to look,' Ruric exclaimed, taking her arm and trying to pull her away.

'Why not?' Briar replied, shaking him loose, her face unusually pale. 'I'm the reason he's dead. I should know what it looks like.'

'If that man is the only one to perish before all is put right, then we shall count ourselves lucky.' Ruric sighed. 'We must find the princess before the regent deems her continued existence too much of a threat and has her killed.'

Joshua's need to argue fell away when Briar allowed herself to be bound. He let himself be secured as well and, true to the man's word, the ropes were loose.

'Between us, we will keep her safe,' Ruric said, pulling a knife.

Joshua stepped back, wary.

'You are remarkably sceptical,' he added, handing over the blade so Joshua could slip it into the scabbard at his waist. 'Keep your arm down so none will see the weapon. It is best if the pair of you appear to be my prisoners. There will be fewer questions that way.'

Now Joshua felt like a total fool, which only darkened his mood. 'Thanks,' he replied half-heartedly.

Briar had once again wandered back to the hole, still transfixed by the remains of the centipede. Pensive, she toed it, and this time it tipped over the edge into the pit.

He and Ruric gravely took the measure of the other.

'You're a prince, aren't you?' Joshua asked. The man nodded. 'Well, that doesn't matter. She's going home with me. I won't let you keep her here.'

Ruric tried to smile, but it proved difficult with the metal. 'Even if she wishes it.'

Joshua groaned. 'This isn't her world. She has a life back home.'

'I know. Still, the decision is hers, not *yours*.' Ruric turned his back on him. 'Come, Briar, let us get out of here. The sentries will be changing soon.'

Despite the fact that he didn't like the prince, Joshua had to admit Ruric's plan worked well: no one was going to challenge a guy whose face was partially silver. Still, Joshua didn't let down his guard. The fact that Ruric had his own ideas for Briar's future, and was going Team Regent, made him increasingly wary.

Though he tried not to be, he was intrigued by Ruric's face, the part that was seamless metal. It was not cutting into the flesh and causing it to die like on some of the other villagers. When he'd asked Ruric why, he'd received a cryptic answer: if the regent enchanted the metal and then it attached to you, it ate away at your skin. If she placed the spell directly, it did not.

It didn't make much sense, but it did explain why not everyone looked the same as the metal conquered them.

Is that a flaw we can exploit?

Joshua tensed when two guards tromped down the hallway towards them, chatting about how much money they'd lost at gambling earlier in the day.

'My wife is going to have my head when she finds out,' one man said.

'Better her than the regent,' the other replied grimly.

'That's the truth.'

265

They passed by the trio with the barest of nods and kept going.

The castle proved a real fortress with thick defensive walls marked by arrow slits, and narrow staircases that wound upward in a clockwise pattern. Those were a marvel of engineering, designed so that one man could defend them against an army. Unfortunately, this time the enemy was already within.

Briar let out a pent-up breath. 'Are we there yet?'

'Soon,' Ruric replied, keeping up the pace.

Ruric only slowed when they entered a broad passageway covered by a wooden-beamed ceiling. Torches hung along the walls, illuminating still figures contorted in odd positions.

'Not all the prisoners are executed on the field,' he explained. 'Some are slain inside the castle and then stuffed and displayed for the regent's amusement. This is her . . . gallery.'

It can't be.

Briar gingerly moved to the nearest figure, that of a middle-aged man. His skull had been split down the middle and each half lay on the corresponding shoulder, as if he was shrugging in two directions at once. All his skin had been peeled away, revealing dried muscles, grey and withered, like an anatomy exhibit.

Did this come from my mind?

She edged her way down the hallway, cataloguing the horrors, one by one, then paused in front of a young man who somehow looked familiar, though his limbs were severed and piled at his feet like trophies.

'Remember Benton, the fellow at the inn, the broken one who drinks so much?' Ruric asked. 'This was his only son.'

'That is so sad,' she whispered. 'But if this is my story, why is it so horrible?'

'It's the curse,' Joshua said. 'It's pulling things from your mind and twisting them. Reena said it'd do that.'

Ruric touched her arm. 'So I am nothing more to you than a mental fancy?'

Looking up into the brown eyes, Briar felt his distress so keenly. It was important to him that he be real in her eyes, not some dream.

'No, you're more than that. You always have been.'

Ruric bowed his head. 'I am gratified to hear that.'

Joshua mumbled something under his breath, but she didn't catch it. Given his deep frown it was probably for the best.

Now silent, the prince led them through the gallery of unfortunates. She wasn't sure if he'd believed her or not. She sort of remembered the prince she'd put in the tale. He'd been named Phillip, and though he was brave and noble he wasn't anything quite like Ruric.

'He isn't real,' Joshua whispered as they continued down the hallway. 'None of this is.'

Briar glared at him. 'Maybe *you* aren't real, either.'

'Of course I am,' he protested.

'How do you know? Maybe you're just in my imagination and instead you're home celebrating that the curse isn't yours any more.'

He grimaced. 'Ouch, that hurt.'

'Good. It was supposed to.'

When they reached one of the circular staircases, Ruric had them hold back.

'I think the princess's chambers are up there, but I'm not sure,' he said quietly. 'Wait here.'

He continued on to the next level and engaged a guard in conversation.

'He has no idea where we're going. He's just trying to look important,' Joshua snarked.

'Why are you being such a jerk to him? He's trying to help us.'

'No, he's trying to help himself. Why else would he bother to wake up a princess? He's hoping to score something out of this.'

Briar seethed, mostly because Joshua was right.

A solid *thunk* of something heavy hitting the floor came from above them.

Shortly thereafter, Ruric reappeared. 'I was right – she is up here. Come. It is safe now.'

A lone guard lay on his side near a doorway, and for a moment Briar thought he was dead.

'Is he . . . ?' she began.

'He's not dead. I am not one of the regent's executioners.'

'At least not yet,' Joshua added.

Briar ignored him. 'There's more metal now.'

Ruric gingerly tapped his face, feeling the meeting point between silver and flesh. 'I know. I can feel it inside me, trying to steal my will. I shall fight it as long as I am able.'

He abruptly turned his back on them and, using a key

he'd apparently taken from the guard, unlocked the room. After he'd dragged the unfortunate man inside, Joshua closed the door behind them. A second set of doors awaited them.

The main room they entered hoarded dust as if it were gold. Inches of it stood on almost every surface, a grey spongy moss. The floor, however, was disturbed, a myriad footsteps criss-crossing here and there. In some places there were little sprinkles of something dried and brown.

Briar found herself drawn to the huge gilt mirror. With a finger, she drew a crown in the dust and put her initials inside. She'd been signing her name like that since kindergarten. Behind her, Joshua tried to stifle a sneeze. It seemed funny that he could work around horses and hay with no problem, but get him in a room that desperately needed a maid and he was a mess.

'People have been in and out of here,' he said, pointing at the marks in between sniffles. 'I'm thinking those dark spots are blood.'

With his goal in sight, Ruric moved resolutely towards the princess. Briar had expected her to be in a canopied bed with lots of lace and frills. Instead, Aurora lay on a simple divan that sat up against the far wall. She was even prettier close up, her gown the same one Briar had seen in the market. She still wore those dancing shoes.

Are your dreams happy, or sad?

The princess's pale eyelashes fanned across creamy skin and her hair was a tumble of honey curls that draped over the side of the bed. Her full lips were bright ruby and her delicate hands crossed just below her chest, clutching a metal rose. She obviously hadn't aged at all in the ten years she had been asleep.

In short, she was a total guy magnet. The effect wasn't lost on the two males in the room.

'Is she not beautiful?' Ruric said, his voice awed. He moved closer as if irresistibly drawn to the girl. 'Her hair is nearly the same gold as yours, Briar. Or what yours once was.'

Joshua stepped forward as well, his watering eyes moving from the sleeping figure to Briar and back again, comparing them. 'She's a babe. You do sort of look like her. That's kind of creepy.'

Briar hadn't missed that he'd said *she* looked like the princess, not the other way round, as if she was a cheap copy. 'Guys, I'm not feeling good about this.'

'Of course you don't,' Ruric said. 'Perhaps you're a bit jealous?'

What? That was a slap-down she hadn't seen coming. 'No, I'm not,' she said, but her disclaimer came out too quickly for either of them not to notice.

'Yes, you are,' Joshua replied. 'What girl wouldn't be? The princess is so . . .'

Wrong?

Briar backed up on instinct. 'If she's so important, why did she only have one guard?'

'It doesn't matter,' Joshua said, his attention never wavering from the sleeping girl. 'She is perfect.'

'I agree,' Ruric replied. 'I shall try to wake her. If I fail—'

'Then I will,' Joshua said dreamily.

You have got to be kidding me. What was wrong with these guys?

As Ruric stepped up on the low platform, the sound of rushing water filled Briar's mind.

'Ruric . . . wait!'

Oblivious, he bent and placed a worshipful kiss on those ruby lips, then stepped back, eager for the princess to wake.

Absolutely nothing happened.

'But I was sure . . .' Ruric began.

'Man, that's a sincere kick in the ego,' Joshua said, grinning. 'My turn.'

Before he could move, Aurora stirred, her lashes fluttering open to reveal deep sapphire-blue eyes. She blinked a couple of times, then sat up, laying the rose aside. When she spied Ruric, she smiled. It was the kind of smile that ruled both men and kingdoms.

He beamed and went down on one knee. 'My princess.'

'My one true prince,' she said, as if there was no question. *Huh?*

That wouldn't have been Briar's first thought after dozing for ten years. Wouldn't Aurora want to know what had happened to her, or how long she'd slept? Or why her parents weren't here?

Not: 'My one true prince.'

'Umm . . . this doesn't feel right. I think we'd better leave,' Briar urged.

'I have no intention of doing any such a thing,' Ruric said, his eyes only for the princess. 'I have found the most

271

beautiful woman in the world and she is mine.'

Still deploying that dazzling smile, the petite royal rose from her bed and placed her delicate arms around Ruric's neck. Eager, he leaned into the embrace, his arms encircling her waist.

'Better get 'em a room,' Joshua grumbled.

As they grew closer, the soft flesh on the princess's hands began to melt away, the creamy skin turning brown as aged brass appeared in its place.

'Ruric!' Briar cried. 'Look out!'

The moment she called out the warning, Aurora's entire body became solid metal, from her hair to her dainty shoes. It was as if she'd been dipped in brass, every fine detail preserved. Not an automaton, but a moving statue.

'How dare you wake me?' the princess demanded, tightening her hands round Ruric's throat. 'Who do you think you are?'

If this had been the real princess, he could have easily escaped, but this version had him in a death grip, and continued to tighten it the more he struggled. The creature did not seem to care that they shared the same metal – or the same mistress – she only saw an enemy that must be destroyed.

Joshua dived to his rescue, hacking at the thing with his knife, but it did no good.

'The guard's sword. Get it!' he cried.

It took some shoving and rolling of the man's sleeping weight for Briar to release the sword from its scabbard. By the time she raced forward, Ruric had been hefted above his captor, his boots barely brushing the floor. His face, at least the skin that remained, was a dusky purple as he fought for each breath. Kicking out, he tried to break her grip.

The metal princess laughed at his feeble efforts.

'They are all the same,' she said. 'None are worthy. All must die.'

Briar hefted the sword and then nearly dropped it. It was amazingly heavy. The second time she put her back into it and got the blade into the air, then let gravity do its worst on the outstretched arm. The sword bounced off the metal, doing it no harm.

'Give it to me,' Joshua ordered. When his blow struck the creature, she broke her grip and staggered back.

As if somehow she'd forgotten her desire to kill now that she'd lost contact with the prince, Aurora sank on to the bed. Without a word, she calmly reclaimed the flower and resumed her resting pose. Metal swiftly yielded to pale skin and golden hair, with no evidence of any injuries.

Stepping closer, for a fraction of a second Briar saw her eyes, pure blue and totally human. Totally afraid.

Then the princess fell asleep once again as the trap was reset.

CHAPTER TWENTY-FIVE

Once Ruric had regained his breath, he croaked, 'Destroy it. It is an unholy monster. Cut off its head.'

'I can't do that, not when she looks like that,' Joshua said, stepping back.

'It will keep killing if we do not stop it,' Ruric insisted, then began to cough again. His colour was returning, but Briar could see the near miss had struck him deeply.

His chance at a kingdom is gone. All that he's hoped for, his only dream.

Would he still want to overthrow the regent?

Briar glanced over her shoulder at the sleeping form. Did she dare tell them what she'd seen in Aurora's eyes? *Not until I understand what it means.*

Joshua gave her a quizzical look and when she shook her head, he laid the sword aside.

'Then if you do not have the courage I shall do the deed, once I have . . . rested,' Ruric replied, slumping down on to the dusty floor. As he leaned himself up against the wall, his quaking hand moved to his throat.

'The metal, it's growing worse,' he said, his words slurring. 'You must leave me while you have the chance.'

'No, you're coming with us,' Briar insisted.

'Briar . . .' Joshua began.

'I'm losing the battle,' Ruric replied soberly, his

tormented eyes meeting hers now. 'Soon I will be all metal and the regent will own me. I may harm you, Briar, though I would have no wish to do so.'

No you won't.

He cleared his throat to little effect. 'The princess is dead and the regent has replaced her with this . . . horror. All my plans are for naught.'

'Do you still want to overthrow the regent?' she asked.

'Yes, but only Aurora could have roused her people to war.'

Unless . . . 'If you had a substitute princess,' Briar said before she could stop herself, 'we can take out the regent and then you'll stop turning all metal.'

He studied her for some time before replying. 'Think long on that offer. If you assume the princess's place, you may well have to remain here. The people will not accept me as their king if Aurora does not share the throne.'

Which means she and Ruric would have to rule together and maybe . . . *get married? Was this what the fortune teller meant?*

'Briar,' Joshua said, the one word laden with abundant warning.

If she ignored the Ruric complications for the moment, it came down to whether she had the guts to pull it off. *Could I do it?* Maybe, once she got the dye out of her hair. In many ways, she'd been rehearsing for the role all her life.

Something must have shown on her face as Joshua exploded. 'Oh, hell no! This is not happening! You're not staying here to play princess with this guy.'

Briar wheeled on him. 'Why not? I can do it.'

275

'For how long? Once the regent's gone, what's to keep him from turning on you?'

'What do I have to go home to? Boring old Bliss? A bunch of sick rumours about why I was cursed? Mike and his lies? At least here I'll be—'

'This *isn't* your life, Briar. You belong with your family and your friends. Not here. Not with . . .' He trailed off, glowering at Ruric now. 'There's no guarantee that if you defeat the regent, that her magic is going to just vanish. You could get stuck with a . . . tin-can prince.'

Now he was just being an ass. 'There are worse things,' she said, glaring. 'At least he won't put a curse on me.'

'You cursed her?' Ruric demanded, his eyes flaring. 'Why in heaven's name would you do that, you fool?'

'I didn't mean to,' Joshua replied. 'It was an accident.'

Ruric eyed the pair of them. 'I give you my word that if Briar assumes the role of princess, I will not harm her in any fashion,' he said, his voice steady. 'If she does not wish to wed, I will not force her to do so. We will find a way around that.'

'Like I believe you,' Joshua snarled. 'She goes home. With me.'

'The decision is mine,' Briar cut in. 'Don't even think you can bully me, Joshua Quinn.'

The prince looked up at her, hopeful. 'Then you will remain, at least long enough to help us overthrow the regent?'

'Long enough for that, yes,' she said, kneeling before

him. 'Then we'll find some way to have the people to accept you as their ruler.'

But, even then, would the curse let her go?

Ruric caught her hand and was about to kiss it, when he paused. 'What is this on your fingers?'

Briar looked down. 'Oh, it's some sort of powdery dust one of the fata gave me.' *Oh, crap, what if . . . ?*

She was on her in feet in a flash.

'Briar?' Ruric asked. 'What is troubling you?'

She pulled out the leaf pouch and held it up for her companions. 'The fata said this stuff was "for all things metal". What if this dust affects it some way?'

'Why would you think that?' Joshua said, his brows furrowed.

'Remember I had some of this on my fingers when we were in the pit? I hit one of the centipedes with my fist and it began to fall apart. That's why I kept staring at it. I was trying to figure out what had happened to it.'

'You didn't mention this . . . why?' Joshua demanded.

'I wasn't sure what was going on.'

'Then if that is the case, you must test it upon me,' Ruric insisted. 'That way we will know if the fata have given us a potent weapon for our battle.'

'Or a really good way to kill you,' Briar cautioned.

'I will take the risk. Put some upon me, and let us determine what this magic is about,' he said, drawing up a sleeve.

'I thought you didn't like the fata.'

'I'm not sure I do, but they are the regent's enemies,

and that may serve our purpose well.'

With a gulp, Briar dipped three fingers in the glittering dust and then handed the pouch over to Joshua so he could close it.

'You sure?' she asked.

Ruric nodded. 'I trust you not to harm me, though others do not deem me worthy of that same gesture,' he said, his flinty gaze on Joshua now.

Briar knelt next to him and then gently wiped her fingers down his arm. They watched it for a few moments, but nothing happened.

'Ohhh, I was wrong. I'm sorry. I thought—'

A shudder rolled through Ruric's body. His face contorted and he collapsed on his side, writhing in agony on the dusty floor, as if he were fighting some mighty battle inside himself.

Briar looked on, hopeless. *Don't let him die, please!*

After some time, Ruric ceased thrashing and he took a long, tortured gasp of air.

With her help, he sat up. 'Your face,' she said, the tears forming in her eyes. 'It's . . . it's . . .' It was red and dotted with sweat that ran down his cheeks in rivulets. 'The metal's gone.'

Ruric extended his once silver-clad arm. It was normal now. 'By heavens, it is true.'

'We have a weapon now,' she exclaimed.

'Not entirely,' the prince replied. 'Her spell is still inside me. I can feel it there. I suspect it will be until the regent is no more.'

Briar looked over at the sleeping princess. 'Are you willing to kiss her again?'

Ruric started at the question. 'Are you mad? I have no intention of going anywhere near that monstrosity. I am not suicidal.'

Maybe that was the point. 'The regent can encase people in metal, so what if this *is* the real princess?' she posed. 'What if she did that to Aurora?'

'It's possible, I guess,' Joshua allowed, wiping his nose on a sleeve after a sneeze. 'But the others stay metal all the time – they don't change back and forth. At least, I've not seen them do that.'

Briar worked that out in her head. 'What if the spell is set up so that she's Aurora *until* someone kisses her? Then she goes full metal and kills the clueless sucker, then reverts back to herself.'

'Why would the regent do such a thing?' Ruric asked.

'Because it's her style,' Briar said, warming to the idea. 'The princess kills anyone who tries to free her. That's really twisted.'

Joshua gave a grudging nod. 'I like it. It has a certain cruelty to it. So give her another kiss, and if she tries to kill you we'll hit her with the dust and see what happens. Worst comes to worst, she turns into a pile of cogs and screws.'

Ruric shook his head, his arms crossed over his chest now, adopting the *I'm so not going there* posture. Briar knew it well – she'd used it off and on over the years.

'I am not willing to risk it,' he said flatly.

'How about if we used the dust *before* you kiss her?' Briar offered.

There was less doubt in his eyes now.

'You've waited all this time to free her, Ruric. We have to give it a shot. If this isn't her, I'll try to get the dye out of my hair, put on some of her clothes and play princess to your prince.'

A low growl came from Joshua, signalling his displeasure.

'We have to try,' she urged.

The prince sighed as he looked heavenward in supplication. She knew she'd won the argument when his arms dropped to his sides in resignation.

'Then you had best prepare yourselves lest this go wrong. Because it shall, I swear,' he said.

Once they were assured they were as ready as possible, the prince stepped closer to the sleeping figure. 'I am such a fool,' he muttered.

'At least you're a brave one,' Briar said, and that earned her a smile.

At his nod, Briar sprinkled the dust over the sleeping form, a very light coat from blonde head to those shoes. The stuff shimmered, almost as if it had movement, changing colours from blue to orange and then back.

'It's kind of pretty,' Briar said.

As the dust sank deep within Aurora's skin, her body shuddered.

'I pray that we have not harmed her, that this wasn't the fata's plan to destroy her,' Ruric murmured.

'They wouldn't have known we were going to do this,'

Briar said. At least she hoped that was the case. *Was I wrong to trust them?*

Warily, Ruric leaned over and kissed the girl once again. This time he did not linger, but stepped away immediately, on guard.

Briar stuffed the pouch back into her corset, then crossed the fingers on both her hands. This *had* to be Aurora.

The figure began to tremble again as the blonde eyelashes fluttered and opened. A deep breath followed as the eyes slowly focused.

'What do you think?' Ruric said.

'We'll know soon enough.' *Come on . . . show us some attitude.* The princess slowly pushed herself up off the divan, just like before. She dropped the rose as if surprised to find herself holding it.

A deep yawn came next, her arms stretching up above her head, tightening the fabric over her ample breasts. A sight that neither of the guys missed.

'My princess,' Ruric said. He did not go down on one knee, still wary.

Aurora stared at him, her eyebrows furrowed in displeasure.

'Who are you?' she demanded, her voice a bit higher than Briar's. It was the kind of tone bred by years of expecting servants to cater to her every whim. 'How *dare* you come into my chambers without my permission?'

Briar grinned. 'Guys, I think this is the real thing.'

For a brief moment, Ruric was speechless. Then he regained his composure and went down on one knee.

'Princess Aurora, I apologize for entering your chambers in such a bold manner. I am Prince Ruric, the third son of King Leovold, from the kingdom of Angevin.'

She wasn't impressed, glaring at him now. 'I do not care who you are. Where is my governess? Why has she allowed you here?'

'Oh, yeah, we got a real piece of work here,' Joshua muttered. 'At least now you get to go home,' he added, giving Briar a sidelong look. 'Right?'

She didn't bother to answer.

Ruric went on a charm offensive. 'Please pardon our intrusion, but it was the only means to break your enchantment.'

The frown deepened. 'I wasn't enchanted. I was resting, you oaf, and you woke me.' She glanced around and grew more confused. 'Why are my chambers in such a state? Why haven't they been cleaned?'

Ruric rose with a frustrated frown of his own. Apparently he'd expected the girl to leap into his arms and proclaim her undying love.

'You have been asleep for a very long time. Ten years, in fact.'

'That is nonsense,' the girl said, rising. Then she saw Briar. 'Who are you and how dare you . . . resemble me?'

Oh boy. We definitely got attitude. 'Actually it's the other way round – you resemble me,' Briar said, stifling a grin. 'Go figure.'

'Who are you? Are you this man's harlot?'

Harlot? Briar's temper unsheathed its claws. 'We're the people who just saved your butt. A little gratitude might be nice, *princess.*'

Aurora stared at her in shock. Apparently nobody had ever called her on being a diva. The next stage would be panic, culminating in her shouting for help.

'Guys, can you give us a moment?' Briar asked. 'I need to bring her up to speed.'

'Good luck with that,' Joshua whispered. He and Ruric promptly backed off, no doubt relieved she was taking the lead.

Briar sat on the princess's bed, despite the glare it earned her.

'How dare you—' the girl began.

'Don't say it!' Briar said, raising a finger for silence. 'The reason your room . . . chambers are a mess is because you're being held prisoner. If we don't get you out of this castle, your kingdom is going to be destroyed.'

'My father will—'

Now Briar did have to be a jerk. 'I sorry, but both your folks are dead. So is all the court. The regent killed them after she enchanted you.'

'Regent? We have no regent in this kingdom. Who is this person?'

'She's your governess,' Ruric chimed in.

Briar shot him a frown. *Now you tell us.*

The princess shook her head, tossing curls in all directions. 'You are lying. Hildretha is a loyal servant. She

283

'saved me from the spell that the fata laid upon me.'

'It is all true, I swear,' Briar replied. 'We need to get you out of here.'

'Might I suggest that you switch clothes with my cousin?' Ruric said.

'With her? Whatever for?' Aurora replied.

'Briar will distract those who might want to harm you, at least long enough for me to help you escape.'

'I am not giving my fine clothes to some village girl,' the princess complained.

Being a village girl was a step up from harlot, but it still rankled.

'Briar is *not* some village girl. She and this young man have risked their lives for you, so show some kindness.'

'I will not—'

'Exchange clothes and let us be off,' he said tartly. 'We do not have time to argue.'

Aurora grumbled under her breath, her eyes promising payback.

'I am sorry for being so abrupt, but after we wed this will only be a bad memory, I promise.'

'Wed?' The girl's expression went from annoyed to suspicious in an instant.

Nooo! That probably hadn't been Ruric's brightest move. Great kissing skills did not equal a guaranteed trip down the aisle. *Or a kingdom.*

The princess eyed her, her expression changing as if she'd come to some decision. 'None of my gowns will fit you. You are too plump.'

Joshua whistled under his breath. 'No people skills there,' he murmured.

'It'll be fine,' Briar replied through clenched teeth. 'Can you two give us space?'

'Come on,' Joshua said, waving Ruric along. 'Let's talk.'

The pair of them exited into the antechamber. As the door closed behind them, they began to murmur in lowered voices, probably Joshua pointing out that Ruric's courting skills needed some serious help.

Briar began unlacing her corset.

'You want my kingdom – I can see it in your face,' the princess said as she fumbled with her own laces.

'No, I want to go home, and the only way that will happen is if your kingdom is regent-free.' *Or at least I hope that's the case.*

'You are mistaken. My governess would never harm me. She has been with me for many years.'

'But she was there when the curse went down, right?'

'If you mean, was she near me when I fell asleep, yes. She promised I would not die. Clearly she told the truth. It is only proper that she has become regent while I was asleep if all my . . . family are . . . gone.'

Briar heard the hitch in her voice. 'I'm sorry about that.'

'You are not lying, are you? About them?'

'No. That's why the regent has to go. She's killed them and she's been torturing and executing people all over the place.'

The girl blinked in consternation. 'Again you lie. You do not know her as I do. Many fear her, but it is only because of the mask she must wear.'

'And why does she wear that and the gloves all the time?'

'Hildretha was burned as a child and hides the scars so none will mock her.'

How convenient. 'Have you *ever* seen her face?'

'I had no need to do so,' was the swift reply.

To speed things along, Briar had to unlace the royal's dress for her, making her wonder if the girl had ever performed such a menial task. The switch was accomplished with a lot of complaining on the princess's part.

'Your clothes are filthy. Do you not wash?'

'I've been a bit busy,' Briar replied.

Somehow that petulant attitude never came across in any of the fairy tales. In those stories, Aurora was portrayed as a demure and kind young woman, not at all like the one wrestling herself into Briar's clothes and bitching up a storm.

Even worse, the princess had been right – her gown didn't fit Briar.

Aurora smirked. 'I did warn you.'

'Just lace it as far you can. You have a cloak, right? It'll hide it.'

The royal did as she asked, despite the four-inch gap at the back.

'We're about ready,' Briar called out to her companions.

She found a comb and began to tidy up her hair in the dusty mirror. The best she could do was braid it and tie it with a small piece of golden cord she'd found near the comb. It was still black and there was nothing she could do about that. If she pulled up the hood of the cloak, maybe all they'd see was her face.

A snort came from behind her. 'Is that the best you can do? Your hair is like an untidy bird's nest.'

Briar whipped round. 'Your people adore you, but I swear I have no idea why. You're just a spoilt brat.' *There's no way I could have dreamed you up.*

Shocked, the princess stepped back, unable to formulate a suitably haughty response.

'Ohhkay,' Joshua said. 'Moving right along . . .'

Briar rummaged through the wardrobe, shoving aside dusty gowns. Finally she pulled out a travelling cloak, which set off another round of sneezing from Joshua.

'Allow me to assist you,' Ruric said, taking the garment from her and placing it on her shoulders. 'Should anyone interfere with your progress, order them to stand aside,' he said. 'Aim for the front gate and when you reach it, run. The princess and I shall find another way out, and then we shall join up with the others in the village.'

'Others?' the princess asked.

The prince turned towards her, his eyes filled with pride. 'There are many who wish to see you free. They will rally to your side and we will wrest your kingdom away from the tyrant.'

Aurora's blue eyes grew chilly. 'I know a way out that none will expect. We will be unchallenged.'

That's optimistic.

Briar paused in front of the exterior door, gathering her courage. She had to be more of a princess than the real thing.

'Don't worry. This will work,' Joshua said from her side. 'You can do it.'

'Thanks,' she said, pleased at the vote of confidence. She gazed over at him, wondering what else she should say that might make it right between them again. 'I'm sorry for what I said. About the curse.'

'Is there some reason we are not moving?' the princess asked. Briar swore she heard the girl's foot tapping in annoyance.

'Just making sure I have the proper bitchy attitude,' Briar replied, pulling up her hood.

Part princess, part Saralyn, part stuck-up snob. Yeah, I've got it.

After a long spiral staircase that required serious concentration, given the weight of her gown, she reached the main floor where she encountered two astonished guards.

'There you are,' Briar said. She doubted anyone would remember the exact timbre of Aurora's voice: it'd been too long since they'd last heard it. It was the delivery that counted. 'I am awake now.'

'Your . . . Your Highness?' one stammered, shooting the other guard a quick look.

'Indeed. Escort me to the front gate without delay,' Briar ordered.

'But—'

'That was not a request,' she said, sweeping ahead as if she knew exactly where she was going. Luckily she'd chosen the right direction and they fell in step around her. If Briar could keep their attention focused on her, they'd not realize

Joshua was creeping along behind them, or that the Ruric and his shrewish wife-to-be were making their own exit.

'How did this happen, Your Highness?' one of the men asked.

'I do not know. I woke, that is all. I yearn for fresh air, for it has been long since I have felt it on my face.'

Hey. Listen to me. I'm pretty good at this. That one summer she'd tried to memorize *Romeo and Juliet* had actually been helpful.

Now that they were strolling through the hallway of very dead suitors, Briar forced herself not to look at them, as she knew they'd upset her. She could do nothing for them now. Instead, she kept her eyes locked on the double doors at the far end of the hallway. The doors that led to the castle's front entrance and freedom.

She marched onward, keeping her chin up and her movements regal. The swish of the skirts on the stone floor was a subtle accompaniment to the heavy-booted steps behind her. They exited the hall and entered the large chamber that led to the doors and the courtyard.

Almost there.

The ambush came so quickly that Briar never had a chance to cry out. One moment she was sailing right along, and the next she found a sword at her throat, held there by a guard who'd seemingly come out of nowhere.

'Be silent or you're dead,' he warned.

'Run, Joshua!' she cried, and then dived away to avoid the blade. The princess's gown was Briar's downfall, tripping her after only a few steps. A shout erupted, then came a solid thud as Joshua hit the floor at her feet.

She looked up to find three guards. The newcomer, the one with an eye patch, nodded appreciatively.

'Get them up,' he ordered.

One of the guards grabbed her arm and hauled her to her feet. Briar shook him free. 'Don't touch me.' She'd sounded so imperial the man backed off, confused.

'You sure about this?' the man demanded.

The one-eyed guard nodded. 'She's not the princess,' he said, pushing back her hood. 'See?'

Joshua was on his feet as well, secured by a pair of guards.

'Sorry, I thought I'd fooled them,' she said.

The lead guard pointed at Joshua. 'Haul this one to the dungeon. The regent wants to see the girl.'

'No!' Joshua lunged, his hand shooting towards her. She reached out as well. Mere inches stood between them, and then the old fear rose once again, but this time she didn't pull back, and neither did he. Instead, Joshua strained harder, his fingers edging closer to hers. If the guards hadn't interfered, they would have touched, for good or ill.

As he was hauled away, he shouted, 'I'll come for you!'

It was a futile boast, but it gave her much-needed strength. He wasn't giving up.

Then neither will I.

The princess led Ruric on a convoluted journey, but she assured him she was headed towards the west side of the castle. Aurora wasn't very stealthy – royalty didn't have to be – but she still managed to be subservient enough for none to bother them as they passed by. It probably helped that she looked like a serving wench, though a very pretty one.

'Down this hall,' she whispered. 'Through that room is a way to the far garden. We can depart through the postern gate.'

'Surely there will be a guard there.'

'He will most likely be in his cups,' was the swift reply.

Ruric had to admit his 'cousin' had been right. Aurora was a spirited young girl, but she was headstrong and immature. *Perhaps she is just frightened.* It had to have been unnerving to wake after such a long sleep and find three strangers in one's chambers. Still, something about her bothered him.

When she opened a door without any great degree of caution and passed through, Ruric followed her, trusting her judgement. It proved a glaring error.

A figure stood in front of a blazing hearth, one he knew all too well.

'It's the regent! Flee!' he said, turning back towards the princess.

'Fiend!' Aurora said, hefting a vase. Before Ruric could dodge out of the way, it united itself with his skull. With a scathing oath on his lips, his consciousness fled in a flash of pain.

The princess they'd risked their lives to free had just sided with their enemy.

CHAPTER TWENTY-SIX

By the time Pat and Reena reached the top of the well, the swarm of fata was gone. Only one remained, the one who had brought them the food. It shivered in terror, its eyes darting from the well to the street around them.

'Where are the others?' Reena asked as she shoved boards across the opening.

Hidden. All will be lost now, the fata said. It held out its hand and on its palm was an object made of leaves, a pouch of some sort. *To save you from the metal.*

It laid it on the well kerb and then skittered off into the night, a flash of colour in the darkness.

Reena picked up the pouch and was about to open it when the first howl split the air.

'What the hell is that?' Pat said, looking around. 'A coyote?'

'No, it sounds like a wolf,' she said, stashing the pouch away. 'I can't imagine it'd be inside the town at night, though.' She looked over at him. 'You OK?'

'Sort of. Couldn't think there for a while. It was like my brain was being sucked out through my ears or something. It was really weird.'

It was more than that, but he had no intention of telling her what he'd really felt. How frightened he'd been. She already despised him, so there was no reason to make it worse.

'Let's get out of here,' she said. 'If we're lucky, we can find that wine cellar again.'

'We should just go home,' he grumbled under his breath. He didn't owe these guys anything, especially when he'd been brought here against his will. Why should he care about the others? That was the Daniels Family Rule #1: always look out for yourself. His dad had pounded that into him since he could walk.

Reena paused to get her bearings. 'What happened down in the well?'

'Don't want to talk about it.'

'OK. A thanks would be nice.'

'For what?' he said, though he knew exactly what she meant.

'For saving your stupid ass,' she replied, ducking her head round the corner. 'I think it's this way.'

'How can you tell?' He certainly couldn't. There was only moonlight to navigate by and all the streets looked the same to him. 'Or are you just faking it to impress me?'

He heard her mutter a swear word under her breath. 'You really do need to get over yourself, Daniels.'

'Hey, it *is* all about me.'

She crooked an eyebrow at him. 'You messing with my head again?'

'No. That's what my dad taught me. You never put yourself at risk for someone else, not unless there's a profit in it.' Now he was somewhere he didn't belong, somewhere that could kill him and not even give a damn that it'd done it.

'Your dad's an asshat. Just saying.'

He should have nailed her for that, but he agreed. Emerson Daniels was a total asshat, and one of the best ways to keep him off your back was to act just like him.

Pat froze when a thin brown dog trotted up to them. It sat and stared at them with baleful eyes.

'Shoo!' he said, waving his arms.

The canine ignored him, turning those sad eyes on Reena. Apparently she was a soft touch because she dug in the canvas bag and tossed it a thick piece of bread. It snapped it up and then waved its tail, no doubt hoping there were more morsels in its future.

'Sorry, that's all I can share right now.'

The hound put its nose to the ground and snuffled off in search of more treats. It was only then Pat noticed that the mutt's tail was metal.

'You shouldn't have wasted the food,' he said as they continued down the street.

Reena gave him a hard frown. 'Animals need love as much as people. They know if you treat them like they matter.'

'Another lecture?' he grumbled. 'What is this – number four or five since we've been here?'

'I lost count a while back. You just keep earning them.'

'I'm not that bad.'

'Convince me otherwise,' she said, hesitating at a crossroads.

'I . . .' To his surprise he had to work to come up with one redeeming quality. 'I like . . . cats. They're cool as long as I don't have to take care of them.'

'That means you have a heart in there somewhere. I had my doubts.'

Why was he bothering with her? She was just some girl. Not important. In a couple of years he'd be out of Bliss and she'd be stuck there doing some dead-end job, probably working as a waitress.

God, now I sound like Dad.

'So what d'you want to do when you get out of college?' Reena asked. She was moving slower now, and he suspected she had no clue where they were.

'My dad wants me to be a corporate lawyer.'

She paused, looking increasingly frustrated. He could tell because she was frowning. 'I repeat, what do *you* want to do?'

He rotated his right arm, trying to loosen it up. Hopefully if he stalled long enough he wouldn't have to answer.

'Daniels? Just tell me. You want be a ballet star or a surf bum or what?'

'I want to join the air force and be a fighter pilot.'

She turned towards him, smiling now, the first time one of those had been aimed at him.

'A fighter pilot? For real?' she said. He nodded. 'That sounds so cool. Those fighter jets haul, don't they?'

'Yeah, I've heard they reach speeds of up to fourteen hundred miles per hour.'

Reena's eyes lit up. 'Wow! Me, I'm into race cars,' she admitted. 'I love speed, and I think being a fighter pilot would be so awesome.'

Somehow he'd managed to impress this impossible girl and that felt good. Maybe it had something to do with the fact that she'd saved his life. There couldn't be any other reason. 'My dad will never go for it so it's just a dream.'

'It's your life, not his.'

'Easier said than lived,' Pat replied. 'He's . . . intense.'

'If it's what you really want to do, get intense right back,' she insisted. 'If he loves you, he'll back down.'

No chance of that.

The howl came again and this time it was much closer. Too close, actually.

'Let's move it!' Reena ordered, and they took off at a jog.

Running through a darkened village proved to be more difficult than Pat had imagined. Though the townspeople were off the streets, there was still their stuff here and there.

'Do you know where we're going?' he demanded as they sprinted down an alley.

'No,' she admitted. At the far end was a stone wall, one about five feet tall.

When they reached it, Reena scrambled up, despite her skirts. A quick leg over and she landed on the other side. 'Come on, Daniels,' she called. 'I thought you were some kick-butt athlete.'

He gritted his teeth and hauled himself over the wall, dropping down next to her. 'I am. Now what?'

'I think I know where we are. If we go down this . . .' she began.

A growl came from above them. They turned in unison to find a wolf on top of the barrier, its bilious green eyes glaring down at them. It sort of resembled a real wolf – fur, teeth, claws and tail – but it didn't move with that wild grace he'd always admired. Parts of its fur were gone, replaced by metal.

'Oh, shit,' he said, backing away. Another wolf sprang up on to the wall next to its companion. 'What are those things?'

'Hungry! Come on!'

As they sprinted, Pat shot a look over his shoulder and counted three beasts trotting along behind them. 'Why aren't they trying to catch up with us?' he asked, his breath coming tighter now.

'That would be why,' Reena said, skidding to a halt.

Two wolves sat in front of them.

'Can't you do some magic? Get us out of here?'

Reena stared at him for a second. 'Maybe I can.' The pouch appeared in her hand and she fumbled it open.

'What are you doing?' he said, snatching up a piece of wood from the street. 'You better be sending us home, you hear?'

'Your bravery is duly noted, wimp,' Reena said testily.

'I'm not a wimp,' he grumbled, 'but even I know when we're out-gunned. You can bring us back later if you want, but we're screwed if we try to fight these things. They'll just rip us apart.'

'I'm going to try something. If it doesn't work, we have to fight our way out of this, OK?'

'Then it damn well better work.'

With a quick start, Reena sprinted towards the two

wolves. One immediately charged her and she rammed her hand down on its back, barely missing getting mauled by its teeth. Dancing around like a hyperactive poodle, she kept on the move.

What are you doing?

She slapped at the second wolf with her hand, making sure to hit a metal patch, then danced back again. It dived directly at her and before Pat could try to help her, he had his own problems. The snap of teeth made him lurch to the side, barely missing having his throat ripped out by one particularly vicious canid.

When it charged again, he whacked it hard on the skull. Then again. When it slumped to the ground, a thick oil slick formed around its muzzle.

'It bleeds oil?' Another lunged and raked its teeth along his calf. He cried out, then fought it off, but it came right back at him.

'Pat, you OK?' Reena called out.

He didn't get a chance to answer, putting his shoulders into the next blow. It cracked hard against the wolf's back and it slumped on the ground, its jaws sparking.

'Yes!' Reena cried. As he spun to see what had happened, he slipped on some of the oil and went down on his knee. A wolf landed on his back, fangs clacking as he landed face first on to the filthy street.

As he struggled to rise before it buried those fangs in his neck, it fell away. He rolled up on to his feet and found Reena standing over him, grinning. The wolf was on the ground nearby, twitching, hacking up cogs and little gears.

Pat bent over to catch his breath, smarting at the pain in his leg.

'You OK?' he wheezed.

'Yeah. You?'

'I'm good.' When he looked up he saw blood on her arm. 'You lie.'

'So do you,' she said, pointing at his bloodied breeches.

He scanned the battlefield and found nothing but defunct enemies.

'How did you do that?'

She held up her hands, both of which glimmered as if they'd been dipped in phosphorescent paint. 'It's the fata's stuff. It destroys the metal. I guess if they're mostly metal it kills them.'

'Well, hell,' he replied as he rose to his feet. 'You're pretty amazing, you know that? Now we can kick some butt in this town.'

Reena cocked her head. 'I thought all you wanted was to go home.'

'No, not yet,' he said, feeling something different take hold of him now. Something that wasn't just about him. 'We need to find the other two, execute some payback. Then we can go home.'

'You know, Daniels, I think I'm beginning to like you.'

'Right back at you, Hill.'

CHAPTER TWENTY-SEVEN

Ruric regained consciousness gradually, the black nothing in his mind slipping away to dull grey. His head ached unmercifully. When he raised it and winced, he felt the crack of dried blood on his skin.

He was secured to a chair with thick ropes. For any man it would be annoying. For a prince it was intolerable. He found one of the sources of his imprisonment sitting primly near the fire. Curiously the regent was not present.

Aurora was still in his 'cousin's' clothes, but there the similarity ended. Briar would never have betrayed him. *What of her and the boy? Are they prisoners too?*

'I expected better treatment from the daughter of a king,' he said.

Aurora's eyes darted to him. 'I hold no loyalty to you or your nefarious companions.'

'I freed you from your spell. I would have put you back on the throne.'

'Only so you could take it from me. Hildretha told me what would happen. I would have been cast aside, or murdered in my sleep. I am fortunate that my governess knows how to deal with your kind.'

'I would have done none of that, and yet you betrayed us. I was a fool to think you worth my time.'

She shot to her feet, fire in her eyes. 'You hold your tongue!'

'Don't like to hear the truth, do you? You have always been pampered and never held accountable for your actions.'

'Why would you believe that?'

'One of my father's nobles met you on your fifteenth birthday. He had little regard for you.'

'I do not care what anyone thinks of me,' she said. Her shoulders shook, but it wasn't from anger. Was he finally breaching her defences?

'Tell me, how many souls lived in this town on your sixteenth birthday?'

'I . . . don't know. Six or seven hundred perhaps.'

'Not now. Many have been made into metal creatures, others slaughtered. Most have run away to spare their families. Only a few hundred remain, praying for the day that their princess is restored to them.' He leaned forward in his bonds. 'And, instead, they got *you*.'

'You churlish oaf!' she stormed. 'I shall see you . . . you . . .'

'What? Hanged? Drawn and quartered? Torn apart by one of the regent's magical horrors? If you wish to be truly evil, you need to be a bit more specific.'

'I . . .'

'But you are not evil,' he said, softer now. 'You are frightened and you have no idea what you're facing.'

'And you do?' she challenged, taking a step forward.

'I know some of it,' he admitted. 'I know enough

301

to be frightened for both of us.'

Aurora glared at the guard near the door, who had wisely remained out of the argument. 'Is it true? Is my governess thought to be a tyrant?'

The man's eyes blinked rapidly, but he did not answer.

'Tell me! Is this truth or lies?'

The guard's eyes saddened and then he pointed to his mouth.

'What is he doing?' she asked, bewildered. 'Why does he not answer me?'

Ruric leaned back in the chair and sighed. 'He is telling you he has no tongue with which to speak. Your precious governess had it removed.'

As the massive wooden door opened and she was escorted inside the room, Briar's question as to who had betrayed them was answered. Aurora stood by the hearth, her arms wrapped round her chest as if to shield herself from life. Or from the truth.

Ruric sat nearby in a chair, a prisoner. 'Briar,' he said. 'I see you fared no better than I. What of Joshua?'

'He's in the dungeon,' Briar replied as she hurried to him, concerned about the blood on his face. It came from an oozing wound on the side of his head. 'You're hurt.'

'Fortunately the princess's aim is not entirely true.'

'You did this?' Briar said, rounding on the girl.

'Of course she did,' the regent said, waving away the guards as she strode into the room. 'Loyalty is a valued commodity in this kingdom.'

The ruler made her way to a wooden table set near the hearth, upon which were charts and parchments and other minutiae of government.

'You may leave us,' she ordered, and her men filed out one by one. Once the door had closed, she turned towards Briar. 'You destroyed the spell that I placed on this usurper. He is no longer mine. How did you do that?'

If Briar told her about the dust, they'd search her and find it. Instead, she clamped her mouth shut.

'Just give her the bracelet,' Ruric cut in. 'It's not worth anyone's life.'

'But . . .' It was a good feint, though she didn't want to lose Joshua's present, not when it seemed to have some effect on their enemy.

The regent eagerly took the bait. 'The silver you wear? That is how you did it?'

Briar delivered a mock glower at Ruric. 'Thanks for that, *cousin.*'

With fumbling fingers, she undid the clasp and held out the bracelet, hoping the regent would come closer to claim it. If the timing was right, maybe she could toss some of the sparkly dust on her. Who knew, maybe she'd melt down like the Wicked Witch of the West.

The regent held her position. 'Claim it from her, Aurora. Place it on the desk.'

So much for that plan.

With cautious steps, the princess approached and then took possession of the bracelet. Briar expected a cry of pain when she touched it. It never came. It appeared that only the regent had a problem with her birthday present.

What does that mean?

'I can't believe you trust her,' Briar said, eager to stir things up.

'Hildretha will always protect me,' the princess replied as she laid the bracelet on the table near a parchment.

Bull. The regent had just altered her plan to allow for an awake Aurora, rather than a sleeping one.

'My princess, I have arranged for new chambers so that you may rest,' the ruler said.

'I have just awoken,' the girl grumbled, sounding sixteen. 'I certainly don't need rest. I need to know what's happening in my kingdom.'

'True, but I shall handle this issue,' the regent said. 'It is not right for you to hear this man's screams.'

'Whatever do you mean?'

The ruler lowered herself into the chair and placed both arms on the table, tenting her gloved hands. 'How do you think we shall learn who is behind this rebellion? Asking this ruffian politely will get us nowhere.'

'But surely—'

'Aurora, your father is no longer here to protect you. That is my role now. You are too . . . delicate for this task.'

The princess's usually creamy skin went a shade paler as she must have realized exactly what the regent intended for Ruric. She steadied herself briefly on the table, then nodded. 'Yes, perhaps I do need to rest.'

When she reached the door, Aurora hesitated, sending a final look over her shoulder at Briar. 'You can keep the dress. It is worth nothing to me now.'

And we rescued you . . . why?

Then it was just the three of them.

'There is more to your metal obsession than just the fata,' Ruric said. 'What is the purpose of all this?'

'The fata were nothing more than a tool. When one of them cursed the princess, I took it a step further.'

'My question remains. Why all the metal?'

'Do you know of the drazak and their ways?' the regent asked.

'Yes. My grandfather fought them many years ago.'

'What are—' Briar began.

'They are creatures who live deep in the earth,' Ruric explained. 'They covet all things metal, be it gold or silver or brass.' He turned to the regent. 'You, however, are not one of them. Drazak are not that clever, or that evil.'

'I am what I was made to be,' the regent replied, her voice deeper now.

At that, the ruler carefully stripped off her leather gloves, dropping them on the table in front of her. The princess had said that her governess had suffered horrific burns, but there were no scars present. Instead, her hands were greyish brown with thick knuckles. They terminated in sharp nails.

Not nails. *Claws.*

'Ruric . . .'

He wriggled his hand and she grasped it for comfort. 'Be brave, cousin. Now we shall know the truth.'

With a click, the mask was unlocked and set aside to

reveal a face that Briar knew no one could ever love, the blend of an older woman and a . . . thing. Thick ridges curved up where cheekbones should rest and the eyes were deep-set and cunning. The mouth held an impressive array of sharpened teeth.

'Ah, I see,' Ruric said, nodding his comprehension. 'I was wrong – you are half drazak and half human. I had heard they exist.'

You've got to be kidding. 'Her mom married a . . .' *Whatever the heck that thing is.*

Ruric cleared his throat. 'It is unlikely nuptials were involved,' he replied. 'Drazak covet humans for their metal, for their jewels and sometimes for . . . other purposes.' His brown eyes pleaded with her not to ask any further questions.

'Ohh . . .' Briar had just got the picture and it was way ugly. This creature was the by-product of some poor girl and . . . *Oh, gross. That's really twisted.*

Seeing that she understood, Ruric turned back to their enemy. 'How did you come to be accepted as Aurora's governess? The queen and king would have been careful not to allow one of your kind near their daughter.'

The regent's smile was the stuff of nightmares, the teeth longer than was normal for a human. 'I used a small magic that hid what I am. Once she saw my supposed burns, Her Majesty was all kindness and I was brought into service, for clearly I was no threat.'

'Got that one wrong,' Briar muttered.

'How did you get that magic?' Ruric pressed.

'My mother had some talent, but not enough to save her.'

'You could have waited until someone woke the princess and continued to serve her as you had before. Instead you made sure her suitors died in their quest. Why?'

'It is easy for those who have never served to speak of it so lightly,' the regent replied. She rose and moved closer to the fire, warming her hands in a human gesture. 'The princess's grandfather drove the drazak out of this kingdom and into the land where my family lived. The ruler there was weak, and he did nothing to stop them from destroying our villages.' The regent turned back towards them, her eyes a reddish brown. 'They swept through our home, pillaging the metal, consuming the flesh and taking their other revenges. I was the child of one of them and there was no place for me with humans, or their kind. I had no home. Until now.'

'You took this one as payback,' Briar said.

The regent nodded. 'Of course. Fitting, isn't it?'

'But why the metal? What *is* its purpose?' Ruric asked again, his voice louder this time. 'I know you crave it, but why are you creating your own?'

'The metal is both a lure and a weapon. The drazak are gaining strength again. They know I rule this kingdom, and the metal will bring them here. They will hope to take it from me.'

'You are seeking a war, but how can you be so sure you win it?'

'I shall greet them as one does family,' she said, her

grin making Briar's stomach lurch. 'I shall grant them food as they need. They will become sated and complacent, believing they can kill me at their whim.'

It took a moment to realize what she meant. 'You'll let them eat your subjects,' Briar said, nearly gagging. 'That's sick.'

'No, it is cunning,' Ruric said, nodding now. 'When drazak consume large quantities of flesh, they grow sluggish. She intends to exploit that weakness.'

'Indeed. They can consume human flesh, but they cannot eat metal,' the regent replied. 'I will turn my warriors loose, and my army will destroy them all. I will have my revenge on *both* the races that cast me out. I will no longer be driven from village to village because of what I am. I will rule here forever.'

Megalomaniac alert.

So far this creature, the physical embodiment of the curse, had been winning.

But how did we change that? Was the princess the key?

Ruric must have been thinking along the same lines. 'What of Aurora?'

'She is of value at present, even if she is awake,' was the chilly reply. 'In time, that will not be the case.'

'My father will know I am lost when I do not return with a report.' He sighed. 'If only there had been help here in the village, but we found none.'

'None at all?' the regent said, stepping closer. 'The princess said otherwise.'

Thank you for that, Aurora.

308

'No,' Ruric replied, but almost too quickly. 'I told her that to make her feel better. In truth, we have no need of assistance. The army of Angevin is mighty enough for the task. It is in your best interests to allow us to leave unharmed.'

'You believe you are my equal?' the regent demanded.

'Yes,' Ruric replied. 'I am *more* than your equal.'

In that moment, Briar knew it was true.

So did the regent, who glowered at both of them. 'You had help, I know it. You are not that clever.' It took her no time for her to don the mask and gloves again. 'Guards!'

They spilt into the room, on alert.

'Take this girl to the dungeon. She and the other boy are to be executed for high treason on the morrow.'

Joshua. No . . .

'The usurper, Your Grace?' one of them asked.

'Let him feel the sting of the whip now. I must know the names of those who have aided him. Tomorrow he is to be taken to the field and impaled. I shall have his head sent home to his father. That should settle the matter.'

'Why not whip the girl?'

The regent's mask turned towards her. 'That is a possibility.'

Briar sucked in a deep breath. If only she could become invisible.

'She doesn't know anything,' Ruric said. 'I never told her. Briar was only useful because of her magic, and the fact that she resembles the princess.'

'You told her nothing?'

He delivered a haughty sneer. 'Why should I? It would

have been my kingdom, not hers. It was easy to convince her that I would share the throne.'

'You lied to me,' Briar said, and, though most of this was for the regent's benefit, for a moment she almost believed him.

'Don't all men lie, cousin?' he said, smiling.

Don't get me started.

As Briar was escorted out of the room, she took a final look over her shoulder. Ruric was stone-faced now, preparing for what lay ahead. As she turned away, she noticed the bracelet was no longer on the table. There was only one person who could have taken it.

Maybe the princess wasn't as gullible as she seemed.

CHAPTER TWENTY-EIGHT

'How bad is your leg?' Reena asked.

'Don't know yet,' Pat replied. 'Not good, the way it's feeling.'

They were keeping close to the buildings, skulking along, trying hard not to encounter any more wolves.

Reena came to a halt. 'OK, I give up. I have no idea where we are.'

He was too weary to be angry. 'I don't either,' he said. 'Maybe we should find a rooftop and get some sleep. It's too dangerous to be on the ground.'

'All right, I can work with that. In the morning, we'll try to get inside the castle. Maybe we can free Briar and Josh, and find this Ruric guy.'

'Sounds good. Then we can kick that cold bitch off the throne. That would rock,' Pat said.

'Wait a minute,' Reena said, turning towards him. 'You were the one who said everything had to be about you. Now you want to go to war with the regent?'

'Yeah, I do. This is totally personal now,' he said.

There was a creak of wood as the door opened behind them. Before either of them could utter a word, a beefy hand came down on each of their shoulders. With a swift tug, they were pulled inside the building and the door closed behind them.

'What do we have here?' a gruff voice asked.

'You're the smithy,' Reena said. 'We saw you earlier today when Briar came to tell you about Ruric.'

The man didn't reply, massive in size with a craggy face.

'We're . . . friends of Briar and . . . the stable guy,' Pat added, hoping that would count for something. 'Unless of course you're one of the regent's people, then we've never heard of them.'

'Oh, that was brilliant,' Reena grumbled.

'I heard you two outside talking about rebellion,' the smithy replied. 'What keeps me from turning you in? I could use the coin.'

'You do that and it all gets worse,' Pat said. 'Ruric dies, so do our friends and you guys get stuck with the ruler from hell for the rest of your lives.'

'You believe you can get her off that throne?' the man asked.

Reena and Pat exchanged looks.

'Who knows?' Pat said, shrugging. 'We can give it a try. That's more than you folks have been doing from what I can see.'

A hand shot out and grabbed him by the collar, dragging him up into the air as if he weighed nothing. 'You have no notion of what we've been doing, lad.'

Struggling not to choke, Pat coughed out, 'Ah, all right. Sorry.'

The man set him free. 'I heard you fell into the fata hole, and yet you're still alive. How did that come to be?'

Reena stepped closer to their questioner. 'They took

care of us. They're not your enemy, but they are definitely the regent's. They gave me something that can destroy her metal.'

The man's eyes widened. 'You speak the truth, girl?'

'I do. It's why she has been killing them. You've had the perfect weapon right under your noses all the time.'

'Why would they help us? They put the curse on the princess.'

'I don't know about that. I just know that the reason the wolves didn't kill us is the fata's magic. It destroyed them, the metal parts at least.'

The smithy thought for a time, then beckoned them to join him. 'Come on, the pair of you, it's safer back here.'

He led the way to the rear of the building where coals still glowed in the forge and the sharp tang of iron filled Pat's nose with each breath.

'We must keep our voices down. My wife and children are asleep inside, and have no knowledge of what this is about. I will put them in great danger if it is learned that I helped you.'

'Thank you,' Reena said. 'What we really need are weapons. A sword, a bow and some arrows. A couple of knives if you have them. Once Ruric wakes the princess, the regent will come after us with all those monsters of hers.'

'By all the saints, that is what I fear most,' the smithy murmured. 'She can conjure at will. It is unholy.' He poked at the forge absentmindedly. 'I remember the day Ruric came to the town. He was wearing nothing that spoke of wealth, but it was his eyes that told me that he was of noble birth. He wasn't haughty or overbearing – it was that quiet strength you see in those who have held power in their hands, and know how to wield it without hurting all they touch.'

'So now you're working together to overthrow the regent?' Reena asked.

'Yes, there are a few of us, but not enough.' He looked over at Pat. 'Help me shift the anvil, lad.'

Pat did as ordered, though to be honest he doubted that he'd contributed much. Compared to the smithy's bulk, he looked like a half-starved chicken. They wrestled the anvil aside and then the smithy moved the log that served as its base. Scraping back the dirt on the floor, he revealed a series of boards. It took some prising, but finally the boards were removed. The smithy began handing out items, all wrapped in burlap.

As Pat unwound one of the bundles, he found two swords and a pair of knives, all in scabbards.

'No bow?' Reena asked.

The smithy shook his head. 'It would not store well in the ground. Help me put this back and I'll show you where to find one.'

Again there was more straining that made Pat's back ache. He had to admit it was a clever hiding place – few would think of looking underneath the anvil.

Then it was Reena's turn as the smithy directed her to climb up into the rafters and then into a far corner. She executed the climb, dug around, gave a slight *eep* when a mouse streaked out, then returned to the ground bearing a wrapped bow and full quiver.

'That do you?' the man asked.

Reena nodded, testing the weapon. 'This is great. Thanks.'

'Any chance you have a quarterstaff or something?' Pat asked. 'I don't handle swords that well.'

The smithy thought for a moment. 'I have something that might serve.'

He tromped off into the back of the structure and began rooting around.

'A staff?' Reena asked.

'I learned *bōjutsu* when I lived in Ohio – it's a Japanese martial art.'

'Colour me impressed,' she said.

'I never fought for real, just in practice. This could get ugly.'

'It already is,' she said, caressing the bow. 'At least now we have weapons.'

The smithy returned and handed Pat a hardwood pole, one about six foot long. 'Will this do?'

Pat judged its weight, then he stepped back and performed a couple of moves. It wasn't too bad, not as finely balanced as the *bō* he had at home, but it would work.

'Yes, thank you.'

The smithy nodded. 'I'll show you out the back.' Then he hesitated. 'If you see Ruric, tell him to send the signal when he wakes the princess and we will come to his aid. If he fails, we have to hold back, to keep our families safe.'

'We'll tell him,' Pat said. 'Thank you for all your help. We appreciate it.'

315

As they left the smithy behind, he couldn't help but notice Reena's strange expression. 'What's wrong?'

'You were very polite in there. I just wondered what happened to the old Patterson Daniels.'

He huffed. 'I think the wolves ate him. Yeah, I'm sure of it.'

With accurate directions from the smithy, they reached the wine cellar in no time, without encountering any wolves. For that, Pat was grateful. Soon a candle was lit and they were settled into the cellar, eating what food was left.

Pat knew his hands were shaking, but he had no way to stop them.

Reena noticed. 'Scared?' she asked.

'No,' he replied, too quickly. 'Well, maybe just a little.'

'I hear you. It all sounds heroic – rescue the princess, save the kingdom – but, if we screw up, the smithy and his family are dead. So are a lot of other people.' She shook her head in dismay. 'I'm not used to being responsible for others.'

'That's not true,' he said. 'You watch over your brothers. From what I hear they're a handful.'

The worried lines on her face diminished. 'The youngest bro is. The others are pretty decent, but that isn't the same. I help get them ready for school, put Star Wars bandages on their skinned knees. Nothing like here.'

At the mention of injuries, Pat rolled up his breeches and checked his leg wound and found it oozing and swollen. There came a ripping sound as Reena tore off a section from the bottom of her skirt. Then she rummaged in her canvas bag and pulled out a small pouch of herbs. She dribbled some into her palm and then gently pressed them against the wound.

He sniffed. 'Is that oregano?'

'Yeah. It's a natural antibiotic. I'm hoping it'll keep your leg from rotting off.'

He angled his head until he could see her face. 'You're joking, right?'

'No, oregano does have some antibiotic properties. Or at least that's what my gran told me.' She tied the strip of cloth round his calf. 'Sorry, it's not that clean,' she said. 'We should have asked the smithy for some bandages.'

'It's OK. He did enough as it was.' Once she was done, he pulled one of the knives from its scabbard and began to sculpt the staff more to his liking, trying to improve its balance.

As he worked, Reena laid out the arrows, examining each one critically. 'They'll do,' she said, nodding to herself. She took one and dipped the metal tip into the pouch holding the fata dust.

'What are you doing?' he asked.

'Testing to see if this stuff works on everything that's metal. If it does, it's not an option as it'll eat right through the arrowhead.'

When the arrowhead didn't disintegrate, Reena cracked a smile. 'All right! We got ourselves a long-distance weapon against the regent's metal creatures.'

'Then this might actually work?' he asked, picking up her enthusiasm.

'Yeah. Maybe. If we get really lucky.' She looked down at the bow and arrows. 'I never thought I'd have to kill someone with one of these.'

'Maybe it won't come to that,' Pat said, though he suspected that was a lie.

After a bit more targeted staff trimming, he pulled himself up to his feet. His calf throbbed, but it wasn't as bad as it had been. Mindful that Reena was watching him, he executed a few test moves and was pleased to find that the staff would do.

'I figured it was all partying with you. I didn't know you're into martial arts.'

'I am full of surprises,' Pat said, arching an eyebrow. Then he grinned. 'Maybe when we get back home the horse dude and me should pay Briar's ex a little visit. Teach that lying jerk some manners.'

Reena's mouth parted in surprise. 'You're going to kick Mike's ass?'

'Why not?' he said, grinning at the thought. 'I bet Quinn would be up for that. You can see by the way he looks at Briar that he's all hot for her.'

'She doesn't see it. She's still looking for her prince. Always has been.'

Pat huffed. 'Good luck with that. They don't exist, at least not in the real world.'

Reena's arched eyebrow matched his now. 'You might be surprised.'

CHAPTER TWENTY-NINE

As Briar descended into the depths of the castle, the acrid stench of stale urine, wet straw and mould nearly choked her. Joshua was down here somewhere. Had they hurt him? Tortured him?

Please, not that. She'd seen the haunted look in his eyes when they'd been separated. The helplessness. The fear. Maybe even regret.

When she and the guards reached the bottom of the stairs, three crude cells awaited her, all set in a row. The floor of each was covered in straw and two buckets sat in opposite corners, one full of water. The other was probably the toilet.

Joshua was in the middle cell. 'Briar!' he called out, managing to roll worry, relief and joy into that one word.

'I want to be in with him,' she said. 'Please.'

'One cell it is,' the jailer said. He clanked the door closed behind her and locked it with an immense key.

Neither she nor Joshua spoke until the guards were gone, just staring at each other as if they'd been apart for years.

'Please tell me no one hurt you,' he said, his face drawn and haggard. 'I've been going mad here, thinking that—'

'I'm good. You?' she asked.

'I'm OK. What about Ruric?'

'They caught him too. It was the princess who sold us out.'

'That doesn't surprise me.'

Would Joshua remember that he'd almost touched her, or would he avoid her now? She had to find out. 'When we were caught, you tried to touch me. Why would you do that?'

'I was afraid they'd hurt you,' he admitted. 'I thought I would never see you again.'

That had come out so easily. *Has he had a change of heart?*

Joshua made her think that was the case when he took a step towards her, his body trembling with emotion.

'If you could have anything you wanted, what would it be?' he asked.

She spread her hands. 'To get out of here.'

'Besides that. Let's say you're home and the curse is history. What would you want the most, Briar?'

To touch you again.

When she didn't reply, he sobered. 'I know what I'd want.' Another step closer. 'I want to hold your hand, touch your face, your hair.'

Briar retreated out of instinct: the cell bars pressed into her back now. 'I don't want you hurt,' she said. 'I don't want you to . . . die because of me.'

'I'm so tired of living our parents' fears. If the curse comes back to me, then that's what happens. I wouldn't want it any other way.' A half-step put Joshua so close she could see deep into his eyes. He was breathing faster now.

'When they took you away, I knew one thing – I don't

want to go to my grave never having touched you again.'

Her breath caught. 'You'd risk your whole life for that?'

'Yes.'

She didn't know how to respond.

'We used to play together all the time, before our families made us enemies. Do you remember those days, Briar?'

Briar did remember the two of them growing up together. The long summers filled with abundant laughter. It had always been her and Joshua, until it wasn't any more.

'Do you have any idea how much you mean to me? How hard it's been to stay away from you all these years?' he asked, his voice quavering now.

She hadn't, not until this moment. A single tear broke loose and tracked down her cheek.

As if drawn to it, he raised his hand.

'No!' she said, flattening against the bars. 'We can't.'

'We can. We must,' he said simply. 'It's the only way for us to regain what we lost in the river.'

Trembling, Briar closed her eyes as his fingers delicately traced the track of the tear. His fingers moved down her cheek, in no rush, as if he were savouring the journey. They curved round her cheek and settled against her neck, his warmth filling her. His other hand sought hers and took hold of it. This time she made no move to pull away.

'See, that wasn't so bad,' he whispered near her ear. 'What were we afraid of?'

'You dying,' she whispered back.

'We're not dead yet.'

'But—'

'Only *now* matters.'

Deep inside she felt something uncurl within her. Briar gasped, fearing it was the curse taking root, but this felt different than that dark night in the river. This was all heat and light, with a sweetness that recalled a spring breeze. It wove through her like a song, erasing the emptiness, leaving peace in its wake.

'It's . . . good?' he asked.

She nodded. 'It doesn't feel like the last time.'

'Want to really push our luck?'

His playful tone caused her eyes to flutter open. 'How?'

'Like this,' he said, and then his lips were on hers.

It was a faint touch, as if he wasn't sure how it should be done. Then it grew and began to take on a life of its own. It was as if Joshua was the only one who knew how to kiss her the way she really wanted.

When it ended, he looked deep into her eyes, judging her reaction. 'Why did we wait so long?' he said.

Because neither of them had had the courage to tempt fate.

He pulled away from her, gazing at her as if she were the most beautiful girl in the world. It made her self-conscious.

'Oh man, I'm a mess. I mean . . . why couldn't this have happened at the party when I looked good?'

'Because you were too busy flirting with Daniels?' Joshua teased, but she could hear the resentment. 'Seriously, you look OK.'

'No, I smell and I'm wearing someone else's clothes that don't even fit.' Then she remembered the princess's jab. 'I'm not plump, am I?'

'No,' he said, laughing. 'You're perfect.' A deep sigh escaped him. 'Unfortunately, we're still here, so that means you're still cursed.'

'I noticed that. At least I'm trapped with a really cool guy.'

He seemed to appreciate that. 'Come on, sit over here. It's less chilly and the floor isn't as gross.'

Briar joined him. The stones were cold under her butt so she wrapped the cloak tight. He put his arms round her and she laid her head on his shoulder. It seemed so natural, as if they'd done it for years.

'What happened with the regent? Do you want to talk about it?'

It was time he knew it all, so Briar told him of what she'd learned, and why the situation was more dangerous than they suspected.

'Man-eating drazaks?' Joshua said, both eyebrows rising.

'Yeah, those. She was way ugly, like something out of a horror movie. I'm going to have nightmares forever.'

'You already do,' he replied.

'It's my fault Aurora ratted us out,' she admitted. 'I really got in her face. I shouldn't have done that.'

'Yeah, well, Ruric didn't help with his *When we wed* line.'

'He's a fairy-tale prince. That's what they do.' She looked up. 'I'm really worried about him.'

'He'll be OK. He seems like a survivor.'

'Are we?'

He placed a quick kiss on her forehead. 'We better be.

When we go home, we're going to have a talk with the folks, both sets. It's not going to be pretty.'

'Mom will have kittens when she finds out we touched. Yours too.'

'You know, I like kittens,' Joshua said, grinning. 'Our barn cat just had a litter. They're really cute, even though they're still blind.'

He's trying to make me feel better. That earned Joshua a lot of points.

Briar wiped a line of dried blood off his cheek.

'Ouch,' he said, but she could tell it hadn't hurt him.

'Big baby,' she replied.

He chuckled. 'You know, I used to talk to Arabella about you. Crazy, huh? Chattering away at a horse about a girl you liked but couldn't get anywhere near. And now . . .'

Now they had a few hours together. Briar hoped it would be enough.

Joshua selected a strand of her hair and studied it with a curious expression. 'Does it just curl like that on its own?'

'Yeah. I hate it.'

'Why? It's so pretty, all those waves.'

She frowned up at him. 'You should try brushing it sometime. It's a pain.'

'At least you don't get burrs in it like Arabella.'

She chuckled. 'You miss her, don't you?' He nodded sadly. 'I miss my peeps too. My parents, even my cat. I always liked snuggling with Dragonfly on rainy days. I'd read fairy tales to her. She's really into "Puss in Boots".'

Joshua snorted. 'Go figure.'

'When we get home . . .' she began. 'What if the curse moves back to you then and—'

'We'll worry about that later,' he cut in. 'Right now, we're together. That's what counts.'

He tipped her chin up to kiss her again. It wasn't rushed and it made Briar wish they were home, near the lake, just him and her.

They jolted apart at the sound of voices and footsteps that came from the stone stairs that led up into the castle. The jailer appeared first, then two guards dragging Ruric who hung limply between them.

'What did you do to him?' Briar demanded, struggling to her feet.

Her question was answered as they hauled the prince past their cell. His back was branded with angry red stripes, and blood oozed through his torn shirt.

Ohmigod. 'Put him in here with us. Please?'

For a time it looked as if the jailer wasn't going to be that helpful, but finally he shrugged and Ruric was dumped in the centre of the cell.

'Let's get him back near the wall. We don't want him lying on this filthy floor,' Joshua said.

It took a lot of pulling and tugging to position Ruric where they wanted him; he seemed all solid muscle. As they did, he kept shivering and issued the occasional moan.

'Oh man, his shirt is stuck to his skin,' Joshua said. 'We'll have to soak it off or it'll hurt like hell.' He returned with the bucket of water, which didn't look that clean.

With considerable effort, Briar ripped off a fist-size

section of her dress and dipped the cloth in the cold water. 'This is going to hurt. Sorry.'

Ruric gave a faint nod, and when she placed the wet rag on his back, he stiffened. A faint oath sailed through the air, then an apology.

'I'd be saying worse than that if it was me,' Joshua said.

Slowly Briar soaked the shirt until it could be removed. With his flesh exposed, Ruric began to shiver harder now. She carefully cleaned each of the welts and the slices, and found herself counting them, anger growing with each mark.

'I told them nothing. I would not give up my friends,' he said. A deep cough. 'This was solely the regent's doing.' Because in his mind Aurora couldn't be capable of such an act.

'Was the princess there?'

'Not as they whipped me. She came afterwards. She was . . . upset.'

But not upset enough to help you.

'Here, he'll need this,' Joshua said, stripping off his jerkin and then his shirt. She couldn't help but note the bruises on his chest, and yet he'd never complained of being hurt.

They replaced Ruric's ruined shirt with Joshua's, but there was no way to keep the open wounds from clinging to the fabric.

'Thank you,' he said, and lay on his side with a groan.

'Just returning the favour, cousin,' she murmured.

Worried that he would only grow more ill, Briar removed her cloak and tucked it around him, hoping it would be enough. A faint nod came her way and then Ruric's eyes closed.

Joshua shifted around the prone man and took a seat next to her. After pulling on the leather jerkin, his cloak went over her shoulders and he tucked her close to his chest. His nearly *unclothed* chest.

Which was when she really noticed that he had muscles, probably from working at the stables. They weren't as defined as Pat's, but they were definitely there.

'That OK?' he asked.

'Just fine,' she said. *Great, even.*

'Why do you call him "cousin"?'

'So no one would think it odd I just showed up out of nowhere.'

'Hmm . . .'

'We're in big trouble. The villagers won't go to war if the princess is supporting the regent, even if she is half drazak.'

'True, but the regent has ruled this kingdom for a long time, so she's used to being in charge. She won't stop issuing orders and prissy princess won't like that. If the regent goes too far, Aurora might rebel.'

'Hopefully before we're all dead,' Briar muttered.

'That's the one flaw in my plan.'

She laid her head on his shoulder and focused on his soft breathing. He didn't seem to be panicking, not like she wanted to.

'I wonder where the others are. If they're still alive.'

'I'm sure they're fine,' Joshua soothed. 'Probably trying

to figure out how to rescue us. Pat would love that part. Then he could play the hero.'

'I wouldn't mind that.'

'Just as long as he doesn't try to kiss you, it's all good.'

Briar grinned as her eyes slipped closed. She tried to believe she was in her own bed, but that proved difficult with her guy holding her. Or maybe they were in the bed together and . . .

Where did that come from?

Joshua shifted a bit, making her wonder if he was having similar thoughts.

'I remember when you were in kindergarten,' he said, his voice barely above a whisper so as not to disturb their companion. 'I loved your long braids. Your mom used different coloured ribbons for each day of the week. Red for Monday, green for Tuesday, and so on. I loved Fridays – you wore blue ribbons then. I really liked those.'

'How do you remember all that?' She sure didn't.

'Just do. That's how I found you in the river. I looked for the ribbons.'

She'd always wondered about that.

'Why didn't you let go of my hand in the water?' he asked, turning towards her now.

'I didn't want to lose you. You were my friend.'

'And now?'

What was he now? 'You're more than that.'

Joshua's hand slid further along her back and his fingers found the open place where the dress didn't meet. They felt warm and comforting against her bare skin. Emboldened, he kissed her.

Briar returned it eagerly and then settled back in his arms.

He risked his life to touch me.

When Briar awoke near dawn, Joshua still had his arms around her, as if he refused to let her go. Ruric hadn't moved all night and was snoring lightly. From the window above them came the thump of boots as guards marched to and fro. It was the day they were supposed to die.

The curse was winning. It had divided them, wounded their champion, and put them on the fast track to the grave.

No, not yet.

Her life rested on her shoulders, not those of some prince or errant hero.

I will own this curse. I will break it.

If not, Briar would lose too many people that she cared about, like the boy next to her. The boy who'd had the courage to touch her and tell her how much he cared for her.

As if he knew she was thinking of her, Joshua muttered in his sleep. She had never really understood what went on inside that mind of his. For so many years she'd thought he hated her because he'd almost died and that's why her mom wouldn't let her talk to him. Later, she came to realize the problem was less about them and more about their families. Now she knew it was the curse that kept derailing their lives.

Joshua really was a handsome guy, soft-spoken most of

the time, blessed with a quiet strength that knew when to hold back, and when to act. She could learn from him.

I already have.

Feeling mischievous, Briar pulled the fata feather from her bodice and trailed it down his cheek, hoping that would wake him. He shifted again, but didn't stir from his slumber. When the feather failed, she stashed it away and kissed his cheek. This time his eyes blinked open. There was confusion for an instant, then a smile.

'That's a good way to wake up,' he said. A frown formed as colour rose in his cheeks. 'Oh, man. I really need . . . to pee.'

So did she. But how? The cell's 'toilet' was a wooden bucket in the far corner. It was noticeably missing that key element: privacy. That was pretty sad even by fairy-tale standards.

'You first,' she said shifting her weight out of his arms. *Anything to buy time.*

'No. You go ahead,' he said, trying to be gallant.

She shook her head.

'This is . . .' he sighed. 'Way embarrassing.'

'Tell me about it. At least you're not wearing a bunch of skirts.' Guys had it so easy.

To give him privacy and to keep from blushing at the thought that a boy was going to be relieving himself within earshot, she turned her back and began to hum. It was a nonsensical song she used to sing to herself when she was little, one all about frogs and princes.

When Joshua tapped her on the shoulder, she jumped,

so fixated on trying not to overhear anything.

'Your turn,' he said.

Briar really wanted to wait it out, but there was no way she could. 'You can't tell anyone this happened. Not *ever*.'

He crossed his fingers over his heart. 'It's our secret.'

Still . . . this was Joshua and . . . now that they'd got so close . . .

This totally sucks. I really like this guy and he's going to remember this every time he sees me.

'You'd better hurry. Ruric will be waking up pretty soon,' he urged.

That would be even worse. Pushing her modesty aside, she did the deed while Joshua stared up at the small cell window and talked about hoof care. How if you didn't keep a horse's hoofs in fine condition they could go lame, and then he detailed exactly how one did that. It was a totally boring topic and allowed her to focus on the job at hand.

When she rejoined him, Briar offered her thanks, still embarrassed.

'For what?' Joshua said, then winked. 'I was just telling you about horse care.'

You really are a cool guy.

He pointed up at the window and then made a sling with his hands. 'Give the bars a shake. Maybe we'll get lucky,' he said.

That proved a no-go.

'It only happens in movies,' she said, as he helped her back down. Briar found herself wedged between him and the stone wall, his arms round her waist. He didn't appear to be in a hurry to remove them.

She really did want him to kiss her again, and when he moved a bit closer his eyes searched hers. Looking for permission or . . .

Ruric chose that moment to sit up and Joshua backed off immediately.

Argh!

'Good morning, all,' the prince said wearily, giving no indication he'd interrupted a romantic moment. With stiff movements, he removed her cloak and handed it over.' No doubt you will need this more than I do.'

Briar had completely forgotten about her lacing issue and that she was flashing two guys. She quickly pulled the cloak over her shoulders. Before either she or Joshua could offer to help, Ruric regained his feet, wincing as the shirt broke free of the wounds, one by one.

'Fine morning for an execution, don't you think?' he said, his face showing the strain.

'I've seen better,' Joshua replied, frowning. 'Any chance of a rescue, O Prince?'

'Not at present,' Ruric replied. 'I trust you still hold the fata's dust.' Briar nodded. 'Then there is some hope.'

They fell silent as the jailer and the guards began the trek into the dungeon.

'All three of you are due for execution within the hour,' he announced.

'What, no breakfast?' Joshua said. 'That's rude.'

The man crooked an eyebrow. 'Don't know how they do

such things your kingdom, young princeling, but we aren't so kind to our traitors.'

Princeling?

Now that Briar studied Joshua anew, she could see why the man had made that assumption. Joshua held himself as if he weren't afraid, his feet apart, his arms crossed over a chest. Just like a royal.

Her eyes caught Ruric's and he gave a subtle nod.

'Maybe not in the blood, but in the heart,' he murmured.

So she *had* found her prince after all, but she was still stuck in the curse.

After their hands were secured in front of them with rough cords, they were escorted out of the dungeon into the early morning sunlight. Briar blinked until her eyes could adjust. It was the beginning of a nice day, which didn't make her feel any better. It should be raining or hailing or something portentous that fitted with being led to her execution. Instead it was as if Mother Nature were shrugging her shoulders, bored with the whole scene.

Nearby was a cart, the same one that had carried so many unfortunate prisoners to their deaths. Even though Joshua went first, it took some doing to get into the back of the thing with her hands tied, though he tried to help her. As she climbed up, she tripped.

'Damned skirts,' she muttered. Not one of the guards offered any assistance.

In their eyes, she was already a corpse.

CHAPTER THIRTY

Briar scooted nearer to Joshua in the back of the cart. He couldn't put his arms around her, not bound as he was, so they had to content themselves with holding hands. It was so strange to see their fingers entwined and thick ropes round their wrists.

'Any chance they'll use a guillotine?' Joshua asked with a weak smile. 'You know, something quick and painless?'

'That'll be it for sure,' she said.

He knew she was lying: the regent wasn't into quick death. She liked people to suffer, to offer a visceral message: 'Obey me and your family won't die. Cross the line and this could be you.'

It was right out of the tyrant's handbook.

'Maybe if anything happens to you, you'll wake up, you know, in the real world,' she said.

Joshua shook his head solemnly. 'Not likely. I'm inside this now. I die here, I die there. Besides, I wouldn't want to wake up and . . . you not be around any more. I couldn't handle that.'

She felt the same way about him.

He shifted uneasily. 'What will my little brothers think if I croaked on them? I was way happy when they left for summer camp because they're so noisy.' He leaned his head back against the wooden frame. 'Now I might never see them again.'

Before he could respond, the cart set off with a jerk. Ruric wasn't a fellow passenger, but forced to march behind them as if he were a prisoner of war, a great general humbled by his capture. Though she knew he was aching, he didn't bow his head, but looked straight forward, unafraid.

'How does he keep it together?' she whispered.

'I have no idea,' Joshua replied. 'Maybe it comes with being a prince.'

As they exited the castle, the gong began to toll. The effect was instant: sleepy villagers came out of their houses, throwing on cloaks and shawls, toting babies and yawning kids.

When Joshua tightened his grip on her hands, she leaned over and placed a kiss on his flushed cheek. As if to punish them, the cart hit a bump and they bounced apart.

'Do you see Pat or Reena?' she asked, searching the crowd that pressed near them.

Joshua shook his head. 'I'm not feeling good about that.'

Briar had the same dread. Maybe they weren't hurt and Reena took them home. In some ways, she wished that were true.

The cart rolled past the inn where she'd stayed with Ruric that night. The innkeeper was on his front porch, gloating.

'Not so high and mighty now, are you?' the man called out.

Jerk. It wouldn't have turned out that way if Ruric had become king.

People stared openly at Briar and Joshua, then at the man they knew as a stablehand. There were murmurs, gasps of surprise. Unlike with the fata, there was no rotten fruit, no jeers. Just shock.

'Is it true he's a prince?' someone asked.

'That's what they say. From Angevin. What has he done?'

'Treason, I heard,' another said.

So the word had got out about Ruric's ancestry. That might work in their favour. Had the regent made a mistake by making their executions public?

As Briar desperately tried to work out some sort of a plan that didn't offer dismal failure, the cart entered the open field, making its way through grazing sheep and the occasional goat.

While the crowd milled around them, the cart jolted to a halt. She searched for familiar faces and found a few. Dimia was a short distance away, crying, no doubt upset that a potential bridegroom was about to become history. The smithy stood nearby, his hand resting on his small son's shoulders. His face was unreadable, probably fearing he and his family might be next.

With effort, Briar worked her way towards the edge of the cart, then on to the ground where Joshua joined her. Ruric halted a few feet away, his mouth set in a grim line. His eyes met hers and she could see he was blaming himself for this.

Sorry, guy. I was supposed to make this right and all I've done is screw up.

'Over here,' the lead guard ordered. He was one of the human ones, but his tone told her it'd be a waste of time to expect any compassion on his part. How did someone become like that? Had all the deaths made him cold inside? At what point did he decide that it was better to be a tool instead?

Briar heard the rattle of the carriage before she saw it, and as before, the regent's elite metal guards escorted the vehicle, their faces reflecting the morning sunlight.

'Oh, damn,' Joshua said.

'What?' she said as she turned back.

He pointed towards the huge oak tree where a noose dangled from one of the main branches. The regent wasn't going to turn one of her metal monsters loose to kill them – she was going to have them hanged, one by one.

'Oh, God . . .' Her hands began to shake and her throat went arid.

Joshua nudged her. 'Come on, don't lose it now. You can do this. This is *your* dream, not hers.'

'But—'

'It's yours!' he insisted. 'You'll find a way to defeat her. I know it. You wrote the story in the first place, right? Reclaim it, and write a new ending.'

He believes in me. It was there in every word, the unyielding faith that somehow she could pull this bloody disaster out of its death spiral.

Briar closed her eyes, trying to scrape together any bit of

courage she could summon. For some absurd reason Elmer Rose came to mind, the scrawny country boy who had run through withering rifle and artillery fire to try to save his home and family. He had failed, but he had done his best in a war that had torn the world apart, no matter if you were blue or grey.

Remembering the portrait of him over the mantel at home, Briar borrowed some of Elmer's strength. Something must have changed on her face because Joshua gave her a nod.

'That's it,' he said. 'Whatever you're doing, keep it up.'

'I'll try.'

The instant the carriage came to a halt, the footman stepped forward and opened the door. As usual, the regent exited, her leather bag in hand, a demonic Mary Poppins without all the merry chimney sweeps.

Another figure emerged from the gloom of the carriage, one Briar hadn't expected. The princess wore a deep blue gown and a matching cloak, her hair stylishly arranged high on her head, as if she were going to a ball rather than an execution. In her hand was a jewelled scabbard, probably some relic of state or something.

Where is my bracelet? What did you do with it?

Now that the princess was here, the only plan that made sense was the *toss the fata dust on the tyrant* strategy, one that could fail spectacularly. Still, if the townspeople found out Hildretha was part drazak, that might tip the scales towards rebellion.

The regent took a position on the low wooden platform,

gazing out at the crowd behind that impenetrable mask. The moment the villagers spied their princess, there were gasps and cries of delight. She really was beloved by these people.

You have no idea what she's like, guys. Nevertheless, a snippy royal brat beat a bloodthirsty tyrant any day.

Aurora cautiously made her way to the steps and up on to the platform with the assistance of a guard, acknowledging the villagers who bowed or curtsied to her. She held her head high with an inborn grace that Briar would have found hard to duplicate. As she gestured to her subjects, there was a glint of silver on her left wrist. The charm bracelet.

'You see it?' Ruric asked. Briar nodded.

A tiny muscle at the corner of Aurora's mouth began to twitch, and her smile faded when her eyes fixed on the rope hanging from the tree.

Had the regent told her what was going down?

I bet not.

Once the prisoners were formed up in front of the platform, Briar found herself studying their enemy with curious detachment. Even if the fata's dust destroyed her mask, would Hildretha then use a spell to hide her face? Make the villagers see a woman instead of the real thing?

The footman appeared, paper in hand as usual.

'Talk about job security,' Joshua muttered.

The man paused and waited until the regent gave him a nod.

'The princess has been awakened!' he cried, as if no one had noticed her presence. 'Let all rejoice!'

339

That strident verbal match set fire to the villagers' enthusiasm, leading to raucous shouts and huzzahs. People hugged each other and cried. It was as if they believed all the darkness would suddenly roll back and goodness would prevail.

Not so much.

Once the noise died down, the regent leaned closer to the princess. It was only because Briar and her friends were near the platform that they heard any of the conversation.

'You should return to the castle now. I will deal with this, Your Highness. You should not soil your hands with such matters.'

'You said that I only needed to greet my people. Why are these prisoners here?' Aurora asked. 'Why is there a hangman's noose in that tree?'

The regent hesitated, then her thick voice grew cunning. 'These three are here to receive justice, Your Highness.'

'Whose justice? I did not order their execution, Hildretha.'

'How do you think I have kept this kingdom in order all these years? Do you believe that it managed itself while you slept like a baby?'

Bad move. She still thinks Aurora's a kid. Someone she can bully.

'My sleep was *not* blissful,' the princess retorted, her hands clenched now. 'There were dark things in my dreams and they hunted me mercilessly.'

'I apologize,' the regent replied, inclining her head. 'I fear you are still suffering from the effects of the curse.

Please return to the castle, Your Highness. I shall see to what is required.'

'No, I shall remain,' the princess said primly. 'I must know of such things.'

The regent held herself very still for a few seconds, then gave another nod. This one wasn't as deep.

'So it shall it be, then.' Hildretha returned her attention to the now uneasy crowd. 'The princess has been awakened, but remains in grave peril,' she said, loud enough for most to hear. 'These three sought to slay her in her sleep.'

There were choruses of 'No!' and 'Traitors!'.

'That's a lie,' Briar retorted, taking a step forward. She was promptly shoved back in place by a guard.

'We only wanted to help you, Your Highness,' Joshua called out.

'That is the truth,' Ruric added. 'I broke the foul curse to save you and your kingdom, Aurora.'

'By taking it from her,' the regent replied slyly.

'No, to return her to her throne,' Ruric retorted. 'You're the one who has stolen it.'

Murmurs grew among the villagers. From what Briar could hear, the news that Ruric had been the one to awaken the princess seemed popular.

'Enough!' the regent replied. 'Take the boy to the centre of the field and give him a sword. Let him show us how brave he is.'

'Joshua?' Briar cried, grabbing on to him before he could be pulled away. He hugged her tight, ruining her plan to slip him the pouch.

'No, you keep it,' he whispered in her ear. 'You have to live through this, you hear?'

'But, Joshua—'

He kissed her, hard. As he was yanked away, he called out, 'I think I'm in love with you, Briar Rose.'

'Wha-what?'

As Joshua was marched towards the centre of the field, he gave her a cocky smile over a shoulder. 'In fact, I'm sure of it!' he added.

Briar's mouth dropped open. *He loves me?*

Why did guys always wait until the last minute to say stuff like that?

CHAPTER THIRTY-ONE

The guards positioned Joshua exactly where the other man had died, and tossed him the same rusty sword. Once they'd retreated, he sawed on his bonds and cut himself free. Then he looked towards her and issued a brave smile, even though he'd refused to take the fata's dust, the one thing that might have saved him.

The first guy to tell her he was in love with her was about to die.

Briar pushed her way towards the platform, only to be halted by a burly guard. 'Your Highness! You must stop this!' she called out. 'Please!'

The princess was frowning now, but gave no reply.

'He risked his life to save yours. Spare him! This is *your* kingdom, not hers.'

'She saved my life,' Aurora replied, but she sounded less sure now.

'The regent slaughtered your family and your people. You owe her nothing.'

That got through. Aurora turned towards their enemy, doubt filling her face. 'You said my family were killed by the fata.'

The regent ignored her, plucking one of those strange metal stars from inside her voluminous bag. Just as before, she placed it on her gloved palm and blew on it, copper particles striking the object. It began as a tiny chick and, after another breath, she tossed it into the air. The closest villagers quickly backed away.

Briar figured it'd be the buzzard again, but that wasn't the case this time. The little bird began to develop a wicked beak and a thick neck, then feathers formed, sharp and pointed along its breast and on the wings that arched over the creature's leonine back. A tail whipped around in agitation.

Part eagle, part lion. All metal.

'It's a . . .' Briar rummaged through her memory for a list of mythological beasts. 'Gryphon?'

With a screeching cry, the magical creature's wings beat a steady rhythm as beneath it dust swirled. After attaining altitude, it began to circle its intended prey. Joshua didn't have a chance against this monstrosity.

Briar's heart chilled. 'Please, spare him!'

The regent shook her head. 'None would spare me such a fate.'

'My father would not have done this,' Aurora said, trembling now. 'He would not have put a young boy to death.'

'Your father was weak,' the regent replied. 'Mercy has no place here.'

Joshua raised the decrepit sword above his head and shouted, 'For Aurora and freedom! Down with the regent!'

It was a masterful moment and murmurs began to run through the crowd.

'For Aurora and freedom! Down with the regent!' a

strident voice called out. It was Pat's.

At least he's still alive.

Others picked up the chant. Was this the moment the villagers turned on their tyrant?

Aurora had grown pale, her brows furrowed now, but she didn't intervene.

'Silence!' the regent ordered, and there was immediate compliance.

High above them, the gryphon issued an ear-splitting screech and began its hunt.

Joshua stared in horror at the silver nightmare diving towards him.

'Oh man, this sucks!'

Running away wasn't an option. Their enemy would just put Briar or Ruric in his place. Panicking seemed the best option, despite his brave declaration. He'd hoped his words would have shifted the villagers into getting with the programme, but they'd remained too frightened to take their chance at freedom.

This was really Briar's show, not his.

Need to buy some time. Or at least stay alive a little longer.

Joshua could hear the wings drawing closer now and he shielded his eyes so he could track the thing. It was huge, and he swore he saw sparks dancing across its extended claws.

He should have taken some of the fata dust with him, but he'd been too busy telling Briar he loved her. *Lot of good that's going to do if I get ripped to pieces.*

Dead dudes never got the girl, unless they were zombies.

The gryphon's wings ceased beating as it glided in for the kill, the wind whistling across the metal, creating dissonant harmonics.

'Come on. A little lower,' Joshua said. The sword in his hand was total junk, but if he struck at just the right place . . .

At the very last second, the gryphon shifted its claws out of harm's reach. As it passed close, one of the wings slapped against him, flinging him across the ground. The beast was playing with him, softening up its meal.

With what sounded like a pleased croak, it sailed upward to begin another run. Joshua climbed to his feet and took stock: his left arm was bleeding and his sword lay in two pieces.

He looked around, desperate to find a weapon. A chain and shackles lay discarded a short distance away, probably from some other dead guy.

'Hey, horse boy. Need some help?' a voice said.

Joshua whirled to find Pat and his trademark smirk striding towards him. He had a quarterstaff in one hand and a sheathed sword round his waist.

'Yeah, I do. You know how to use that stick thing?' Joshua asked.

The question was promptly answered when one of the regent's human guards tried to intervene. A quick swipe at knee level and the guy was on the ground, writhing in pain. The others took note and backed off.

'Not bad,' Joshua allowed. When the scabbard landed at his feet, he pulled the sword out, pleased to find it was in good condition. He smiled: he knew this blade from the History Channel, it was a hand-and-a-half sword, sometimes called a bastard sword. Sturdy and reliable.

'Thanks,' he said. 'Is Reena OK?'

'She's good. She's keeping an eye on Briar.'

That was exactly what Joshua wanted to hear.

Above them, the gryphon turned and began another approach.

Pat peered up, shielding his eyes. 'Damn, that thing is big.'

They instinctively spread out, trying to judge how it would attack. Would it try to pick them both off at once or choose one as its target?

Joshua adjusted his position, and then had to do it again.

'What is it doing?' Pat called out as the creature changed course yet again.

'Duck!' Joshua shouted as it overflew him and dived at his companion. One of its claws caught Pat's cloak and dragged him along the ground. He dropped his staff and fought with the clasp at his neck.

Joshua raced to free him. Striking with his sword, he severed one of the claws, which fell into dirt, tiny cogwheels whirring inside as it spun in a slow circle. The gryphon screamed its fury and rose higher in the air.

Pat climbed to his feet, breathing heavy as the claw completed two more circles, then ground to a stop. 'Reena's got some dust stuff that takes out the metal. It's way cool.'

'I know,' Joshua said. 'Briar has some too.'

They traded looks.

'They have the ultimate weapon and we have none?' Joshua observed.

'Yeah.' Pat sighed wearily as he picked up the quarterstaff. 'So a chick has to save our butts? That's totally depressing.'

'Beats being dead.'

'Just barely.'

Briar had cheered when she saw Pat come to Joshua's aid. If Pat was alive, that meant Reena might be as well. They might still pull this off.

First, she had to get close to the regent.

Before she could make her move, a metal hand clamped on Briar's shoulder and dragged her backwards towards the oak tree. She fought, digging her heels into the dirt, but it was useless. Kicking and striking the guard proved futile as his metal skin protected him from her blows.

'You must stop this!' the princess insisted.

Finally!

Villagers pressed in from all sides, ringing Briar and her captor. They weren't trying to stop him, but they were slowing him down. The guard began pushing them out of the way, barking orders, which they ignored.

'Set the girl free,' the princess ordered. 'The young man as well. The executions are stayed.'

The guard paid no attention, but the distraction gave Briar the time she needed to reach inside her corset and extract the pouch. She didn't dare waste the dust, so she fumbled with the strings. Her captor abruptly surged forward, ramming his way through the onlookers, and the bag went flying out of her hands.

She cried out and tried to break loose, but it was impossible, the man's grip was too tight. Then she spied the smithy's son.

'The pouch! Get it!' she cried, pointing. For a second she thought he didn't understand her plea, but then he dived in between the legs of his fellow villagers and disappeared.

When he reappeared, the lad had the pouch in his hand. The instant she had it back in her grasp, Briar pulled open the strings and stuck three fingers inside to coat them. Tugging the strings closed with her one hand and her teeth, she stashed the pouch back in her corset to keep it safe. Wriggling around as best as she could, all the while moving inexorably towards the tree and the rope, Briar threaded her fingers down the guard's arm, leaving sparkly streaks in their wake.

'Tag, you're it!'

He continued across the field, unaffected. *Why didn't it work?*

As they approached the tree, Briar began to flail in mounting panic.

Her captor halted so abruptly she bounced off him. His hand began to ripple like lake water in a breeze, the metal disintegrating as whole sections fell away, revealing a tanned arm and a homespun shirt. The guard's bizarre metallic hair fell out in clumps, leaving behind short brown curls. With a cry, the man shook himself like a wet dog and pieces of silver went flying like shrapnel.

Briar shielded her face from the storm of debris, and

when it ended she found the startled eyes of a fully human young man peering at her.

'You freed me!' he said. 'How is this possible?'

'Reg?' a woman called out. 'Is that you?'

He turned slowly, as if still encased in the metal, and then was engulfed by the arms of a young woman.

'I thought you dead,' she said, tears rolling in a great flood.

'I was worse than dead, my love,' he replied, then caressed her. 'Now I am whole.'

Cool.

Gasps came from around them as the villagers' awestruck faces registered what they'd just witnessed.

'She destroyed the metal,' one of them exclaimed.

'The regent can be defeated!'

'No!' the princess cried out. 'Unhand me!'

Briar spun round to discover two of the elite metal guards forcibly dragging the princess towards the carriage. Apparently the regent had decided Aurora was no longer a lovely prop.

'Stop them!' Briar called out.

Once the princess was back inside the palace, it was a good bet she'd never be seen alive again. No Aurora, no revolt. As much as the two guys needed Briar's help, the royal came first.

With a roar of fury, Ruric broke free of his guards. 'To the princess!' he shouted. When some of the village men joined him, they swiftly encountered an unyielding line of the regent's elite warriors, who hacked at them unmercifully.

That only enraged the peasants more. To her credit, Aurora put up a good fight, kicking and shouting as she was being manhandled towards the carriage.

Briar sprinted towards the melee, knowing if she could just get some of the fata's dust on the metal, the guards would revert back to human form and give Ruric and the others a chance to rescue the princess. But she was running out of time – Aurora was at the carriage now, struggling not to be shoved inside.

'Get out of the way!' Briar shouted, frustrated, as she tried to manoeuvre through the jostling bodies. Then she saw Reena just in front of her, notching an arrow in a curved bow, her apparent target one of the elite guards.

'No!' Briar said, snagging on to her arm. 'There's a guy underneath all that metal.'

Reena stared at her and then lowered the bow. 'Hey, you're still alive,' she said.

'Right back at you,' Briar replied. 'We have to help the princess. I have some dust that will destroy the metal on the guards but I can't get close enough.'

'I have some of that too,' Reena said, frowning. 'It's on my arrows.'

Briar thought for a second, then searched around the crowd. She beckoned and the smithy's son trotted up to them. 'Can I borrow your slingshot?'

He peered up at her, nodding. The weapon and a small pouch of stones came her way.

'Thanks. Now go hide, will you? It's too dangerous for you.'

'Not for me. I'm brave like my father,' he said, then took off into the fray.

'Kids,' she muttered.

Reena relieved her of the pouch of stones. 'I'll dip them in the dust, you do the slinging. You're better at that than I am.'

'Maybe when I was seven,' Briar said. She tested the pull on the weapon and was pleased to find it proved sturdy and well-made.

As she waited for Reena to ready the missiles, she popped up on her tiptoes, casting a worried glance towards the two guys – they were still fighting the gryphon. More ominously, the regent was digging into that bag of hers again. What would it be this time? Another flying thing, or something worse?

Reena handed her the first sparkly rock. It would have been ideal to allow plenty of time to set up the shot, but Briar didn't have it. She took the shot and groaned when the pebble bounced harmlessly off the side of the carriage, missing one Aurora's captors entirely.

'Wow, should I go get the kid?' her friend said.

Briar grumbled under her breath as she loaded another stone. Now that she had a feel for the slingshot, the next missile struck one of Aurora's guards on the shoulder. He didn't even flinch.

'Any . . . time . . . now.'

The warrior's shoulder turned darker, then began to disintegrate, revealing the human underneath.

'Yes!' Reena shouted, executing a fist pump. 'Get the other one.'

Briar did as she was told and suddenly the princess had two confused humans at her side. They quickly figured out what had happened and became her protectors.

Meanwhile, Ruric had been hemmed in by three of the warriors and, though having secured himself a sword, was dangerously close to being gutted. With a pleased grin, Briar helped even the odds. One by one the warriors lost their metal cladding.

Around her, families reunited with their missing sons, brothers, fathers or husbands. After the tears and the hugs, the anger rose. Those same men picked up their swords and began to clear a path to their ruler, keen for revenge.

Game on!

Briar turned her sights on the regent. 'Payback time,' she murmured, loading another stone. Moving sideways, she cautiously lined up the shot, hoping for a miracle. As the stone flew through the air, Briar whispered a prayer that it'd do the trick.

It slammed into the regent's mask, causing the woman to reel backwards.

'Yes!'

The regent turned towards her, but the copper didn't disintegrate. 'Kill her!' the ruler ordered. 'Kill her now!'

'Why didn't it work?' Briar said, backing up nervously.

'It doesn't on regular metal. Just her magical stuff,' Reena said, backing up with her, an arrow notched.

Now you tell me.

A village man staggered up, his shoulder bleeding in two places. 'The princess . . . wanted you to have . . . this,' he said. He held out the charm bracelet.

'Thank you!'

Briar took it, and then hunted for Aurora in the scrum. The princess sat on one of the horses now, surveying the battle from a distance. Briar gave her a wave and a regal nod returned.

Briar tucked the slingshot in her corset and then slipped on the bracelet, some of the fata dust coating it as she snapped the clasp. The moment the silver touched her skin, it gave a sharp ping of recognition.

What else can I do with this thing?

When an enraged shout came from Joshua, they turned as one to find the guys reeling from the latest attack.

'Oh, God. I can't hit that creature, it moves too fast. Can't you do anything?' Reena demanded.

'Maybe I can.' As Briar set off towards the guys, her friend called out to her. 'Do not let Pat get dead or I will be seriously pissed, do you hear me?'

Without knowing exactly why, Briar wrapped her dust-covered fingers round the one charm that might just give her a chance to defeat the gryphon. As she picked up her pace, she made a single, crazy wish.

Because, sometimes, wishes come true.

CHAPTER THIRTY-TWO

The gryphon's last pass had earned Pat three deep cuts on his forehead and a couple down his back. Though he'd pounded at it with his quarterstaff, it had had little effect. Joshua had managed to hack off a few feathers and part of a leg, but that was it. They were both tiring and their weapons were pretty much useless. It was only a matter of time before the gryphon won this battle.

Joshua was relieved to see the townspeople had experienced a change of heart, cheerfully bashing their way towards the regent with anything they could lay their hands on. He and Pat needed to be there as well, not fighting some wind-up monster.

Above them, their menace circled, as if it were stalling.

Why? He began to suspect it was intentionally keeping them occupied so they wouldn't be able to join the battle.

But where was Briar? Joshua's eyes darted to the tree in fear. The noose was empty.

Thank God.

The gryphon still glided around above them.

'I wish Reena would shoot down this idiot bird,' Joshua replied.

'If she could hit it, she would have. I think it's too fast for her,' Pat replied.

'Where is Briar?' Joshua demanded. If she was hurt or dead . . .

'Found her,' his companion cried, pointing upward. 'Whoa, check out *that* ride!'

A sleek golden-white horse floated to the ground near them, its iridescent wings forming swirls in the air behind them. Sitting astride the steed was Briar, her cloak and unbound hair trailing behind her.

'Are you *serious*?' Joshua called out.

She beckoned to him. 'Sure! Come on, let's go kick some gryphon butt.'

Pat leaned on his staff, getting his breath. 'You know how to fly one of these things?'

'It's a horse, right?' Joshua replied. 'How hard can it be?'

Briar scooted further back, giving him space on the mount. Joshua sheathed his sword and tied the scabbard round his waist, then moved the blade out of the way as he climbed up to join her. The horse moved a few paces to the left and settled.

'This is the weirdest thing that's ever happened to me,' he said, causing the mare's ears to twitch. 'And that's saying something right now.'

'Isn't she cool?' Briar said. 'Screw driver's ed, I'm turning up to class on this baby next year.'

'You conjured her up on your own?'

'Yeah. I didn't know I could do that. I think it had something to do with the fata dust. I wished for her and there she was.'

'Works for me.'

A series of howls rent the air as a new menace joined the hunt, called to the battle by their mistress. Grey predators streaked across the open field from the village, encircling their prey.

'Wolves,' Briar said, her momentary joy gone. 'So many wolves.'

'Ah, damn,' Reena said. 'Just what we need.' With one last concerned look towards Pat, she began to stalk the new threats. She didn't dare take a shot unless there was a good chance the wolf she was targeting would go down. There just weren't that many arrows.

An idea came to mind, and when she spied the smithy's son, she waved him over and handed him the pouch.

'This is special magic. It destroys the regent's metal. Have your people put it on their weapons. You understand?'

The eager boy nodded and took off towards a knot of village men. He wriggled his way into their midst, and after a lot of hand waving and explanation they began dispensing the fata magic.

Knowing that was the best she could do, Reena returned to the hunt. As she stalked the closest wolf, a primordial bellow came from the centre of the field.

'Oh God, now what?'

The winged horse shied away in fright as a column of dirt surged upward from where the regent had been standing. The ruler's magic transformed her into a figure with thick arms and chubby legs. The limbs continued to elongate as the creature rose in height, first ten, then some twenty feet above the field. Its round, pudgy face sat above a massive chest and neck. It was female and completely nude.

Joshua winced. 'Oh man, my eyes are scarred for life. What is that thing?'

'I think it's a drazak. It's what the regent looks like, at least the parts that aren't human.'

He shook his head in disgust. 'Whatever it is, I just wish it wore clothes. Can't unsee that.'

The creature hoisted a massive club on her shoulders while grinning a mouthful of mismatched teeth. Apparently dental care wasn't a priority for her kind.

A shadow covered them.

'Gryphon!' Joshua cried out as he kicked the horse in the sides to avoid the creature. As they cantered forward, Briar grabbed on to his waist to keep from falling off. Once they were airborne, the winged horse had a mind of its own, veering away towards safety.

'No!' he cried out. 'We have to fight that thing.'

The mare shook her head, clearly thinking that idea was blazingly stupid.

With great effort Joshua brought the steed under control and swung them back towards the gryphon. And found it missing.

'Where did it go?' he asked, looking around.

'Above us!' Briar cried, pointing.

The beast executed a power dive, forcing the horse to sheer away from it. Even before Briar could load a dust-coated stone into the slingshot, the gryphon passed agonizingly close. Just like it had with Pat, a talon shot out and hooked on to her cloak. She tried to hold on to Joshua, but was dragged off the back of the horse. As her feet found nothing but air beneath them, her scream was cut off by the rushing wind. The slingshot tumbled out of her grasp.

With a desperate effort, Briar clutched on to the beast's rear leg with her left hand, trying to avoid the talons. Behind her, the cloak broke free and sailed away causing the wind to whistle through the opening in her dress and up her skirts. She was flashing the entire field. Aware that it had a passenger, the gryphon's sharp metal tail lashed at her, coming perilously close to her face.

She dared not touch the thing with her right hand, or it would disintegrate. But how long could she hang on with only one hand?

'Bring her to me!' the regent demanded in a deep voice.

The gryphon dutifully circled round and began to descend, eager to deliver its cargo. Briar's left arm cramped fiercely, like thousands of sharp knives digging into her flesh. Tears formed in her eyes from the pain.

Joshua flew just below the beast, trying to get in position.

'Jump!' he cried.

Briar shook her head. Gritting her teeth, she tried to wait out the ride, hoping to touch the beast a short time before it landed so she'd have an opportunity to escape.

Another sharp turn. Briar's grip faltered and she slid down the leg. Flinging out her right hand in a desperate effort to keep from plummeting to her death, she grabbed on.

Too soon!

The reaction was instant: the gryphon went into a barrel roll, screeching as if it were on fire from within. Where she'd touched it, the metal began to lose cohesion, some unfathomable chemical reaction that would not halt even though they were still in the air.

As she watched in horror, the process worked its way forward, across the back, the neck and on to the head. Then it reversed its course, aimed towards her.

'Jump!' Joshua cried again.

Terror locked her in place. Beneath Briar's fingers she felt the metal begin to flex as the beast lost its ability to fly. Out of control, it careened towards the old oak tree.

Either she jumped or she fell. With a prayer stuck in her throat, Briar let go. She heard Joshua shout out as his hands brushed hers, and then she was gone. There was no way he could catch her now. He would forever remember her falling away from him like some golden autumn leaf, at least until her bones and her body shattered when she hit the ground.

Momentum tumbled her into the tree and Briar clipped something, crashing into a tangle of branches. The one beneath her cracked, sending her plunging downward. Then she caught hold of a solid limb, cushioned in leaves and tiny branches, which absorbed her landing and poked her in a hundred different places.

For a moment it was hard believe she wasn't still falling. Brushing hair out of her eyes, Briar stared out at the battlefield through the leaves. A wolf went down, an arrow in its side, courtesy of Reena. The prince and the smithy were fighting back to back. Aurora was surrounded by villagers, safe for the moment.

Which left the regent.

'Get out of there!' Joshua called out. He hovered on the flying horse a short distance away, his eyes wild with fear. 'Go!' Then he veered off as a mighty fist tried to snatch him out of the air, like one would catch a pesky fly.

Two massive legs thumped in her direction: their enemy had not forgotten her.

Briar scrambled from limb to limb, ignoring the pain, but the faster she moved, the closer the solid *thump thump* came. A squirrel fled past her, chittering in blind panic. She was still too far up to jump.

A whistling sound hissed through the air, and out of the corner of her eye she saw the club racing towards the oak.

As it struck the aged tree dead centre, Briar leaped into the nothingness.

CHAPTER THIRTY-THREE

Flailing, Briar landed on her back in the grass, every point of contact sending waves of misery throughout her body. Above her, the air filled with the tortured crack of green wood, the death shriek of a tree that had lived for centuries. People screamed and fled as the wood splintered into lethal missiles. Some were impaled nonetheless, their cries nearly overwhelming that of the dying hardwood.

The ground beneath Briar began to melt as giant roots flung themselves out of the earth, like eager new shoots seeking the sun for the first time. Shredded leaves rained down on her in a torrent of green. Her body jumped with the ground as the world-jolting impact of the trunk heralded the oak tree's brutal demise.

Trapped under the leafy blanket, Briar worked to free herself, but her legs were lodged under a limb. Joshua called out her name but when she tried to answer, no words came.

'Briar!' he called again, more frantic this time.

Branches went in all directions as he tore his way to her. Then the weight lifted off her legs and she was in his arms. His breath was ragged against her face and his arms shook.

'Come on, don't be dead,' he pleaded. 'You can't die on me.'

No, she couldn't. Then the curse would win.

Besides, she liked his arms around her. *Really* liked his kisses.

Briar blinked open her eyes and tried to grin into the

panicked face of the boy who'd said he was in love with her.

'Hey, you,' she said, then coughed hard. There had to be a sackful of dirt in her lungs.

Joshua exhaled nosily in relief and whispered something that sounded like *Thank you, God.*

Briar touched his cheek, feeling the sweat. Or were they tears? 'Can I just take a nap? I'm kind of tired.'

He shook his head. 'We've got a buck-naked giant to slay. Then you can sleep, princess.'

That made her laugh, but when she tried to move the clothes fought back.

'Damn this gown! Will you help me with this thing?' Briar pleaded.

Joshua produced a knife and began to make some alterations, slicing off the bottom third of the dress, leaving the back long. When she stood, to her horror she found the gown now ended well above her knees, exposing her legs and those ugly-duckling boots.

After Joshua sheathed the knife, he studied his work. 'Oops. I might have got it a little short,' he said, shrugging.

You think? 'Thanks a bunch.' At least it would be easier to run now.

A near-deafening roar split the air as the regent turned her murderous attentions towards a small band of townspeople. Their three friends were at the front of the group.

Oh God, they're going to get themselves killed.

Reena was thinking the same thing. She'd seen the tree explode with her best friend in the middle of it, and was sure that Briar was dead. Then she'd seen Josh pull her out of the tangled branches.

'OK, girlfriend, this is *your* curse, not ours. We're running out of time here.'

As the regent squared up with them, Reena looked around for the fata. Why weren't they here? They had as much to lose as anyone else. Not that she could blame them. Who wanted to take on a two-storey psycho monster?

My great-gran was right. Sometimes it's better not to get involved.

As she notched an arrow, she swore under her breath. 'Have I mentioned how much this sucks?'

'Right there with you,' Pat replied. He'd traded his staff for a sword now, though he swore he wasn't particularly good with sharp, pointy objects. 'So how do you kill one of these things?'

'They love metal so I doubt the dust will work.'

'We shall have to fight it hand to hand,' Ruric said. He gave the princess a worried look. 'No matter what happens, please keep Aurora safe.' He took a deep breath and marched towards the regent, blade in hand.

'Just a note: that whole prince/hero thing he's got going, it doesn't work for me,' Pat said, shaking his head in despair. 'She is just going to flatten him.'

'Then we have to make sure she doesn't,' Reena replied. 'No prince, no happy ending, remember?'

'I was afraid you'd say that.' He rolled his shoulders. 'Then let's go do something totally suicidal. It's been at least a couple of minutes since someone's tried to kill me.'

Reena grinned over at him, enjoying his sardonic sense of humour. 'You're pretty cool. Not that I'll ever admit I said that.'

'Right back at you, girl.' He gave her a hopeful look. 'Maybe when this is all over we could . . . you know, hang together?'

'Yeah, maybe, if we're still in one piece,' she said. 'But I don't put out, just so you know that up front. That's a no-go.'

Pat nodded. 'Word. I appreciate the heads-up. Keeps me from making an ass out of myself.'

She eyeballed him, trying to figure out exactly what had happened to the Pat Daniels she'd found in the pillory.

What made you change?

Though it looked flash, Ruric's swordplay was pretty much a waste of time, even if he did get some vicious slices into the regent's feet as the beast was busily playing Stomp the Prince. She wasn't doing well – bad eye-foot coordination apparently. Every time she missed, she bellowed in frustration, which only made Reena's eardrums ache.

Yeah, yeah, you're big and noisy. I got that.

In an equally lunatic exhibition of testosterone, Pat raced up and jammed his blade into the beast's leg. It had little effect other than raising the thing's bellow even louder. He'd barely scurried away when a huge hand tried to grab him.

'Guys,' Reena muttered, shaking her head. 'What *is* it with them?'

She moved laterally, trying to find the best place to embed an arrow.

Pat cried out as the regent kicked at him, sending him tumbling across the grass. Her heart raced until she saw him crawl back to his feet. Still, he was moving too slowly and if she didn't do something . . .

Something sharp pricked her in the back and Reena froze.

'You release the arrow and you die,' a firm voice said. A swift glance over her shoulder proved the knife wielder was well dressed and portly, probably an official of some sort. It'd been a miracle he'd bothered to issue the warning.

Then the knife was gone, along with the threat, who crumpled to the ground in an unconscious heap.

'Go ahead, take care of that thing,' the smithy said from behind her. 'The reeve won't be troubling you no more.'

'Thank you!'

Reena studied her target again. *Brain or heart? Which one will take you down?*

'You OK with this?' Joshua asked as they regrouped, his eyes on Pat in particular. *Say yes, you idiot. We can't have Ruric take one for the team.*

Pat nodded, and then the prince as well, though reluctantly.

It was an insane plan: while the other two made a bunch of noise to gain the regent's attention, Joshua would circle behind the beast, positioning himself behind one of the massive feet. If he could reach one of the Achilles tendons

366

and sever it, the thing would no longer be mobile. Or at least that's what he hoped.

Joshua gave a quick look in Briar's direction, but she wasn't where he'd left her. He growled under his breath. He'd tried to convince her to stay hidden, but clearly she hadn't listened. With a concerned sigh, he turned back to the task at hand.

He waved that he was ready, and at that his two companions began a series of catcalls designed to enrage their enemy. Pat, in particular, was crudely inventive, and that earned him the beast's anger. With a snarl the regent abruptly shifted a clawed foot backwards and Joshua had to scramble out of reach to keep from being squashed.

'Will you just stay put?' he complained.

He lined up the sword crosswise to the tendon and then threw himself at the target. The blade caught the back of the creature's foot and nicked the thick skin, but didn't sever the muscle.

The monster reacted accordingly, kicking backwards, throwing Joshua into the air. He landed, hard. If his breath hadn't been knocked out of him, there would have been enough swear words to earn him a week's worth of chores back home.

Above him, the massive body turned as two gleaming eyes searched for the troublesome gnat. Stubby fingers dived down to grab him.

'Run!' Pat shouted.

Joshua scrambled to his feet and broke out in a sprint. He'd gone only a short distance when one of the fingers slapped at him, causing him to do a face plant.

Though Pat and Ruric charged the regent at the same time, yelling and slashing, trying to deflect the creature's attention, it proved futile as the massive hand scooped him up into the air.

'Oh God, no,' Reena said as her friend was carried closer to the beast's gaping maw. She tried to calm herself as she zeroed in on the area just above the left breast. She took a calming breath and set the arrow free. It zipped into the air, the fletching guiding it to its intended target. Even before it reached the beast, the regent moved and the arrow flew past, harmless.

'Dammit!' Reena shouted, pulling the final arrow from her quiver.

'Closer!' Briar urged.

The horse obeyed her, responding to her commands without question as just ahead of them the massive hand lifted Joshua higher. When he struggled in the creature's grip, he gained a bit of leverage, but was still trapped.

I have to get him free. But how?

The charm bracelet tingled on her wrist, a reminder that it was the one thing that the regent feared. Briar pulled it off, clutching it in her palm. As she tried to concoct a plan, Joshua managed to free himself and scrambled up the arm like a monkey.

'Incoming!' Reena shouted a second before the arrow embedded itself deep in the regent's breast. The beast roared, thrashing in pain, nearly sending Joshua hurtling to the ground.

Now it was Briar's turn. This was her against the curse, one on one. If it was going to kill her, it would be now. Briar flew so close she could feel the regent's hot breath, see the madness in her eyes.

'Eat this and die!' Briar called out, flinging the bracelet towards the open mouth. An unlikely missile, the silver tumbled over and over, gaining momentum. Recognizing the danger, the regent made a swipe at the bracelet, but missed, her hand knocking into the winged horse when it passed by.

As Briar and the steed tumbled over and over in the air, she clung tightly to the mare, her thighs cramping, hands knotted in the mane. When the horse finally regained control and levelled off, she shook her hair out of her face. Briar looked back at their enemy, hoping for some good news. The scene had changed: the regent clutched at her throat, eyes wide now that she had just swallowed her enemy's magic. The one thing that could hurt her.

A thick groan issued from her mouth, before she began to choke. As the regent's spell failed, the creature sank towards the ground, shrinking like a collapsing fountain, while Joshua clung to her arm, an ant on a falling redwood. He tried to leap away at the last minute, but his timing was off. A huge cloud of dust swirled in the air as the regent disappeared from sight.

Briar cried out his name, but there was no sign of the boy who loved her.

CHAPTER THIRTY-FOUR

Even before the horse had landed and come to a halt, Briar slid off the mare's back. She sprinted across the field, terror making her cover the distance at top speed. The dust settled, revealing a body.

'Joshua!'

She'd just reached him when he pulled himself up.

'Oh man, that hurts,' he said. His hair was filthy and he had fresh blood on his face. He coughed a couple of times and then gave her a lopsided grin. 'Hey, look, it's a real princess. Love the dress.'

Briar grabbed him, hugging him so hard he struggled to breathe. 'You OK?'

'I'm . . . good . . .' he wheezed.

She let up the pressure, then swiped her hair out of his face. 'You sure?'

He nodded wearily. 'Did we win?'

'I don't know.' *But if we did, why are we still in the curse?*

When she helped Joshua to his feet, he caught her and pulled her towards him. The kiss was quick and dusty, but appreciated.

'More later,' he promised.

'Deal. Thanks for not dying on me.'

'Yeah, let's get this done so we can go home,' he replied.

Moving slowly, hand in hand, they made their way

towards the gathering in the centre of the field. There were no metal monsters storming around, the regent's bag of tricks now useless. Hildretha was on her knees, her mask fallen away, still wearing that strange dress of hers. Her hair hung in tangles as drops of black blood sank into the soil. Her claws dug into the earth, as if she thought she could find sanctuary there.

When she raised her head, the arrow in her shoulder was clearly visible, snapped off near the skin. The regent strained, as if trying to change her features, to hide her true nature, but the charm bracelet had rendered her magic impotent. Now it was plain to see she was the unholy blend of human and drazak.

Around them, people gasped.

'This is my kingdom,' Hildretha said, and then spat blood. 'I would destroy you all rather than lose the only home I've ever had.'

Before Briar could reply, voices rose from behind them as guards swept through the villagers, opening a path for their princess. Aurora was a mess: her dress stained, her fancy cloak ripped. There was a red mark on her cheek where she had suffered a blow.

Briar couldn't find the energy to gloat. She knew she didn't look much better.

Aurora seemed dazed, her attention moving across the field from face to face. She still held the sheathed knife, gripping the hilt so tightly her fingers were bone white.

'That's her father's blade,' someone nearby murmured. 'She has reclaimed the kingdom.'

Boy, I hope so.

As the princess drew closer, Briar knew what was expected and she curtsied as best she could, while Joshua bowed. Only Ruric held his position, and for a moment Briar wondered if there was going to be trouble.

'Princess Aurora,' he said, inclining his head slightly, his way of reminding her they were equals.

'Prince Ruric,' she said.

After a long look at him, Aurora turned towards her people, her hand still clutching the sheathed knife. Briar wondered if she knew she was holding it.

It was vital that the princess say something that would help her subjects begin the healing process. From her blank expression, Aurora clearly had no idea where to begin. She'd always been the pretty flower in the background while her father had handled the affairs of state. Now the kingdom was hers and she was overwhelmed.

'Selfish child,' Hildretha said. 'You have no bones for this. I should have killed you, just as you killed so many of the others.'

Aurora's blank stare faded. 'What do you mean?'

'The creature is lying,' Ruric said, stepping up. 'She killed your courtiers and your family.'

'What do you mean?' the princess repeated, ignoring him.

'I only killed the king and queen,' Hildretha said. She pointed a clawed finger at the princess. 'You killed the rest. You strangled your servants and any who came to free you. It was the best part of my spell, for their blood is on *your* hands, as much as mine.'

Aurora's face had gone alabaster, and Briar feared that she might faint.

'Is this true?' the princess asked in a tremulous voice.

Ruric bowed his head in acknowledgement.

'Why did you not tell me?' she demanded.

'I felt it would do great harm to you to know such things.'

'You had no right to keep it from me.' The princess's ire faded as her expression saddened. 'I remember some of them. In my sleep, there were men talking to me. Kissing me. I longed to wake, but I couldn't until . . .' She looked over at Ruric. 'Until you.'

'What is your command, Your Highness?' one of the guards called out. 'Do you wish the fiend executed?'

Aurora didn't respond, her eyes fixed in the middle distance, no doubt seeing those faces in her dreams again. The crowd grew restless, muttering among themselves.

'Your Highness?' the guard nudged.

The princess's arms fell loosely at her sides, her chest rising and falling with each quickened breath. There was no rejoicing in her eyes, only a decade's worth of nightmares.

Aurora took a step closer to her former servant. 'Hildretha of the Drazaks, you chose to make war rather than live among us in peace. You hid your true form and refused our friendship. Yet I owe you for sparing my life. You could have killed me at any time, and you did not.'

What? She's letting the thing go? Beside her, Ruric sighed heavily.

'Girl's gotta grow a pair . . .' Reena murmured. A grunt of agreement came from Pat.

'I do not blame you,' Hildretha said, her eyes narrowing, full of malice as she glowered at Briar. 'It is *this* one who has brought the evil here,' she said.

'No,' Aurora said, 'you did. You killed my mother and my father.'

The regent didn't seem to hear the change in tone, but instead launched herself at Briar, claws poised to rip out her throat. Suddenly Aurora was between them, her knife buried deep in her governess's chest. The drazak slashed at her, but her efforts fell short. When the princess pulled the blade free, Hildretha slumped to the ground, dying.

A stunned silence fell around them.

'Turn away, please,' Ruric said, raising his sword. 'We must be sure that she is truly dead.'

'Strike the blow,' Aurora said, then watched with glazed eyes as Hildretha's head rolled into the grass.

'So it ends,' he said. 'Your enemy is no more.'

The princess's bloodied hand slowly lowered to her side, the knife and its scabbard dropping from her grasp. Her skin was so pale it nearly matched her hair.

'Where do you wish it buried, Your Highness?' the guard asked.

'Ah . . .' After an extended deep breath, Aurora appeared to regain her composure. 'Take her outside our kingdom. I do not want her body corrupting our soil.'

'What of the regent's metal?' a gruff voice called out. 'What shall we do with it?'

Leave it to a smithy to ask that question.

'Gather it together and have it melted down. If fire will cleanse it of her dark magic, then have it distributed to all. If not, it shall be buried at our borders, to act as a warning to those who would try to harm us in future.'

When the princess turned towards Briar, she seemed to have aged.

'Thank you,' Briar said simply. 'You saved my life.'

'As you saved mine.' Her flurry of orders complete, Aurora wavered on her feet. In an instant, Ruric's hand was on her elbow, steadying her.

'Are you unwell?' he asked.

She studied him, as if seeing him for the first time, and tugged her arm from his grasp. 'Prince Ruric, you have my gratitude for breaking my slumber and killing the . . . drazak. No doubt you are eager to return to your own kingdom. Please send my regards to your father.'

Pat whistled under his breath. 'Bitch slap.'

Ruric's jaw tightened. 'It was my honour to serve you and your people. I shall depart for my home on the morrow. I would not have it said that I had unduly interfered in your realm in any way.'

'That is a wise choice,' Aurora replied, though her voice quavered at the end. 'Take your companions with you,' she said, her eyes back on Briar now. 'No doubt they are missing their families as well.'

They were all being shown the door.

Aurora swept away, and was handed into the carriage, a dishevelled young woman who had just inherited a kingdom and needed abundant courage to rule it.

Once she was out of earshot, Pat shook his head. 'What a hag.'

Ruric glowered at him. 'Mind your tongue.'

It would have been easy to hate the princess, but Briar understood her better than most. Aurora was, after all, part of her own imagination.

'She never thought she'd have to govern a kingdom,' she said. 'Her parents always sheltered her and now . . . she's on her own.' Briar looked over at her friends. 'I know how that feels.'

'Yeah, but you got with the programme,' Reena said. 'I'm not sure she ever will.'

She has to. She has no other choice.

It was then she noticed Ruric staring wistfully at the retreating carriage, as flecks of blood dried along his cheek.

'Cousin?' Briar nudged him, breaking his concentration. 'You all right?'

'What?' he said, startled. 'Yes.' Agitated, he cleaned the princess's knife and paired it with the scabbard. 'She will make a poor ruler and a poorer wife to whoever falls for her charms.'

Yeah, your ego is bruised.

Without another word, he handed one of the guards the knife, then set off towards the cart which was being loaded with the wounded. When he encountered the smithy, they fell to talking, but she could see that the prince wore his bitterness like a heavy cloak.

'No happy ending here,' Joshua said as he touched her arm. 'Well, not for those two.'

Something was wrong. Briar had found her prince and they'd defeated the regent. 'Why haven't I woken up? I broke the curse. Didn't I?' she asked.

'Maybe you're not done yet,' he replied.

Reena tossed Briar her cloak. 'Here. You need this more than I do.'

'Thanks.'

'We'll see you two later,' Pat said, offering Reena his arm. 'Come on, archer lady, let's find some food. I'm hungry.'

'I thought you were all about getting home,' Reena retorted.

His smile faded a bit. 'Yeah, I was. This is more . . . exciting.'

'Meaning your dad isn't here to give you any shit.'

'Yup. Besides, you want to hang with me, because I'm a hero. Didn't you see how I whaled on that gryphon? That thing was totally my bitch,' he said, his eyes twinkling now.

'Pleeease,' Reena said, grinning as she pushed a stray lock of hair out of his eyes.

With a laugh, she took Pat's arm as they strolled towards the town, trading good-natured barbs.

'You know, I never would have seen those two together,' Briar said, pulling on the cloak. 'Not ever.'

'It's simple: she doesn't let him be a jerk, and he likes that,' Joshua replied. 'He respects her. I doubt there are many people who reach that bar with him.'

'He respects you too. You ruled, dude.'

'So did you, Briar.'

She took his hand, mindful of the shale cuts he'd received, and they strolled towards the town, following behind the wagon. Other villagers limped along, some wounded, some crying, some still stunned at how it'd all fallen out.

'The princess is in big trouble,' Briar said. 'She has no idea how to run a kingdom. She has to get strong real soon or this place will be at war in a week.' Or there would be mass slaughter when the drazaks showed up.

'I don't know, she seems capable enough,' Joshua replied. 'She killed the regent. That showed some guts. She doesn't really need a prince to tell her what do to.'

Briar really liked it that he felt a girl could handle things as well as guy. Unfortunately, he was probably wrong in this case – at least until Aurora had gained some experience on that throne.

'She's as naive as I was. Every jerk will offer to help her. If she doesn't go along with what they want, they kill her and take over.'

Joshua thought it through. 'That was one of the regent's mistakes – she didn't murder the princess right off. The next one won't make that error.'

'Aurora knows it and that's why she's afraid. She needs someone she can trust, someone who might have his own agenda, but would be honourable anyway. Someone who has risked his life to save her.'

'You mean like the prince she just ordered out of her kingdom?' he asked.

'That would be the dude.'

CHAPTER THIRTY-FIVE

The village's usual routine was superseded by two things – the treating of the wounded and the need to celebrate. The locals were in the streets now, and though some had lost family and friends, they were mourning their losses by acknowledging their freedom. Food had come from inside homes and shops, and the ale was being handed out without coins changing hands.

As Briar and Joshua made their way towards the castle, they were frequently accosted, offered hugs and congratulations. The pillories were being put to good use, now holding people who had once sold out their neighbours to the regent. Boys cheerfully hurled all manner of refuse at them, most of it horse dung. Briar was pleased to see that one of the men locked up was the reeve. He swore and shouted, but it did him no good.

As the celebration ramped up, Briar found that all this happiness wasn't being shared equally.

'Come on,' she said, tugging Joshua towards the alley with the abandoned well. It took a bit of time to weave through the raucous celebrants, including one very talented man juggling knives. Eventually they reached the well.

'What are we doing here?' Joshua asked.

'Letting the fata out. They have as much right to party as we do.'

'You sure the locals are going to buy that?'

When Briar looked up, her face must been pretty fierce, as Joshua raised his hands in surrender. 'OK, I'm good with it. Here, let me help.'

Even before they could move the boards out of the way, someone tugged on her dress. Briar looked down to find one of the little beings peering up at her.

'Hey, you guys need to come out. The regent's gone. Your dust stuff worked great.'

To her surprise, it shook its head vigorously and tugged on her hand, apprehensive.

Not there now, it said.

'So what is down there now?' Briar asked.

Only darkness.

'What happened?'

It shook its head again as if it was too painful to explain.

In time, they found that the creatures had taken refuge in an abandoned building at the far edge of the village. Once inside, in the dim light, curious faces peered at them.

Briar lit up to see so many of them had survived. 'Hey, guys. Good news! You need to come out now. The regent is dead.' For some reason that silly song from *The Wizard of Oz* began to play in her mind. 'You need to come out now.'

There was much anxious twittering. Finally a brave soul climbed out from its hiding place, its body shaking in fright. Briar took its hand to comfort it, and after some hesitation it smiled up at her. When a second fata appeared, she did the same. When Briar reached the street, she looked back to find that Joshua had a pair of fata of his very own. A steady stream of coloured bodies followed behind them, two by two, all holding hands.

They were taking a great risk and all knew it.

The moment they came near to the centre of the village, oaths flew their way. Then a knot of people drew closer, ringing them. The menace grew like a growing thunderstorm.

Please let this work. They can't be the enemy forever.

'Why are you staring?' she demanded.

'Them!' a man said, and spat in disgust. 'They all deserve to die.'

'It was their dust that destroyed the regent's metal,' she countered.

'You're lying, wench.'

Pat came out of nowhere, suddenly in the guy's face. 'Watch your mouth. That girl saved your ass.'

'Is there a problem?' Ruric said, appearing at the edge of the crowd. His hand sat on the pommel of his sword, promising pain for anyone who crossed him.

'The fata need their freedom,' Briar said firmly.

'They do indeed,' he replied. 'They have done us much good of late.'

He took his place behind Joshua and offered his hands. Two of the fata gingerly took hold. It would have been funny – a tall warrior with a pair of diminutive beings on either side of him – if the stakes hadn't been so high.

Reena joined them. Two fata came up to her and she hugged them tight.

'Are you OK?' They both nodded. 'What about the things in the well?'

Dead. The drazak's magic killed them. We are sad. They were once us.

'I'm sorry, guys. Really. At least you're safe now.'

To Briar's surprise the smithy joined the group, his massive paws engulfing the tiny blue hands of the fata on each side of him. One of them stood on its tiptoes as if to get a better view of this mountain of a man.

The menace didn't ease up, but at least it remained in check as Briar led the entire procession to where Aurora sat on a wooden chair, a makeshift throne of sorts. Her face was still pale, but she had straightened her hair and changed her gown. The blood was gone from her hand.

She rose as they approached. 'What is this?' she asked. 'Why are these creatures here?'

'Your Highness,' Briar said, keeping her voice respectful, 'the fata wish to rejoin your kingdom. Their dust is what destroyed the regent's magic.'

'Is this true?' Aurora asked, addressing the nearest one.

All the fata nodded at once.

'Still, they put a curse me,' the princess said. 'How can I forgive that? Why should I allow you to live amongst my people?'

One of us was wrong. She hurt you. It shall not happen again, the closest fata said.

Unsure if the princess could hear it, Briar translated. 'They admit they were wrong, but they've learned their lesson. They wish you and your people no harm. They only want to live in the sunlight again.'

'What keeps them from turning into those monsters I have heard speak of?'

'It was the regent's magic that did that,' Reena said, stepping forward. 'Your Highness,' she added, 'they cared for us when we were hurt. They are no threat to you or your kingdom.'

The princess wasn't looking at her now. 'What would you do, Prince Ruric? Would you show mercy or would you cast them out?' the princess asked. It almost sounded as if she were testing him.

'If the fata had not shared their magic with us, I would be one of the regent's men by now, more metal than human. I owe them my life, so I am biased in their favour.'

'My father once said that gratitude is not a weakness,' the princess replied. Her tired blue eyes met Briar's again. 'So it shall be.' She stepped forward and reached out a slim hand towards one of the fata.

It shied back, but Briar reassured it. 'She will not hurt you.'

The fata, a younger one, shyly took the royal's hand.

'I forgive your kind for cursing me and I thank you for saving my people,' Aurora said. 'Hear me! All fata are under my protection, and if you harm one of them it is as if you are harming me.'

'What keeps them from cursing you again?' a man called out.

Ruric glowered at him and the guy cowered under his gaze.

Never again, the fata said. *Too much death. Too much sadness.*

'Indeed,' the princess replied. 'They will live among us from this day forward.'

'Mazie, no!' a woman called out.

Ignoring her mother's warning, a little brown-haired girl skipped up, clearly not concerned that she was approaching a princess without permission. Even as her mother called her back, she offered a flower to one of the fata. It smiled, touched the yellow bloom and turned it pink, causing the child to squeal in joy.

It gave Briar an idea. 'Can you fix my hair? Make it the right colour again?' she asked the closest one. A nod came, and when she bent down, a small lavender finger touched her head.

From the gasps around her, Briar knew it had changed back to blonde again.

'That's better,' Joshua said. When she rose, she found the princess staring at her.

'Your hair is as mine. You are nearly a twin to me,' Aurora began. 'You could have taken my place any time you wished.'

'But I didn't. This kingdom isn't mine. This isn't my home.'

Pensive now, the princess beckoned her forward. 'Walk with me,' she said. Leaving the others behind, they strolled under the portcullis, then inside the castle, pausing only at the entrance to the hallway of dead suitors.

'Is it true I killed all these men?'

'Some. Not all,' Briar said.

The princess turned towards her, her hands clasped in front of her. 'I don't know whom to trust,' Aurora admitted. 'Not after . . .'

'You will, in time. You've got friends here. The smithy, for one. But you need to get control soon. There's more danger coming your way.'

'What do you mean?'

Briar told her about Hildretha's prediction that the drazaks would soon come to the kingdom, eager for war and to plunder the metal.

'So that was her plan,' Aurora said solemnly. 'How shall I defeat them?'

'You won't, not on your own. Find yourself some allies,' Briar said. 'From the kingdom of Angevin, perhaps. I hear their third son is an honourable man.'

A faint smile came to the princess's face now. 'Strangely enough, I have heard the same.' She brushed imaginary dirt off her sleeve. 'I am not strong like you. I was not born to rule.'

'You're stronger than you think. Just don't let anyone kick you around.'

'Is it that simple?'

'No. It's hard. I'm still learning.'

With a nod, the princess and Briar headed back the way they'd come, the silence holding between them.

When they emerged into the sunlight, Briar smiled at the sight. It seemed as if there weren't enough fața to go around. A few of the townspeople still hung back, but most had came forward and taken the hands of their former enemies.

Laughter came from all quarters and bright butterflies flitted among the crowd, some of the fata's magic, no doubt.

She found Joshua and gave him a peck on the cheek.

'Well done,' he said, slipping his arm round Briar's waist. 'You truly are a princess, you know that?'

'That makes you my prince, right?'

He executed a sweeping bow with his free hand. 'I live to serve, Your Highness.'

A strange thought popped into her head. 'Do you know how to make mead?'

He was momentarily confused. 'What? Ah, no, but a friend of my dad's does. Mr Roper makes it every summer. It's good stuff.'

'Score!' she said, grinning.

'Is that all you want?'

She moved closer. 'For now. No, wait, a kiss would be nice.'

'My pleas—'

Briar *eep*ed as Pat caught her and spun her away from Josh into an impromptu dance in the middle of the dirt street. A drummer and a man with some sort of whistle played a lively tune, and she did her best to mimic the moves of the others. People were pointing at her savaged gown and laughing.

I look like a complete dork, but I don't care!

As she danced by, she noted Ruric. He hadn't joined the festivities, but stood at the edge of the gathering, a tankard in hand. From time to time his eyes would wander towards the princess, his brow furrowed in thought. Was he mourning the loss of a throne or was it more than that?

A short time later Joshua took over from Pat and guided her out of the throng.

'Come on, let's go for a walk. It's too loud here.'

He fell silent as he led her down the street past energetic children chasing chickens. When they reached the edge of the village, he pointed towards a stretch of grass.

'Here will do,' he said.

Briar could feel his tension. 'Joshua, what's up?' she asked, growing more worried with each step.

He swallowed heavily. 'Do you know who put this curse on me? On us?'

'No, I don't. My mom wouldn't tell me.'

'Oh. It's just that I want payback, you know, but I can't do that if I don't know who laid the spell in the first place.'

'Ask Reena. Maybe she'll tell you.'

'I will.' He gathered her in his arms and planted a kiss on her nose. 'You are awesome and I never want to lose you again.'

'Hey, you're the brave one. I was just trying not to get killed.'

'Same here.'

'No one's going to believe us, you know? Metallic monsters, fata, magical tyrants? They'll swear we've been smoking something.'

'That's if we even remember all this when we wake up.'

That hit her like a stone. 'What if we don't know that we . . . touched. That we're OK together?'

'I've been thinking the same thing. We could go right

back to the way it was before this all happened.'

'No, we will remember all of it. We have to,' she said, touching his chin fondly.

He leaned in to kiss her. As if they'd woven their own spell, the town seemed to vanish around them, as did the aches in her bones, the worries of what faced them at home. Right now, his kiss was sunlight and magic and she wanted it to last forever.

'This is what I've always wanted – you as my girl,' he said softly. 'Now all the guys will be sooo jealous.'

'Bragging rights, huh? Even if they think I'm a slut?'

His eyes went flinty. 'Anyone says that and they're eating my fist.'

All her life Briar had hunted for her prince, the guy with the nifty castle and the fancy horse who'd carry her away from boring little Bliss, Georgia. Though he did own a really fine horse, Joshua Quinn had no castle, no title, no jewels or money to speak of. He was just an ordinary boy who did extraordinary things.

That's enough for me.

Pat looked over at the girl sitting next to him. Reena's dense black curls lay softly across her shoulders. She had a scrape on her arm and her clothes were dirty. To him, she looked great.

He didn't know when it'd happened, but he had a thing for Reena Hill, the sassy girl who never cut him any slack. She wasn't in awe of him for who he was or how much money his family had. She wasn't a sports groupie. Her respect for him had been for what he'd done for others, not for what he could do for her.

But, more than that, she'd risked her life to save him, hadn't left him behind to be eaten by those evil things in the well. That had touched him in a way he hadn't thought possible.

Since they were both hungry, he'd managed to secure a small feast: fresh bread, cheese and some fruit. There'd been little talking as they ate, ravenous as they were. Every now and then someone would walk by and stare openly at Reena.

'I feel like I'm in a glass cage,' she murmured.

'They're not used to seeing such a pretty girl,' he countered.

Did I just say that?

Reena must have thought the same thing as she gave him a look that said she wasn't sure if he was BSing her.

'Honest. You are smokin', at least when you're not giving me hell,' he said.

'Nothing you didn't deserve,' she retorted.

'True, but, right now, I'm golden. I killed some bad guys, scored myself some food and a pretty wench. Doesn't get much better than that.'

'Wench?' Reena nailed him on the arm with a mock punch, but returned the grin, which told him she hadn't taken it personally.

Pat scored a piece of roasted meat from a serving lad and presented it to her with a bow.

'You make a great servant, you know that?' she teased.

The good vibes faded away. 'God, don't ever say that in front of my father.'

'Your old man really brings you down, doesn't he?' she asked.

'Yeah. He's good at that. If we start hanging together, you'll have to meet him and my mom.'

She choked on the cheese and he thumped her back until she waved her arm to indicate she was OK.

'If you're fine with that, I mean,' he added.

'Your dad is *not* going to like me,' Reena said, running a hand up and down her body. 'I'm not his *type*, if you get my meaning.'

'Because you're black?' he joked. 'Well, I don't care. Feel free to get in his face. You killed a bunch of mechanical wolves and wounded the regent. You can stand up to my old man, no sweat.'

The light in her eyes dimmed.

'Hey, what happened? You're not smiling any more. What did I say?' Pat said as he jostled her elbow.

'Why are you interested in me?'

His brows lowered. 'You know, that's a good question. I've been trying to figure that out myself. I think it's because you're not trying to impress me just because my family has money. You're . . . real, you know?'

'So you're not using me to get back at your folks because I'm black?'

'What? Hell, no.' But she'd read him right, at least in the past. 'I used to do that kind of thing, try to shock them, but not now. It's not worth the hassle because my folks never got it anyway. And it always hurt whoever I was with at the time.'

He tried not to hold his breath while she thought that through. 'Look, if you're not good meeting the parentals, then we don't have to do that.'

'No, I'm OK with it now I know where you stand. I just didn't want to get . . . hurt again,' she said, quieter now.

He gently touched one of her curls. 'I don't either.'

Reena drew a deep breath. 'It goes both ways – you'll have to meet my folks too and, trust me, they'll grill you within an inch of your life.'

'Since I'm not into ripping off cars I should be fine.' Then he realized there might another issue. 'Are they going to have a hassle about me being . . . white?'

'No. They just don't like jerks.'

'No sweat, then,' he said. Pat offered her another piece of cheese and then stole it back the moment her lips came close to it. He kissed her cheek instead.

'You dog!' she said, laughing. Then she leaned in to kiss him again.

He put his arm round her and she laid her head on his shoulder as the celebrations continued around them.

So much had changed while he'd been here, in ways he'd never anticipated. He'd found something inside of himself he liked, a strength that didn't come from his father or his family name. It was something he could claim as his, alone.

Let's hope it's still there once we get home.

CHAPTER THIRTY-SIX

As she'd hoped, Briar found Ruric in the stable, curry-combing the mare who had been reclaimed from the reeve. She looked in good shape, her coat glossy and not in need of care: Ruric was just finding things to do to keep himself from brooding about Aurora. It wasn't working.

His face harboured a thundercloud and his movements were so abrupt that he was spooking the horse.

'Sorry,' he said. 'Don't worry, we'll be out of here soon enough. No one will miss us.'

'I will, cousin,' Briar said, leaning in the doorway, her arms crossed over her chest.

'You're about the only one,' Ruric replied without turning round.

'You're giving up too easily,' she said. 'I didn't expect that from you.'

He did turn this time, and his expression made her wonder if she'd gone too far.

'I have been informed I am not needed. It is *her* kingdom, after all. She'll learn her lessons soon enough.'

'With scheming courtiers or some loser of a prince?'

'Just so. Those kinds are only interested in feathering their own nests. If she does not do what they wish, a slip of poison in her wine or a push down the stairs will solve their problem. They are just as dangerous as the regent, only more subtle.'

He wouldn't be so worried if he didn't care.

'Aurora's worth fighting for. She's not as stuck up as you think.'

The prince snorted. 'You are just grateful she saved your life.'

'Yes, I am. But she's still worth it.'

'No. I journeyed to this village to claim a wife and a kingdom, and found myself fighting a tyrant. Now everything feels wrong somehow. I blame you for that, all that nonsense about marrying for love,' he said, picking up the closest hoof and examining it critically. He apparently discovered something he didn't like as he began to dig at it with a hoof pick.

Briar sank on to a milking stool. 'I was right, you know. You shouldn't marry someone for duty or to please your parents.'

'That only works for those who do not have noble blood in their veins.'

'Don't give me that,' she retorted. 'You royals are in charge of everything, so change the rules. If peasants can marry for love, so can you.'

'This conversation is a waste of time,' he growled. 'The princess has no interest in me, and so I shall not plague her with my attentions.'

'You really like her, don't you?'

He let loose the hoof and straightened up. A deep sigh came next.

'I admit I admire her. Who may fathom how horrific those nightmares were as she slept, yet she survived them.

She appears intelligent and is very pretty. She would make someone a fine wife.' He groaned. 'God's blood, you are right – I am smitten good and proper, and it has nothing to do with her throne.'

Briar kept the grin to herself. Placing her elbows on her knees, she leaned her chin on a palm. When she noted that Ruric's attention was now on her legs, she pulled the cloak around to cover them.

'What is it with you boys? You'll take on an ogress or a pack of wolves all by yourself, but if you like a girl you get all stupid.'

Ruric frowned in her direction, but didn't dispute the point.

'Just tell her you like her.'

'No, that will seem self-serving,' he said. 'She knows I came here to claim a kingdom through marriage. I *do* have my pride.'

'So what? You both know where you stand. It's what you do after this moment that counts.'

Ruric's face grew troubled, as if he foresaw a loss he could not bear. 'Do you believe she will even listen to me, or will she just order me thrown out of the kingdom like some troublesome beggar?'

'Only one way to find out.' *No guts, no glory.*

He took a deep breath then sighed. 'I shall try, then. My pride demands that I leave, but my heart says . . .'

'That love might be yours.'

He gave a soft smile. 'And what of you, cousin? Have you found your true love now?'

'Yes, I think I have. Joshua is . . . everything I ever wanted.'

'Has he a kingdom?' Ruric joked.

'No, but that doesn't matter. When I'm with him, I feel that I can fly. He makes me so happy. I can't imagine losing that, you know?'

'Ah, I seem to suffer from a similar affliction when it comes to Aurora,' he admitted. 'I had no idea such an emotion could strike me down so quickly.'

'Told you.' She rose. 'I have to go home now. I can't stay here.'

They embraced and he placed a chaste kiss on her cheek.

'Be well, Briar Rose,' Ruric said, his dark eyes sad. 'You are a marvel. I have learned much under your tutelage.'

'As I have with you, Prince Ruric, son of whomever it was.'

He laughed, then quickly sobered. 'I shall miss you very much.'

'Same here. You're now my most favourite cousin *ever*.'

With one last look at her fairy-tale prince, Briar exited the stable, melancholy. It would be hard to leave him behind, he was so real to her.

She'd only gone a few paces to find Aurora waiting a short distance away. Two guards loitered behind her at a respectful distance.

'You heard all that?' Briar said softly as she drew near.

The princess nodded.

'Ruric's right – you are smart, but you're going to need help, at least in the beginning. I know that scares you, but it's for the best.'

'I am truly my father's daughter. I am stubborn, and I often say words I regret. He always said I did not need to know how to command men or negotiate treaties.'

'Parents can be wrong. Trust me on this. Mine have been.'

Aurora inclined her head towards the stable. 'You truly believe Prince Ruric is a good and honourable man?'

'Yes,' Briar replied earnestly. 'When I first came here, he could have turned over to the regent, but he didn't. He kept me safe, even though it nearly cost him his life. He is a man worth caring for.'

There were noises from inside the stable now.

'He is brave,' Aurora admitted, a shy smile in place. 'He is also quite handsome.'

Briar waggled an eyebrow. 'That never hurts when it comes to princes.'

'Then I shall trust your intuition, Briar Rose. I pray you are not wrong.'

'Just live your own story, not someone else's. I made that mistake. I won't ever do it again.'

'Thank you. You are welcome to visit again, if you wish.'

'I will remember that,' Briar said politely. *But I won't be back.*

Aurora flowed past her and came to a halt just outside the stable doors.

She cleared her throat. 'Prince Ruric, I hear you are departing my realm.'

'I was told I was no longer needed,' he responded from within, his tone chilly.

Briar crossed her fingers. *Come on, go for it, you two!*

'What do you know of King Taltin?' Aurora asked. 'Is he an honest man or a craven one?'

There was a pause before Ruric answered. 'The old king was a good soul. His son, the current ruler, is . . . vile. Why do you ask?'

'Word of the regent's death will spread quickly. I suspect that Taltin will be sending emissaries to my court very soon. What will they say to me?'

'Nothing but lies. Taltin wishes this kingdom as his own, so he will propose a hasty marriage.'

'Is he worthy?'

'Hardly,' Ruric said, his voice hardening. 'He is a liar and a debaucher. You would do better to wed a venomous snake than that man.'

'I see,' the princess said pensively. 'You know him well?'

'I met him once. He tried to obtain my sister's hand in marriage. My father sent him packing.'

After giving Briar a quick glance, the princess stepped further inside the stable.

'Would you consider . . . remaining here until such time as I have rebuffed his offer, lest the viper feel the need to employ his fangs?'

There was a very long pause this time.

Say yes, you idiot!

'I would be honoured to assist you in any way possible, my princess.'

'I am pleased to hear that. Perhaps you would care to move your horse to the royal stables?'

'No, not just yet,' he said. 'I do not want to . . . unnerve her.'

'I see,' the princess replied, taken aback.

No, he's not going to just roll over. You're both going to have to work for this.

'Dine with me on the morrow,' Aurora said. 'We have much to discuss.'

'I am at your service, Your Highness.'

Yes!

Briar scooted down the street before Ruric knew she'd helped orchestrate the whole encounter. In her mind she saw how this might play out: as soon as the snaky King What's-his-face had been dealt with, there would be another issue, then another. Some day, hopefully soon, the stubborn royals would realize they couldn't live without each other.

Then they'll live happily ever after.

Bubbling, and in a terrific mood, Briar found her friends waiting for her at the end of the street. They, on the other hand, were sombre.

'And?' Joshua asked. 'How'd it go?'

'Ruric is staying. It's up to them now.'

'You did good,' Reena said. 'Now let's go home.'

'Yeah,' Pat added. 'It's been real, but I'm missing hot showers.'

It *was* time to leave, though that was proving harder than Briar had anticipated. Despite all the horrors, there were parts of this little village she would miss.

The fata. Ruric. Even the princess.

'So how does this work?' she asked.

Her friends traded looks.

'Um . . . I used a crossroads key to get us here so that's how we go home,' Reena explained.

That sounded pretty thin. 'Ohhkay . . . but I have to get home on my own, right?'

Her friend nodded.

They hiked out of the village and along the way, Briar paused to study the battleground and the decimated tree. The regent's body was gone and a small mound of metal had begun to form. No doubt, the villagers would keep collecting it over time. Who knew, maybe some day a beautiful oak would grow once more.

'Hey, we're almost home,' Joshua said, his hand taking hers.

'I can't wait to see my parents' faces when I wake up.'

He kissed her and they walked on.

Once Reena had found a likely spot, she made her preparations: they proved more involved than Briar had anticipated. First her friend lit a candle and buried its base in the dirt. By its weak glow, she drew lines around it, though Briar couldn't figure out what they meant. Then Reena sprinkled some sort of herbs here and there.

'She did this stuff to get you guys here?' Briar whispered to Joshua.

'Yeah, I guess. I was in my bed at home and then – *bam* – I was here.'

'OK, guys, we need to sit in a circle,' Reena said, beckoning.

'Just like at camp,' Pat said, plopping down next to her. 'Do we get to hold hands?'

'If that keeps you from losing it, sure.'

Joshua grabbed Briar's hand and then pulled her into his arms. The kiss they shared was beyond her imagining, a physical duet of emotion and yearning. Their tongues touched and her body set on fire.

When it ended, he sighed deeply and caressed her hair. 'See you on the other side.'

He joined the other two in the circle. Pat's face was easy to read – he was totally freaked out. Reena, however, appeared calm as she tugged a ribbon from under her dress. At the end of it was a skeleton key along with something Briar recognized as hers.

'Is that from my charm bracelet?' she asked.

Her friend nodded and then winked. 'See you soon, girlfriend.'

Briar moved some distance away, then watched their faces in the dim candlelight as Reena began her ritual. When she had finished, Joshua asked her something, though Briar couldn't hear what was being said. Her friend gave him a sharp shake of the head. He asked again, more forcefully.

This time Reena answered him. The reaction was instant: Joshua went rigid. His eyes met Briar's and she saw shock and anger reflected in them.

'Joshua, what's wrong?'

Before he could answer her, a swirling tunnel popped out of nowhere and encompassed her friends. A blast of chilly air struck her straight on, throwing Briar on to her butt in the earth. Before she could regain her feet, the tunnel had sucked them away.

Her friends were gone, and she was still inside the curse.

Briar hiked back to the town where braziers flamed high on the castle and the festivities continued. With each step her dread grew. What if she was wrong and the curse *had* won and she was dead back home? Was this her home now?

Knowing nowhere else to go, she returned to the stable. The doors were locked so with considerable effort she got herself in through the rear window, landing in the hay below.

This was where she'd started. Well, not quite – she'd actually begun this tale in an alley, but she wasn't going there. Instead, Briar stretched out on a patch of fresh hay in the back corner, staring up at the hewn beams faintly illuminated by the moonlight streaming in the window.

Trying not to cry, she began to make a list of things to do if she was stuck here. She certainly didn't want to take care of horses forever. *I could become Aurora's lady-in-waiting.*

No, that didn't sound good. There would be no Reena, no parents. *No Joshua.*

'I need a pair of ruby slippers,' she murmured. She'd be clicking them together right about now. 'Hey! Whoever is listening up there! I want to be back in Bliss, with my family. I want to hang with my friends and my guy. I don't belong here. I never did. I fixed the tale. I want to go home.'

As time crept by, her eyes drifted shut and the nightmare began anew.

CHAPTER THIRTY-SEVEN

Briar was on the side of the road again, the one near Bliss, as the boy walked next to her. The accident nightmare was repeating itself again.

No. This can't be. I broke the curse.

Or had she?

The lights of the oncoming car drew closer, then came the sound of brakes and the skid of tires on gravel. On instinct, Briar brought her hand up to shield herself, but it was a futile gesture as the agonizing impact tossed her into the air, just as it had every other time.

Then it began again, a seemingly endless loop.

'No!' she shouted. 'I won't die here.' Not after all she'd been through.

Heart pounding, Briar waited until the last minute, then walked straight towards the car lights, accepting her fate like she had the last time. Maybe that was key.

This time the seconds slowed, like individual frames of a movie. She witnessed the gradual movement of the car towards her, the headlights catching her in their stark glow. Ignoring everything else, Briar sought the face of whoever was behind the wheel. At first she couldn't see who it was, but gradually the driver came into focus.

As the car struck Briar for the final time, she cried out: 'I accept this curse! I accept it and break it, *now!*'

Briar woke because something fuzzy licked her face, probably the ewe checking her out again. She waved a hand and the licking stopped.

Then started up again.

She really didn't want to open her eyes. What if all she saw was the sheep, the horses and the stable? The longer she kept them shut the longer she could imagine this was Dragonfly running her rough tongue across Briar's cheek. Or that the hay felt more like her own bed.

Holding her breath, she gave in and opened her eyes, which took some time to adjust to the light. Fake stars hung above her. If she saw them, Ruric and the stable were history.

Ohmigod, I'm home!

She sat up in bed, her heart hammering, and the sudden movement made her cat bolt out of the door. A quick look at the digital clock told her it was close to seven in the evening. Shadows were lengthening outside, and from the open window came the lulling sounds of small town Bliss. There were no carts in the streets, no howling wolves or the screeching of evil things. Instead there was the throaty roar of Mr Anchor's gas-powered weed eater and the Cromptons' antisocial mutt kicking up a fuss.

Briar checked herself over, looking for bruises or cuts. There were none. Her nail polish was back in place and the charm bracelet was on her wrist, minus the little woodsman and his axe.

'I'm really home,' she said, astounded. 'I did it.'

Her joy slipped, breaking apart at the seams. Now she

knew what had happened the night of her Aunt Sarah's accident and what it meant. What her aunt's death had cost both her and Joshua.

Briar located her cellphone on her desk and fired it up. She wasn't surprised to find that Reena's text sat on the very top.

All of us are home. You better be too! Call me.

She wasn't in the mood to talk, not yet, so Briar sent back a message.

Home. What was Joshua upset about?

Briar waited for a reply, fidgeting as time passed, but there was none.

Why was he so upset? What did Reena say to him?

The creak of the stairs told her someone was headed upstairs, her dad, she thought, as his steps were heavier than her mom's. They sounded weary because he usually moved faster than that. She set the phone aside as her father walked in the door, unshaven, with dark bags under his eyes, as if he hadn't slept in days.

He stared at her, blinking rapidly.

'Hey,' Briar said, feeling the tears build. 'I'm back. Do I get a hug for that or what?'

'Maralee!' her father shouted, and then dived for the bed. He scooped Briar in his arms and hugged her so tight that his whiskers scraped against her face. She didn't care. She was home.

Her mother flew into the room, her eyes wide and her mouth quivering.

'Briar . . .' she whispered, then sank on to the bed. She touched her hair, her face. 'Oh, God, you're awake.'

It all went totally emotional. There was no way it couldn't be with two parents crying and hugging her and Briar doing the same thing back. Even the cat got into the middle of it, figuring it was a great place to score a few scratches.

Finally Briar prised herself free and leaned back against the headboard, wiping away the tears. The toll on her parents was evident: rumpled clothes, gaunt faces, her mom's hair in a ponytail – something she never did unless she was sick.

'How long did I sleep?' she asked. *Months, years? Did I miss my junior prom?*

'It's Monday night, so it's only been a couple of days,' her father replied.

'Really?' Briar said, surprised. 'It felt longer than that. Time must have been different inside the curse.'

'Lily told us you weren't alone in there. She said Reena and the Quinn boy found a way in. Is that true?'

'Yeah, it is,' Briar said, smiling now. 'And Pat Daniels, a guy from my class. But he was kind of there by mistake.'

'I never would have expected the Quinn boy to take that risk,' her mother said as she dabbed at her tears. 'Not after . . .'

Their eyes met and the truth sat between them like an unwanted guest.

'Who put the curse on him?' Briar asked. 'Was it you, Mom?'

Her mother hung her head, which was answer enough.

That must have been what Reena told Joshua right before they left the village.

He knows. Now he'll hate me.

Briar wiped a final tear away, her emotions see-sawing back and forth. Part anger, part she didn't know what. At the heart of the matter, she knew her mom wasn't evil.

'It's because of the accident, right?' she asked.

'Yes. I didn't mean it to be that way,' her mom said, looking up now. 'I was in the car with Lora that night, and she was driving, because I'd been drinking. We'd celebrated my engagement to your father.'

Briar's dad pulled her closer. 'Go on, Maralee. She has to know all of it.'

She nodded weakly. 'We were laughing and joking and then there were these two kids in the road and she hit them. I didn't realize until we got out of the car that one was . . . Sarah. She'd snuck out of the house. She was always doing that.'

'Who was the boy?' Briar asked.

'Randy Miller. He ended up with a concussion,' her dad replied. 'Your aunt took the full hit. No charges were filed – Lora wasn't drunk, and you know how dark that road is at night. It was just an accident.'

'Which nearly destroyed two families,' Briar said. Four, if you counted Pat and Reena's people. 'You aren't into magic, Mom. At least I've never see you do it. Who made the spell?'

'A woman in Savannah,' her mother replied. 'I . . . swear I didn't tell her to kill the boy. I just wanted Lora to feel the pain I was feeling, how much it hurt to lose someone you loved. I was so angry, you see. I just couldn't get over Sarah's death. She was my favourite sister.'

Briar waited her out, sensing there was more.

'The woman gave me a bag of some strange powder to put outside the Quinn's house,' her mom said. Her eyes met Briar's now. 'One night I slipped over and did just like she said. When nothing happened, I forgot about it. Lora never even knew, and we just drifted apart. I didn't know that she was pregnant at the time and that the curse would go after her son.'

Lily had said the spell had got out of hand and for whatever reason it had latched on to Joshua and then moved to Briar. Which, in a karmic sort of way, was righteous since her mom had started the whole thing.

'When did you know the curse had crossed over to me?' she asked.

Her mom's upper lip trembled, but she didn't answer.

Her father stepped in. 'Lily saw you at a picnic a couple of weeks after you nearly drowned. She knew something was wrong with you. It took her a while to figure it out. She told Lora what had happened. She was furious that I'd put the curse on her in the first place, and terrified that you would somehow pass it back to Joshua.'

'It was equally my fault,' her dad added. 'I never really believed any of this until . . .'

'I fell asleep for forever?' Briar asked, irritated.

He nodded.

They'd both let her down, made arbitrary decisions without telling her what was going on. Parents often did that, but this was bigger than that.

'How did you break the curse?' her father asked, clearly uncomfortable with her silence.

'I fought it on my terms,' Briar said. 'It was . . . hell.'

The high colour on her mother's cheeks faded, as if she were trying to imagine that hell.

'There's some good out of this – I'm not dead,' Briar said, which was kind of obvious. 'And . . .' *Just tell them.* 'Joshua and I are . . . a couple now.'

She waited for the reaction, so tense her back ached in protest. If her parents tried to ruin this, she'd lose it. Not after all she and her guy had been through. 'We . . . really like each other,' she added. 'I know how you feel about the Quinns, but you guys owe us this one. We're together now.'

Her father's instant frown told her she was skating perilously close to a reprimand. She didn't care.

'I'm not the same Briar that fell asleep. While I was in the curse, I learned things about myself. I fought monsters and I kicked butt.' Briar took a deep breath to give her time to get her thoughts in order. This was so important she had to get it right.

'Since there's no more curse, my life is no longer on pause. I want to get my driver's licence, go to Disneyland, do all sorts of stuff you never let me do before. I'm not your little girl any more. I'm . . . a new me. I can handle it, really.'

With a thick sob, her mother fled the room.

Briar groaned and thumped her skull against the padded headboard. 'Oh man, I just want a life. Why is that such a big deal?'

Her father stared at her. 'You are different,' he said, and from his tone she wasn't sure if he liked that or not. 'It'll take a while for us to adjust to this new . . . Briar. Especially your mom. She's spent so many years trying to keep you safe from imaginary threats.'

'Some of which were totally real.'

Her dad nodded ruefully. 'Give her some time. She made a huge mistake, grieving too long for a sister she loved so very much. She never meant to hurt either of you.'

Briar quirked an eyebrow. 'So do you guys get grounded when you screw up? I mean, it'd only be fair since I get nailed when I do.'

Her father blinked and then a faint smile curved up the corners of his mouth.

'Sorry, no. Part of being a parent. You'll find that out some day.' His eyes misted. 'God, now that's a possibility, isn't it? Boys and college. Maybe even a wedding.'

She thought of Joshua. Would they still be together after high school? College? Could this whole curse thing have set them up for a life together?

'Yeah, I get all that now,' she said, smiling.

Her father bent over and kissed her forehead. 'Come downstairs when you're ready. We'll make you some food. What do you want?'

'Breakfast. Lots of it. I'm starving.'

'Coming right up.'

When he reached the door, Briar called out. 'Tell Mom I still love her, no matter what. But no more magic, OK?'

'I think you'll find she'll be a lot better now.'

'Only if she makes peace with Joshua's mom.'

He sighed, his smile fading. 'I know. That will be harder than you can imagine, for both of them.'

CHAPTER THIRTY-EIGHT

Briar took her worries to the shower and made the water hotter than normal. Slowly her muscles came back online, so that by the time she was dressing she could move around with few twinges or aches. Fortunately there were no bruises, nothing other than the feeling that she'd been in bed too long.

As Briar towelled off, she checked her cellphone – no call from Joshua, but then he wouldn't have her number. *Just chill. You'll see him soon.*

As she dressed, quiet conversation floated up the stairs from the kitchen, the kind that only allowed you to catch every tenth word or so. Parents were masters at that. When she heard Joshua's name, it made her smile.

Her parents were waiting for her at the kitchen table, and from the heavenly smells, the covered dishes promised a feast. Briar loaded up her plate with eggs, bacon and pancakes, and began eating faster than was wise.

'Whoa, you must be hungry,' her dad said.

'There was lots of peasant food,' Briar explained with her mouth full. 'It was pretty good. You guys should make some mead. That stuff rocked.'

'Maybe some day,' he said, clearly ill at ease. At his side, her mom's eyes bored holes in the tablecloth.

Briar cleaned up the last strip of bacon and then took

a huge gulp of milk. Feeling the resulting moustache, she wiped it off. 'Thanks, Mom, that was good. I missed your cooking.'

Her mother's puffy eyes rose. 'What happened inside the curse?'

That wasn't where Briar wanted to go, mostly because it was only going to make her mom feel worse, but when her father gave her a nod of encouragement, Briar told them the full tale, leaving out only the really cool kissing parts with Joshua. She told them about Ruric, the regent, the sleeping princess and the monsters. How in some ways the curse had mirrored the story she'd written when she was little, and how it kept trying to find ways to kill her.

Halfway through the tale, her mother's mouth formed an O.

'You actually saved a kingdom?' her dad said. In any other situation that would have been a really weird comment.

'Yeah, I did.' Briar allowed herself a smile. 'All four of us kicked butt. I wouldn't ever want to do that again, but . . . it was . . . amazing.'

The look traded between the parents was one of astonishment. And pride.

'I'm not sure Lora is going to allow Joshua to see you. You have to know that going in. She's very angry at me,' her mother warned.

'Then we have to convince her it's a good thing,' Briar said. 'Because it is.'

He's mine now. I'm not letting him go.

Her phone rang, and she didn't recognize the number. It had to be Josh. He must have scored her number from Reena.

'It's him. I gotta take this.'

Briar raced up the stairs and plopped on her bed as she answered the phone.

'Hello?'

'Briar?'

'Hey! I'm back! Can you believe it?'

'Yeah, I can,' Joshua said. There was no joy in the voice. In fact, she heard something that made her body stiffen.

'What's wrong?'

'You lied to me. You knew your mother cursed me and you didn't tell me,' he accused.

'No, I figured it out right before I woke up. Joshua, I'm so sorry.'

'Your mother tried to kill me!' he shouted. 'Sorry doesn't cover it.'

'But—'

'I should have known it was her all along. Now my mom and dad are talking about getting a divorce because of you people. Are you happy now?' There was a knock on the door, and Reena poked her head into the room.

'Josh—' But she was talking to a dial tone. 'Oh God, he hung up on me.'

'You're surprised?' Reena asked as she closed the bedroom door behind her.

Briar's hurt found a new target. 'You told him, didn't you? Right before you *poof*ed them all home. I saw his face.'

412

'He said he wouldn't leave unless he knew.'

'You ruined it all! How could you do that to me?' Briar flopped back on the bed, staring upward at the faint stars. 'He hates me now.'

'Josh is just upset. He'll chill out.'

'But what if he doesn't?' Her whole *happy ever after* was disintegrating like one of the regent's monsters.

Around her, all the trappings of a naive childhood mocked her clueless innocence. Infuriated, Briar launched off the bed, yanked 'Sleeping Beauty' out of the bookshelf and hunted for the page where the prince arrives to wake the sleeping princess. When she found that scene, she ripped it apart, the colourful illustrations falling from her hands like tattered dreams.

'Hey, what are you doing?' Reena asked, moving closer.

In a rage, Briar reached for another book and tore it to pieces.

'Happy ever after? It's a lie!'

Reena caught her, embracing her before she could continue her vicious literary destruction. Briar struggled, then let the tears roll free. She sobbed, her heart emptying out.

'He said he loved me,' she said. 'One minute I'm his beautiful princess and then I'm the ogress. How does love just stop like that?'

'It doesn't. He still loves you – he's just hurting.' Her friend guided her to the bed and they sank on to the mattress. 'Josh is facing something really ugly and he's afraid.'

'His parents? He said they were getting a divorce.'

Reena issued a long sigh. 'It's more than that. You need to be there for him.'

She did not want to see that face again, see his lips, remember what they felt like when he kissed her. Remember how bad it hurt when he threw her away like she was nothing.

'No, I'm not crawling to him. Joshua Quinn can go to hell,' Briar exploded. 'I don't ever want to see him again.'

'What would that prove?' Reena asked. 'All it would do is move this mess into another generation. Maybe if you or Josh get mad enough, there'll be another curse and then one of *your* kids will find themselves inside some nightmare.'

Briar couldn't imagine that happening. Joshua wouldn't hurt her. Would he? '*No* . . .'

'All things are possible,' Reena said. 'That's why feuds last. No one wants to be the first to say they're sorry and make it right.'

While Briar stewed on that, her friend made a trip to the bathroom, and returned with a handful of tissues. 'Here.'

She took them and blew her nose. From downstairs she heard voices. One in particular.

'Lily's here?'

'Yes. Josh needs you tonight. He's facing something very dangerous.'

'What do you mean? The curse is history.'

'My gran will explain. I just need to know if you're willing to be there for him.' Reena paused. 'Like he was there for you.'

'Is he really in big trouble?' Briar asked.

'Yeah, you could say that. A matter of life and death.'

Briar blew her nose again, weighing all that Reena had told her and what she hadn't. Her friend was nervous, spooked even. Whatever Joshua was facing was truly nasty, and she didn't think it had anything to do with the now-defunct curse.

It was time to set her wounded heart aside, at least for tonight.

'OK, even if he hates me, I'm there for him. Let me know what I need to do.'

Briar fixed her make-up, because if she was going to see the boy who had once loved her she refused to look bad. This time she used waterproof mascara just in case she lost it when the former love of her life blew up in her face again.

Which he will. Joshua had said he wanted payback and now he had a target. When they entered the kitchen, her mother looked marginally better, as if somehow Lily's presence had helped. The adults were at the kitchen table, along with cups of coffee and a plate of brownies. The latter hadn't been touched.

'Mrs Foster,' Briar said politely. As the old woman's eyes checked her out, she felt as if she'd just undergone a full body scan.

'I'm pleased to see yer up and goin', girl.'

'Yes, ma'am. Thank you for helping me get through that.'

'Ya did most the work.' Lily creaked to her feet. 'Yer folks have allowed ya to come with us tonight. I have some

415

things I want to do to make sure that curse is gone for good. Ya all right with that?'

Reena had coached her on this part. 'Yeah, I'm good.'

'Don't stay out too late,' her father said. 'We'll be waiting up.'

'I'll have her back as soon I'm done,' Lily added.

Remembering Reena's warning that tonight could be dangerous, even as she refused to give her any details, Briar took the opportunity to hug both her parents. Her mother's embrace told she didn't want her daughter to leave.

'I love you, Mom,' she said.

'I love you too. Be careful, OK?'

'I will.' *Or not.*

Then they were headed down the front stairs towards Reena's car. It was slow going because Lily moved at the same speed as an arthritic turtle.

As she waited for her to catch up, Briar paused by the front rose garden. She bent and broke off a rose, a pink one that was just beginning to bloom. It reminded her of the ones on the tarot card and the bud's scent filled her with hope.

'How long were you asleep?' she asked her friend.

'One day. The parents freaked when I didn't wake up, even though I left them a note. Lily settled them down.'

A *humpf* came from the old lady.

'You knew what I was going to do,' Reena said, opening the car door for her great-gran. 'You left the spell right out where I could see it.'

'Me?' Lily said, all innocence. 'Must be getting senile in my old age.'

'Riiight.'

'I made sure to go to the Quinns so I could tell them why their son was sleepin' so long. His momma didn't take it very well, him going in to help you. I didn't know about the Daniels boy.'

'His folks were out of town anyway,' Reena said. 'He lives out there on his own during the remodelling.'

At least Briar's parents watched over her, but it seemed that Pat didn't have that kind of love in his life. 'No wonder he's a jerk sometimes,' she said.

'Reformed jerk. He is starting to see the light, as they say,' Reena replied.

'Is he going to be here tonight?'

'No. This isn't his battle,' Reena said. 'He already did his thing inside the curse.'

At least one of us ended up with a good guy.

Once they headed down the street, Briar leaned forward over the seat.

'So what's really going on?'

Lily sighed, a slight wheeze at the end of the breath. 'To get inside the curse, my Reena here summoned the Dark Rider. That's a spirit that lies at the crossroads and he'll share his power with those who call him proper like. But he is a trickster and that's where it went wrong.'

'You summoned a spirit?' Briar said, her eyes widening. 'Wow. I'm impressed.'

'It went OK,' Reena said. 'Well, at least until Josh turned

round. He wasn't supposed to see the dude. The Dark Rider made him agree to a horse race so I could get the power we needed to enter the curse.'

'OK, so where's the problem? Arabella can beat any horse out there.'

'It's not just the horse – it's who he's riding against,' Reena explained.

A cold shiver curved up Briar's spine.

'Once Reena was awake and told me what had happened, I did some scryin'. The Dark Rider has another spirit sharin' that ground with him, and he wants that one gone.'

'If this guy's got all that power, why doesn't he do it himself?'

'That's not how the Dark Rider works. He likes messin' with people.'

'Who is Joshua racing against?' Briar asked as the car turned south on the old road.

'Someone this town hoped they'd never see again.' The old woman adjusted the seatbelt across her bony shoulder. 'Back in 1864 we had a traitor in our midst, a fella named Jebediah Rawlins,' she explained. 'Rawlins was an evil man and he'd made a deal with the enemy that he'd show them where all the jewels and silver were hidden, if they gave him a cut.'

Briar remembered some of this from her history class. 'He killed a couple of sentries so Bliss didn't get any warning that the Yankees were coming.'

'That's right. What he didn't know is that most folks had moved their family treasures out of town and buried them.

That way when the Yankees came callin' they didn't find much, except some food and livestock.'

'They still burned most of the town.'

'True, but Rawlins paid the price because his neighbours knew he'd betrayed them. When he was wounded, the bluecoats left him behind and he was taken prisoner. The townsfolk didn't bother with a trial – just strung him up in the square.

'From what *my* great-gran told me, he didn't die real quick; they made sure of it. Right before they dropped him, he swore he'd come back from the grave and take his revenge. That frightened the townsfolk so much that he was buried at the crossroads so his spirit wouldn't ever rise again.'

Briar had never heard *that* part in history class.

'Rawlins will be the one racin',' Lily said. 'If he wins, his ghost will be set free and he'll roar through town, hacking and killin'. If ya believe in them, a haint can murder folks just as easily as the livin'. And this town does believe in Jebediah Rawlins.'

Hacking and killing? She realized exactly what Lily meant. *My mom, my dad, all my friends.* 'What if this Rawlins guy loses?'

'I'm bettin' he's not gonna go back to the crossroads without a fight.'

'And Joshua?' Briar asked, fearing the answer.

'He'll be the first to die. Rawlins hates Quinns, even though they were relations. He hates you Roses too. It was yer families that hung him and my family sealed his spirit at the crossroads. All of us will be in his sights.'

'Does Joshua know all this?' Briar asked.

'I told him just after he woke up. He said he'd honour his word, though we had to do a bit of lyin' to his folks or they'd never let him out of the house.'

'No wonder he was so upset,' she murmured.

'I'm sure that findin' out that yer mamma was the one who brought down the curse didn't help.'

That's for sure.

'I admit, I set my Reena up to do the summonin' on purpose, wantin' her to take the next step in her trainin', but I didn't anticipate Rawlins's part in this. That's my mistake.'

'Lots of blame to go round,' Reena said softly.

Lily slowly turned her head until she could see into Briar's eyes. Hers were bloodshot and revealed the strain. 'We can leave ya off at my house if ya don't want part of this, now that ya know what yer facin'. We won't think poorly of ya if ya did.'

The answer came without thought. 'No, Joshua needs me. I'll be there.'

Even if he doesn't love me any more.

CHAPTER THIRTY-NINE

Briar stared out of the side window at a pale landscape lit by a quarter moon and scudding clouds. According to Lily, another storm was coming in from Alabama, but she didn't think it would hit until later.

Probably at dawn, just in time to wash the blood off Bliss's streets. At least that might be case if they didn't get that ghost back in the ground.

Now that she thought about it, she'd been too caught up in her part of the curse to realize it had the power to ricochet through their lives like a stray bullet.

Please let Joshua win this race. I can't handle all those people's blood on my hands. I would rather die than let that happen.

There was no answer, as was often the case when she prayed. Briar just hoped someone upstairs was listening and would maybe give them a hand tonight.

Near the intersection of the two roads, Reena pulled the car off to the side, careful to avoid the ditch. While her friend pulled a bag out of the trunk, Briar walked to the crossroads. It appeared that it'd rained that afternoon so the earth was damp, but not muddy, which would be good for Joshua's horse. Too wet and it would be really slippery. As she studied the red clay, nothing about it suggested that a magical spirit lived underneath. Or, for that matter, a Civil War traitor.

Briar turned in a slow circle, like a compass wheel. Three miles to the west was Bliss. The South Carolina state line a number of miles north, and to the east traffic barricades indicated that the road ended about a half-mile down the way. Facing south now, her eyes tracked the stretch of road as it headed along the river, where it would eventually pass by the old bridge, the lane to Lily's place and Potter's Mill.

'Here he comes,' Reena called out.

As Briar returned to the car, a horse and rider came up the road from the south. Joshua drew closer. She could see his face – he seemed different, his jaw set and eyes dull. Nothing like the adventurous guy she'd come to love.

Just hold it together. He needs me here.

Joshua climbed down from Arabella, his heart pounding, feeling sick inside. He'd awakened to find his parents at war with each other, his dad blaming it all on his mom, and his mother furious that Joshua would risk his life for *that Rose girl*.

Apparently even Lily's intervention hadn't helped, only stoking the fires more. His return to the real world had given them something to rejoice about, then it'd fallen apart almost instantly.

My fault. He'd totally lost it at his mom, furious that she'd kept the truth from him all these years. If he'd known Mrs Rose had tried to kill him, he'd never have helped Briar. Why should he? Her family hated his people.

But he'd been doing a lot of lying recently. First, to his parents – he'd told them he needed to go for a ride tonight to get his head straight, which wasn't entirely wrong. He just failed to mention the race and the possible outcome.

Joshua had been lying to himself as well. No matter how mad he was, he wanted to believe he would have gone into the curse to save Briar. That he was better than Briar's mom, who had taken her deep grief and fashioned it into a potent weapon.

At the heart of all this was *that Rose girl*. If Briar really had known about the curse and who had placed it on him, how would that have played out?

Hi, I think you're really cute, Briar, and by the way my mother ran over your aunt and then your mom cursed me to die. But I didn't die so now you get to. No big deal, right?

'Hey, Josh,' Reena called out, breaking his dark thoughts.

It was then he noticed Briar standing by the car, her stance rigid, as if fearing another wound to her heart.

'What are you doing here?' he demanded.

Lily waved a bony hand. 'Come on, child, let's give 'em some room. Just keep it civil, ya hear?'

As Reena went by him, she whispered. 'Don't be an asshat. I won't ever forgive you if you are.'

'I'm not the one who curses people,' he fired back.

'Neither does she.'

To his surprise, Briar made the first move, moving towards him. Her face was paler than normal, with blotchy colour on her cheeks.

'Uh, hi. Uh . . . where's Kerry?' she asked.

'Home. Didn't figure she should be here.' *Like you shouldn't be.*

Briar blinked rapidly like tears were in her future. 'Look, I'm sorry, Joshua. I really didn't know, not until tonight.'

'Lot of good that does,' he replied, his arms crossed over his chest now.

'My mom didn't mean it to happen that way.'

'That's what Lily said, but I'm having trouble wrapping my mind around that.'

'You don't know her. She leaves flowers on my aunt's grave every month. She just can't let go.'

'So killing me was going to make it better?' he demanded.

'No. She never thought that way. She made a big mistake.'

'There's a lot of that going around.' He dropped his arms. 'You haven't answered my question. Why are you here?'

'Because when I was stuck in some hellish nightmare, you did me a solid. You were there for me, and I won't ever forget that.'

'You're here just because you feel you owe me?'

'That and . . . yeah, that.'

Joshua looked away, annoyed. Why had he hoped it was more than gratitude? Wasn't he over this girl? Why did he feel guilty now?

Near the crossroads, Reena and Lily were talking back and forth, ignoring them.

'I . . . know it's not your fault,' he said, looking back. 'That doesn't mean you have to be here. This could get real bad.'

'I know that.' Briar took another step closer. 'Do you remember what you said when they were going to execute you?'

He held his breath.

'Well, I do.'

Another step closer. He could see her shining eyes so clearly now, awash in tears.

'What of it?' he snapped.

She winced, but his cruel words didn't deter her. 'I think I love you, Joshua. In fact, I'm sure of it. Sounds familiar, doesn't it?'

His mouth dropped open, then slowly closed. 'You love me even though I'm a Quinn?'

'Yeah, even that. Can you ignore that I'm a Rose?'

'No,' he said, years of training making that answer automatic.

Briar's expression flattened as the light drained out of her eyes. 'Then it won't work. It has to go both ways. We both have to forgive.'

As she turned away, she hesitated at the last moment. 'Once this is over, I'll give you space. I won't chase after someone who hates me.'

'Hate? Oh God, Briar, it's not that. It's—'

'What? What else would it be if you turned away from me now?' She shook her head. 'I had hoped we could end this, tonight. End it forever.'

Forever? He just wanted to live until dawn.

'I don't hate you,' he admitted. 'I can't even hate your mom, and that pisses me off. What I don't like is what it took to get us here tonight. All the death and suffering, for everyone, Quinn and Rose.'

'I'm there with you. I'm just trying to make it right.'

Like he'd wanted to when he went into the curse.

Joshua ran a hand through his hair, agitated now. 'You serious, you really do love me?'

'Yeah, I'm thinking so,' she said, a faint smile trying to claim her face. 'You're in my heart now and I've never felt that way before.'

'Just kiss her, you wimp!' Reena called out. Lily promptly shushed her.

A faint blush appeared on Briar's cheeks. 'Good luck with the race. You'll win. I know it.'

As she began to walk away, Joshua dismounted, caught her arm and pulled her towards him.

'No more hate,' he whispered into her ear. 'We start over, tonight. You and me. Our folks will just have to catch up.'

Briar reached out to touch his cheek, her hand cold and shaking. He caught it in his own and kissed it.

'I'm glad you're here,' he said. 'I missed you.'

That shy smile he loved came alive again. It was so sweet and innocent, though he knew she had a tough streak that toppled tyrants.

They drew together. He had meant the kiss to be gentle, but it seared their flesh. It didn't end there, but built in strength until he felt his lungs would burst.

The instant the kiss ended he felt empty again. No, not entirely. Briar's eyes shone with happiness. With desire. All of it was for him.

He bent over and kissed her delicately on the tip of her nose. 'I'd best go get ready.'

She refused to release him and the next kiss was deeper, stronger, filled with so many promises. When they broke apart, Joshua smiled.

'Wow. That was amazing.'

'You get another one like that when you win,' she said coyly.

'Promise?' he said.

'On the Rose family name.' Then she grimaced. 'Sorry.'

After a quick peck on Briar's cheek, he returned to Arabella to prepare for what lay ahead. As Briar walked away, she kept sneaking glances at him, her eyes full of love. It made Joshua feel like a giant. For once, his heart and his mind were in total agreement: he was going to win this race no matter what it cost.

CHAPTER FORTY

'Move that white candle over a bit the other way,' Lily instructed.

Reena did as she asked, her knees more flexible than her great-gran's.

'That's good,' Lily said. 'Tonight I'll do the summonin'. Just know, we can't help the boy. It's his race.'

'You have to do something to even the score,' Briar insisted.

'Nope, we don't. That would be cheatin'.'

When Reena looked up, Briar caught something in her friend's eyes.

I know that look. Reena wasn't one to step back and let things go, but then neither was Lily, not when her great-granddaughter's life was on the line. Briar bet they had a plan cooked up, but why weren't they telling her about it?

'If Joshua hadn't made it back from the curse, there would be no race. So what happens if we don't call up this spirit?' Briar said.

Lily was shaking her head even before she'd stopped talking. 'Reena and the boy made a deal and that meant Rawlins was gonna be freed one way or another. The Dark Rider would see to that. It's best we try to control how that happens.'

Joshua, meanwhile, was patiently checking each of

Arabella's hoofs. He'd cleaned out a bit of gravel from one, then reassured himself that the saddle was well secured. In his own way, he was fidgeting. All Briar could do was gnaw on a fingernail.

'We got company,' he called out.

In the distance the glare of headlights illuminated the dirt road. As the pick-up drew closer, Briar and her friends melted back into the shadows, Joshua keeping a firm hand on the horse's bridle.

Would the vehicle roll right over the crossroads, destroying all their work? Why wasn't Lily trying to warn them off? The truck slowed, stopped, and then backed up. Instead of going south, it turned right, heading into town. As it passed, its lights caught them for a brief moment, making Briar blink.

'Only crazy fools are out here this time of night,' Lily muttered.

You mean like us? 'Why didn't they come down here?'

'I had Reena put a little something on the road to send them in the other direction,' the old woman replied, smiling. 'Works every time.'

More magic.

Lily hobbled back to the very centre of the crossroads and double-checked Reena's preparations. She nudged something with a toe of an orthopaedic shoe and then nodded her approval.

'Good job,' she said, and her great-granddaughter smiled at the rare compliment. To Briar, the roots and herbs and little strange things made no sense. Maybe some day she'd have Reena explain it all.

'Do we need to turn round this time?' her friend asked, her own voice thicker now.

'No need. He knows who we all are.'

Even me?

Lily began to sing an old Negro spiritual, deep and resonant, even though her voice was frail with age. Briar could feel the power brushing across her skin, raising the hairs on the back of her neck.

'This is it,' Joshua whispered. He was standing beside her now and his hand took hold of hers. 'No matter what, you'll still be my girl?'

'Forever.'

'Then it's all good,' he said. After a hasty kiss, he was up in the saddle.

Briar gently caressed Arabella's velvety nose, then went up on tiptoes to whisper in the horse's ear. 'Run fast. Keep him safe. Don't get hurt, OK?'

The ear twitched as the horse bobbed its head, just like she understood.

Maybe she does.

The centre of the road began to quake, causing Lily to retreat. Though the magical stuff remained in place, the earth melted, and swirled like a whirlpool. Out of the centre of the swirl rose a spectral horse built of greyish black smoke, and, seated on it, a figure clad in mismatched clothes from another time. A thick noose hung round his neck.

'Oh my God,' Joshua murmured. 'Lily was right.'

The ghost of Jebediah Rawlins edged his horse off the

crossroads, then came to a halt, his gaze never leaving Reena's great-gran. 'I know yer blood. Yer one of those old witch ladies.'

'My father's great-great-grandmama helped ya be born, Rawlins. She saw the mark of Cain on ya then, but didn't tell no one. That was a mistake.'

The ghost spat. 'So ya say.' His obsidian eyes moved to Joshua. 'That the nag yer gonna ride, Quinn?'

'Sure is,' Joshua said, keeping a firm hand on Arabella's bridle as she danced around, spooked by the ghost and his unearthly mount.

'Hear me, Rawlins. Do this race proper,' Lily said, 'or there will be hell comin' yer way, do ya understand?'

The haint reared back in brittle laughter, the kind that seemed to flay at Joshua's skin. The sound sent Arabella skittering sideways, nostrils flaring.

'Ain't any different from the hell I've been livin'. People been ridin' over my grave since the day I was hung. Some even pissed on me.'

'You sold out the town to Sherman's raiders. What did you expect?' Briar called out.

He zeroed in on her, making Joshua wish she'd kept silent.

'I figured there had to be a Rose here.' He grinned. 'It was me that made sure that Elmer died that day. One bullet was all it took. Couldn't have him bringin' no more rebels to the fight, could I?'

Briar's mouth fell open. '*You* killed him?'

'Sure nuff. He had his eyes on a girl I fancied. Name was

Emmie. Fine little lady. Course she didn't like my kind.'
Rawlins laughed again. 'When I'm done, there won't be
any of yer families left in this county. I will find every one of
them and I will kill them.'

Joshua glared. 'How's about you shut the hell up and we
race?'

His mouth earned him the ghost's fury, which was
exactly what he'd hoped.

'Ya Quinns were never kindly to us Rawlins. Said we
was white trash, but I know yer no better than me and I'm
gonna prove it.' Rawlins adjusted himself on the horse. 'So
where are we goin'? We racin' to Atlanta and back? Is it still
on fire like I heard tell?'

Joshua shook his head. 'We are running south on the
road to where the ford used to be. There's a footbridge
there now. Go over that and then back up the other side of
the river to the road that goes to Bliss. The finish line is here
at the crossroads.'

'The hell it is,' the ghost growled. 'I ain't no damned fool.
I'm not goin' anywhere near this place again.' He pointed
at Lily. 'Not with that old witch around. She'll just try to
bind me again and I won't stand for that.'

Joshua gave Lily a panicked look.

She shrugged. 'Smarter than I figured him for. Then it
don't matter now.'

'OK,' Joshua began, then sighed. 'Whoever crosses the
river first at the bridge wins.'

The ghost nodded his approval. 'It ain't gonna matter
where we race cuz I'm gonna beat ya.' He leaned forward

on the horse. 'When I'm free, I'll be sure to treat *yer* family real special, Quinn. It was them that put this noose round my neck.'

If I'm lucky, we'll do it again.

The course Joshua had picked was one he knew intimately. Over the years, he'd gone for hundreds of rides on that very stretch of ground, starting a couple years after he'd nearly drowned and Briar had been made off limits. Out here he could cry without anyone seeing him, and that way no one would make fun of him. Luckily his dad had understood.

Now this very same course was a matter of life and death, for all of them. When he'd checked the route earlier in the evening, there was a small pine tree down close to the ford but he'd made no effort to shift the obstruction: Arabella would sail right over it. She loved to jump, and so did he.

He stroked the horse fondly. 'Easy, girl. I know it's scary, but we'll get through this.' Arabella stomped nervously. She wasn't liking the ghost one bit and his smoke-coloured mount looked as if it had been sired in hell.

Joshua glanced at Briar, to gain strength, and maybe to say goodbye. His distraction proved an error. With a rebel yell, Rawlins kicked his horse and took off down the road.

'You bastard!' Joshua shouted.

Arabella took off at a gallop, ears back and legs stretching. She lived for speed and that was the danger. They were racing at night and any little hole or tree root could send her crashing to the ground. The recent rain wasn't helping the situation as clumps of mud flew from her hoofs.

To his dismay, Rawlins remained in the lead as they reached the first curve, one of two before the footbridge. It was clear the ghost knew this path just as well as he did.

Slowly Arabella began to gain ground as Joshua kept his profile low to cut the wind drag. The longer she went the more her pace evened out and soon she was eating road with every step. The pride hit him head on – this was the most magnificent animal he'd ever ridden, and she was doing all the work.

'Good girl,' he called, though he doubted she could hear him with the wind blowing past them. In the distance, the faint figure of the ghost appeared in front of him. 'We're gaining!' he shouted. Could he win after all?

As if his words were a spur in her side, Arabella picked up speed. She hated to lose and maybe, with some horsey instinct, she knew the stakes were far higher than bragging rights.

The first curve came and went, leaving behind the side road that led to the old bridge. As they angled closer to the second curve they drew neck and neck. Rawlins was whipping his mount and Joshua swore he saw fire coming out of the horse's mouth.

Oh my God.

The ghost glowered at him and the whip came his way, barely missing his eyes. Joshua instinctively dug in his heels and Arabella responded. The second curve was just ahead and beyond that, the downed tree he'd found earlier.

Behind he could hear swearing and the cry of his opponent's horse as Rawlins applied the whip even harder.

The curve came and went and then Joshua was sailing over the pine like it wasn't even there. Arabella didn't land solid, but regained her footing and kept moving. Joshua leaned down, worried that she'd injured a foot, but there was no further break in stride.

'That's it, girl. You go!'

And go she did. The last stretch to the river evaporated in what seemed to be a heartbeat. Joshua had to rein her back to make the footbridge – it was fairly new, only eight feet wide, and he didn't want her to take it full gallop. The horse fought him, loving the speed, but he took control.

Just as Arabella's hoofs hit the ground on the far side, Rawlins came tearing up behind them. Joshua gave his horse a sharp kick and she took off on the path that led back up the river. He didn't let her go, it was much narrower than the road, more treacherous.

When he looked back, Rawlins was right on his tail and gaining. On instinct Joshua ducked as something bright flashed towards him as the ghost's shimmering sword missed him by inches.

'I'll have ya yet, ya little rat!' the man cried.

Then they were neck and neck again, and his blade shot across Joshua's forehead. Joshua gasped in pain. Arabella shied in fear and stumbled. His grip faltered and he was off her back and flying through the air before he had a chance to right himself. He hit the ground hard, and rolled, the breath knocked out of him.

Rawlins's laughter mocked him. For a moment he feared the ghost would run him through before he could rise, but instead the fiend spurred his horse and thundered down the path.

Joshua swore as he climbed to his feet. Using his shirt sleeve, he wiped blood off his face. To his relief, Arabella stood a short distance away, panting, her eyes wild. He walked up to her slowly and patted a sweaty flank.

Swinging himself up into the saddle, he kicked her in the flanks. The race was lost and he knew it. Now it was a matter of protecting Briar and the others from the ghost's wrath.

'Come on, girl, let's finish it, one way or another.'

CHAPTER FORTY-ONE

Once the riders were gone, Reena had loaded her great-gran and Briar into the car and driven south a short distance to the road that led to the old bridge. It wasn't in use now, with barricades and warning signs to keep people away – none of which were a deterrent to them as they used flashlights to make their way on foot towards the dilapidated structure.

The bridge had been built before the Civil War, a handy way to cross the river when it was running too high and Pike's Ford was out of commission. Now it was in bad condition, a rotting reminder of the past.

'This will have to do,' Lily said. 'Think ya can make it across there?'

'I better or we're in big trouble,' Reena replied, her flashlight flitting here and there as she studied the gnarled structure.

'But why here?' Briar asked, puzzled.

'Rawlins was too smart to go back to where we started,' Lily explained. 'But what he doesn't know is that a bridge over a body of water will act as a crossroads. I can bind him here, but he has to be in the middle of it or it won't work.'

'Does Joshua know about this?'

'I warned him it might happen this way, so we planned ahead. Once Rawlins is on the bridge, Reena will lay the conjure down on the other side. I'll have done the same here. If all goes right, he won't ever rise again.'

Reena is going across the bridge. Though it was totally selfish, Briar heaved a sigh of relief. Her best friend heard it.

'We all have our own fears,' Reena said. 'Mine isn't water.'

'So what can I do?' Briar asked.

'You can help me put down the trick on this side,' Lily said as she handed Reena a burlap bag. 'Good luck. Be safe, ya hear?'

'Same for you two. Love you, Gran.'

Briar watched with growing trepidation as her friend began testing the planking on their side of the bridge.

'Man, this wood is way brittle,' Reena reported. She walked forward a few steps, using her arms for balance. Boards bent under her weight and one cracked in two, causing her to readjust quickly or she'd have tumbled into the river below.

'Keep those herbs dry,' Lily warned.

'I know, Gran,' she replied patiently.

'Come on, girl. Let's get this ready.'

Eager to have something to do, Briar nodded. 'Yes, ma'am.'

While her friend manoeuvred her way across the river, Briar was put to work laying down the magic on their side. It started with a line of red dust.

'What is this stuff?'

'Brick dust.'

There were other curious things – bones and shells and whatnot. If Reena hadn't found a way into the curse using this kind of magic, Briar would have thought it just plain silly.

Her friend had barely made it to the middle of the bridge when it began to creak underneath her.

'You OK out there?' Briar called out.

'Don't know.' Reena went down on her hands and knees, but the sounds continued to grow in intensity. 'Don't you dare break!' she commanded as she jammed the bag between two boards.

A moment later there was a deafening crack and she plunged into the swift and muddy river below.

'Reena!' The instant her friend's head vanished under the water, Briar's memories seized her. To her shame, her legs locked up and she couldn't move to help her friend.

'Reena? Ya OK, girl?' Lily called, hobbling down the bank.

Move. You've got to help her.

She'd barely taken a few steps when there was a splash a short way downstream. It was followed by a muted swear word, then, 'Yeah, I'm good. Give me minute and I'll get back up there.'

Briar let loose a joyous whoop as Lily came back up the bank. The old woman paused, listening, then shook her head.

'There's no time. Rawlins is on the other side now.' Her old eyes turned towards Briar and she could hear the unspoken question.

Do ya have what it takes to save us?

Reena would not make it back to the bridge in time,

439

and Lily was nearly ninety. There was only one person who could carry the magic to the other side of the river.

Briar whimpered. 'No, I can't . . . The water—'

'Ya can and ya must, girl,' Lily said, grabbing hold of her arm in a tight grip. 'Reena told me what ya did in that curse. Ya got the strength for it.'

'But—'

'There is no other choice. It's that or yer young man dies. And a lotta other people.'

Briar had never learned how to swim and even a few inches of bath water frightened her, the reason she only took showers. Was it possible to face the monster that lived in the river?

'Girl?' Lily said, shaking her. 'Rawlins will be here soon. Ya have to be on the other side or this won't work. Ya hear?'

Briar shot a desperate look down the river and found Reena was still swimming towards the bank.

It has to be me.

'OK, I'll try.'

Lily explained exactly what she had to do, but it was hard for Briar to hear any of the instructions. She was too busy staring at the bridge.

'Ya got that?'

'Ah, yeah. Maybe.'

'Go on, then.'

Briar tried to convince herself this wasn't any big deal, at least until the toe of her tennis shoes touched the first plank. Below her, the river monster woke from its slumber and snarled, licking its lips in anticipation.

'Yer doin' OK – just keep goin',' Lily urged.

The first few feet of bridge were pretty good, and then the holes grew wider. The worst part was that she could see the water rushing below. Shaking with each step, she kept moving forward, keeping in mind what Rawlins would do to them if he won. How the town would burn once again.

She was a Rose, and while Joshua's people might not like that name, it came with certain responsibilities. Elmer had fulfilled his. Now it was her turn. Maybe some day down the line a descendant of hers would re-enact this very crossing.

In time, Briar couldn't remain upright with any degree of security, so she went down on to her hands and knees just as Reena had. The stifling smell of the river rose up and choked her.

'That's it!' her friend called out. 'You're doing it!'

As she crawled forward, she thought of Joshua, of his sweet smile, of how empty her life would be if he weren't around. Despite everything, they were still a couple.

I'll be damned if I let some old ghost take him away from me.

A sharp pain pierced her palm, a broken nail cutting into her flesh. Muttering under her breath, she wiped the hand on her jeans and kept moving. Luckily her tetanus shot was current.

Just ahead of her was the bag Reena had left behind, and when she reached it Briar jammed it down her shirt. The heady scent of herbs cloaked the river's stench and seemed to give her added courage.

With a moan of despair, she realized she was only

halfway across while beneath her the water continued to call out to her.

'Go faster!' Lily called out

Sure. How hard can that be?

Briar pushed on, then had to halt because there was a vast open section in front of her. As she calculated the best way to get round it, there was the sound of pounding hoofs. Joshua? Or the ghost?

Unsure, she angled to the edge of the bridge, a move that offered up other perils as one of the boards might break and pitch her into the water below.

The hoofbeats grew closer, along with the sound of a labouring horse. Down the path came the hellish mount, Rawlins on its back, his eyes alight with fire.

Where's Joshua? Is he hurt or . . .

As she flattened herself on one of the planks, Rawlins reined his horse to a stop at the edge of the bridge.

'Ah, hell,' Reena swore, for once not fearing her elders' wrath.

The sound of another horse drew closer as Joshua rode into sight. The moment Arabella saw the ghost, she snorted and reared, refusing to come any closer.

'You cheated, you bastard!' Joshua shouted as he fought to control her.

'Yeah, so what?' Rawlins called back. 'Ya see that?' he said, pointing to the other side of the bridge. 'Just a little further and I win. Ain't that somethin'?'

'Not unless you're across the water,' Joshua replied. He slid off his horse and began walking towards the bank.

'It's whoever crosses first. I still might win.'

Rawlins snorted. 'If that's what ya want, boy. Just know that when I get on the other side my sword is gonna to be buried deep in those womenfolk.'

'No! This is between us, no one else.'

The ghost wasn't listening to him. 'Where are you, girl? I smell ya.' He shifted his horse around, searching the bridge. 'Come out, now!'

Briar had no choice but to stand and reveal her position. He would have found her eventually. 'I'm here,' she said, trying hard to balance on a couple of partially rotted planks. He and his mount were in front of her now. She had to get past him to set the magic before he reached the far bank.

'Briar?' Joshua said in astonishment.

'Yeah, look at me. Standing on a rickety bridge over a bunch of —' she couldn't say the 'w' word — 'moving stuff.'

Rawlins laughed as if he knew her fear. Then he proved it by causing the river to jet up and splash her. She cried out, but didn't move. Another wave came up and this time she was ready for it.

'No wonder they hanged you,' she said, glaring up at the fiend.

His sword flashed and then it was pointed directly at her. Given the vicious slice on Joshua's face, it'd already been put to use.

Rawlins's horse clambered forward, hovering in open air where no planking existed, the sword shining silver in the dark night. Joshua plunged down the bank and into the water, wading as fast as he could, Arabella right behind.

The strength of the river's current nearly pulled him off his feet.

As Rawlins moved closer to her, Briar dodged, hoping to scurry around him, but was forced to lurch backwards just as the sword's tip flew past her nose. The spectral horse pranced around and she swore she could feel flames on her back.

A wave of water burst upward again, trying to slap her down. Briar's fingers desperately grasped on to a rough-hewn board, the splinters digging into her palms. Beneath her the water sang to her, urging her to let go, to allow it to carry her away in its cold arms.

No way.

She wriggled her butt, trying to move closer to the next board. Above her the faint moonlight was blocked out by the glimmering underside of Rawlins's mount as it stood in the middle of the bridge.

'Briar!' Joshua called out as the water knocked at her again. Briar reached out and found the next board, her hands burning and her muscles straining. She grasped another, then the next one after that.

In her mind, she wasn't on some old broken bridge – she was seven and climbing across the monkey bars at school. There was no water beneath her, only soft sand. It was a sunny day, not the dark of night. Soon playtime would be over and . . .

Briar picked up speed now, stretching out a hand to test the next board, then moving forward. If it was loose, she chose another. Finally she reached a place where the bridge felt more solid, and with tremendous effort she hoisted herself up on the planking, leaving her feet to dangle beneath her.

Over her left shoulder was the butt of the spectral horse. It pawed at the planking beneath it as if it could unearth her. Rawlins shifted in his saddle and spied her.

'There ya are.'

Briar desperately tried to pull herself up, but her arms were too tired.

'Jump!' Joshua shouted from somewhere in the river.

If she did, the herbs would get wet and they wouldn't work. Then Rawlins would win.

Lily called out to him. 'Leave that child alone,' she ordered. 'She's no trouble to ya.'

'I won the race, old woman. I have my freedom now!'

'Not till ya cross the river,' she replied.

Briar finally got a leg on the bridge and pulled herself up. Adrenalin fuelling her now, she scrambled over the remaining ten feet or so. To her relief, the boards gave way to earth and she dived for solid ground.

Rawlins's horse began to fight him, prancing around. Did it recognize the danger she posed?

Briar pulled the burlap bag out of her shirt and frantically poured out the line of red dust on the ground. Then she laid out roots and little strange bits in the same pattern as Lily had on the other side. Her hands were so sore the herbs made them sting, but she didn't stop.

'Ya sold yer soul for a few gold pieces,' Lily called out. 'Yer one of the devil's own, Rawlins. It's time ya went to hell for good.'

The ghost laughed again. 'I'll show ya hell, old woman,'

he said, spurring his horse forward, the sword glowing in the night.

'Done!' Briar yelled, praying that somehow she'd got it right.

A flash came from other side of the bridge, spooking both horses. Like a magical detonation cord, it ran down the sides of the structure towards Rawlins, then past him to where Briar knelt in the mud. The magic ignited there and flared so brightly she had to shield her eyes.

'What is this? What're ya doin'?' Rawlins demanded. 'Ah, hell, yer tryin' to bind me again.'

Words tumbled out of Lily's mouth now, loud and strong, the names of saints and patriarchs, all interwoven with a spell of immense power.

The ghost spurred his mount, but the horse was caught in place, crying out in terror. The power grew around them, focusing on the centre of the bridge. Planks began to rise into the air as the structure shook itself free of its moorings.

'Jebediah Rawlins, I bind ya to this place, to be held here for all eternity!' Lily cried, her arms in the air, and her body lit from within. 'May God Almighty judge yer dark soul and find it wantin'!'

A second passed, long enough for Briar to fear the spell had failed, before a solid column of water and fire spiralled upward into a funnel, like an infernal twister. It caught the ghost and horse, sucking them into its vortex.

'Noooo!' Rawlins cried.

Before Briar could take another breath, the bridge exploded in a rainbow of light and splinters.

CHAPTER FORTY-TWO

Hands grabbed Briar and threw her to the ground. Joshua landed on top of her, sheltering her with his wet body as planks and nails and water pelted down upon them. From behind them, the river roared its fury, like a watery lion, then it grew quiet.

Too quiet.

'You OK?' he gasped, still holding her tight.

'Yeah. You?'

He slowly rose on an elbow, blood running down the side of his face. 'Yeah, I think. A little dizzy.'

'You're bleeding,' she said, touching his cheek.

'Rawlins nicked me with his sword,' he replied, as if it weren't a big deal.

You protected me. Just like she had protected him. *How could I not love this guy?*

'Briar? Josh?' Reena called out from across the river. 'You still with us?'

'Yes!' Briar called back as she got to her feet. 'What about you guys?'

'We're good. A little dirty, but OK.'

'Is Rawlins really gone?'

'Of course he is, girl,' Lily snapped. 'Ya can thank me later. Now get me off the ground, Reena B.'

Briar chuckled. The old lady had actually pulled it

off. When she turned to say something to Joshua, he was transfixed, staring at the empty space where the bridge had once stood.

'It's gone,' he said. 'Like *totally* gone.'

'Not entirely. I've got some of it in my hands,' she said, raising her palms as proof.

'Oh God, Arabella,' Joshua said, whirling round. 'She might be hurt.'

'I'm sure she's OK.' She was probably headed for home. The horse had more sense than they did.

As he hurried into the woods, calling for his mare, Briar stared out at the river. 'That one was for you, Elmer. I'm sorry you died because of a traitor. You're still a hero to me.'

Her cellphone *bing*ed in her pocket. It was Reena, who had apparently grown tired of shouting across the river.

Meet u @ Josh's place. Gran needs rest.

OK. Will find mare then head that way.

Hell & damn, we did it, girlfriend!

Briar grinned. That was the other reason for the text – Lily didn't allow any swearing.

'Yeah, we freakin' rock, every one of us.'

Joshua crept along, keeping his movements unhurried. With what had just gone down at the bridge, Arabella had to be beyond spooked. He still was.

'Hey, girl, where are you? The bad guy's all gone. Same with that creepy stallion thing. Come on, it's safe now.'

Nothing. Was she lying somewhere, injured? *No, not that.*

'Arabella, where are you? Don't scare me like this.'

A whinny came from his right as Briar led the mare out of a stand of trees.

'Oh, thank God, you found her. Is she OK?'

'Seems to be,' Briar replied. 'Scared and wet, but so are the rest of us.'

Arabella nuzzled Joshua's hand and then sneezed, shooting snot all over it.

'Thanks for that,' he said, wiping his hand on his jeans.

Though Briar had said the horse was fine, he checked her nonetheless. 'A few scratches, but she's good.' He patted her neck. 'You're a wonder, girl.'

Then he looked over at Briar. 'Both of you are.' He reached over to touch her face and she backed off.

'Ewww . . . that hand is so off limits.'

He laughed. 'I'll wash it in the river. Besides, you owe me a kiss.'

'Really? You didn't win the race,' she teased, but he could see the sparkle in her eyes.

'Neither did Rawlins, so I call it a draw.'

'Hmm . . . maybe we can bend the rules.' She looked over the river. 'Reena's taking Lily to your place. She'll meet us there.'

'OK. I want to walk the horse for a while, let her cool down, then we can ride back home.' Then it hit him. 'Ah, damn. If they're going to my place, the folks are going to know what really went down tonight.'

'It's time they knew anyway,' Briar said. 'I told my parents about you. How we are . . . together now.'

He froze at that admission. 'How'd it go?'

'Better than I thought,' she said. 'They didn't lock me in a tower or anything.'

He laughed. 'It'll be harder for my folks, I think. Mom, at least.'

'I'm not giving you up. Not now.'

'Same here,' he said.

As they headed down the path, Joshua took one last look at the empty section of water. 'Someone is going to take some heat for the bridge being gone,' he said. 'You know the county sheriff – he's always bitching about how us kids are wrecking everything.'

'That's totally bogus,' Briar said, falling in step with him. 'Usually it's just a couple of old drunk dudes from the Moose Lodge.'

'Not to hear the sheriff tell it.'

They reached the footbridge far too soon for Briar's liking.

'You OK going over this?' he asked, pausing on the bank.

'Yeah. It's got, like, real planks and everything. Major improvement over the last one.'

Joshua handed over the reins and then edged down the bank to wash his hands and then wet his face. He used the bottom of his damaged T-shirt to dry himself. When he returned, Briar grimaced in sympathy.

'That looks bad,' she said, gently touching near the wound. It was bleeding again.

'Wounded warriors always get a kiss, right?' he said,

pulling her close. He smelt like sweat and blood and the river. She didn't care.

The kiss they shared was breathtaking, as if they'd traded parts of their souls. When it ended, he smoothed her tangled hair.

'I think you're the bravest girl I've ever met.'

'Really?' He made her feel so good. 'That works since you're the bravest guy I've ever seen.'

'I like how this turns up at the end,' he said, tweaking her nose. 'It's cute.'

'I always loved your eyes. They are so . . . expressive.'

'You are supposed to love my bulging muscles, not my eyes,' he said, grinning.

'Yeah, yeah. Come on, we need to get you a bandage,' she said, tugging him forward. 'Can't have my hero fainting in my arms. That would ruin your street cred.'

Instead of walking, he climbed on the horse and then pulled her up in front of him. As they clopped over the footbridge, he muttered, 'You going to visit me when I'm grounded for life?'

She moaned. 'Maybe our folks will let it all slide this time, because we did good things.'

'You *do* believe in fairy tales,' he retorted.

Sometimes they even come true.

Trouble lay in wait at Joshua's house.

'Oh no, that's my parents' car,' Briar moaned. 'What are *they* doing here?'

'Lily must have called them. We are seriously busted.'

After they dismounted, he tied Arabella to the fence near a water trough, then stripped off her saddle. 'I'll be back, girl. Gotta go get my butt kicked, then I'll give you a good brush down and some grain. You deserve it.'

Once they reached the door, Joshua held it open for Briar. She knew he didn't want to go in first.

'You're being a chicken,' she said.

He made clucking noses. '"Abandon hope all ye who enter here."'

'No matter what, we stay together,' she said.

'There's no other way it *can* be.'

'Joshua, is that you?' his dad called out.

'Yes. Briar's with me.' Maybe that would keep his father from tearing into him too much.

They barely got inside the door when they were mobbed. Briar's parents pulled her into a tight hug, her mother crying. Joshua's dad gave him a bear hug, then pounded his back like he'd just scored the winning touchdown. His mom gasped at the sight of the blood on his face and shirt.

'Oh God, you're hurt,' and then she began to cry as well.

Throughout it all, Lily sat in the corner of the living room, a cup of tea in hand as if this kind of drama happened all the time. Reena sat next to her, watching the whole scene with a bemused smile.

Maybe we're not as screwed as we think.

'Thank God, you're safe, son,' his father said. 'Come on over here and sit down. I'll get the first-aid kit.'

'It's OK, Dad. Really. Arabella is too. She was magnificent.'

Another bear hug came his way.

Briar was still trapped in her parents' arms. Finally she managed to wriggle free and after insisting she was unharmed other than a few splinters, they all settled in various chairs. Mrs Rose kept sniffling.

'You told them about the bet and the race,' Joshua said.

Lily nodded. *And they believed you?* She nodded again, as if she'd heard him.

His dad returned with the first-aid kid and began cleaning the wound. Joshua grimaced as he worked on it.

'I don't know if it's going to need stitches or not. What do you think, Mrs Rose?' he asked, sending a look towards Briar's mom.

Though Joshua blinked in surprise, Briar jumped right in.

'Please, Mom. You were a nurse, you know best.' She looked over at him. 'You wouldn't mind, would you, Josh?'

Joshua shook his head, though a bit reluctantly, as his mother was frowning at the notion.

'Do you mind, Lora?' Briar's mother asked.

His mom took a deep breath, like most everyone else in the room. 'I'm not sure you should be touching my boy after what you did to him.'

'I told you I was sorry for what happened. I never meant to hurt him. I wouldn't do that to a child. You know that.'

Joshua's mom swallowed hard. 'Doesn't make it any better.'

'So that's it?' Briar cut in. 'We're going to let Aunt

453

Sarah's death rule us until the end of time? That's not fair to any of us. Especially Joshua and me.'

The silence stretched out until it was painful.

'Yer children are wiser than their parents, at least in this case. Time to put it behind y'all,' Lily said quietly. 'Too much blood has been spilt. Too much pain has been endured.'

Joshua's mother gave a faint nod, then looked away. 'Go on, see if he needs stitches.'

He kept his eyes down as Briar's mom checked the wound and found Mrs Rose's touch surprisingly gentle.

'I think you can get away with Steri-Strips,' she said. 'Do you have some of those?' His dad nodded. 'It might scar, though. You should prepare yourself for that.'

'Just like Harry Potter,' Reena said. 'Well, not quite.'

Joshua grimaced as his dad applied some stingy antiseptic, followed by the strips.

Briar chortled. 'Now one of your eyebrows is higher than the other.'

Of course it is.

'So am I grounded like . . . a couple days?' Joshua asked, hopefully.

His dad eyed him. 'I'm thinking it should be until you're at least forty. That might do it.'

'Oh, come on, Dad! I didn't do anything illegal.' *Other than some bridge destruction.*

'Even if I half believed everything that Ms Lily told us — and I'm not sure I do — you were wildly out of control, son. Way over the mark. You risked your life *twice* and you didn't tell us what you were doing or what you were facing. That's not right.'

Yeah, I'm screwed. His dad never used guilt unless he was really upset.

'What he said,' Mr Rose added, frowning over at his daughter. 'Why didn't you tell us where you were going, Briar?'

Joshua noted that question hadn't been aimed at Lily. The parents were tiptoeing around the old woman for good reason.

'You wouldn't have let us do anything,' Briar replied. 'It was our job, not yours.'

Mr Rose sighed. 'We are not going to agree on this. You're giving your mother and me grey hair way too early.'

'Hair dye is your friend,' Briar said brightly. 'I know that first hand.'

The humour didn't blunt the parental disapproval.

'Just tell me – how long am I grounded?' she asked.

Briar's fingers crossed as the parents thought it through.

'Two weeks ought to do it,' her father replied. 'I've been meaning to clean out the garage and now it's your job.'

'Two weeks!' Briar groaned. 'But school starts right after that and the garage is a mess. There's a lot of junk in there and it's way hot and—'

'Yes, to all that,' Mr Rose replied, wearing the *This isn't a democracy* look her parents employed when they held the upper hand. 'However, you can still do the re-enactment on Saturday.'

'Really?' She caught Joshua's eyes and smiled. 'That works.'

'Same deal for you, son,' his dad said. 'Fourteen days should be just about right for you to paint the house.'

Joshua added his own groan to the mix. *Not that.*

'Sounds fair to me,' Lily said as she rose from the chair with Reena's help. 'I need to go talk to my great-granddaughter's folks. They'll probably hear what went on tonight and it's best they know just how fine a daughter they have. Before they ground her.'

'Oh, man,' Reena murmured. 'Do good and get busted for it.'

'That's often the case,' Lily replied. 'Don't expect these kids to be the same as they were a week ago. They've grown up in a hurry. Had no choice about that.'

'I know. I can see it already,' Briar's mom said, and took hold of her daughter's hand. 'We're just happy she's alive.' She looked up at Joshua. 'That all of you are alive. I mean that.'

Briar nudged her mom and gave her a pointed look.

'I apologize for what I did to your family, Lora. Daniel. It wasn't right. I had no idea it would get as bad as it did. I am truly sorry.'

Joshua's mother only gave a stiff nod, but it was a start.

'I can't speak for my wife, but I accept your apology,' his dad said. 'This is done. We need to move on, all of us.'

A'-freakin'-men!

*

456

As Joshua and Briar headed towards the barn, he murmured, 'This was so Shakespearean, you know. Like one of his tragedies.'

' "See, what a scourge is laid upon your hate, that heaven finds means to kill your joys with love! And I, for winking at your discords too, have lost a brace of kinsmen. All are punish'd." '

He looked at her in awe. 'What was that from?'

'*Romeo and Juliet*. Talk about a high body count. Even the lovers die and that is *so* wrong. Everyone knows there's supposed to be a happy ending, except old Will apparently.'

When Joshua laughed, it pulled at the cut on his face. 'I'll see you Saturday at the battle. I'll try to call you if I can,' he said. 'Or email you. It depends on whether Dad takes away both my phone *and* my computer.'

'Same here.'

They drifted closer, then gradually became aware that both sets of parents were on the porch, watching them far too closely. Joshua gave her a kiss on the cheek. 'I'll be dreaming about flying around on that crazy horse with you.'

She beamed. 'So will I.'

As her dad pulled out of the drive, Briar waved at her new boyfriend, then sank back into the seat, immensely tired.

'Briar?'

'Yeah, Mom?'

'You really crawled across the bridge on your own?'

'Yes I did.' *I still can't believe it.*

There was silence for a time and then, 'I never really let

457

you do much over the years. I was too scared something would happen to you. It'll take a while for me to loosen up.'

Briar blinked. This was not a conversation she'd ever thought she'd have with her mother. 'OK. I'll be careful from now on, but . . . I want to do more things. I just don't want to stay at home and watch my life go by, you know?'

'I'd say we all need to be thinking like that,' her father cut in. 'We've had our lives on hold for too long.'

'How about a driving lesson, Dad? You up for that?' *Come on, go for it.*

He sighed. 'OK.'

Score!

'Mom, if I make it on the tennis team, will you car pool me and some of the others to practice?'

A moment's hesitation and then, 'Sure, if you make the team, and I have no doubt you will.'

'You might want to rethink that, hon,' Briar's father began, his tone light. 'You'll get stuck driving a car full of raging hormones. Trust me, it's not pretty.'

'I hadn't thought of that. Just how bad is it?' she asked, grinning now. It'd been so long since Briar had seen her mother happy.

'Unbearable,' he said, and grinned. 'Right, daughter?'

'No comment, Dad.'

As her parents parried back and forth, Briar leaned against the window, smiling to herself. It appeared that she and her folks would all be stretching their wings very soon.

How cool is that?

CHAPTER FORTY-THREE

The next few days were a blur of work. When Briar finished cleaning the garage in record time – all the while hoping that her sentence would be lifted early – her parents had just come up with a new project. And then another. By the time Saturday morning came she had managed to accomplish more scut work than she had the entire summer.

Each evening's phone call to Joshua proved that he'd employed the same tactic with similarly disappointing results. According to him, Reena and Pat had dropped by one afternoon and helped with the house, though Joshua claimed they'd spent more time messing with each other's heads and stealing kisses than getting paint in the proper places.

While Briar had slaved away, there had been a steady stream of visitors to the Rose house. Everyone wanted to know what had happened to their daughter because the rumour mill was working overtime. Luckily her mom had extra baked goods in the freezer because every visitor wanted sit and talk over coffee. The first had been the pastor, worried about the rumour that Briar was 'into magic' like the Hill girl. Her mom had reassured him that wasn't the case and sent him home with a Bundt cake. That had proved a mistake as others dropped by just on the off-chance of some Rose-quality baked goods. Her mom didn't win first prize at the county fair each year for nothing.

A more ominous visitor was Sheriff Johnson, who was investigating the 'wanton destruction' of the old bridge. Apparently the guys in the pick-up had made note of a young man on a black horse and girl with blonde hair along the road that night and had readily offered up that information to avoid a speeding ticket.

This time Briar's mother took the lead. 'Yes, my daughter was out there,' she'd said. 'She and Joshua Quinn were riding along the old road.'

'That late?' the cop asked dubiously as he claimed another peanut-butter cookie. It was his fifth.

'Yes. We knew they were out there. The Quinn boy is a . . . nice kid and I trust him with my daughter. Besides, we were just up the road at his parents' place for a visit.'

'I thought you and the Quinns had some . . . problems.'

'We did. We got that sorted out . . . recently. Briar and Joshua are dating now so it seemed only fair we get to know his parents better.'

After more questioning that led absolutely nowhere, the sheriff departed with a bag full of cookies and brownies. He claimed his next stop was going to be the Quinn house, then he'd be seeing Reena Hill's folks.

Briar wasn't worried. She knew that none of their parents, or Lily, would allow anything bad to happen to them.

The following Saturday Briar was granted respite from her detention. Since her birthday had hardly been one of celebration, a party had been scheduled for that evening.

460

As always, Briar's mom was baking, but this time it wasn't stress relief. In fact, she was humming along to the radio. She'd even signed up for art classes in Statesboro.

'I'm out of here,' Briar said, shouldering her pack that held her uniform. 'It's time to get all hot and sweaty.'

Her mom chuckled. 'You used to hate that.' She removed a sheet of cookies from the oven. The scent was absolutely mind altering.

'I've been worse,' Briar said. *Like covered in wolf drool, for one.*

'My little girl has changed.'

'So have you. I like my new mom a lot.'

'Even when she makes you scrub the kitchen floor?' her mother teased.

That hadn't been fun. 'Yeah, even then.'

They hugged and then a kiss landed on her forehead. 'Just don't forget how to be my little girl every now and then, OK?'

'I won't. Thanks for being cool about Joshua.'

'He's a good kid. I'm sorry we kept you guys apart.'

'Yeah, me too. He said his parents are getting counselling. I'm hoping that works for them.'

'All we can do is hope. Lora and I are meeting for lunch next week in Statesboro. Fewer busybodies watching us that way. It's not going to be easy, but I think we'll try to mend fences as best we can.'

Yes!

'Cookie to go?' her mother offered.

Briar took one, popped a kiss on her mom's cheek, and

then scooted out the side door at warp speed, letting the screen bang shut behind her. As she headed through town for the field, she couldn't keep her smile under wraps.

No one knew it yet, but Elmer Rose's sad story was about to change for the better.

In deference to the heat, the last re-enactment of the year was scheduled an hour earlier, though it was almost as hot at eleven as it would be at noon. The moment Briar pulled on the heavy uniform she began to wilt. How did the soldiers wear these things? At least she wasn't allergic to wool like one of the other re-enactors who'd broken out in hives.

She'd just finished buttoning up her uniform coat, twitching at the itchy fabric, when Joshua appeared, leading his mare on to the field, Kerry trotting at his side. He was in full uniform and had hidden his wound under an old-fashioned bandage.

Wow, is he cute or what?

'There you are,' he said, smiling. 'I've missed you.' He placed a kiss on her cheek.

'It's been, like, forever,' she said. They kissed more earnestly now.

'Briar?'

They jumped at her father's voice. He was standing behind them.

How did he sneak up on us? Wasn't he supposed to be working in the beer tent?

Her cheeks warmed in embarrassment. 'Ah, hi, Dad.'

'Hi there. Joshua, can I talk to you a minute?' he said.

'Sure, Mr Rose.' With a shrug, Joshua handed off the reins and then tailed behind him until they reached a suitable distance away. Then her dad began to chat with her boyfriend, a friendly hand laid on his shoulder.

'What is that all about?' Briar murmured.

Reena coasted up, assessed the scene and delivered her verdict. 'My dad did the same with Pat yesterday. It's the *You mess with my girl and I'll kill you* lecture.'

'He really said that?' Briar asked, astounded.

'Yup. Pat was still freaked about it last night. You know how big my dad is.'

'Yeah, linebacker big. How are you and the Ego doing?'

'Just fine,' Reena said, waggling her eyebrows and grinning. 'Pat's a total kick once you get to know him. Who would have thought there was a nice guy beneath all that jerkiness?'

'What about his parents? How are they taking you two being together?'

'His mom was pretty cool. She's interested in local history and because my family's been here since forever she likes that. Especially since they used to be slaves at the Ashland Plantation.' Reena snorted at that. 'His dad? Well . . .'

'Bad?' Briar asked, still keeping an eye on her own dad and her boyfriend, wishing she could hear what her father was saying.

'The first time we met was *way* awkward,' Reena explained. 'Mr Daniels stared at me like I had horns growing out of my head. Then he found out that my dad used to be a pro football player and suddenly I was golden. Seems he's hoping to score tickets to the Super Bowl.'

'Wow. He's a user, isn't he?'

'Totally. Oh, and Pat's coming to your party with me tonight.'

'Oh, man,' Briar said, realizing the implications. 'Did you warn him about some of my relatives?'

Reena grinned. 'No, I didn't. I figured it'd be more fun that way. Especially your great-aunt. I'm hoping she wears that hat with the flamingo on it. That'd rock.'

Briar groaned at the memory.

'I'm off to the ice-cream tent and then I'm meeting Pat at the lake. See you later, girlfriend.'

'OK, bye!'

Joshua returned, his cheeks crimson.

'What did my dad say to you?'

He shot a look at her father, who was currently talking to a re-enactor.

'He said . . .' Joshua sighed. 'He said, and I quote, that "having grandchildren appear before my daughter gets married *and* in college would give me homicidal tendencies". In short, if I crossed the line with his little girl, he would rip my head off and feed it to me.'

'What? Is that, like, even anatomically possible?'

'He made it sound like it would be,' Joshua admitted. 'And I believe him.'

'I'm sorry. He can be kinda weird sometimes.'

'No weirder than my dad. I got the *Let's review the birds and the bees* lecture over breakfast. Bottom line is *Don't go there no matter what*. At least not yet.'

'I'm surprised there isn't a chastity belt involved.'

'Don't give them any ideas.' He hugged her. 'Don't worry. I'm not like Mike, but I will need a lot of kissing to compensate.'

'That I can handle.'

As Briar wound her hair round and pinned it up – it was always hard to get it under the cap – she worked out the final parts of her plan.

'You have a very devious look going on there,' Joshua observed.

She leaned close and whispered the plan in his ear, along with a question.

'Arabella could handle it. But are you sure? These guys will freak out.'

'Exactly,' Briar replied, smiling. 'It's time Elmer won for a change.'

The re-enactment went down like clockwork: the Union forces moved across the battlefield towards Bliss as the Rebs took cover behind various trees and bushes. Gunfire was exchanged and then the Union unleashed their field cannons and the bodies began to fall. It was December 1864 all over again.

Briar held her ground, just like Elmer had. Then she began her run, flying across the field, dodging Union soldiers and their bayonets. At first she stuck to the script, but at the last minute she veered towards a Union officer who was destined to fall from his horse, wounded.

Five, four, three, two . . .

The guy went down and this time Elmer Rose swung up on to the saddle, wheeled Arabella around and took off like Sherman himself was on his heels. Riding past stunned faces, Briar made sure to avoid any bodies lying on the ground.

When she reached the fence that was the Union line, she vaulted it and kept going. Behind her came shouts and then raucous cheers. Further down the field, she reined the horse in. She turned round to find chaos. Emboldened, many of the re-enactors had broken ranks and were attacking the bluecoats with unrestrained and totally non-historic glee.

Once the final bugle sounded, Briar nudged Arabella back towards the Confederate lines. Joshua trotted up to her, winded. 'That. Was. Awesome!'

Briar hooted in celebration. She knew some of the re-enactors would be upset with her, but it didn't matter. The fact that Rawlins had been the one to kill Elmer had cut her deeply, that her ancestor had died at the hands of a traitor. That didn't mean she couldn't give Elmer Rose his own moment of glory.

Briar slid off the horse and claimed a hug from Joshua who placed a kiss on her sweaty neck.

'I'm so proud of you.'

She beamed at the praise. It meant so much coming from *her* guy.

When she looked around for her father, he shot a thumb up in the air and she returned it.

After more photo opportunities than usual, they encountered Sergeant Nickleby at the edge of the battlefield.

Since he was in charge of the re-enactment, she'd expected a lot of yelling because of her flagrant misuse of history. Instead, he was so upset he could only wave his hands and croak incoherently.

'That was totally farb, but I loved it, Briar!' one of the Union soldiers called out. Translation: historically inaccurate, but it still rocked.

'Thanks!'

Nickleby sputtered along, beyond words. One of his aides helped him to a folding chair where he sank down and put his head in his hands. Briar suspected that in future the part of Elmer Rose wouldn't be assigned to a headstrong girl. No doubt generations of Rose women would sing her praises for that.

After she'd stripped out of the uniform and touched up her make-up, she hunted down Joshua. He was near the horse tank, waiting as Arabella loaded up on water. Kerry sat nearby, chomping on an ice cube.

'Good news. We've both been given a reprieve this afternoon,' he announced.

'Honest?'

'Yup. Your dad told me to have you home in time for the party at six, which *I am* invited to, by the way.'

'For real? That's cool! So what should we do?'

He gestured towards the saddle where a canvas bag hung from the side. 'Your mom packed a picnic lunch for us. I'm thinking we should head for the lake. How about you?'

My mom packed us lunch?

'Deal!'

Joshua didn't head to their usual spot on the beach, but further round the edge of the lake to a private cove. It was quiet and remote, and Briar loved it on sight.

'How did you find this?'

'I know all the ground around here. Comes from spending a lot of time on a horse.'

While Arabella grazed on grass and Kerry chased squirrels, they dined on cold chicken and three-bean salad, laughed at each other's jokes and fooled around. There was even apple pie.

'Your mom is a great cook. Mine is just OK,' Joshua observed.

'How's she doing?'

'Better, I think. Still . . . confused.'

'She'll get better, I'm sure of it.'

With Kerry on guard for any rampaging wildlife, they stretched out in the grass under a shady tree, watching the clouds form weird shapes above them. Where Briar came up with all sorts of different names for the formations, Joshua claimed every one of them was a horse.

He pointed at another cloud. 'That looks like a—'

'Horse, I know.'

'I was going to say it looked like a zebra.'

'Which is nothing more than a horse with stripes,' she countered.

They laughed together and then he kissed her.

'I proclaim this a perfect day,' Briar said, feeling loved like never before.

'Who knows, it might get even more perfect,' he replied, his eyes promising mischief.

'How?' *Could that even be possible?*

Joshua rose up, dug for something in his pack and returned with a small box. 'I was going to give you this tonight at the party, but with all your relatives around it'd get awkward.'

Inside the box was a charm, a silver rose. 'Wow, that's really pretty. It'll work great on my bracelet. Thank you!'

'Thought you'd like that. Turn it over.'

She found 'BR + JQ' engraved on the back of the charm. 'Awww . . .'

Joshua touched her face in genuine fondness. 'See, I'm good with Roses now.'

Briar laughed, and they were just about to kiss when someone charged up to them at full speed.

'I found them!' Pat called out.

Reena quickly joined him. 'Hey, girlfriend. We're not interrupting you or anything?' she asked, then sniggered.

'What are you doing here?' Briar muttered.

'Breaking up your PDAs, what else?'

Her two friends quickly stripped down to their swimsuits and, though she wasn't supposed to be looking, Briar couldn't help but notice that Pat looked pretty good.

'Avert your eyes, woman!' Joshua said, turning her head towards him.

She laughed and stole a kiss.

'Race you!' Reena said, and then took off for the water. Pat was right on her heels and when they reached the lake they began splashing each other like small kids, laughing and joking. Kerry bounced around and barked at their antics.

'I thought you said no one knew where we were,' Briar murmured.

'I might have told some friends about this place. Well, those two, at least. I didn't figure you'd mind.'

'No. Pat's cool.'

Briar leaned back into Joshua's arms, listening to the sounds of the summer.

This was like their own little kingdom, no castle needed.

'Happy?' he asked.

'Totally.'

'Let's keep it that way from now on. No drama.'

'You got it.'

Even if their summer break was almost over, she'd done a lot of cool stuff. What other princess had rode a flying horse, fought with mechanical wolves and defeated a cunning magical enemy?

Even better, Briar had found her very own prince and saved *his* life a couple of times.

'Do you believe in happy endings?' she asked, curling up Joshua's arms.

'I do now,' he replied and moved in for another kiss.

So do I.

AUTHOR'S NOTE

Where would we be without fairy tales? Be they the sweet Disney kind or the blood-drenched Brothers Grimm versions, they have remained our constant companions throughout the centuries. One of the most iconic – 'Sleeping Beauty' – still has meaning today. A young girl's awakening, the weight of a curse that refuses to quit. There was so much here to work with and I'm thrilled I had a chance to tell Briar's tale. I hope you enjoyed it as well.

ACKNOWLEDGEMENTS

My deepest gratitude goes to Rachel Petty, my incredible editor, who suggested I try my hand at a Southern retelling of a classic fairy tale. Thank you for making the process painless and, dare I say, fun?

As always, a hug and much love to my literary agent, Meredith Bernstein, who was willing to go in a new direction. You rock, lady!

Also thanks go to my critique partners Berta Platas, Carla Fredd, Maureen Hardegree and Michele Roper, who quizzed me about the plot, the magic and the emotional landscape of *Briar Rose*. These talented authors threw out the strangest ideas, many of which made it into the story (the creepy metal worm in the apple, for instance). Thank you for everything, ladies, even if your excellent cakes and baked goods added a few pounds!

I owe many an Innis & Gunn to Shane Burton, who grew up near Briar's fictional town. His tales of quicksand, alligators, armadillos and cotton fields helped make Bliss come alive.

The hoodoo portions of the story came from various references books, including Catherine Yronwode's *Hoodoo Herb and Root Magic* and Jim Haskins' *Voodoo and Hoodoo*. Any mistakes are on my head, not theirs.

Finally, a hug for my very own prince, who shares my daydreams and helps make them come true.